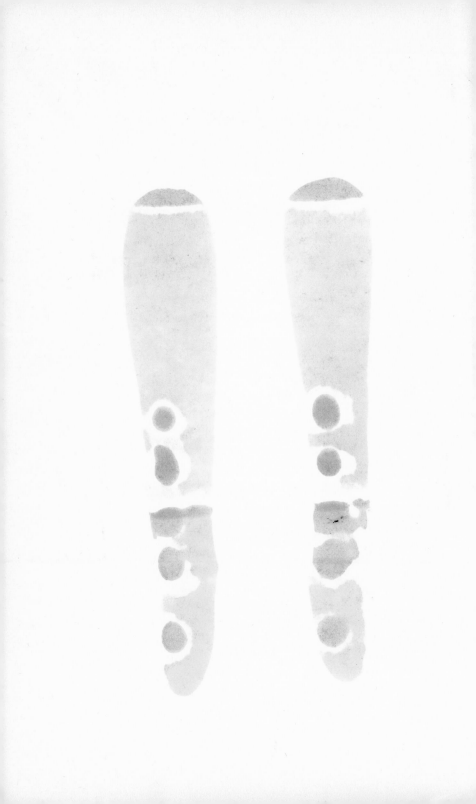

Wanderer of the Wasteland

Wanderer of the Wasteland

Zane Grey™

Thorndike Press • Chivers Press
Thorndike, Maine USA   Bath, Avon, England

This Large Print edition is published by Thorndike Press, USA
and by Chivers Press, England.

Published in 1995 in the U.S. by arrangement with The
Golden West Literary Agency and HarperCollins Publishers.

Published in 1995 in the U.K. by arrangement with the Author's
estate, c/o The Golden West Literary Agency.

U.S. Hardcover   0-7862-0405-2   (Western Series Edition)
U.K. Hardcover   0-7451-3030-5   (Chivers Large Print)

The text of this Large Print edition is unabridged.
Other aspects of the book may vary from the original edition.

Set in 16 pt. News Plantin by Warren Doersam.

Printed in Great Britain on permanent paper.

British Library Cataloguing in Publication Data available

Library of Congress Cataloging in Publication Data

Grey, Zane, 1872–1939.
    Wanderer of the wasteland / Zane Gr
      p.   cm.   6/14/95
   ISBN 0-7862-0405-2 (lg. print : hc)   FELD
   1. Large type books. I. Title.
[PS3513.R6545W36 1995]
813'.52—dc20   94-46890

Dedicated to my wife
LINA ELISE GREY
Without whose love, faith, spirit
and help I never could have
written this novel

ZANE GREY

1

Adam Larey gazed with hard and wondering eyes down the silent current of the red river upon which he meant to drift away into the desert.

The Rio Colorado was no river to trust. It chafed at its banks as if to engulf them; muddy and thick it swirled and glided along in flood, sweeping in curves back and forth from Arizona to California shore. Majestic and gleaming under the hot sky, it swung southward between wide green borders of willow and cottonwood toward a stark and naked upflung wilderness of mountain peaks, the red ramparts of the unknown and trackless desert.

Adam rushed down the bank and threw his pack into a boat. There his rapid action seemed checked by the same violence that had inspired his haste. He looked back, up at the dusty adobe town of Ehrenberg, asleep now under the glaring noonday heat. It would not wake out of that siesta till the return of the weary gold diggers, or the arrival of the stagecoach or the steamer. A tall Indian, swarthy and unkempt, stood motionless in the shade of a wall, watching stolidly.

Adam broke down then. Sobs made his utterance incoherent. "Guerd is no brother — of mine — any more!" he burst out. His accent was one of humiliation and cheated love. "And as for — for *her* — I'll never — never think of her — again."

When once more he turned to the river, a spirit wrestled with the emotion that had unnerved him. Adam Larey appeared to be a boy of eighteen, with darkly tanned, clear-cut, and comely face, and a lofty stature, straight and spare and wide. Untying the boat from its mooring, he became conscious of a singular thrill. Sight of the silent river fascinated him. If it had been drink that had fortified his reckless resolve, it was some strange call to the wildness in him that had stirred exaltation in the prospect of adventure. But there was more. Never again to be dominated by that selfish Guerd, his brother who had taken all and given nothing! Guerd would be stung by this desertion. Perhaps he would be sorry. That thought gave Adam a pang. Long habit of being influenced, and strength of love fostered in playmate days, these made him waver. But the tide of resentment surged up once more; and there flowed the red Colorado, rolling away to the southwest, a gateway to the illimitable wastes of desert land, with its mystery, its adventure, its gold and alluring freedom.

"I'll go," he declared, passionately, and with a shove he sent the boat adrift and leaped over the bow to the rowing seat. The boat floated till it edged into the current, then, as if grasped by unseen power, it glided downstream. Adam seemed to feel the resistless current of this mysterious river take hold of his heart. There would be no coming back — no breasting that mighty flood with puny oars. The moment was sudden and poignant in its revelation. How swiftly receded the cluster of brown adobe huts, the somber, motionless Indian! He had left Ehrenberg behind, and a brother who was his only near relative, and a little sum of love that had failed him.

"I'm done with Guerd forever," he muttered, looking back with hard dry eyes. "It's his fault. Mother always warned me. . . . Ah! if she had lived I would still be home. Home! and not here — in this awful desert of heat and wastelands — among men like wolves and women like. . . ."

He did not finish the thought, but from his pack he took a bottle that glittered in the sunlight, and, waving it defiantly at the backward scene of glare and dust and lonely habitation, he drank deeply. Then he flung the bottle from him with a violent gesture of repulsion. He had no love for strong drink. The bottle fell with hollow splash, rode the muddy swirls, and sank. Whereupon Adam applied himself to the oars with long and powerful sweep.

In that moment of bitter soliloquy there had

flashed through Adam Larey's mind memories and pictures of the past — the old homestead back East, vivid and unforgettable — the sad face of his mother, who had loved him as she had never loved his brother Guerd. There had been a mystery about the father who had died in Adam's childhood. Adam thought of these facts now, seeing a vague connection between them and his presence there alone upon that desert river. When his mother died she had left all her money to him. But Adam had shared his small fortune with Guerd. That money had been the beginning of evil days. If it had not changed Guerd it had awakened slumbering jealousy and passion. Guerd squandered his share and disgraced himself in the home town. Then had begun his ceaseless importunity for Adam to leave college, to see life, to seek adventures, to sail round the Horn to the California gold fields. Adam had been true to the brother spirit within him and the voice of the tempter had fallen upon too thrilling ears. Yearning to be with his brother, and to see wild life upon his own account, Adam yielded to the importunity. He chose, however, to travel westward by land. At various points *en route* Guerd had fallen in with evil companions, among whom he seemed to feel freer. At Tucson he launched himself upon the easy and doubtful career of a gambler, which practice did not spare even his brother. At Ehrenberg, Guerd had found life to his liking — a mining and outfitting post remote from

10

civilization, where he made friends compatible with his lately developed tastes, where he finally filched the favor of dark eyes that had smiled first upon Adam.

It was a June sun that burned down upon the Colorado desert and its red river. Adam Larey had taken to rowing the boat with a powerful energy. But the fiery liquor he had absorbed and the intense heat beating down upon him soon prostrated him, half drunk and wholly helpless, upon the bottom of the leaky boat, now at the mercy of the current.

Strangest of all rivers was the Rio Colorado. Many names it had borne, though none so fitting and lasting as that which designated its color. Neither crimson nor scarlet was it, nor any namable shade of red, yet somehow red was its hue. Like blood with life gone from it! With its source at high altitude, fed by snow fields and a thousand lakes and streams, the Colorado stormed its great canyoned confines with a mighty torrent; and then, spent and leveled, but still tremendous and insatiate, it bore down across the desert with its burden of silt and sand. It was silent, it seemed to glide along, yet it was appalling.

The boat that carried Adam Larey might as well have been a rudderless craft in an ocean current. Slowly round and round it turned, as if every rod of the river was an eddy, sweeping near one shore and then the other. The hot hours of the afternoon waned. Sunset was a glaring blaze without clouds. Cranes and bitterns swept in lumbering flight over the wide green crests of the bottom lands, and desert buzzards sailed down from the ruddy sky. The boat drifted on. Before darkness fell the boat had drifted out of the current into a back eddy, where slowly it rode round and round, at last to catch hold of the arrowweeds and lodge in a thicket.

At dawn Adam Larey awoke, sober enough, but sick and aching, parched with thirst. The eastern horizon, rose-flushed and golden, told him of the advent of another day. He thrilled even in his misery. Scooping up the muddy and sand-laden water, which was cold and held a taste of snow, he quenched his thirst and bathed his hot face. Then opening his pack, he took out food he had been careful to bring.

Then he endeavored to get his bearings. Adam could see by the stain on the arrowweeds that the flood had subsided a foot during the night. A reasonable calculation was that he had drifted a good many miles. "I'll row till it gets hot, then rest up in a shady place," he decided. Pushing away from the weeds, he set the oars and rowed out to meet the current. As soon as that caught him the motion became exhilarating. By and by, what with the exercise and the cool breeze of morning on his face and the sweet, dank smell of river lowlands, he began to wear off the effects of the liquor and with it the disgust and sense of unfitness with which it had left him. Then at length gloom faded from his mind, though a pang abided in his breast. It was not an unfamiliar sensation. Resolutely he faced that wide traveling river, grateful for something nameless that seemed borne on its bosom, conscious of a strange expansion of his soul, ready to see, to hear, to smell, to feel, to taste the wildness and wonder of freedom as he had dreamed it.

The sun rose, and Adam's face and hands felt as if some hot material thing had touched them. He began to sweat, which was all that was needed to restore his usual healthy feeling of body. From time to time he saw herons, and other long-legged waterfowl, and snipe flitting over the sand bars, and somber, gray-hued birds that he could not name. The spell of river or desert hovered over these birds. The fact brought to Adam the strange nature of this silence. Like an invisible blanket it covered all, water and brush and land.

"It's desert silence," he said, wonderingly.

When he raised the oars and rested them there seemed absolutely no sound. And this fact struck him overpoweringly with its meaning and with a sudden unfamiliar joy. On the gentle wind came a fragrant hot breath that mingled with the rank odor of flooded bottom lands. The sun, hot as it was, felt good upon his face and back. He loved the sun as he hated cold.

"Maybe Guerd's coaxing me West will turn out well for me," soliloquized Adam, with resurging boyish hope. "As the Mexicans say, *Quien sabe?*"

At length he espied a sloping bank where it appeared safe to risk landing. This was a cove comparatively free of brush and the bank sloped gradually to the water. The summit of the bank was about forty or fifty feet high, and before Adam had wholly ascended it he began to see the bronze tips of mountains on all sides.

"By Jove!" exclaimed Adam. "No sign of man! No sign of life!"

Some distance from the river bank stood a high knoll. Adam climbed to the top of it, and what he saw here made him yearn for the mountain peaks. He had never stood at any great elevation. Southward the Colorado appeared to enter a mountain gateway and to turn and disappear.

When he had refreshed himself with food and drink he settled himself into a comfortable position to rest and sleep a little while. He had plucked at the roots of love, but not yet had he torn it from his heart. Guerd, his brother! The old boyhood days flashed up. Adam found the pang deep in his heart and ineradicable. The old beautiful bond, the something warm and intimate between him and Guerd, was gone forever. For its loss there could be no recompense. He knew every hour would sever him the farther from this brother who had proved false. Adam hid his face in the dry grass, and there in the loneliness of that desert he began to see into the gulf of his soul.

"I can fight — I can forget!" he muttered. Then he set his mind to the problem of his immediate future. Where would he go? There were two points below on the river — Picacho, a mining camp, and Yuma, a frontier town — about both of which he had heard strange, exciting tales. And at that moment Adam felt a reckless eagerness for adventure, and a sadness for the retreating of his old dream of successful and useful life. At length he fell asleep.

When he awoke he felt hot and wet with sweat. A luminous gold light shone through the willows and there was vivid color in the west. He had slept hours. When he moved to sit up he heard rustlings in the willows. These unseen creatures roused interest and caution in Adam. In his travels across Arizona he had passed through wild places and incidents. And remembering tales of bad Indians, bad Mexicans, bad white men, and the fierce beasts and reptiles of the desert, Adam fortified himself to encounters that must come.

When he stepped out of the shady covert it was to see river and valley as if encompassed by an immense loneliness, different somehow for the few hours of his thought and slumber. The river seemed redder and the mountains veiled in ruby haze. Earth and sky were bathed in the hue of sunset light.

He descended to the river. Shoving the boat off, he applied himself to the oars. His strong strokes, aided by the current, sent the boat along swiftly, perhaps ten miles an hour. The rose faded out of the sky, the clouds turned drab, the blue deepened, and a pale star shone. Twilight failed. With the cooling of the air Adam lay back more powerfully upon the oars. Night fell, and one by one, and then many by many, the stars came out. This night ride began to be thrilling. There must have been danger ahead. By night the river seemed vast, hurrying, shadowy, and silent as the grave. Its silence wore upon Adam until it seemed unnatural.

As the stars multiplied and brightened, the deep cut where the river wound changed its character, becoming dark and clear where it had been gloomily impenetrable. The dim, high outlines of the banks showed, and above them loomed the black domes of mountains. From time to time he turned the boat and, resting upon his oars, he drifted with the current, straining his eyes and ears. These moments of inaction brought the cold, tingling prickle of skin up and down his back. It was impossible not to be afraid, yet he thrilled even in his fear. In the clear obscurity of the night he could see several rods ahead of him over the gleaming river. But the peril that haunted Adam seemed more in the distant shadows, round the bends. What a soundless, nameless, unintelligible river! To be alone on a river like that, so vast, so

16

strange, with the grand and solemn arch of heaven blazed and clouded white by stars, taught a lesson incalculable in its effects.

The hour came when an invisible something, like a blight, passed across the heavens, paling the blue, dimming the starlight. The intense purity of the sky sustained a dull change, then darkened. Adam welcomed the first faint gleam of light over the eastern horizon. It brightened. The wan stars faded. The mountains heightened their clearness of silhouette, and along the bold, dark outlines appeared a faint rose color, herald of the sun. It deepened, it spread as the gray light turned pink and yellow. The shadows lifted from the river valley and it was day again.

"Always I have slept away the great hour," said Adam. An exhilaration uplifted him.

He drifted round a bend in the river while once more eating sparingly of his food; and suddenly he espied a high column of smoke rising to the southwest. Whereupon he took the oars again and, having become rested and encouraged, he rowed with a stroke that would make short work of the few miles to the camp.

"Picacho!" soliloquized Adam, remembering tales he had heard. "Now what shall I do? . . . I'll work at anything." He carried a considerable sum of money in a belt round his waist — the last of the money left him by his mother, and he wanted to keep it as long as possible.

Adam was not long in reaching the landing, which appeared to be only a muddy bank. A

17

small, dilapidated sternwheel steamer, such as Adam had seen on the Ohio River, lay resting upon the mud. On the bow sat a gaunt weather-beaten man with a grizzled beard. He held a long crooked fishing pole out over the water, and evidently was fishing. The bank sloped up to fine white sand and a dense growth of green, in the middle of which there appeared to be a narrow lane. Here in a flowing serape stood a Mexican girl, slender and small, with a single touch of red in all her darkness of dress.

Adam ran the boat ashore. Lifting his pack, he climbed a narrow bench of the bank and walked down to a point opposite the fisherman. Adam greeted him and inquired if this place was Picacho.

"Mornin', stranger," came the reply. "Yes, this here's the gold diggin's, an' she's hummin' these days."

"Catching any fish?" Adam inquired, with interest.

"Yep; I ketched one day before yestiddy," replied the man, complacently.

"What kind?' went on Adam.

"I'll be doggoned if I know, but he was good to eat," answered the angler, with a grin. "Where you hail from, stranger?"

"Back East."

"So I reckoned. No Westerner would tackle the Colorado when she was in flood. I opine you hit the river at Ehrenberg. Wal, you're lucky. Goin' to prospect for gold?"

18

"No, I'd rather work. Can I get a job here?"

"Son, if you're as straight as you look you can get a good job. But a husky lad like you, if he stayed sober, could strike it rich in the diggin's."

"How about a place to eat and sleep?"

"Thet ain't so easy to find up at the camp. It's a few miles up the canyon. But say, I'm forgettin' about the feller who stayed here with the Mexicans. They jest buried him. You could get his place. It's the 'dobe house — first one. Ask Margarita, there. She'll show you."

Thus directed, Adam saw the Mexican girl standing above him. Climbing the path to the top of the bank, he threw down his pack.

"*Buenas dias*, señor." The girl's soft, liquid accents fitted a dark, piquant little face, framed by hair as black as the wing of a raven, and lighted by big eyes, like night.

Adam's Spanish was not that of the Mexicans, but it enabled him to talk fairly well. He replied to the girl's greeting, yet hesitated with the query he had on his lips. He felt a slight shrinking as these dark eyes reminded him of others of like allurement which he had willed to forget. Yet he experienced a warmth and thrill of pleasure in a pretty face. Women invariably smiled upon Adam. This one, a girl in her teens, smiled with half-lowered eyes, the more provocative for that; and she turned partly away with a lithe, quick grace. Adam's hesitation had been a sudden chill at the proximity of something

19

feminine and attractive — of something that had hurt him. But it passed. He had done more than boldly step across the threshold of a new and freer life.

2

For Adam's questions Margarita had a shy, "*Si*, señor," and the same subtle smile that had attracted him. Whereupon he took up his pack and followed her.

Back from the river the sand was thick and heavy, clean and white. The girl led down a path bordered by willows and mesquites which opened into a clearing where stood several squat adobe houses.

Margarita stopped at the first house. The girl's mother appeared to be an indolent person, rather careless of her attire. She greeted Adam in English, but when he exercised some of his laborsome Spanish her dark face beamed with smiles that made it pleasant to behold. The little room indoors, to which she led Adam, was dark, poorly ventilated, and altogether unsatisfactory. Adam said so. The señora waxed eloquent. Margarita managed to convey her great disappointment by one swift look. Then they led him outdoors and round under the low-branching mesquites, where he had to stoop, to a small structure. The walls were made of two rows of long slender poles, nailed upon heavier uprights at the corners, and between these rows had been poured wet adobe mud. The hut contained two rooms, the closed one full of wood and rubbish, and the other, which had an open front, like a porch, faced the river. It was empty, with a floor of white sand. This appeared very much to Adam's liking, and he agreed upon a price for it, to the señora's satisfaction and Margarita's shy rapture. Adam saw the latter with some misgiving, yet he was pleased, and in spite of himself he warmed toward this pretty señorita who had apparently taken a sudden fancy to him. He was a stranger in a strange land, with a sore and yearning heart. While Adam untied his pack and spread out its contents the women fetched a low bench, a bucket of water, and a basin. These simple articles constituted the furniture of his new lodgings. He was to get his meals at the house, where, it was assured, he would be well cared for. In moving away, Margarita, who was looking back, caught her hair in a thorny branch of the mesquite. Adam was quick to spring to her assistance. Then she ran off after her mother.

"What eyes! Well, well!" exclaimed Adam, sensible of a warmth along his veins. Suddenly at that moment he thought of his brother Guerd. "I'm glad he's not here." Margarita had prompted that thought. Guerd was a handsome devil, irresistible to women. Adam went back to his unpacking, conscious of a sobered enthusiasm.

He hung his few clothes and belongings upon the walls, made his bed of blankets on the sand, and then surveyed the homely habitation with pleasure.

He found the old fisherman in precisely the same posture. Adam climbed on board the boat.

"Get any bites?" he queried.

"I believe I jest had one," replied the fisherman.

Adam saw that he was about fifty years old, lean and dried, with a wrinkled tanned face and scant beard.

"Have a smoke," said Adam, proffering one of the last of his cigars.

"Lordy!" ejaculated the fisherman, his eyes lighting. "When have I seen one of them? . . . Young man, you're an obligin' feller. What's your name?"

Adam told him, and that he hailed from the East and had been a tendertoot for several memorable weeks.

"My handle's Merryvale," replied the other. "I came West twenty-eight years ago when I was about your age. Reckon you're about twenty."

"No. Only eighteen. Say, you must have almost seen the old days of 'forty-nine."

"It was in 'fifty. Yes, I was in the gold rush."

22

"Did you strike any gold?" asked Adam, eagerly.

"Son, I was a prospector for twenty years. I've made an' lost more than one fortune. Drink an' faro an' bad women! . . . And now I'm a broken-down night watchman at Picacho."

"I'm sorry," said Adam, sincerely. "I'll bet you've seen some great old times. Won't you tell me about them? You see, I'm foot-loose now and sort of wild."

Merryvale nodded sympathetically. He studied Adam with eyes that were shrewd and penetrating, for all their kindliness. Wherefore Adam talked frankly about himself and his travels West. Merryvale listened with a nod now and then.

"Son, I hate to see the likes of you hittin' this gold diggin's," he said.

"Why? Oh, I can learn to take care of myself. It must be a man's game. I'll love the desert."

"Wal, son, I oughtn't discourage you," replied Merryvale. "An' it ain't fair for me to think because I went wrong, an' because I seen so many boys go wrong, thet you'll do the same. . . . But this gold diggin's is a hell of a place for a tough old timer, let alone a boy runnin' wild."

And then he began to talk like a man whose memory was a vast treasure store of history and adventure and life. Gold had been discovered at Picacho in 1864. In 1872 the mill was erected near the river, and the ore was mined

23

five miles up the canyon and hauled down on a narrow-gauge railroad. The machinery and construction for this great enterprise, together with all supplies, were brought by San Francisco steamers round into the Gulf of California, loaded on smaller steamers, and carried up the Colorado River to Picacho. These steamers also hauled supplies to Yuma and Ehrenberg, where they were freighted by wagon trains into the interior. At the present time, 1878, the mine was paying well and there were between five and six hundred men employed. The camp was always full of adventurers and gamblers, together with a few bad women whose capacity for making trouble magnified their number.

"Down here at the boat landin' an' the mill it's always sorta quiet," said Merryvale. "You see, there ain't many men here. An' the gamblin' hells are all up at the camp, where, in fact, everybody goes of an evenin'. Lord knows I've bucked the tiger in every gold camp in California. There's a fever grips a man. I never seen the good of gold to the man thet dug it. . . . So, son, if you're askin' me for a hunch, let me tell you, drink little an' gamble light an' fight shy of the females!"

"Merryvale, I'm more of a tenderfoot than I look, I guess," replied Adam. "You'd hardly believe I never drank till I started West a few months ago. I can't stand liquor."

Adam's face lost its brightness and his eyes shadowed, though they held frankly to Merryvale's curious gaze.

'Son, you're a strappin' youngster an' you've got looks no woman will pass by," said Merryvale. "An' in this country the preference of women brings trouble. Wal, for thet matter, all the trouble anywheres is made by them. But in the desert, where it's wild an' hot an' there's few females of any species, the fightin' gets bloody."

"Women have been the least of my fights or troubles," rejoined Adam. "But lately I had a — a little more serious affair — that ended suddenly before I fell in deep."

"Lordy! son, you'll be a lamb among wolves!" broke in Merryvale. "See here, I'm goin' to start you right. This country is no place for a nice clean boy, more's the shame and pity. Every man who gets on in the West, let alone in the desert where the West is magnified, has got to live up to the standard. He must work, he must endure, he must fight men, he must measure up to women. I ain't sayin' it's a fine standard, but it's the one by which men have survived in a hard country at a hard time."

"Survival of the fittest," muttered Adam soberly.

"You've said it, son. Thet law makes the livin' things of this desert, whether man or otherwise. *Quien sabe?* You can never tell what's in a man till he's tried. Son, I've known desert men whose lives were beyond all understandin.' But not one man in a thousand can live on the desert.

Thet has to do with his mind first; then his endurance. But to come back to this here Picacho. I'd not be afraid to back you against it if you meet it right."

"How is that?"

"Lordy! son, I wish I could say the right word," returned Merryvale, in pathetic earnestness. "You ain't to be turned back?"

"No. I'm here for better or worse. Back home I had my hopes, my dreams. They're gone — vanished. . . . I've no near relatives except a brother who — who is not my kind. I didn't want to come West. But I seem to have been freed from a cage. This grand wild desert! It will do something wonderful — or terrible with me."

"Wal, wal, you talk like you look," replied Merryvale, with a sigh. "Time was, son, when a hunch of mine might be doubtful. But now I'm old, an' as I go down the years I remember more my youth an' I love it more. You can trust me." Then he paused, taking a deep breath, as if his concluding speech, involved somehow his faith in himself and his good will to a stranger. "Be a man with your body! Don't shirk work or play or fight. Eat an' drink an' be merry, but don't live jest for thet. Lend a helpin' hand — be generous with your gold. Put aside a third of your earnin's for gamblin' an' look to lose it. Don't ever get drunk. You can't steer clear of women, good or bad. An' the only way is to be game an' kind an' square."

"Game — kind — square," mused Adam, thoughtfully.

"Wal, I need a new fishin' line," said Merryvale, as he pulled in his rod. "We'll go up to the store an' then I'll take you to the mill."

While passing the adobe house where Adam had engaged board and lodging he asked his companion the name of the people.

"Arallanes — Juan Arallanes lives there," replied Merryvale. "An' he's the whitest greaser I ever seen. He's a foreman of the Mexicans employed at the mill. His wife is nice, too. But thet black-eyed hussy Margarita —"

Merryvale shook his grizzled head, but did not complete his dubious beginning. The suggestion piqued Adam's curiosity. Presently Merryvale pointed out a cluster of huts and cabins and one rather pretentious stone house, low and square, with windows. Both white and dark-skinned children were playing on the sand in the shady places. Idle men lounged in front of the stone house, which Merryvale said was the store. Upon entering, Adam saw a complete general store of groceries, merchandise, hardware, and supplies; and he felt amazed until he remembered how the river steamers made transportation easy as far as the border of the desert. Then Merryvale led on to the huge structure of stone and iron and wood that Adam had espied from far up the river. As Adam drew near he heard the escape of steam, the roar of heavy machinery, and a sound that must have been a movement and crushing of ore, with a rush of flowing water.

Merryvale evidently found the manager, who was a man of medium height, powerfully built, with an unshaven broad face, strong and ruddy. He wore a red-flannel shirt, wet with sweat, a gun at his belt, overalls thrust into cowhide boots; and together he looked a rough and practical miner.

"Mac, shake hands with my young friend here," said Merryvale. "He wants a job."

"Howdy!" replied the other, proffering a big hand that Adam certainly felt belonged to a man. Also he was aware of one quick all-embracing glance. "Are you good at figures?"

"Why, yes," answered Adam, "but I want to work."

"All right. You can help me in the office where I'm stuck. An' I'll give you outside work, besides. To-morrow." And with this brusque promise the manager strode away in a hurry.

"Mac don't get time to eat," explained Merryvale.

Adam had to laugh at the incident. Here he had been recommended by a stranger, engaged to work for a man whose name he had not heard and who had not asked his, and no mention made of wages. Adam liked this simplicity. A man must pass in this country for what he was.

Merryvale went his way then, leaving Adam alone. It seemed to Adam, as he pondered there,

28

that his impressions of that gold mill did not augur well for a satisfaction with his job. He had no distaste for hard labor, though to bend over a desk did not appeal to him. Then he turned his gaze to the river and valley. What a splendid scene! The green borderland offered soft and relieving contrast to the bare and grisly ridges upon which he stood. At that distance the river shone red gold, sweeping through its rugged iron gateway and winding majestically down the valley to lose itself round a bold bluff.

Adam drew a long breath. A scene like this world of mountain wilderness, of untrodden ways, was going to take hold of him. And then, singularly, there flashed into memory an image of the girl Margarita. Just then Adam resented thought of her. It was not because she had made eyes at him — for he had to confess this was pleasing — but because he did not like the idea of a deep and vague emotion running parallel in his mind with thought of a roguish and coquettish little girl, of doubtful yet engaging possibilities.

"I think too much," declared Adam. It was action he needed. Work, play, hunting, exploring, even gold digging — anything with change of scene and movement of muscle — these things that he had instinctively felt to be the need of his body, now seemed equally the need of his soul.

3

Arallanes, the foreman, did not strike Adam as being typical of the Mexicans among whom he lived. He was not a little runt of a swarthy-skinned man, but well built, of a clear olive complexion and regular features.

After supper Arallanes invited Adam to ride up to the camp. Whereupon Margarita asked to be taken. Arallanes laughed, and then talked so fast that Adam could not understand. He gathered, however, that the empty ore train traveled up the canyon to the camp, there to remain until morning. Also Adam perceived that Margarita did not get along well with this man, who was her stepfather. They appeared on the verge of a quarrel. But the señora spoke a few soft words that worked magic upon Arallanes, though they did not change the passion of the girl. How swiftly she had paled! Her black eyes burned with a dusky fire. When she turned them upon Adam it was certain that he had a new sensation.

"Will not the gracious señor take Margarita to the dance?"

That was how Adam translated her swift, eloquent words. Embarrassed and hesitating, he felt that he cut a rather sorry figure before her. Then he realized the singular beauty of her big eyes, sloe black and brilliant, neither half veiled nor shy now, but bold and wide and burning, as if the issue at stake was not trivial.

Arallanes put a hand on Adam. "No, señor," he said. "Some other time you may take Margarita."

"I — I shall be pleased," stammered Adam. The girl's red lips curled in pouting scorn, and with a wonderful dusky flash of eyes she whirled away.

Outside, Arallanes led Adam across the sands, still with that familiar hand upon him.

"Boy," he said, in English, "that girl — she no blood of mine. She damn leetle wild cat — mucha Indian — on fire all time."

If ever Adam had felt the certainty of his youthful years, it had been during those last few moments. His collar was hot and tight. A sense of shock remained with him. He had not fortified himself at all, nor had he surrendered himself to recklessness. But to think of going to a dance this very night, in a mining camp, with a dusky-eyed little Spanish girl who appeared exactly what Arallanes had called her — the very idea took Adam's breath with the surprise of it, the wildness of it, the strange appeal to him.

"Señor veree beeg, but young — like colt," said Arallanes, with good nature. "Tenderfeet, the gamblers say. . . . He mos' dam' sure have tough feet soon on Picacho!"

"Well, Arallanes, that can't come too soon for me," declared Adam, and the statement seemed to give relief.

They climbed to the track where the ore train stood, already with laborers in almost every car. After a little wait that seemed long to the impatient Adam the train started. The track was built a few feet above the sand, but showed signs of having been submerged, and in fact washed out in places. The canyon was tortuous, and grew more so as it narrowed. Adam descried tunnels dug in the red walls and holes dug in gravel benches, which place Arallanes explained had been made by prospectors hunting for gold. It developed, however, that there was a considerable upgrade. That seemed a long five miles to Adam. The train halted and the laborers yelled merrily.

Arallanes led Adam up a long winding path, quite steep, and the other men followed in single file. When Adam reached a level once more, Arallanes called out, "Picacho!"

But he certainly could not have meant the wide gravelly plateau with its squalid huts, its adobe shacks, its rambling square of low flat buildings, like a stockade fort roofed with poles and dirt. Arallanes meant the mountain that dominated the place — Picacho, the Peak.

Adam faced the west as the sun was setting. The mountain, standing magnificently above the bold knobs and ridges around it, was a dark purple mass framed in sunset gold; and from its frowning summit, notched and edged, streamed a long ruddy golden ray of sunlight that shone down through a wind-worn hole. With the sun blocked and hidden except for that small aperture there was yet a wonderful effect of sunset. A ruddy haze, shading the blue, filled the canyons and the spaces. Picacho seemed grand there, towering to the sky, crowned in gold, aloof, unscalable, a massive rock sculptured by the ages.

Arallanes laughed at Adam, then sauntered on. Mexicans jabbered as they passed, and some of the white men made jocular comment at the boy standing there so wide eyed and still. A little Irishman gaped at Adam and said to a comrade:

"Begorra, he's after seein' a peanut atop ole Picacho. . . . What-th'-hell now, me young fri'nd? Come hev a drink."

The crowd passed on, and Arallanes lingered, making himself a cigarette the while.

Adam had not been prepared for such a spectacle of grandeur and desolation. He seemed to feel himself a mite flung there, encompassed by colossal and immeasurable fragments of upheaved rock, jagged and jutted, with never a softening curve, and all steeped in vivid and intense light. The plateau was a ridged and scarred waste, lying under the half circle of range behind, and sloping down toward where the

33

river lay hidden. The range to the left bore a crimson crest, and it lost itself in a region of a thousand peaks. The range to the right was cold pure purple and it ended in a dim infinity. Between these ranges, far flung across the Colorado, loomed now with exquisite clearness in Adam's sight the mountain world he had gotten a glimpse of from below. But now he perceived its marvelous all-bracing immensity, magnified by the transparent light, its limitless horizon line an illusion, its thin pale distances unbelievable. The lilac-veiled canyons lay clear in his sight; the naked bones of the mountains showed hungrily the nature of the desert earth; and over all the vast area revealed by the setting sun lay the awful barrenness of a dead world, beautiful and terrible, with its changing rose and topaz hues only mockeries to the lover of life.

A hand fell upon Adam's shoulder.

"Come, let us look at games of gold and women," said Arallanes.

Then he led Adam into a big, poorly lighted, low-ceiled place, as crudely constructed as a shed, and full of noise and smoke. The attraction seemed to be a rude bar, various gambling games, and some hawk-faced, ghastly spectacles of women drinking with men at the tables. From an adjoining apartment came discordant music. This scene was intensely interesting to Adam, yet disappointing. His first sight of a wild frontier gambling hell did not thrill him.

It developed that Arallanes liked to drink and talk loud and laugh, and to take a bold chance at a gambling game. But Adam refused, and meant to avoid drinking as long as he could. He wandered around by himself, to find that everybody was merry and friendly. Adam tried not to look at any of the women while they looked at him. The apartment from which came the music was merely a bare canvas-covered room with a board floor. Dancing was going on.

Adam's aimless steps finally led him back to the sand-floored hall, where he became absorbed in watching a game of poker that a bystander said had no limit. Then Adam sauntered on, and presently was attracted by a quarrel among some Mexicans. To his surprise, it apparently concerned Arallanes. All of them showed the effects of liquor, and, after the manner of their kind, they were gesticulating and talking excitedly. Suddenly one of them drew a knife and lunged toward Arallanes. Adam saw the movement, and then the long shining blade, before he saw what the man looked like. That action silenced the little group.

The outstretched hand, quivering with the skewerlike dagger, paused in its sweep as it reached a point opposite Adam. Instinctively he leaped, and quick as a flash he caught the wrist in a grip so hard the fellow yelled. Adam, now that he possessed the menacing hand, did not know what to do with it. With a powerful jerk he pulled the Mexican off his feet, and then, exerting his strength to his utmost, he swung him round, knocking over men and tables, until his hold loosened. The knife flew one way and the Mexican the other. He lay where he fell. Arallanes and his comrades made much of Adam.

"We are friends. You will drink with me," said Arallanes, grandly.

Though no one would have suspected it, Adam was really in need of something bracing.

"Señor is only a boy, but he has an arm," said Arallanes, as he clutched Adam's shoulder and biceps with a nervous hand. . . . "When señor becomes a man he will be a giant."

Adam's next change of emotion was from fright to a sense of foolishness at his standing there. Then he had another drink, and after his feelings changed again, and for that matter the whole complexion of everything changed.

He never could have found the narrow path leading down into the canyon. Arallanes was his guide. Walking on the sandy floor was hard work and made him sweat. The loose sand and gravel dragged at his feet. Not long was it before he had walked off the effects of the strong liquor. He became curious as to why the Mexican had threatened Arallanes, and was told that during the day the foreman had discharged this fellow.

"He ran after Margarita," added Arallanes, "and I kicked him out of the house. The women, señor — ah! they do not mind what a man is! . . . Have a care of Margarita. She has as many loves and lives as a spotted cat."

For the most part, however, the two men were silent on this laborious walk. By and by the canyon widened out so that Adam could view the great expanse of sky, fretted with fire, and the mountain spurs, rising on all sides, cold and dark against the blue. At last Arallanes announced that they were home. Adam had not seen a single house in the gray shadows. A few more steps, however, brought tangible substance of walls to Adam's touch. Then he drew a long deep breath and realized how tired he was. The darkness gradually changed from pitch black to a pale obscurity. He could see dim, spectral outlines of mesquites, and a star shining through. At first the night appeared to be absolutely silent, but after a while, by straining his ears, he heard a rustling of mice or ground squirrels in the adobe walls. The sound comforted him, however, and when one of them, or at least some little animal, ran softly over his bed the feeling of utter loneliness was broken.

"I've begun it," he whispered, and meant the lonely life that was to be his. The silence, the darkness, the loneliness seemed to give him deeper thought. The thing that puzzled him and alarmed him was what seemed to be swift changes going on in him. If he changed his mind every hour, now cast down because of memories he could not wholly shake, or lifted to strange exaltation by the beauty of a desert sunset, or again swayed by the appeal of a girl's dusky eyes, and then instinctively leaping into a fight with a Mexican — if he were going to be as vacillating and wild as these impulses led him to suppose he might be, it was certain that he faced a hopeless future.

But could he help himself? Then it seemed his fine instincts, his fine principles, and the hopes and dreams that would not die, began to contend with a new uprising force in him, a wilder something he had never known, a strange stirring and live emotion.

"But I'm glad," he burst out, as if telling his secret to the darkness. "Glad to be rid of Guerd — damn him and his meanness! . . . Glad to be alone! . . . Glad to come into this wild desert! . . . Glad that girl made eyes at me! I'll not lie to myself. I wanted to hug her — to kiss her — and I'll do it if she'll let me. . . . That gambling hell disgusted me, and sight of the greaser's knife scared me cold. Yet when I got hold of him — felt my strength — how helpless he was — that I could have cracked his bones — why, scared as I was, I felt a strange wild something that is not gone yet. . . . I'm changing. It's a different life. And I've got to meet things as they come, and be game."

Next morning Adam went to work and it developed that this was to copy MacKay's lead-pencil scrawls, and after that was done to keep accurate account of ore mined and operated. Several days passed before Adam caught up with his work to the hour. Then MacKay, true to his word, said he would set him on a man's job part of the time. The job upon which MacKay put Adam was no less than keeping up the fire under the huge boilers. As wood had to be used for fuel and as it was consumed rapidly, the task of stoking was not easy. Besides, hot as the furnace was, it seemed the sun was hotter. Adam sweat till he could wring water out of his shirt.

That night he made certain MacKay was playing a joke on him. Arallanes confided this intelligence, and even Margarita had been led into the secret. MacKay had many laborers for the hard work, and he wanted to cure the tenderfoot of his desire for a man's job, such as he had asked for. It was all good-natured, and amused Adam. He imagined he knew what he needed, and while he was trying to find it he could have just as much fun as MacKay.

Much to MacKay's surprise, Adam presented himself next afternoon, in boots, overalls, and undershirt, to go on with his job of firing the engine.

"Wasn't yesterday enough?" queried the boss.

"I can stand it."

Then it pleased Adam to see a considerable evidence of respect in the rough mill operator's expression. For a week Adam kept up with his office work and labored each afternoon at the stoking job. No one suspected that he suffered, though it was plain enough that he lost flesh and was exceedingly fatigued. Then Margarita's reception of him, when he trudged home in the waning sunset hour, was sweet despite the fact that he tried to repudiate its sweetness. Once she put a little brown hand on his blistered arm, and her touch held the tenderness of woman. All women must be akin. They liked a man who could do things, and the greater his feats of labor or fight the better they liked him.

The following week MacKay took a Herculean laborer off a strenuous job with the ore and put Adam in his place. MacKay maintained his good humor, but he had acquired a little grimness. This long-limbed tenderfoot was a hard nut to crack. Adam's father had been a man of huge stature and tremendous strength; and many a time had Adam heard it said that he might grow to be like his father. Far indeed was he from that now; but he took the brawny and seasoned laborer's place and kept it. If the other job had been toil for Adam, this new one was pain. He learned there what labor meant. Also he learned how there was only one thing that common men understood and respected in a co-laborer, and it was the grit and muscle to stand the grind. Adam was eighteen years old and far from having reached his growth. This fact might have been manifest to his fellow workers, but it was not that which counted. He realized that those long hours of toil at which he stubbornly stuck had set his spirit in some immeasurable and unquenchable relation to the strange life that he divined was to be his.

Two weeks and more went by. MacKay, in proportion to the growth of his admiration and friendship for Adam, gradually weakened on his joke. And one day, when banteringly he dared Adam to tip a car of ore that two Mexicans were laboring at, and Adam in a single heave sent the tons of ore roaring into the shaft, then MacKay gave up and in true Western fashion swore his defeat and shook hands with the boy.

So in those few days Adam made friends who changed the color and direction of his life. From Merryvale he learned the legend and history of the frontier. MacKay opened his eyes to the great health for mind and body in sheer toil. Arallanes represented a warmth of friendship that came unsought, showing what might be hidden in any man. Margarita was still an unknown quantity in Adam's development. Their acquaintance had gone on mostly under the eyes of the señora or Arallanes. Sometimes at sunset Adam had sat with her on the seat of the river bank. Her charm grew. Then the unexpected happened. A break occurred in the machinery and a small but invaluable part could not be repaired. It had to come from San Francisco.

Adam seemed to be thrown back upon his own resources. He did not know what to do with himself. Arallanes advised him not to go panning for gold, and to be cautious if he went up to Picacho, for the Mexican Adam had so roughly handled was the ringleader in a bad gang that it would be well to avoid. All things conspired, it seemed, to throw Adam into the company of Margarita, who always waited around the corner of every hour, watching with her dusky eyes.

So as the slow, solemn days drifted onward, like the wonderful river which dominated the desert valley, it came to pass that the dreaming, pondering Adam suddenly awakened to the danger in this dusky-eyed maiden.

The realization came to Adam at the still sunset hour when he and Margarita were watching the river slide like a gleam of gold out of the west. They were walking among the scattered mesquites along the sandy bank, a place lonesome and hidden from the village behind, yet open to the wide space of river and valley beyond. The air seemed full of marvelous tints of gold and rose and purple. The majestic scene, beautiful and sad, needed life to make it perfect. Adam, more than usually drawn by Margarita's sympathy, was trying to tell her something of the burden on his mind, that he was alone in the world, with only a hard gray future before him, with no one to care whether he lived or died.

Then had come his awakening. It did not speak well for Margarita's conceptions of behavior, but it proved her a creature of heart and blood. To be suddenly enveloped by a wind of flame, in the slender twining form of this girl of Spanish nature, was for Adam at once a revelation and a catastrophe. But if he was staggered, he was also responsive, as in a former moment of poignancy he had vowed he would be. A strong and shuddering power took hold of his heart and he felt the leap, the beat, the burn of his blood. When he lifted Margarita and gathered her in a close embrace it was more than a hot upflashing of boyish passion that flushed his face and started tears from under his tight-shut eyelids. It was a sore hunger for he knew not what, a gratefulness that he could express only by violence, a yielding to something deeper and more far-reaching than was true of the moment.

Adam loosened Margarita's hold upon his neck and held her back from him so he could see her face. It was sweet, rosy. Her eyes were shining, black and fathomless as night, soft with a light that had never shone upon Adam from any other woman's.

"Girl, do you — love me?" he demanded, and if his voice broke with the strange eagerness of a boy, his look had all the sternness of a man.

"Ah . . . !" whispered Margarita.

"You — you big-hearted girl!" he exclaimed, with a laugh that was glad, yet had a tremor in it. "Margarita, I — I must love you, too — since I feel so queer."

Then he bent to her lips, and from these first real kisses that had ever been spent upon him by a woman he realized in one flash his danger. He released Margarita in a consideration she did not comprehend; and in her pouting reproach, her soft-eyed appeal, her little brown hands that would not let go of him, there was further menace to his principles.

Adam, gay and teasing, yet kindly and tactfully, tried to find a way to resist her.

"Señorita, some one will see us," he said.

"Who cares?"

"But, child, we — we must think."

"Señor, no woman ever thinks when love is in her heart and on her lips."

Her reply seemed to rebuke Adam, for he sensed in it what might be true of life, rather than just of this one little girl, swayed by unknown and uncontrollable forces. She appeared to him then subtly and strongly, as if there was infinitely more than willful love in her. But it did not seem to be the peril of her proffered love that restrained Adam so much as the strange consciousness of the willingness of his spirit to meet hers halfway.

44

Suddenly Margarita's mood changed. She became like a cat that had been purring under a soft, agreeable hand and then had been stroked the wrong way.

"Señor think he love me?" she flashed, growing white.

"Yes — I said so — Margarita. Of course I do," he hastened to assure her.

"Maybe you — a gringo liar!"

Adam might have resented this insulting hint but for his uncertainty of himself, his consequent embarrassment, and his thrilling sense of the nearness of her blazing eyes. What a little devil she looked! This did not antagonize Adam, but it gave him proof of his impudence, of his dreaming carelessness. Margarita might not be a girl to whom he should have made love, but it was too late. Besides, he did not regret that. Only he was upset; he wanted to think.

"If the *grande* señor trifle — Margarita will cut out his heart!"

This swift speech, inflexible and wonderful with a passion that revealed to Adam the half-savage nature of a woman whose race was alien to his, astounded and horrified him, and yet made his blood tingle wildly.

"Margarita, I do not trifle," replied Adam, earnestly. "God knows I'm glad you — you care for me. How have I offended you? What is it you want?"

"Let señor swear he love me," she demanded, imperiously.

Adam answered to that with the wildness that truly seemed flashing more and more from him; and the laughter and boldness on his lips hid the gravity that had settled there. He was no no clod. Under the softness of him hid a flint that struck fire.

As Margarita had been alluring and provocative, then as furious as a barbarian queen, so she now changed again to another personality in which it pleased her to be proud, cold, aloof, an outraged woman to be wooed back to tenderness. If, at the last moment of the walk home, Margarita evinced signs of another sudden transformation, Adam appeared not to note them. Leaving her in the dusk at the door where the señora sat, he strode away to the bank of the river. When he felt himself free and safe once more, he let out a great breath of relief.

"Whew! Now I've done it! . . . So she'd cut my heart out? And I had to swear I loved her! The little savage! . . . But she's amazing — and she's adorable, with all her cat claws. Wouldn't Guerd rave over a girl like Margarita? . . . And here I am, standing on my two feet, in possession of all my faculties, Adam Larey, a boy who thought he had principles — yet now I'm a ranting lover of a dark-skinned, black-eyed slip of a greaser girl! It can't be true!"

With that outburst came sobering thought. Adam's resolve not to ponder and brood about himself was as if it had never been.

He knew he would never make such a resolve again. For hours he strolled up and down the sandy bank, deep in thought, yet aware of the night and the stars, the encompassing mountains, and the silent, gleaming river winding away in the gloom. As he had become used to being alone out in the solitude and darkness, there had come to him a vague awakening sense of their affinity with his nature. Success and people might fail and betray him, but the silent, lonely starlit nights were going to be teachers, even as they had been to the Wise Men of the Arabian waste.

Adam at length gave up in despair and went to bed, hoping in slumber to forget a complexity of circumstance and emotion that seemed to him an epitome of his callow helplessness. The desert began to loom to Adam as a region inimical to comfort and culture. He had almost decided that the physical nature of the desert was going to be good for him. But what of its spirit, mood, passion as typified by Margarita Arallanes?

Adam could ask himself that far-reaching query, and yet, all the answer he got was a rush of hot blood at memory of the sweet fire of her kisses. He saw her to be a simple child of the desert, like an Indian, answering to savage impulses, wholly unconscious of what had been a breach of womanly reserve and restraint. Was she good or bad? How could she be bad if she did not know any better? Thus Adam pondered and conjectured, and cursed his ignorance, and lamented his failings, all the time honest to acknowledge that he was fond of Margarita and drawn to her. About the only conclusion he formed from his perplexity was the one that he owed it to Margarita to live up to his principles.

At this juncture he recollected Merryvale's significant remarks about the qualities needed by men who were to survive in the desert, and his nobler sentiments suffered a rout. The suddenness, harshness, fierceness of the desert grafted different and combating qualities upon a man or else it snuffed him out, like a candle blown by a gusty wind.

Next morning, as every morning, the awakening was sweet, fresh, new, hopeful. Another day! And the wonderful dry keenness of the air, the colors that made the earth seem a land of enchantment, were enough in themselves to make life worth living. In the morning he always felt like a boy.

Margarita's repentance for her moods of yesterday took a material turn in the preparation of an unusually good breakfast for Adam. He was always hungry and good meals were rare. Adam liked her attentions, and he encouraged them; though not before the señora or Arallanes, for the former approved too obviously and the latter disapproved too mysteriously.

When, some time later, a boat arrived, Adam was among the first to meet it at the dock.

He encountered MacKay coming ashore in the company of a man and two women, one of whom was young. The manager showed a beaming face for the first time in many days. Repairs for the mill engine had come. MacKay at once introduced Adam to the party; and it so turned out that presently the manager, who was extremely busy, left his friends for Adam to entertain. They were people whom Adam liked immediately, and as the girl was pretty, of a blond type seldom seen in the Southwest, it seemed to Adam that his task was more than agreeable. He showed them around the little village and then explained how interesting it would be for them to see the gold mill. How long a time it seemed since he had been in the company of a girl like those he had known at home! She was merry, intelligent, a little shy.

He was invited aboard the boat to have lunch with the mother and daughter. Everything tended to make this a red-letter day for Adam. The hours passed all too swiftly and time came for the boat to depart. When the boat swung free from the shore Adam read in the girl's eyes the thought keen in his own mind — that they would never meet again. The round of circumstances might never again bring a girl like that into Adam's life, if it were to be lived in these untrodden ways. He waved his hand with all the eloquence which it would express. Then the obtruding foliage on the bank hid the boat and the girl was gone. His last thought was a selfish one — that his brother Guerd would not see her at Ehrenberg.

Some of MacKay's laborers were working with unloaded freight on the dock. One of these was Regan, the little Irishman who had been keen to mark Adam on several occasions. He winked at MacKay and pointed at Adam.

"Mac, shure thot boy's a divil with the wimmen!"

MacKay roared with laughter and looked significantly past Adam as if this mirth was not wholly due to his presence alone. Some one else seemed implicated. Suddenly Adam turned. Margarita stood there, with face and mien of a tragedy queen, and it seemed to Adam that her burning black eyes did not see anything in the world but him. Then, with one of her swift actions, graceful and lithe, yet violent, she wheeled and fled.

"O Lord!" murmured Adam, aghast at the sudden-dawning significance of the case. He had absolutely forgotten Margarita's existence. Most assuredly she had seen every move of his with her big eyes, and read his mind, too. He could not see the humor of his situation at the moment, but as he took a short cut through the shady mesquites toward his hut, and presently espied Margarita in ambush. What fiendish glee this predicament of his would have aroused in his brother Guerd! Adam, the lofty, the supercilious, had come a cropper at last — such would have been Guerd's scorn and rapture!

Margarita came rushing from the side, right upon him even as he turned. So swiftly she came that he could not get a good look at her, but she appeared a writhing, supple little thing, instinct with fury. Hissing Spanish maledictions, she flung herself upward, and before he could ward her off she had slapped and scratched his face and beat wildly at him with flying brown fists. He thrust her away, but she sprang back. Then, suddenly hot with anger, he grasped her and, jerking her off her feet, he shook her with far from gentle force, and did not desist till he saw that he was hurting her. Letting her down and holding her at arm's length, he gazed hard at the white face framed by disheveled black hair and lighted by eyes so magnificently expressive of supreme passion that his anger was shocked into wonder and admiration. Desert eyes! Right there a conception dawned in his mind — he was seeing a spirit through eyes developed by the desert.

"Margarita!" he exclaimed, "are you a cat — that you —"

"I hate you," she hissed, interrupting him. The expulsion of her breath, the bursting swell of her breast, the quiver of her whole lissom body, all were exceedingly potent of an intensity that utterly amazed Adam. Such a little girl, such a frail strength, such a deficient brain to hold all that passion. What would she do if she had real cause for wrath?

"Ah, Margarita, you don't mean that. I didn't

51

do anything. Let me tell you."

She repeated her passionate utterance, and Adam saw that he could no more change her then than he could hope to move the mountain. Resentment stirred in him.

"Well," he burst out, boyishly, "if you're so darned fickle as that I'm glad you do hate me."

Then he released his hold on her arms and, turning away without another glance in her direction, he strode from the glade. He took the gun he had repaired and set off down the river trail. When he got into the bottom lands of willow and cottonwood he glided noiselessly along, watching and listening for game of some kind.

In the wide mouth of a wash not more than a mile from the village Adam halted to admire some exceedingly beautiful trees. The first was one of a species he had often noted there, and it was a particularly fine specimen, perhaps five times as high as his head and full and round in proportion. The trunk was large at the ground, soon separating into innumerable branches that in turn spread and drooped and separated into a million twigs and stems and points. Trunk and branch and twig, every inch of this wonderful tree was a bright, soft green color, as smooth as if polished, and it did not have a single leaf. As Adam gazed at this strange, unknown tree, grasping the nature of it and its exquisite color and grace and life, he wondered anew at the marvel of the desert.

As he walked around to the side toward the

river he heard a cry. Wheeling quickly, he espied Margarita running toward him. Margarita's hair was flying. Blood showed on her white face. She had torn her dress.

"Margarita!" cried Adam, as he reached her. "What's the matter?"

She was so out of breath she could scarcely speak.

"Felix — he hide back there — in trail," she panted. "Margarita watch — she know — she go round."

The girl labored under extreme agitation, which, however, did not seem to be fright.

"Felix? You mean the Mexican who drew a knife on your father? The fellow I threw around — up at Picacho?'

"*Si* — señor," replied Margarita.

"Well, what of it? Why does Felix hide up in the trail?"

"Felix swore revenge. He kill you."

"Oh-ho! . . . So that's it," ejaculated Adam, and he whistled his surprise. A hot, tight sensation struck deeply inside him. "Then you came to find me — warn me?"

She nodded vehemently and clung to him, evidently wearied and weakening.

"Margarita, that was good of you," said Adam, earnestly, and he led her out of the sun into the shade of the tree. With his handkerchief he wiped the blood from thorn scratches on her cheek. The dusky eyes shone with a vastly different light from the lurid hate of a few hours

53

back. "I thank you, girl, and I'll not forget it. . . . But why did you run out in the sun and through the thorns to warn me?"

"Señor know now — he kill Felix before Felix kill him," replied Margarita, in speech that might have been naïve had its simplicity not been so deadly.

Adam laughed again, a little grimly. This was not the first time there had been forced upon him a hint of the inevitableness of life in the desert. But it was not his duty to ambush the Mexican who would ambush him. The little coldness thrilled out of Adam to the close, throbbing presence of Margarita. The fragrance, the very breath of her, went to his head like wine.

'But girl — only a little while ago — you slapped me — scratched me — hated me," he said, in wonder and reproach.

"No — no — no! Margarita love señor!" she cried, and seemed to twine around him and climb into his arms at once. The same fire, the same intensity as of that unforgettable moment of hate and passion, dominated her now, only it was love.

And this time it was Adam who sought her red lips and returned her kisses. Again that shuddering wild gust in his blood! It was as strange and imperious to him then as in a sober reflection it had been bold, gripping, physical, a drawing of him not sanctioned by his will. In this instance he was weaker in its grip, but still he conquered. Releasing Margarita, he led her to a shady place in the sand under the green tree, and found a seat where he could lean against a low branch. Margarita fell against his shoulder, and there clung to him and wept. Her dusky hair rippled over him, soft and silky to the touch of his fingers. The poor, faded dress, of a fabric unknown to Adam, ragged and dusty and torn, and the little shoes, worn and cracked, showing the soles of her stockingless feet, spoke eloquently of poverty. Adam noted the slender grace of her slight form, the arch of the bare instep, and the shapeliness of her ankles, brown almost as an Indian's. And all at once there charged over him an overwhelming sense of the pitifulness and the wonderfulness of her — a ragged, half-dressed little Mexican girl, whose care of her hair and face, and the few knots of ribbon, betrayed the worshipful vanity that was the jewel of her soul, and whose physical perfection was in such strange contrast to the cramped, undeveloped mind.

"My God!" whispered Adam, under his breath. Something big and undefined was born in him then. He saw her, he pitied her, he loved her, he wanted her; but these feelings were not so much what constituted the bigness and vagueness that waved through his soul. He could not grasp it. But it had to do with the life, the beauty, the passion, the soul of this Mexican girl; and it was akin to a reverence he felt for the things in her that she could not understand.

Margarita soon recovered, and assumed a demeanor so shy and modest and wistful that Adam could not believe she was the same girl. Nevertheless, he took good care not to awaken her other characteristics.

"Margarita, what is the name of this beautiful tree?" he asked.

"*Palo verde*. It means green tree."

It interested him then to instruct himself further in regard to the desert growths that had been strange to him; and to this end he led Margarita from one point to another, pleased to learn how familiar she was with every growing thing.

Presently Margarita brought to Adam's gaze a tree that resembled smoke, so blue-gray was it, so soft and hazy against the sky, so columnar and mushrooming. What a strange, graceful tree and what deep-blue blossoms it bore! Upon examination Adam was amazed to discover that every branch and twig of this tree was a thorn. A hard, cruel, beautiful tree of thorns that at a little distance resembled smoke!

"*Palo Christi*," murmured Margarita, making the sign of the cross. And she told Adam that this was the Crucifixion tree, which was the species that furnished the crown of thorns for the head of Christ.

Sunset ended several happy and profitable hours for Adam. He had not forgotten about the Mexican, Felix, and had thought it just as well to let time pass and to keep out of trouble as long as he could. He and Margarita reached home without seeing any sign of Felix. Arallanes, however, had espied the Mexican sneaking around, and he warned Adam in no uncertain terms. Merryvale, too, had a word for Adam's ear; and it was significant that he did not advise a waiting course. In spite of all Adam's reflections he did not need a great deal of urging. After supper he started off for Picacho with Arallanes and a teamster who was freighting supplies up to the camp.

Picacho was in full blast when they arrived. The dim lights, the discordant yells, the raw smell of spirits, the violence of the crude gambling hall worked upon Adam's already excited mind; and by the time he had imbibed a few drinks he was ready for anything. But they did not find Felix.

Then Adam, if not half drunk, at least somewhat under the influence of rum, started to walk back to his lodgings. The walk was long and, by reason of the heavy, dragging sand, one of considerable labor. Adam was in full possession of his faculties when he reached the village. But his blood was hot from the exercise, and the excitement of the prospective battle of the early evening had given way to an excitement of the senses, in the youthful romance felt in the dark, starlight, the wildness of the place. So when in the pale gloom of the mesquites Margarita glided to him like a lissom spectre, to enfold him and cling and whisper, Adam had neither the will, nor the heart, nor the desire to resist her.

5

Adam's dull eyelids opened on a dim, gray desert dawn. The coming of the dawn was in his mind, and it showed pale through his shut lids. He could not hold back the hours. Something had happened in the night and he would never be the same again. With a sharp pang, a sense of incomprehensible loss, Adam felt die in him the old unreasoning, instinctive boy. And there was more, too deep and too subtle for him to divine. It had to do with a feminine strain in him, a sweetness and purity inherited from his mother and developed by her teachings. It had separated him from his brother Guerd and kept him aloof from a baseness common to their comrades. Nevertheless, the wildness of this raw, uncouth, primitive West had been his undoing.

It was with bitterness that Adam again faced the growing light. All he could do was to resign himself to fate. The joy of life, the enchantments — all that had made him feel different from other boys and hide his dreams — failed now in this cool dark morning of reality. He could not understand the severity of the judgment he meted out to himself. His spirit suffered an ineffaceable blunting. And the tight-drawing knot in his breast, the gnawing of remorse, the strange, dark oppression — these grew and reached a climax, until something gave way within him and there was a sinking of the heart, a weary and inscrutable feeling.

Then he remembered Margarita, and the very life and current of his blood seemed to change. Like a hot wave the memory of Margarita surged over Adam, her strange new sweetness, the cunning of her when she waylaid him in the dead of the night, the clinging lissomeness of her and the whispered incoherence that needed no translation, the inevitableness of the silent, imperious demand of her presence, unashamed and insistent.

Adam leaped out of his blankets, breaking up this mood and thought by violent action. For Adam then the sunrise was glorious, the valley was beautiful, the desert was wild and free, the earth was an immense region to explore, and nature, however insatiable and inexorable, was prodigal of compensations. He drank a sweet cup that held one drop of poison bitterness. Life swelled in his breast. He wished he were an Indian. As he walked along there flashed into mind words spoken long ago by his mother: "My son, you take things too seriously, you feel too intensely the ordinary moments of life." He understood her now, but he could not distinguish ordinary things from great things. How could anything be little?

Margarita's greeting was at once a delight and a surprise. Her smile, the light of her dusky eyes, would have made any man happier. But there was a subtle air about her this morning that gave Adam a slight shock, an undefined impression that he represented less to Margarita than he had on yesterday.

Then came the shrill whistle of the downriver boat. Idle men flocked toward the dock. When Adam reached the open space on the bank before the dock he found it crowded with an unusual number of men, all manifestly more than ordinarily interested in something concerning the boat. By slipping through the mesquites Adam got around to the edge of the crowd.

A tall, gaunt man, clad in black, strode off the gangplank. His height, his form, his gait were familiar to Adam. He had seen that embroidered flowery vest with its silver star conspicuously in sight, and the brown beardless face with its square jaw and seamy lines.

"Collishaw!' ejaculated Adam, in dismay. He recognized in this man one whom he had known at Ehrenberg, a gambling, gun-fighting sheriff to whom Guerd had become attached. As his glance swept back of Collishaw his pulse beat quicker. The next passenger to stride off the gangplank was a very tall, superbly built young man. Adam would have known that form in a crowd of a thousand men. His heart leaped with a great throb. Guerd, his brother!

Guerd looked up. His handsome, heated face, bold and keen and reckless, flashed in the sunlight. His piercing gaze swept over the crowd upon the bank.

"Hello, Adam!" he yelled, with gay, hard laugh. Then he prodded Collishaw and pointed up at Adam. "There he is! We've found him."

Adam plunged away into the thickest of mesquites, and, indifferent to the clawing thorns, he did not halt until he was far down the bank.

It died hard, that regurgitation of brother love. It represented most of his life, and all of his home associations, and the memories of youth. The strength of it proved his loyalty to himself. How warm and fine that suddenly revived emotion! How deep seated, beyond his control! He could have sobbed out over the pity of it, the loss of it, the fallacy of it. Plucked out by the roots, it yet lived hidden in the depths of him. Adam in his flight to be alone had yielded to the amaze and shame and fury stirred in him by a realization of joy in the mere sight of this brother who hated him. For years his love had fought against the gradual truth of Guerd's hate. He had not been able to prove it, but he felt it. Adam had no fear of Guerd, nor any reason why he could not face him, except this tenderness of which he was ashamed. When he had fought down the mawkish sentiment he would show Guerd and Collishaw what he was made of. Money! That was Guerd's motive, with an added possibility of desire to dominate and hound.

"I'll fool him," said Adam, resolutely, as he got up to return.

Adam did not know exactly what he would do, but he was certain that he had reached the end of his tether. He went back to the village by a roundabout way. Turning a sharp curve in the canyon, he came suddenly upon a number of workmen, mostly Mexicans. They were standing under a wooden trestle that had been built across the canyon at this narrow point. All of them appeared to be gazing upward, and naturally Adam detected his gaze likewise.

Thus without warning he saw the distorted and ghastly face of a man hanging by the neck on a rope tied to the trestle. The spectacle gave Adam a terrible shock.

"That's Collishaw's work," muttered Adam, darkly, and he remembered stories told of the sheriff's grim hand in more than one act of border justice. What a hard country!

In front of the village store Adam encountered Merryvale, and he asked him for particulars about the execution.

"Wal, I don't know much," replied the old watchman, scratching his head. "There's been some placer miners shot an' robbed up the river. This Collishaw is a regular sure-enough sheriff, takin' the law to himself. Reckon there ain't any law. Wal, he an' his deputies say they tracked thet murderin' gang to Picacho, an' swore they identified one of them. Arallanes stuck up for thet greaser. There was a hot argument, an', by gosh! I jest swore Collishaw was goin' to draw on Arallanes. But Arallanes backed down, as any man not crazy would have done. The greaser swore by all his Virgins thet he wasn't the man, an' was swearin' he could prove it when the rope choked him off. . . . I don't know, Adam. I don't know. I was fer waitin' a little to give the feller a chance. But Collishaw came down here to hang some one an' you bet he was goin' to do it."

"I know him, Merryvale, and you're betting right," replied Adam, forcefully.

"Adam, one of his men is a fine-lookin' young chap thet sure must be your brother. Now, ain't he?"

"Yes, you're right about that, too."

"Wal, wal! You don't seem powerful glad. . . . Son, jest be careful what you say to Collishaw. He's hard an' I reckon he's square as he sees justice, but he doesn't ring right to an old timer like me. He courts the crowd. An' he's been askin' fer you. There he comes now."

The sheriff appeared, approaching with several companions, and halted before the store. His was a striking figure, picturesque, commanding, but his face was repellent. His massive head was set on a bull neck of swarthy and weathered skin like wrinkled leather; his broad

63

face, of similar hue, appeared a mass of criss-crossed lines, deep at the eyes, and long on each side of the cruel, thin-lipped, tight-shut mouth; his chin stuck out like a square rock; and his eyes, dark and glittering, roved incessantly in all directions, had been trained to see men before they saw him.

Adam knew that Collishaw had seen him first, and, acting upon the resolution that he had made down in the thicket, he strode over to the sheriff.

"Collishaw, I've been told you wanted me," said Adam.

"Hello, Larey! Yes, I was inquirin' about you," replied Collishaw, with the accent of a Texan.

"What do you want of me?" asked Adam.

Collishaw drew Adam aside out of earshot of the other men.

"It's a matter of thet little gamblin' debt you owe Guerd," he replied, in low voice.

"Collishaw, are you threatening me with some such job as you put up on that poor greaser?" inquired Adam, sarcastically, as he waved his hand up the canyon.

Probably nothing could have surprised this hardened sheriff, but he straightened up with a jerk and shed his confidential and admonishing air.

"No, I can't arrest you on a gamblin' debt," he replied, bluntly, "but I'm shore goin' to make you pay."

"You are, like hell!" retorted Adam. "What

had you to do with it? If Guerd owed you money in that game, I'm not responsible. And I didn't pay because I caught Guerd cheating. I'm not much of a gambler, Collishaw, but I'll bet you a stack of gold twenties against your fancy vest that Guerd never collects a dollar of his crooked deal."

With that Adam turned on his heel and strode off toward the river. His hard-earned independence added something to the wrong done him by these men. He saw himself in different light. The rankling of the injustice he had suffered at Ehrenberg had softened only in regard to the girl in the case. Remembering her again, it seemed her part in his alienation from Guerd did not loom so darkly and closely. Margarita had come between that affair and the present hour. This other girl had really been nothing to him, but Margarita had become everything. A gratefulness, a big, generous warmth, stirred in Adam's heart for the dark-eyed Mexican girl. What did it matter who she was? In this desert he must learn to adjust differences of class and race and habit in relation to the wildness of time and place.

In the open sandy space leading to the houses near the river Adam met Arallanes. The normally genial foreman appeared pale, somber, sick. To Adam's surprise, Arallanes would not talk about the hanging. Adam had another significant estimate of the character of Collishaw. Arallanes, however, was not so close lipped concerning Guerd Larey.

"*Quien sabe,* señor?" he concluded. "Maybe it's best for you. Margarita is a she-cat. You are my friend. I should tell you. . . . But, well, señor, if you would keep Margarita, look out for your brother."

Adam gaped his astonishment and had not a word for Arallanes as he turned away. It took him some time to realize the content of Arallanes's warning and advice. But what fixed itself in Adam's mind was the fact that Guerd had run across Margarita and had been attracted by her. How perfectly natural! How absolutely inevitable! Adam could not remember any girl he had ever admired or liked in all his life that Guerd had not taken away from him. Among the boys at home it used to be a huge joke, in which Adam had good-naturedly shared. All for Guerd! Adam could recall the time when he had been happy to give up anything or anyone to his brother. But out here in the desert, where he was beginning to assimilate the meaning of a man's fight for his life and his possessions, he felt vastly different. Moreover, he had gone too far with Margarita, regrettable as the fact was. She belonged to him, and his principles were such that he believed he owed her a like return of affection, and besides that, loyalty and guardianship. Margarita was only seventeen years old. No doubt Guerd would fascinate her if she was not kept out of his way.

"But — suppose she likes Guerd — and wants

him — as she wanted me?" muttered Adam, answering a divining flash of the inevitable order of things to be. Still, he repudiated that. His intellect told him what to expect, but his feeling was too strong to harbor doubt of Margarita. Only last night she had changed the world for him — opened his eyes to life not as it was dreamed, but lived!

Adam found the wife of Arallanes home alone.

"Señora, where is Margarita?"

"Margarita is there," she replied, with dark, eloquent glance upon Adam and a slow gesture toward the river bank.

Adam soon espied Guerd and Margarita on the river bank some few rods below the landing place. Here was a pretty sandy nook, shaded by a large mesquite, and somewhat out of sight of passers-by going to and fro from village to dock. Two enormous wheels connected by an iron bar, a piece of discarded mill machinery, stood in the shade of the tree. Margarita sat on the cross-bar and Guerd stood beside her. They were close together, facing a broad sweep of the river and the wonderland of colored peaks beyond. They did not hear Adam's approach on the soft sand.

"Señorita, one look from your midnight eyes and I fell in love with you," Guerd was declaring, with gay passion, and his hand upon her was as bold as his speech. "You little Spanish princess! . . . Beautiful as the moon and stars! . . . Hidden in this mining camp, a desert flower born to blush unseen! I shall —"

It was here that Adam walked around the high wheels to confront them. For him the moment was exceedingly poignant. But despite the tumult within him he preserved a cool and quiet exterior. Margarita's radiance vanished in surprise.

"Well, if it ain't Adam!" ejaculated her companion. "You son-of-a-gun! . . . Why, you've changed!"

"Guerd," began Adam, and then his voice halted. To meet his brother this way was a tremendous ordeal. And Guerd's presence seemed to charge the very air. Worship of this magnificent brother had been the strongest thing in Adam's life, next to love of mother. To see him again! Guerd Larey's face was beautiful, yet virile and strong. The beauty was mere perfection of feature. The big curved mouth, the square chin, the straight nose, the large hazel-green eyes full of laughter and love of life, the broad forehead and clustering fair hair — all these were features that made him singularly handsome. His skin was clear brown tan with a tinge of red. Adam saw no change in Guerd, except perhaps an intensifying of an expression of wildness which made him all the more fascinating to look at. For Adam the mocking thing about Guerd's godlike beauty was the fact that it deceived. At heart, at soul, Guerd was as false as hell!

"Adam, are you goin' to shake hands?" queried Guerd, lazily extending his arm. "You sure strike me queer, boy!"

"No," replied Adam, and his quick-revolving thoughts grasped at Guerd's slipshod speech. Guerd had absorbed even the provincial words and idioms of the uncouth West.

"All right. Suit yourself," said Guerd. "I reckon you see I'm rather pleasantly engaged."

"Yes, I see," returned Adam, bitterly, with a fleeting glance at Margarita. She had recovered from her surprise and now showed cunning feminine curiosity. "Guerd, I met Collishaw, and he had the gall to brace me for that gambling debt. And I've hunted you up to tell you that you cheated me. I'll not pay it."

"Oh yes, you will," replied Guerd, smilingly.

"I will not," said Adam, forcefully.

"Boy, you'll pay it or I'll take it out of your hide," declared Guerd, slowly frowning, as if a curious hint of some change in Adam had dawned upon him.

"You can't take it that way — or any other way," retorted Adam.

"But, say — I didn't cheat," remonstrated Guerd, evidently making a last stand of argument to gain his end.

"You lie!" flashed Adam. "You know it, I know it. . . . Guerd, let's waste no words. I told you at Ehrenberg — after you played that shabby trick on me — over the girl there — I told you I was through with you for good."

Guerd seemed to realize with wonder and chagrin that he had now to deal with a man. How the change in his expression thrilled Adam! What relief came to him in the consciousness that he was now stronger than Guerd! He had never been certain of that.

"Through and be damned!" exclaimed Guerd, and he took his arm from around Margarita and rose from his leaning posture to his lofty height. "I'm sick of your milksop ideas. All I want of you is that money. If you don't pony up with it I'll tear your clothes off gettin' it. Savvy that?"

"Ha-ha!" laughed Adam, tauntingly. "I say to you what I said to Collishaw — you will, like hell!"

Guerd Larey's lips framed curses that were inaudible. He was astounded. The red flamed his neck and face.

"I'll meet you after I get through talking to this girl," he said.

"Any time you want," rejoined Adam, bitingly, "but I'll have my say now, once and for all. . . . The worm has turned, Guerd Larey. Your goose has stopped laying golden eggs. I will take no more burdens of yours on my shoulders. You've bullied me all my life. You've hated me. I know now. Oh, I remember so well! You robbed me of toys, clothes, playmates. Then girl friends! Then money! . . . Then — a worthless woman! . . . You're a fraud — a cheat — a liar. . . . You've fallen in with your kind out here and you're

70

going straight to hell."

The whiteness of Guerd's face attested to his roused passion. But he had more restraint than Adam. He was older, and the difference of age between them showed markedly.

"So you followed me out here to say all that?" he queried.

"No, not altogether," replied Adam. "I came after Margarita."

"Came after Margarita?" echoed Guerd, blankly. "Is that her name? Say, Adam, is this one of your goody-goody tricks? Rescuing a damsel in distress sort of thing! . . . You and I have fallen out more than once over that. I kick — I —"

"Guerd, we've fallen out forever," interrupted Adam, and then he turned to the girl. "Margarita, I want you —"

"But it's none of your damned business," burst out Guerd, hotly, interrupting in turn. "What do you care about a Mexican girl? I won't stand your interference. You clear out and let me alone."

"But, Guerd — it is my business," returned Adam, haltingly. Some inward force dragged at his tongue. "She's — my girl."

"What!" ejaculated Guerd, incredulously. Then he bent down to peer into Margarita's face, and from that he swept a flashing, keen glance at Adam. His eyes were wonderful then, intensely bright, quickened and sharpened with swift turns of thought. "Boy, you don't mean you're on friendly terms with this greaser girl?"

"Yes," replied Adam.

"You've made love to her!" cried Guerd, and the radiance of his face then was beyond Adam's understanding.

"Yes."

Guerd violently controlled what must have been a spasm of fiendish glee. His amaze, deep as it was, seemed not to be his predominant feeling, but that very amaze was something to force exquisitely upon Adam how far he had fallen. The moment was dark, hateful, far-reaching in effect, impossible to realize. Guerd's glance flashed back and forth from Adam to Margarita. But he had not yet grasped what was the tragic thing for Adam — the truth of how fatefully far this love affair had fallen. Adam's heart sank like lead in his breast. What humiliation he must suffer if he betrayed himself! Hard he fought for composure and dignity to hide his secret.

"Adam, in matters of the heart, where two gentlemen admire the lady in question, the choice is always left to her," began Guerd, with something of mockery in his rich voice. A devil gleamed from him then, and the look of him, the stature, the gallant action of him as he bowed before Margarita, fascinated Adam even in his miserable struggle to appear a man.

"But, Guerd, you — you've known Margarita only a few moments," he expostulated, and the sound of his voice made him weak. "How can you put such a choice to — to her? It's — it's an insult."

"Adam, that is for Margarita to decide," responded Guerd. "Women change. It is something you have not learned." Then as he turned to Margarita he seemed to blaze with magnetism. The grace of him and the beauty of him in that moment made of him a perfect physical embodiment of the emotions of which he was master. He knew his power over women. "Margarita, Adam and I are brothers. We are always falling in love with the same girl. You must choose between us. Adam would tie you down — keep you from the eyes of other men. I would leave you free as a bird."

And he bent over to whisper in her ear, with his strong brown hand on her arm, at once gallant yet masterful.

The scene was a nightmare to Adam. How could this be something that was happening? But he had sight. Margarita seemed a transformed creature, shy, coy, alluring, with the half-veiled dusky eyes, heavy-lidded, lighted with the same fire that had shone in them for Adam.

"Margarita, will you come?" cried Adam, goaded to end this situation.

"No," she replied, softly.

"I beg of you — come!" implored Adam.

The girl shook her black head. A haunting mockery hung around her, in her slight smile, in the light of her face. She radiated a strange glow like the warm shade of an opal. Older she seemed to Adam and surer of herself and somewhat deeper in that mystic obsession of passion he had often sensed in her. No spiritual conception of what Adam regarded as his obligation to her could ever dawn in that little brain. She loved her pretty face and beautiful body. She gloried in her power over men. And the new man she felt to be still unwon — who was stronger of instinct and harder to hold, under whose brutal hand she would cringe and thrill and pant and fight — him she would choose. So Adam read Margarita in that moment. If he had felt love for her, which he doubted, it was dead. A great pity flooded over him. It seemed that of the three there, he was the only one who was true and who understood.

"Margarita, have you forgotten last night?" asked Adam, huskily.

"Ah, señor — so long ago and far away!" she said.

Adam whirled abruptly and, plunging into the thicket of mesquites, he tore a way through, unmindful of the thorns. When he reached his quarters there was blood on his hands and face, but the sting of the thorns was as nothing to the hurt in his heart. He lay down.

"Again!" he whispered. "Guerd has come — and it's the same old story. Only worse! . . . But, it's better so! I — I didn't know — her! . . . Arallanes knew — he told me. . . . And

74

I — I dreamed so many — many fool things. Yes — it's better — better. I didn't love her right. It — it was something she roused. I never loved her — but if I did love her — it's gone. It's not loss that — that stabs me now. It's Guerd — Guerd! Again — and I ran off from him. . . . 'So long ago and far away,' she said! Are all women like that? I can't believe it. I never will. I remember my mother."

6

That night in the dead late hours Adam suddenly awoke. The night seemed the same as all the desert nights — dark and cool under the mesquites — the same dead, unbroken silence. Adam's keen intentness could not detect a slightest sound of wind or brush or beast. Something had pierced his slumbers, and as he pondered deeply there seemed to come out of the vagueness beyond that impenetrable wall of sleep a voice, a cry, a whisper. Had Margarita, sleeping or waking, called to him? Such queer visitations of mind, often repeated, had convinced Adam that he possessed a mystic power or sense.

When Adam awoke late, in the light of the sunny morning, unrealities of the night dispersed like the gray shadows and vanished. He arose eager, vigorous, breathing hard, instinctively seeking for action. The day was Sunday. Another idle wait, fruitful of brooding moods! But he vowed he would not go to the willow brakes, there to hide from Guerd and Collishaw. Let them have their say — do their worst! We would go up to Picacho and gamble and drink with the rest of the drifters. Merryvale's words of desert-learned wisdom rang through Adam's head. As for Margarita, all Adam wanted was one more look at her face, into her dusky eyes, and that would forever end his relation to her.

At breakfast Arallanes presented a thoughtful and forbidding appearance, although this demeanor was somewhat softened by the few times he broke silence. The señora's impassive serenity lacked its usual kindliness, and her lowered eyes kept their secrets. Margarita had not yet arisen. Adam could not be sure there was really a shadow hovering over the home, or in his own mind, coloring, darkening his every prospect.

After breakfast he went out to stroll along the river bank and then around the village. He ascertained from Merryvale that Collishaw, Guerd, and their associates had found lodgings at different houses for the night, and after breakfast had left for the mining camp. As usual, Merryvale spoke pointedly: "Your brother said they were goin' to clear out the camp. An' I reckon he didn't mean greasers, but whisky an' gold. Son, you stay away from Picacho today."

For once, however, the kind old man's advice fell upon deaf ears. Adam had to fight his impatience to be off up the canyon; and only a driving need to see Margarita held him there. He walked to and fro, from village to river and back again. By and by he espied Arallanes and his wife, with their friends, dressed in their best, parading toward the little adobe church. Margarita was not with them.

Adam waited a little while, hoping to see her appear. He did not analyze his strong hope that she would go to church this Sunday as usual. But as no sign of her was forthcoming he strode down to the little brown house and entered at the open door.

"Margarita!" he called. No answer broke the quiet. His second call, however, brought her from her room, a dragging figure with a pale face that Adam had never before seen pale.

"Señor Ad-dam," she faltered.

The look of her, and that voice, stung Adam out of the gentleness habitual with him. Leaping at her, he dragged her into the light of the door. She cried out in a fear that shocked him. When he let go of her, abrupt and sharp in his motions, she threw up her arms as if to ward off attack.

"Do you think I would hurt you?" he cried harshly. "No, Margarita! I only wanted to see you — just once more."

She dropped her arms and raised her face. Adam, keen in that poignant moment, saw in her the passing of an actual fear of death. It struck him mute. It betrayed her. What had been the dalliance of yesterday, playful and passionate in its wild youth, through the night had become dishonor. Yesterday she had been a cat that loved to be stroked; to-day she was a maimed creature, a broken woman.

"Lift your face — higher," said Adam, hoarsely, as he put out a shaking hand to touch her. But he could not touch her. She did lift it and looked at him, denying nothing, still unashamed. But now there was soul in that face. Adam felt it limned on his memory forever — the stark truth of her frailty, the courage of a primitive nature fearing only death, yearning for brutal blows as proof of the survival of jealous love, a dawning consciousness of his honesty and truth. Terrible was it for Adam to realize that if she had been given that choice again she would have decided differently. But it was too late.

"*Adios,* señorita," he said, bowing, and backed out of the door. He stopped, and the small pale face with its tragic eyes, straining, unutterably eloquent of wrong to him and to herself, passed slowly out of his sight.

Swiftly Adam strode up the canyon, his fierce energy in keeping with his thoughts. He overtook the Irishman, Regan, who accosted him.

"Hullo, Wansfell, ould fri'nd!" he called. "Don't yez walk so dom' fast."

78

"Wansfell! Why do you call me that?" asked Adam. How curiously the name struck his ear!

"Ain't thot your noime?"

"No, it's not."

"Wal, all right. Will yez hev a dhrink?" Regan produced a brown bottle and handed it to Adam.

They walked on up the canyon, Regan with his short, stunted legs being hard put to it to keep up with Adam's long strides. The Irishman would attach himself to Adam, that was evident; and he was a most talkative and friendly fellow. Whenever he got out of breath he halted to draw out the bottle. The liquor in an ordinary hour would have befuddled Adam's wits, now it only heated his blood.

"Wansfell, if yez ain't the dom'dest foinest young feller in these diggin's!" ejaculated Regan.

"Thank you, friend. But don't call me that queer name. Mine's Adam."

"A-dom?" echoed Regan. "Phwat a hell of a noime! Adom an' Eve, huh? I seen yez with thot black-eyed wench. She's purty."

They finished the contents of the bottle and proceeded on their way. Regan waxed warmer in his regard for Adam and launched forth a strong argument in favor of their going on a prospecting trip.

"Yez would make a foine prospector an' pard," he said. "Out on the desert yez are free an' happy, b'gorra! No place loike the desert, pard, whin yez come to know it! Thar's air to breathe an' long days wid the sun on yer back an' noights whin a mon knows shlape. Mebbe we'll hev the luck to foind Pegleg Smith's lost gold mine."

"Who was Pegleg Smith and what gold mine did he lose?" queried Adam.

Then as they plodded on up the canyon, trying to keep to the shady strips and out of the hot sun, Adam heard for a second time the story of the famous lost gold mine. Regan told it differently, perhaps exaggerating after the manner of prospectors. But the story was impelling to any man with a drop of adventurous blood in his veins. The lure of gold had not yet obsessed Adam, but he had begun to feel the lure of the desert.

Adam concluded that under happier circumstances this Regan would be a man well worth cultivating in spite of his love for the bottle. They reached the camp about noon, had a lunch at the stand of a Chinaman, and then, entering the saloon, they mingled with the crowd, where Adam soon came separated from Regan. Liquor flowed like water, and gold thudded in sacks and clinked musically in coins upon the tables. Adam had one drink and that incited him to take another. Again the throb and burn of his blood warmed out the coldness and bitterness of his mood. Deliberately he drank and deliberately he stifled the voice of conscience until he was in a reckless and dangerous frame of mind. There seemed to be a fire consuming him now, to which liquor was only fuel.

He swaggered through the crowded hall, and for once the drunken miners, the painted hags, the cold-faced gamblers, did not disgust him. The smell of rum and smoke, the feel of the thick sand under his feet, the sight of the motley crowd of shirt-sleeved and booted men, the discordant din of music, glasses, gold, and voices — all these sensations struck him full and intimately with their proof that he was a part of this wild assembly of free adventurers. He remembered again Merryvale's idea of a man equipped to cope with this lawless gang and hold his own. Suddenly when he espied his brother Guerd he shook with the driving passion that had led him there.

Guerd sat at table, gambling with Collishaw and MacKay and other men of Picacho well known to Adam. Guerd looked the worse for liquor and bad luck. When he glanced up to see Adam, a light gleamed across his hot face. He dropped his cards, and as Adam stepped near he rose from the table and in two strides confronted him, arrogant, menacing, with the manner of a man dangerous to cross.

"I want money," demanded Guerd.

Adam laughed in his face.

"Go to work. You're not slick enough with the cards to hide your tricks," replied Adam, in deliberate scorn.

Temper, and not forethought, actuated Guerd then. He slapped Adam, with the moderate force of an older brother punishing an impertinence.

Swift and hard Adam returned that blow, staggering Guerd, who fell against the table, but was upheld by Collishaw. He uttered a loud and piercing cry.

Sharply the din ceased. The crowd slid back over the sand, leaving Adam in the center of a wide space, confronting Guerd, who still leaned against Collishaw. Guerd panted for breath. His hot face turned white except for the red place where Adam's fist had struck. MacKay righted the table, then hurriedly drew back. Guerd's fury of astonishment passed to stronger controlled passion. He rose from Collishaw's hold and seemed to tower magnificently. He had the terrible look of a man who had waited years for a moment of revenge, at last to recognize it.

"You hit me! I'll beat you for that — I'll smash your face," he said, stridently.

"Come on," cried Adam.

At this instant the Irishman, Regan, staggered out of the crowd into the open circle. He was drunk.

"Sic 'em, Wansfell, sic 'em," he bawled. "I'm wid yez. We'll lick thot — loidy face — an' ivery dom' —"

Some miner reached out a long arm and dragged Regan back.

Guerd Larey leaned over to pound with fist on the table. A leaping glow radiated from his face, as if a genius of hate had inspired some word or speech that Adam must find insupportable. His look let loose a bursting gush of blood through Adam's throbbing veins. This was no situation built on a quarrel or a jealous rivalry. It was backed by years, and by some secret not easily to be divined, though its source was the very soul of Cain.

"So that's your game," declared Guerd, with ringing passion. "You want to fight and you make this debt of yours a pretense. But I'm on to you. It's because of the girl I took from you."

"Shut up! Have you no sense of decency? Can't you be half a man?" burst out Adam, beginning to shake.

"Ha! Ha! Ha! Listen to Goody-Goody! . . . Mother's nice boy —"

"By Heaven, Guerd Larey, if you speak of — my mother — here — I'll tear out your tongue!"

They were close together now, with only the table between them — Cain and Abel — the old bitter story plain in the hate of one flashing face and the agony of the other. Guerd Larey had divined the means to torture and to crucify this brother whose heart and soul were raw.

"Talk about the fall of Saint Anthony!" cried Guerd, with a voice magical in its steely joy. "Never was there a fall like Adam Larey's — the Sunday-school boy — too sweet — too innocent — too pure to touch the hand of a girl! . . . Ha-ha! Oh, we can fight, Adam. I'll fight you. But let me talk — let me tell my friends what a damned hypocrite you are. . . . Gentlemen, behold the immaculate Saint Adam whose Eve was a little greaser girl!"

There was no shout of mirth. The hall held a low-breathing silence. It was a new scene, a diversion for the gamblers and miners and their painted consorts, a clash of a different kind and spirit. Guerd paused to catch his breath and evidently to gather supreme passion for the delivery of what seemed more to him than life itself. His face was marble white, quivering and straining, and his eyes bland with a piercing flame.

Adam saw the living, visible proof of a hate he had long divined. The magnificence of Guerd's passion, the terrible reality of his hate, the imminence of a mortal blow, locked Adam's lips and jaws as in a vise, while a gathering fury, as terrible as Guerd's hate, flooded and dammed at the gates of his energy, ready to break out in destroying violence.

"She told me!" Guerd flung the words like bullets. "You needn't bluff it out with your damned lying white face. She told me! . . . You — you, Adam Larey, with your pure thoughts and lofty ideals . . . the *rot* of them! *You* — damn your milksop soul! — you were the slave of a dirty little greaser girl who fooled you, laughed in your face, left you for me — for me at the snap of my fingers. . . . And, by God! my cup would be full — if your mother could only know —"

84

It was Collishaw's swift hand that knocked up Adam's flinging arm and the gun which spouted red and boomed heavily. Collishaw grappled with him — was flung off — and then Guerd lunged in close to save himself. A writhing, wrestling struggle — quick, terrible; then the gun boomed with muffled report — and Guerd Larey, uttering a cry of agony, fell away from Adam, backward over the table. His gaze, conscious, appalling, was fixed on Adam. A dark crimson spot stained his white shirt. Then he lay there with fading eyes — the beauty and radiance and hate of his face slowly shading.

Collishaw leaned over him. Then with hard, grim gesture he shouted, hoarsely: "Dead, by God! . . . You'll hang for this!"

A creeping horror was slowly paralyzing Adam. But at that harsh speech he leaped wildly, flinging his gun with terrific force into the sheriff's face. Like an upright stone dislodged Collishaw fell. Then Adam, bounding forward, flung aside the men obstructing his passage and fled out of the door.

Terror lent wings to his feet. In a few moments he was beyond the outskirts of the camp. Even here, fierce in his energy, he bounded upward, from rock to rock, until he reached the steep jumble of talus where swift progress was impossible. Then with hands and feet working in unison, as if he had been an ape, he climbed steadily.

From the top of the first rocky slope he gazed

back fearfully. Yes, men were pursuing him, strung out along the road of the mining camp; and among the last was a tall, black-coated, bareheaded man that Adam took to be Collishaw. This pursuer was staggering along, flinging his arms.

Adam headed straight up the ascent. Picacho loomed to the right, a colossal buttress of red rock, wild and ragged and rugged. But the ascent that had looked so short and easy — how long and steep! Every shadow was a lie, every space of slope in the sunlight hid the truth of its width. Sweat poured from his hot body. He burned. His breath came in labored bursts. A painful stab in his side spread and swelled to the whole region of his breast. He could hear the mighty throb of his heart, and he could hear it in another way — a deep muffled throb through his ears.

At last he reached the height of the slope where it ended under a wall of rock, the backbone of that ridge, bare and jagged, with no loose shale on its almost perpendicular side. Here it took hard labor of hand and foot to climb and zigzag and pull himself up. Here he fell exhausted.

But the convulsion was short lived. His will power was supreme and his endurance had not been permanently disabled. He crawled before he could walk, and when he recovered enough to stagger erect he plodded on, invincible in his spirit to escape.

From this height, which was a foothill to the

great peak, he got his bearings and started down.

"They can't — trail me — here," he whispered, hoarsely, as he looked back with the eyes of a fugitive. "And — down there — I'll keep off the road."

After that brief moment of reasoning he became once more victim to fear and desperate passion to hurry. He had escaped, his pursuers could not see him now, he could hide, the descent was tortuous; yet these apparent facts, favorable as they were, could not save him. Adam pushed on, gaining strength as he recovered breath. As his direction led him downhill, he went swiftly, sometimes at a rapid walk, again sliding down here and rushing there, and at other places he stepped from rock to rock, like a balancing rope walker.

The descent here appeared to be a long, even slant of broken rocks, close together like cobblestones in a street, and of a dark-bronze hue. They shone as if they had been varnished. And a closer glance showed Adam the many reddish tints of *bisnagi* cactus growing in the cracks between the stones.

His misgivings were soon verified. He had to descend here, for the afternoon was far gone, and whatever the labor and pain, he must reach the road before dark. The rocks were sharp, uneven, and as slippery as if they had been wet. At the very outset Adam slipped, and, falling with both hands forward, he thrust them into a cactus. The pain stung, and when he had to pull hard to free himself from the thorns, it was as if his hands had been nailed. He could not repress moans as he tried to pull out the thorns with his teeth. They stuck tight. The blood ran in little streams. But he limped on, down the black slope.

The white road below grew closer and closer. It was a goal. This slope of treacherous rocks and torturing cacti was a physical ordeal that precluded memory of the past or consideration of the present. When Adam at last reached the road, there to fall exhausted and wet and burning upon a flat rock, it seemed that he had been delivered from an inferno.

Presently he sat up to look around him. A wonderful light showed upon the world — the afterglow of sunset. Picacho bore a crown of gold. All the lower tips of ranges were purpling in shadow. To the southward a wide gray barren led to an endless bleak plateau, flat and dark, with dim spurs of mountains in the distance. Desolate, lifeless, silent — the gateway to the desert! Adam felt steal over him a sense of awe. The vastness of seen and suggested desert seemed flung at him, as if nature meant to reveal to him the mystery and might of space. The marvelous light magnified the cacti and the rocks, and the winding ranges and the bold peaks, and the distances, until all were unreal. Adam felt that he had overcome a great hardship, accomplished a remarkable feat, had climbed and descended a range as sharp toothed as jagged

lava. But to what end! Something in the bewildering light of the west, in the purple shadows growing cold in the east, in the tremendous
oppression of illimitable space and silence and
solitude and desolation — something inexplicable repudiated and mocked his physical sense
of great achievement.

All at once, in a flash, he remembered his
passion, his crime, his terror, his flight. Not
until that instant had intelligence operated in
harmony with his feelings. He lifted his face
in the cool, darkening twilight. The frowning
mountains held aloof, and all about him seemed
detached, rendering his loneliness absolute and
immutable.

"Oh! Oh!" he moaned. "What will become
of me? . . . No family — no friends — no
hope! . . . Oh, Guerd — my brother! His blood
on my hands! . . . He ruined my life! He's
killed my soul! . . . Oh, damn him, damn him!
he's made me a murderer!"

Adam fell face down on the rock with breaking
heart. His exceeding bitter cries seemed faint
and lost in the midst of the vastness of desert
and sky. The deepening of twilight to darkness, the cold black grandeur of the great peak,
the mournful wail of a desert wolf, the pure
pale evening star that pierced the purple sky,
the stupendous loneliness and silence of that solitude — all these facts seemed Nature's pitiless
proof of her indifference to man and his despair.
His hope, his prayer, his frailty, his fall, his

burden and agony and life — these were nothing to the desert that worked inscrutably through its millions of years, nor to the illimitable expanse of heaven, deepening its blue and opening its cold, starry eyes. But a spirit as illimitable and as inscrutable breathed out of the universe and over the immensity of desert space — a spirit that breathed to the soul of the ruined man and bade him rise and take up his burden and go on down the naked shingles of the world.

Despair and pride and fear of death, and this strange breath of life, dragged Adam up and drove him down the desert road. For a mile he staggered and plodded along, bent and bowed like an old man, half blinded by tears and choked by sobs, abject in his misery; yet even so, the something in him that was strongest of all — the instinct to survive — made him keep to the hard, gravelly side of the road, that his tracks might not show in the dust.

And that action of blood and muscle, because it came first in the order of energy, gradually assumed dominance of him, until again he was an escaping fugitive, mostly concerned with direction and objective things. The direction took care of itself, being merely a matter of keeping along the edge of the road that gleamed pale in front of him. Objects near at hand, however, had to be carefully avoided. Rocks were indistinct in the gloom; *ocatilla* cacti thrust out long spectral arms; like the tentacles of an octopus; and shadows along the road took the alarming shape of men and horses and wagons. All around him, except to the west, was profound obscurity, and in that direction an endless horizon, wild and black and sharp, with sweeping bold lines between the spurs, stood silhouetted against a pale-blue, star-fired sky. Miles and miles he walked, and with a strength that had renewed. He never looked up at the heavens above. Often he halted to turn and listen. These moments were dreaded ones. But he heard only a faint breeze.

Morning broke swiftly and relentlessly, a gray, desert dawning. Dim columns of smoke scarce a mile away showed him that Yuma was close. Fields and cattle along the road, and then an Indian hut, warned him that he was approaching the habitations of men and sooner or later he would be seen. He must hide by day and travel by night. Bordering the road to his left was a dense thicket of arrowweed, indicating that he had reached the bottom lands of the river. Into this Adam crawled like a wounded and stealthy deer. Hunger and thirst were slight, but his whole body seemed a throbbing ache. Both mind and body longed for the oblivion that came at once in sleep.

7.

Adam's heavy slumbers were punctuated by periods when he half awakened, drowsily aware of extreme heat, of discomfort and sluggish pain, and of vague sounds.

Twilight had fallen when he fully awakened, stiff and sore, with a gnawing at his stomach and a parching of mouth and throat from thirst. He crawled out of the copse of arrowweed, to the opening by which he had entered it, and, stealthily proceeding on to the road, he peered out and listened. No man in sight — no sound to alarm! Consciousness of immense relief brought bitterly home to him the fact that he was a fugitive. Taking to the road, he walked rapidly in the direction of the lights. He passed low, dark huts somewhat back from the road, and he heard strange voices, probably of Indians.

In about a quarter of an hour he came to the river basin, where the road dropped down somewhat into the outskirts of Yuma. Most of the lights were across the river on the Arizona side. He met both Mexicans and Indians who took no apparent notice of him, and this encouraged Adam to go on with them down to a ferryboat.

The boat was shoved off. Adam saw that it was fastened to the cable overhead by ropes and pulleys. The current worked it across the river. Adam got out with the rest of the passengers, and, leaving them, he walked down the bank a few rods. He found a little dock with a skiff moored to it, and here he lay flat and drank his fill. The water was full of sand, but cool and palatable. Then he washed his face and hands. The latter were swollen and stiff from the cactus thorns, rendering them clumsy.

Next in order for him was to find a place to eat, and soon he came at once upon an eating house where several rough-looking white men and some Mexicans were being served by a Chinaman.

When he ended this meal he had determined upon a course to take. He needed a gun, ammunition, canteen, burro, and outfit; and he hardly expected to be able to purchase them after dark, without exciting suspicion. All the same, he set out to look.

A short walk brought Adam to a wide street, dimly lighted by the flare of lamps from open doors of saloons and stores. He halted in a shadow on the corner. A stream of men was passing — rugged, unshaven, dusty-booted white men, and Mexicans with their peaked sombreros and embroidered jackets and tight braided trousers.

Presently Adam ventured forth and walked up the street. The town resembled Picacho in its noisiest hours, magnified many times. He felt a wildness he could not see or hear. It dragged at him. It somehow made him a part of the frontier life. He longed to escape from himself.

A glimpse of a tall man in black frock coat startled Adam. That coat reminded him of Collishaw. He sheered down a side street into the gloom. He saw wagons and heard the munch of horses in stalls. Evidently this place was a barnyard and might afford him a safe retreat for the night. The first wagon he examined contained straw. Climbing into it, he lay down. For a long time he lay there, worrying over the risk he must run next day, until at length he fell asleep.

When day dawned, however, Adam had not such overpowering dread. The sun was rising in red splendor and the day promised to be hot. As it was early, but few people were to be encountered, and this fact lent Adam more courage. He had no difficulty in finding the place where he had eaten the night before. Adam ate as heartily as he could, not because he was hungry, but for the reason that he had an idea he might have to travel far on this meal.

That done, he sallied forth to find a store where he could purchase the outfit he needed; and he approached the business section by a street that climbed to what was apparently the highest point in Yuma.

Adam entered a store, and almost forgot himself in the interest of the purchases he wanted to make. He needed a small mule, or burro, to pack his outfit, and while the storekeeper went out to get it for Adam several Mexicans entered. One of them recognized Adam. He cried out, "Santa Maria!" and ran out, followed by his amazed but less hurried comrades. It took Adam a moment to place the man in mind. Felix! the Mexican that had drawn a knife on Arallanes.

Therefore Adam pondered. He must take risks to get away with this necessary outfit. The storekeeper, who had gone out through the back of the store, returned to say he could furnish a good burro ready to be packed at once. Adam made a deal with him for the whole outfit and began to count out the money. The storekeeper did not wait, and, gathering up an armful of Adam's purchases, he carried them out through the back door. This gave Adam opportunity to have a look from the front door into the street. There rode Felix, gesticulating wildly to the white man Adam had seen before, the black-coated tall Collishaw, significant and grim, with a white bandage over his face.

A shock pierced Adam's heart, and it was followed by a terrible icy compression, and then a bursting gush of blood, a flood of fire over all his body. Leaping like a deer, he bounded back through the store, out of the door, and across an open space full of implements, wagons, and obstacles he had to run around or jump over. He did not see the storekeeper. One vault took him over a high board fence into an alley, and through this he ran into a street. He headed for the river, running fleetly, blind to all around him but the ground flying under his feet and the end of the street. He gained that. The river, broad and swirling, lay beneath him. Plunging down the bank, he flew toward the dock. Upon reaching the dock, Adam espied a skiff, with oars in place, with bow pulled up on the sand. One powerful shove sent it, with him aboard, out into the stream. He bent the oars in his long, strong sweeps, and it took him only a few moments to cross. Not yet had any men appeared in pursuit or even to take notice of him. As he jumped out on the California shore of the river and began to run north, he found that he faced the long black mountain peak which dominated the rise of the desert. The dust was ankle deep. It stifled him, choked him, and caked on his sweaty face and hands. He strode swiftly, oppressed by the dust and intolerant of the confining borders of yellow brush. The frequent bends in the road were at once a relief and a dread. They hid him, yet obstructed his own view. He seemed obsessed by a great, passionate energy to escape. When he looked back he thought of Collishaw, of sure pursuit; when he looked ahead he thought of the road, the dust, the brush into which he wanted to hide, the physical things to be overcome.

By and by he climbed and passed out of the zone of brush. He was on the open gravel ridges, like the ridges of a washboard, up and down, and just as bare. Yet, as a whole, there was a distinct slope upward. He could not see the level of the desert, but the lone mountain peak, close at hand now, red and black and shining, towered bleakly over him.

Adam derived satisfaction from the fact that the hard gravel ridges did not take imprint of his boots. Assured now that escape was in his grasp, he began to put his mind upon other considerations of his flight. He was not such a fool as to underrate the danger of his venturing out upon the desert without food, and especially without water. Already he was thirsty. These thoughts, and counter ones, pressed hard upon him until he surmounted the long slope to the top of the desert mesa. Here he looked back.

First he saw clouds of dust puffing up from the brush-covered lowlands, and then, in an open space where the road crossed, he espied horsemen coming at a gallop. Again, and just as fiercely, did his veins seem to freeze, his blood to halt, and then to burst into flame.

"Collishaw — and his men!" gasped Adam, his jaw dropping. "They've trailed me! . . . They're after me — on horses!"

The apparent fact was terrific in its stunning

force. Adam reeled; his sight blurred. It was a full moment before he could rally his forces. Then, gazing keenly, he saw that his pursuers were still miles away.

At first he ran fleetly, with endurance apparently unimpaired, but he meant to slow down and husband his strength as soon as he dared. Before him stretched a desert floor of fine, shining gravel, like marbles, absolutely bare of any vegetation for what seemed hundreds of yards; and then began to appear short bunches of low meager brush called greasewood, and here and there isolated patches of *ocatilla*. These multiplied and enlarged in the distance until they looked as if they would afford cover enough to hide Adam from his pursuers. Hot, wet with sweat, strong, and panting, he ran another mile, to find the character of the desert changing.

Reaching the zone of plant life, he soon placed a thin but effective barrier of greasewood and *ocatilla* behind him. Then he slowed down to catch his breath. Before him extended a vast hazy expanse, growing darker with accumulated growths in the distance. To the right rose the chocolate mountain range, and it ran on to fade in the dim horizon. Behind him now stood the lone black peak, and to the left rose a low, faint wavering line of white, like billows of a sea. This puzzled him until at length he realized it was sand. Sand — and it, like the range, faded in the distant horizon.

Adam also made the discovery that as he

looked back over his shoulder he was really looking down a long, gradual slope. Plainly he could see the edge of the desert where he had come up, and often, as he traveled along at a jog trot, he gazed around with fearful expectancy. He had imagined that his running had given rise to the breeze blowing in his face. But this was not so. A rather stiff wind was blowing straight at him. It retarded his progress, and little puffs of fine, invisible sand or dust irritated his eyes. Then the tears would flow and wash them clear again. With all his senses and feelings there mingled a growing preponderance of the thought or realization of the tremendous openness of the desert. He felt as though a door of the universe had opened to him, and all before him was boundless. He had no fear of it; indeed, there seemed a comfort in the sense of being lost in such a vastness; but there was something intangible working on his mind. The wind weighed upon him, the coppery sky weighed upon him, the white sun weighed upon him, and his feet began to take hold of the ground. How hot the top of his head and his face! All at once the sweat appeared less copious and his skin drier. With this came a strong thirst. The saliva of his mouth was pasty and scant. He swallowed hard and his throat tightened. A couple of pebbles that he put into his mouth mitigated these last sensations.

Intelligence gave him pause then, and he halted in his tracks. If death was relentlessly pursuing him, it was no less confronting him there to the fore, if he passed on out of reach of the river. Death from thirst was preferable to capture, but Adam was not ready to die. He who had loved life clung to it all the more fiercely now that the sin of Cain branded his soul. He still felt unlimited strength and believed that he could go far. But the sun was hotter than he had ever experienced it; the heat appeared to strike up from the earth as well as burn down from above; and it was having a strange effect upon him. He had sensed a difficulty in keeping to a straight line of travel, and at first had put it down to his instinct for zigzagging to his greasewood bush and that *ocatilla* plant to place them behind him. Moving on again, he turned toward the chocolate mountain and the river.

It seemed close. He saw the bare gray desert with its green growths slope gradually to the rugged base of the range. Somewhere between him and there ran the river. He strained his eyesight. How strangely and clearly the lines of one ridge merged into the lines of another! There must be distance between them. But it could not be seen. The range looked larger and farther away the more he studied it — the air more full of transparent haze, the red and russet and chocolate hues more quiveringly suggestive of illusion.

"Look here," panted Adam, as he halted once more. "I've been told about the desert. But I

100

didn't pay particular attention and now I can't remember. . . . I only know it's hot — and this won't do."

It was just then that Adam, gazing back down the gray desert, saw puffs of dust and horses.

Panic seized him. He ran directly away from his pursuers, bending low, looking neither to right nor to left, violent, furious, heedless, like an animal in flight. And with no sense of direction, with no use of reason, he ran on till he dropped.

Then his breast seemed to split and his heart to lift with terrified pressure, agonizing and suffocating. He lay on the ground and gasped, with his mouth in the dust. Gradually the paroxysm subsided.

He arose to go on, hot, dry, aching, dizzy, but still strong in his stride.

"I've — got — away," he said, "and now — the river — the river."

Fear of Collishaw had been dulled. Adam could think of little besides the heat and his growing thirst, and this thing — the desert — that was so strange, so big, so menacing. It did not alarm him that his skin was no longer wet with sweat, but the fact struck him singularly.

The wind was blowing sand in his face, obstructing his sight. Suddenly his feet dragged in sand. Dimly then he made out low sand dunes with hollows between, and farther on larger dunes waving and billowing on to rise to what seemed mountains of sand. He saw them as through a veil of dust. Turning away, he plodded on, half blinded, fighting the blast of wind that was growing stronger. The air cleared somewhat. Sand dunes were all around him, and to his right, in the direction he thought was wrong, loomed the chocolate range. He went that way, and again the flying sand hid a clear view. A low, seeping, silken rustle filled the air, sometimes rising to a soft roar. He thought of what he had heard about sandstorms, but he knew this was not one. Unwittingly he had wandered into the region of the dunes, and the strong gusty wind swept up the fine sand in sheets and clouds. He must get out. It could not be far to the level desert again. He plodded on, and the way he chose, with its intermittent views of the mountains, at last appeared to be the wrong one. So he turned again. And as he turned, a stronger wind, now at his back, whipped up the sand till all was pale yellow around him, thick and opaque and moaning, through which the sun shone with strange magenta hue. He did not dare rest or wait. He had to plod on. And the way led through soft, uneven sand, always dragging at his feet.

After a while Adam discovered that when he trudged down into the hollows between dunes he became enveloped in flying sand that forced him to cover mouth and eyes with his scarf and go choking on, but when he climbed up over a dune the air became clearer and he could breathe easier. Thus instinctively he favored the ascents, and thus he lost himself in a world of curved and sculptured sand dunes, gray and yellow through the flying mists, or steely silver under the gleaming sunlight. The wind lulled, letting the sand settle, and then he saw he was lost as upon a trackless ocean, with no landmarks in sight. On all sides heaved beautiful white mounds of sand, ribbed and waved and laced with exquisitely delicate knife-edged curves. And these crests changed like the crests of waves, only, instead of flying spray, these were curled and shadowed veils of sand blowing from the scalloped crowns. Then again the wind, swooping down, whipped and swept the sand in low thick sheets on and on over the dunes, until thin rising clouds obscured the sky.

Adam climbed on, growing weaker. As the heat had wrought strangely upon his blood, so the sand had dragged strength from his legs. His situation was grave, but, though he felt the dread and pity of it, a certain violence of opposition had left him. That was in his will. He feared more the instinctive reaction — the physical resistance that was growing in him. Merryvale had told him how men lost on the desert could die of thirst in one day. But Adam had scarcely credited that; certainly he did not believe it applicable to himself. He realized, however, that unless he somehow changed the present condition sun and sand would overwhelm him. So when from a high knoll of sand he saw down into a large depression, miles across, where clumps of mesquites showed black against the silver, he descended toward them and eventually reached them, ready indeed to drop into the shade.

Here under a thick-foliaged mesquite he covered his face with a handkerchief, his head with his coat, and settled himself to rest and wait. It was a wise move. At once he felt by contrast what the fierce sun had been. Gradually the splitting headache subsided to a sensation that seemed to Adam like a gentle boiling of blood in his brain. He could hear it. His dry skin became a little moist; the intolerable burn left it; his heart and pulse ceased such labored throbbing; and after a time his condition was limited to less pain, a difficulty in breathing, and thirst. These were bearable.

From time to time Adam removed the coverings to look about him. The sun was westering. When it sank the wind would cease to blow and then he could find a way out of this wilderness of sand dunes. Leaning back against a low branch of the tree, he stretched out, and such was his exhaustion and the restfulness of the posture that he fell asleep.

When he awoke he felt better, though half smothered. He had rested. His body was full of dull aches, but no more pain. His mouth did not appear so dry or his tongue so swollen; nevertheless, the thirst remained, giving his throat a sensation of puckering, such as he remembered he used to have after eating green persimmons.

Then Adam, suddenly realizing what covered his head, threw off the coat and handkerchief. And his eyes were startled by such a sight as they had never beheld — a marvelous unreality of silver sheen and black shadow, a starry tracery of labyrinthine streams on a medium as weird and beautiful and intangible as a dream.

"O God! am I alive or dead?" he whispered in awe. And his voice proved to him that he and his burden had not slipped into the oblivion of the beyond.

Night had fallen. The moon had arisen. The stars shone lustrously. The sky burned a deep rich blue. And all this unreal beauty that had mocked him was only the sculptured world of sand translating the magnificence and splendor of the heavens.

More than all else, Adam grew sensitive to the oppressiveness of the silence. His first steps were painful, a staggering, halting gait, that exercise at length worked into some semblance of his old stride. The cold desert air invigorated him, and if it had not been for the discomfort of thirst he would have been doing well under the circumstances.

A sense of direction that had nothing to do with his intelligence prompted him to face east. He obeyed it. And he walked for what seemed hours over a moon-blanched sea of sand, to climb at last a high dune from which he saw the dark, level floor of the desert, and far across the shadowy space a black range of mountains. He thought he recognized the rugged contour, and when, sweeping his gaze southward, he saw the lone mountain looming like a dark sentinel over the desert gateway, then he was sure of his direction. Over there to the east lay the river. And he had long hours of the cool night to travel.

From this vantage point Adam looked back over the silver sea of sand dunes; and such was the sight of it that even in his precarious condition he was stirred to his depths. The huge oblong silver moon hung low over that vast heaving stretch of desert. It was a wasteland, shimmering with its belts and plains of moonlit sand, blank and mysterious in its shadows, an abode of loneliness. An inexplicable sadness pervaded Adam's soul. This wasteland and he seemed identical. How strange to feel that he did not want to leave it! Life could not be sustained in this sepulcher of the desert. But it was not life that his soul yearned for then — only peace. And peace dwelt there in that solitude of the sands.

Gray dawn found Adam many miles closer to the mountain range. Yet it was still far and his former dread returned. On every side what interminable distances!

A deepening rose color over the eastern horizon appeared to be reflected upon the mountain peaks, and this glow crept down the dark slopes. Gray dawn changed to radiant morning with an ethereal softness of color. When the blazing disk of the sun shone over the ramparts of the east all that desert world underwent a wonderous transfiguration. The lord of day had arisen and this was his empire. Red was the hue of his authority, emblazoned in long vivid rays over the ranges and the wastelands. Then the great orb of fire cleared the horizon and the desert seemed aflame.

One moment Adam gave to the marvel and glory of the sunrise, and then he looked no more. That brief moment ended in a consciousness of the gravity of his flight. For the first touch of sun on face and hands burned hot, as if it suddenly aggravated a former burn that the night had soothed.

"Got to reach — river soon," he muttered, thickly, "or never will."

He walked on while the sun climbed.

Desert vegetation increased. Adam toiled on, breathing hard, careless now of the reaching thorns and heedless of the rougher ground.

He was perfectly conscious of a subtle changing of his spirit, but because it seemed a drifting farther and farther from thought he could not comprehend it. Courage diminished as fear augmented. More and more his will and intelligence gave way to sensorial perceptions. More and more he felt the urge to hurry, and, though reason warned against the folly of this, it was not strong enough to compel him to resist. He did hurry more and stumbled along. Like breath of a furnace the heat rose from the rocky, sandy soil; and from above there seemed to bear down the weight of the leaden fire.

His skin became as dry as dust and began to shrivel. It did not blister. The pain now came from burn of the flesh underneath. He felt that his blood was drying up. A stinging sensation as of puncture by a thousand thorns throbbed in his face and neck. The heat burned through his clothes, and the soles of his boots were coals of fire. Doggedly he strove forward. A whistle accompanied his panting breaths. Most intolerable of all was thirst — the bitter, astringent taste in the scant saliva that became pasty and dry, the pain in his swelling tongue, the parched constriction in his throat.

At last he reached the base of a low rocky ridge which for long had beckoned to him and mocked him. It obstructed sight of the slope to the mountain range. Surely between that ridge and the slope ran the river. The hope spurred him upward.

As he climbed he gazed up into the coppery sky, but his hot and tired eyes could not endure the great white blaze that was the sun. Halfway up he halted to rest, and from here he had measureless view of the desert. Then his dull brain revived to a final shock. For he seemed to see a thousand miles of green-gray barrenness, of lifting heat veils like transparent smoke, of wastes of waved sand, and of ranges of upheaved rock. How terribly it confronted him! Pitiless mockery of false distances on all sides! A sun-blasted world not meant for man!

Then Adam ascended to the summit of the ridge. A glaring void seemed flung at him. His chocolate-hued mountain range was not far away. From this height he could see all the gray-green level of desert between him and the range. He stared. Again there seemed flung in his face a hot glare of space. There was no river.

"Where, where's — the river?" gasped Adam, mistrusting his eyesight.

But the wonderful Rio Colorado, the strange red river beloved by desert wanderers, did not flow before him — or to either side — or behind. It must have turned to flow on the other slope of this insurmountable range.

"God has — forsaken me!" cried Adam, in despair, and he fell upon the rocks.

But these rocks, hot as red-hot plates of iron, permitted of no contact, even in a moment of horror. Adam was burned to stagger up, to plunge and run and fall down the slope, out upon the level, to the madness that awaited him.

He must rush on to the river — to drink and drink — to bathe in the cool water that flowed down from the snow-fed lakes of the north. Thoughts about water possessed his mind — pleasant, comforting, hurrying him onward. Memory of the great river made pictures in his mind, and there flowed the broad red waters, sullen and eddying and silent. All the streams and rivers and lakes Adam had known crowded their images across his inward eye, and this recall of the past was sweet. He remembered the brook near his old home — the clear green water full of bright minnows and gold-sided sunfish; how it used to flow swiftly under the willow banks where violets hid by mossy stones, and how it tarried in deep dark pools under shelving banks, green and verdant and sweet smelling; how the ferns used to bend over in graceful tribute and the lilies float white and gold, with great green-backed frogs asleep upon the broad leaves. The watering trough on the way to school, many and many a time, in the happy days gone by, had he drunk there and splashed his brother Guerd. Guerd, who hated water and had to be made to wash, when they were little boys! The old well on Madden's farm with its round cobblestoned walls where the moss and lichen grew, and where the oaken bucket, wet and dark and green, used to come up bumping and spilling, brimful of clear cold water — how vividly he remembered that! His father had called it granite water, and the best, because it flowed through the cold subterranean caverns of granite rock. Then there was the spring in the orchard, sweet, soft water that his mother used to send him after, and as he trudged home, burdened by the huge bucket, he would spill some upon his bare feet.

Yes, as Adam staggered on, aimlessly now, he was haunted more and more by memories of water. That dear, unforgettable time of boy-hood when he used to love the water, to swim like a duck and bask like a turtle — it seemed far back in the past, across some terrible interval of pain, vague now, yet hateful. Where was he — and where was Guerd? Something like a blade pierced his heart.

Suddenly Adam was startled out of his pleasant reminiscence by something blue and bright that danced low down along the desert floor. A lake! He halted with an inarticulate cry. There was a lake of blue water, glistening, exquisitely clear, with borders of green. He could not help but rush forward. The lake shimmered, thinned, shadowed, and vanished. Adam halted and, rubbing his eyes, peered hard ahead and all around. Behind him shone a strip of blue, streaked up and down by desert plants, and it seemed to be another lake, larger, bluer, clearer, with a delicate vibrating quiver, as if exquisitely rippled by a gentle breeze. Green shores were marvel-ously reflected in the blue. Adam gaped at this. Had he waded through a lake? He had crossed that barren flat of greasewood to reach the spot upon which he now stood. Almost he was forced to run back. But this must be a deceit of the desert or a madness of his sight. He bent low, and the lake of blue seemed to lift and quiver upon a thin darkling line of vapor or transparent shadow. Adam took two strides back — and the thing vanished! Desert magic! A deception of nature! A horrible illusion to a lost man growing crazed by thirst!

"Mirage!" whispered Adam, hoarsely. "Blue water! Ha-ha! . . . Damned lie — it shan't fool me!"

But as clear perception failed these mirages of the desert did deceive him. All objects took on a hazy hue, tinged by the red of blood in his eyes, and they danced in the heat-veiled air. Shadows, glares, cactus, and brush stood as immovable as the rocks of ages. Only the illusive and ethereal mirages gleamed as if by magic and shimmered and moved in that midday trance of the sun-blasted desert.

The time came when Adam plunged toward every mirage that floated so blue and serene and mystical in the deceiving atmosphere, until hope and despair and magnified sight finally brought on a mental state bordering on the madness sure to come.

Then, as he staggered toward this green-bordered pond and that crystal-blue lake, already drinking and having in his mind, he began to hear the beautiful sounds of falling rain, of gurgling brooks, of lapping waves, of roaring rapids, of gentle river currents, of water — water — water sweetly tinkling and babbling, of wind-laden murmur of a mountain stream. And he began to wander in a circle.

8
●

Consciousness returned to Adam. He was lying under an ironwood tree, over branches of which a canvas had been stretched, evidently to shade him from the sun. The day appeared to be far spent.

His head seemed to have been relieved by a hot metal band; his tongue was no longer bursting in his mouth; the boil of his blood had subsided. His skin felt moist.

Then he heard the rough voice of a man talking to animals, apparently burros. Movement of body was difficult and somewhat painful; however, he managed to sit up and look around. Hide-covered boxes and packsaddles, with duffle and utensils of a prospector, were littered about, and conspicuous among the articles near him were three large canvas-covered canteens, still wet. Upon the smoldering embers of a camp fire steamed a black iron pot. A little beyond the first stood a very short, broad man, back turned; and he was evidently feeding choice morsels of some kind to five eager and jealous burros.

"Spoiled — every darn one of you!" he was

saying, and the kindness of his voice belied its roughness. "Why, I used to have burros that could lick labels off tin cans an' call it a square meal!"

Then he turned and espied Adam watching him.

"Hullo! You've come to," he said, with interest.

Adam's gaze encountered an extraordinary-looking man. He could not have been taller than five and a half feet, and the enormous breadth of him made him appear as wide as he was long. He was not fat. His immense bulk was sheer brawn, betokening remarkable strength. His dusty, ragged clothes were patched like a crazy-quilt. He had an immense head, a shock of shaggy hair beginning to show streaks of gray, and a broad face tanned dark as an Indian's, the lower half of which was covered with a scant grizzled beard. His eyes, big, dark, rolling, resembled those of an ox. His expression seemed to be one of set tranquillity — the impassiveness of bronze.

Adam's voice was a husky whisper: "Where am — I? Who are you?"

"Young man, my name's Dismukes," came the reply, "an you're ninety miles from anywhere — an' alive, which's more than I'd bet on yesterday."

The words brought Adam a shock of memory. Out there the desert smoked, sweltering in the spent heat of the setting sun. Slowly Adam lay back upon the blanket and bundle that had been placed under him for a bed. The man sat down on one of the hide-covered boxes, fastening his great eyes upon Adam.

"Am I — all right?" whispered Adam.

"Yes, but it was a close shave," replied the other.

"You said — something about yesterday. Tell me."

Dismukes fumbled in his patched vest and, fetching forth a stumpy pipe, he proceeded to fill it. It was noticeable that he had to use his little finger to press down the tobacco into the bowl, as the other fingers of his enormous hands were too large. Adam had never before seen such scarred, calloused hands.

"It was day before yesterday I run across you," began Dismukes, after a comfortable pull at his pipe. "My burro Jinny has the best eyes of the pack outfit. When I seen her ears go up I got to lookin' hard, an' presently spied you staggerin' in a circle. I'd seen men do that before. Sometimes you'd run, an' again you'd wag along, an' then you'd fall an' crawl. I caught you an' had to tie you with my rope. You were out of your head. An' you looked hard — all dried up — tongue black an' hangin' out. I thought you were done for. I poured a canteen of water over your head an' then packed you over here where there's wood an' water. You couldn't make a sound, but all the same I knew you were ravin' for water. I fed you

115

water a spoonful at a time, an' every little while I emptied a canteen over you. Was up all night with you that night. You recovered awful slow. Yesterday I'd not have gambled much on your chances. But to-day you came round. I got you to swallow some soft grub, an' I guess you'll soon be pretty good. You'll be weak, though. You're awful thin. I'm curious about how much you weighed. You look as if you might have been a husky lad."

"I was," whispered Adam. "Hundred and eighty-five — or ninety."

"So I thought. You'll not go over one hundred an' twenty now. You've lost about seventy pounds. . . . Oh, it's a fact! You see, the body is 'most all water, an' on this desert in summer a man just dries up an' blows away."

"Seventy — pounds!" exclaimed Adam, incredulously. But when he glanced at his shrunken hands he believed the incomprehensible fact. "I must be skin — and bones."

"Mostly bones. But they're long, heavy bones, an' if you ever get any flesh on them you'll be a darned big man. I'm glad they're not goin' to bleach white on the desert, where I've seen so many these last ten years."

"You saved my life?" suddenly queried Adam.

"Boy, there's no doubt of that," returned the other. "Another hour would have finished you."

"I — I thank you. . . . But — so help me God — I wish you hadn't," whispered Adam, poignantly.

Dismukes spent a strange gaze upon Adam. "What's your name?" he asked.

Adam halted over the conviction that he could never reveal his identity; and there leaped to his lips the name the loquacious Regan had given him.

"Wansfell," he replied.

Dismukes averted his gaze. Manifestly he divined that Adam had lied. "Well, it's no matter what a man calls himself in this country," he said. "Only everybody an' everythin' has to have a name."

"You're a prospector?"

"Yes. But I'm more a miner. I hunt for gold. I don't waste time tryin' to sell claims. Years ago I set out to find a fortune in gold. My limit was five hundred thousand dollars. I've already got a third of it — in banks an' hid away safe."

"When you get it — your fortune — what then?" inquired Adam, with thrilling curiosity.

"I'll enjoy life. I have no ties — no people. Then I'll see the world," replied the prospector, in deep and sonorous voice.

A wonderful passion radiated from him. Adam saw a quiver run over the huge frame. This Dismukes evidently was as extraordinary in character as in appearance. Adam felt the man's strangeness, his intelligence, and the inflexible will and fiery spirit. Yet all at once Adam felt steal over him an emotion of pity that he could not understand. How strange men were!

At this juncture the prospector was compelled to drive the burros out of camp. Then he attended to his cooking over the fire, and presently brought a bowl of steaming food to Adam.

"Eat this slow — with a spoon," he said, gruffly. "Never forget that a man starved for grub or water can kill himself quick."

During Adam's long-drawn-out meal the sun set and the mantle of heat seemed to move away for the coming of shadows. Adam found that his weakness was greater than he had supposed, rendering the effort of sitting up one he was glad to end. He lay back on the blankets, wanting to think over his situation rather than fall asleep, but he found himself very drowsy, and his mind vaguely wandered until it was a blank. Upon awakening he saw the first gray of dawn arch the sky. He felt better, almost like his old self, except for that queer sensation of thinness and lightness, most noticeable when he lifted his hand. Dismukes was already astir, and there, a few rods from camp, stood the ludicrous burros, as if they had not moved all night. Adam got up and stretched his limbs, pleased to find that he appeared to be all right again, except for a little dizziness.

Dismukes evinced gladness at the fact of Adam's improvement. "Good!" he exclaimed. "You'd be strong enough to ride a burro to-day. But it's goin' to be hot, like yesterday. We'd better not risk travelin'."

"How do you know it's going to be as hot

as yesterday?" inquired Adam.

"I can tell by the feel an' smell of the air, an' mostly that dull lead-colored haze you see over the mountains."

Adam thought the air seemed cool and fresh, but he did see a dull pall over the mountains. Farther toward the east, where the sunrise lifted an immense and wondrous glow, this haze was not visible.

The remark of Dismukes anent the riding of a burro disturbed Adam. This kindly prospector meant to take him on to his destination. Impossible! Adam had fled to the desert to hide, and the desert must hide him, alive or dead. The old, thick, clamoring emotions knocked at his heart. Adam felt gratitude toward Dismukes for not questioning him, and that forbearance made him want to tell something of his story. Yet how reluctant he was to open his lips on that score! He helped Dismukes with the simple morning meal, and afterward with odds and ends of tasks, all the time cheerful and questioning, putting off what he knew was inevitable. The day did come on hot — so hot that life was just bearable for men and beasts in the shade of the big ironwood tree. Adam slept some of the hours away. He awoke stronger, with more active mind. Of the next meal Dismukes permitted Adam to eat heartily. And later, while Dismukes smoked and Adam sat before the camp fire, the moment of revelation came, quite unexpectedly.

"Wansfell, you'll not be goin' to Yuma with me to-morrow," asserted Dismukes quietly.

The words startled Adam. He dropped his head. "No — no! Thank you — I won't — I can't go," he replied, trembling. The sound of his voice agitated him further.

"Boy, tell me or not, just as you please. But I'm a man you can trust."

The kindness and a nameless power invested in this speech broke down what little restraint remained with Adam.

"I — I can't go. . . . I'm an outcast. . . . I must hide — hide in the — desert," burst out Adam, covering his face with his hands.

"Was that why you came to the desert?"

"Yes — yes."

"But, boy, you came without a canteen or grub or burro or gun — or anythin'. In all my years on the desert I never saw the like of that before. An' only a miracle saved your life. That miracle was Jinny's eyes. You owe your life to a long-eared, white-faced burro. Jinny has eyes like a mountain sheep. She saw you — miles off. An' such luck won't be yours twice. You can't last on this desert without the things to sustain life. . . . How did it happen that I found you here alone — without anythin'?"

"No time. I — I had to run!" panted Adam.

"What'd you do? Don't be afraid to tell me. The desert is a place for secrets, and it's a lonely place where a man learns to read the souls of

120

men — when he meets them. You're not vicious. You're no — But never mind — tell me without wastin' more words. Maybe I can help you."

"No one can — help me," cried Adam.

"That's not so," quickly spoke up Dismukes, his voice deep and rolling. "Some one can help you — an' maybe it's me."

Here Adam completely broke down. "I — I did — something — awful!"

"No crime, boy — say it was no crime," earnestly returned the prospector.

"O my God! Yes — yes! It was — a crime!" sobbed Adam, shuddering. "But, man — I swear, horrible as it was — I'm innocent! I swear that. Believe me. . . . I was driven — driven by wrongs, by hate, by taunts. If I'd stood them longer I'd have been a white-livered coward. But I was driven and half drunk."

"Well — well!" ejaculated Dismukes, shaking his shaggy head. "It's bad. But I believe you an' you needn't tell me any more. Life is hell! I was young once. . . . An' now you've got to hide away from men — to live on the desert — to be one of us wanderers of the wastelands?"

"Yes. I must hide. And I want — I need to live — to suffer — to atone!"

"Boy, do you believe in God?" asked the prospector.

"I don't know. I think so," replied Adam, lifting his head and striving for composure. "My mother was religious. But my father was not."

"Well — well, if you believed in God your

121

case would not be hopeless. But some men —
a few out of the many wanderers — find God
out here in these wilds. Maybe you will. . . .
Can you tell me what you think you want to
do?"

"Oh — to go alone — into the loneliest place
— to live there for years — forever," replied
Adam, with passion.

"Alone. That is my way. An' I understand
how you feel — what you need. Are you goin'
to hunt gold?"

"No — no."

"Have you any money?"

"Yes. More than I'll ever need. I'd like to
throw it all away — or give it to you. But it
— it was my mother's. . . . And I promised
her I'd not squander it — that I'd try to save."

"Boy, never mind — an' I don't want your
money," interrupted Dismukes. "An' don't do
any fool trick with it. You'll need it to buy
outfits. You can always trust Indians to go to
the freightin' posts for you. But never let any
white men in this desert know you got money.
That's a hard comparison, an' it's justified."

"I'm already sick with the love men have for
money," said Adam, bitterly.

"An' now to figure out an' make good all
that brag of mine," went on Dismukes, reflectively. "I'll need only two days' grub to get
to Yuma. There's one sure water hole. I can
give you one of my canteens, an' Jinny, the
burro that saved your life. She's tricky, but a

blamed good burro. An' by makin' up enough bread I can spare my oven. So, all told, I guess I can outfit you good enough for you to reach a canyon up here to the west where Indians live. I know them. They're good. You can stay with them until the hot weather passes. No danger of any white men runnin' across you there."

"But you mustn't let me have all your outfit," protested Adam.

"I'm not. It's only the grub an' one burro."

"Won't you run a risk — with only two days' rations?"

"Wansfell, every move you can make on this desert is a risk," replied Dismukes, seriously. "Learn that right off. But I'm sure. Only accidents or unforeseen circumstances ever make risks for me now. I'm what they call a desert rat."

"You're most kind," said Adam, choking up again, "to help a stranger — this way."

"Boy, I don't call that help," declared Dismukes. "That's just doin' for a man as I'd want to be done by. When I talked about help I meant somethin' else."

"What? God knows I need it. I'll be grateful. I'll do as you tell me," replied Adam, with a strange thrill stirring in him.

"You are a boy — no matter if you're bigger than most men. You've got the mind of a boy. What a damn pity you've got to do this hidin' game!" Under strong feeling the prospector got up, and, emptying his pipe, he began to take short strides to and fro in the limited shade cast by the ironwood tree. The indomitable force of the man showed in his step, in the way he carried himself. Presently he turned to Adam and the great ox eyes burned intensely. "Wansfell, if you were a man I'd never feel the way I do. But you're only a youngster — you're not bad — you've had bad luck — an' for you I can break my rule — an' I'll do it if you're in earnest. I've never talked about the desert — about its secrets — what it's taught me. But I'll tell you what the desert is — how it'll be your salvation — how to be a wanderer of the wasteland is to be strong, free, happy — if you are honest, if you're big enough for it."

"Dismukes, I swear I'm honest — and I'll be big, by God! or I'll die trying," declared Adam, passionately.

The prospector gave Adam a long, steady stare, a strange gaze such as must have read his soul.

"Wansfell, if you can live on the desert you'll grow like it," he said, solemnly, as if he were pronouncing a benediction.

Adam gathered from this speech that Dismukes meant to unbosom himself of many secrets of this wonderful wasteland. Evidently, however, the prospector was not then ready to talk further. With thoughtful mien and plodding gait he resumed his short walk to and fro. It struck Adam then that his appearance was almost as ludicrous as that of his burros, yet at the same time his presence somehow conveyed a singular sadness. Years of loneliness burdened the wide bowed shoulders of this desert man. Adam divined then, in a gust of gratitude, that this plodding image of Dismukes would always remain in his mind as a picture, a symbol of the actual good in human nature.

The hot day closed without Adam ever venturing out of the shade of the tree. Once or twice he had put his hand in a sunny spot to feel the heat, and it had burned. The night mantled down with its intense silence, all-embracing, and the stars began to glow white. As Dismukes sat down near Adam in the glow of the camp fire it was manifest, from the absence of his pipe and the penetrating, possession-taking power of his eyes, that he was under the dominance of a singular passion.

"Wansfell," he began, in low, deep voice, "it took me many years to learn how to live on the desert. I had the strength an' the vitality of ten ordinary men. Many times in those desperate years was I close to death from thirst — from starvation — from poison water — from sickness — from bad men — and last, though not least — from loneliness. If I had met a man like myself, as I am now, I might have been spared a hell of sufferin'. I did meet desert men who could have helped me. But they passed me by. The desert locks men's lips. Let every man save his own life — find his own soul.

That's the unwritten law of the wastelands of the world. I've broken it for you because I want to do by you as I'd have liked to be done by. An' because I see somethin' in you."

Dismukes paused here to draw a long breath. In the flickering firelight he seemed a squatting giant immovable by physical force, and of a will unquenchable while life lasted.

"Men crawl over the desert like ants whose nests have been destroyed an' who have become separated from one another," went on Dismukes. "They all know the lure of the desert. Each man has his own idea of why the desert claims him. Mine was gold — is gold — so that some day I can travel over the world, rich an' free, an' see life. Another man's will be the need to hide — or the longin' to forget — or the call of adventure — or hate of the world — or love of a woman. Another class is that of bad men. Robbers, murderers. They are many. There are also many men, an' a few women, who just drift or wander or get lost in the desert. An' out of all these, if they stay in the desert, but few survive. They die or they are killed. The Great American Desert is a vast place an' it is covered by unmarked graves an' bleached bones. I've seen so many — so many."

Dismukes paused again while his broad breast heaved with a sigh.

"I was talkin' about what men think the desert means to them. In my case I say gold, an' I say that as the other man will claim he loves the silence or the color or the loneliness. But I'm wrong, an' so is he. The great reason why the desert holds men lies deeper. I feel that. But I've never had the brains to solve it. I do know, however, that life on this wasteland is fierce an' terrible. Plants, reptiles, beasts, birds, an' men all have to fight for life far out of proportion to what's necessary in fertile parts of the earth. You will learn that early, an' if you are a watcher an' a thinker you will understand it.

"The desert is no place for white men. An oasis is fit for Indians. They survive there. But they don't thrive. I respect the Indians. It will be well for you to live awhile with Indians. . . . Now what I most want you to know is this."

The speaker's pause this time was impressive, and he raised one of his huge hands, like a monstrous claw, making a gesture at once eloquent and strong.

"When the desert claims men it makes most of them beasts. They sink to that fierce level in order to live. They are trained by the eternal strife that surrounds them. A man of evil nature survivin' in the desert becomes more terrible than a beast. He is a vulture. . . . On the other hand, there are men whom the desert makes like it. Yes — fierce an' elemental an' terrible, like the heat an' the storm an' the avalanche, but greater in another sense — greater through that eternal strife to live — beyond any words of mine to tell. What such men have lived —

the patience, the endurance, the toil — the fights with men an' all that makes the desert — the wanderin's an' perils an' tortures — the horrible loneliness that must be fought hardest, by mind as well as action — all these struggles are beyond ordinary comprehension an' belief. But I know. I've met a few such men, an' if it's possible for the divinity of God to walk abroad on earth in the shape of mankind, it was invested in them. The reason must be that in the development by the desert, in case of these few men who did not retrograde, the spiritual kept pace with the physical. It means these men never forgot, never reverted to mere unthinking instinct, never let the hard, fierce, brutal action of survival on the desert kill their souls. Spirit was stronger than body. I've learned this of these men, though I never had the power to attain it. It takes brains. I was only fairly educated. An' though I've studied all my years on the desert, an' never gave up, I wasn't big enough to climb as high as I can see. I tell you all this, Wansfell, because it may be your salvation. Never give up to the desert or to any of its minions! Never cease to fight! You must fight to live — an' so make that fight equally for your mind an' your soul! Thus you will repent for your crime, whatever that was. Remember the secret is never to forget your hold on the past — your memories — an' through thinkin' of them to save your mind an' apply it to all that faces you out there."

Rising from his seat, Dismukes made a wide, sweeping gesture, symbolical of a limitless expanse. "An' the gist of all this talk of mine — this hope of mine to do for you as I'd have been done by — is that if you fight an' think together like a man meanin' to repent of his sin — somewhere out there in the loneliness an' silence you will find God!"

With that he abruptly left the camp fire to stride off into the darkness; and the sonorous roll of his last words seemed to linger on the quiet air.

Every one of his intense words had been burned into Adam's sensitive mind in characters and meanings never to be forgotten. Dismukes had found eager and fertile soil for the planting of the seeds of his toil-earned philosophy. The effect upon Adam was profound, and so wrought upon his emotions that the black and hateful consciousness which had returned to haunt him was as but a shadow of his thought. Adam stared out into the night where Dismukes had vanished. Something great had happened. Was the man Dismukes a fanatic, a religious wanderer of the wasteland, who imagined he had found in Adam an apt pupil, or who had preached a sermon because the opportunity presented? No! The prospector had the faith to give out of his lesson of life on the desert. His motive was the same as when he had risked much to follow Adam, staggering blindly across the hot sands to his death. And as Adam felt the mounting passion of conviction, of gratitude, his stirred mind seemed suddenly to burst into a radiant and scintillating inspiration of resolve to be the man Dismukes had described, to fight and to think and to remember as had no one ever before done on the desert. It was all that seemed left for him. Repentance! Expiation! True to himself at the last in spite of a horrible and fatal blunder!

"Oh, Guerd! Guerd, my brother!" he cried, shuddering at the whisper of that name. "Wherever you are in spirit — hear me! . . . I'll rise above wrongs and hate and revenge! I'll remember our boyhood — how I loved you! I'll atone for my crime! I'll never forget. . . . I'll fight and think to save my soul — and pray for yours! . . . Hear me and forgive — you who drove me out into the wastelands!"

9

Adam lay awake for some length of time, waiting for Dismukes to return, but he did not come. Adam at length succumbed to drowsiness. It was Dismukes's call that awakened him. The sun already tipped the eastern range, rosy red, and all the open land lay fresh and colorful in the morning light. Adam felt no severe effects from his hard experience, except an inordinate hunger, which Dismukes was more disposed to appease. Still he cautioned Adam not to eat too much.

"Now, Wansfell, you must learn all about burros," began Dismukes. "The burro is the most important part of your outfit. This desert would still be a blank waste, unknown to the white man, if it had not been for those shaggy, lazy, lop-eared little donkeys. Whenever you get sore at one an' feel inclined to kill him for some trick or other, just remember that you could not get along without him.

"Most burros are alike. They hang near camp, as you see mine, hopin' they can steal a bite of somethin' if you don't give it to them. They'll eat paper, or 'most anythin' except greasewood. They love paper off bacon. I had one once that ate my overalls. They never get homesick an' seem contented in the most desolate places. I had a burro that was happy in Death Valley, which 's the hell hole of this wasteland. Burros are seldom responsive to affection. They'll stand great abuse. Never expect any thanks. Always patient. They are usually easy to catch. But they must know you. Only way to catch them is to head them off. Then they stop. Young burros are easily broke an' will follow others. They must be driven. Never knew but one that I could lead. Don't forget this. They have the most wonderful endurance — never stumble or fall — an' can exist on practically nothin'. When you turn them loose they'll nibble around awhile, then stop an' stand like rocks, never movin' for hours an' hours, as if they were wrapped in prehistoric thought. In the mornin' when you start off on your day's travel the burros are fresh an' they drive fine. But in the afternoon, when they get tired, they think of tricks. They'll lie down — roll over on a pack — knock against a rock or tree. They'll get together in a bunch to tangle the packs. When a burro intends to lie down he humps his back an' wriggles his tail. It's hard to get burros across streams. Scared of water! Strange, isn't that? I've had to carry my burros many a time. But they'll climb or go down the steepest, roughest mountain trail without fear. They can slide down a steep slope that a man will not stick on. Burros have more patience and good qualities, an' also cussedness, than any other beasts. They pick out pardners an' stick together all the time. A big bunch of burros will pair off regardless of sex. Never give each other up! They bray at night — an awful sound till you get used to it. Remember this quick some night when you're lifted out of a sleep by a terrible unearthly roar. . . . Well, I guess that's an introduction to desert burros. It's all serious fact, Wansfell, as you'll learn, an' to your cost, unless you remember."

How singular for Adam to have the closing words of Dismukes reveal the absorbing interest of this simple and practical talk about burros! It amazed Adam to find that he had even been amused, ready to laugh.

"I'll remember," he asserted, with conviction.

"Dare say you will," replied Dismukes, "but the idea is you must remember before you get in trouble, not after. I can't tell you when to know a burro is goin' to trick you. I'm just givin' you facts as to the nature of burros in general. You must study an' learn them yourself. A man could spend his life studyin' burros an' then have lots to learn. Most prospectors lose half their time trackin' their burros. It's tryin' to find burros that has cost many a desert man his life. An' this is why, if you've chosen the desert to live in, you must learn the habits of the burro. He's the camel of this Sahara."

With that the prospector appeared to have talked himself out for the present, and he devoted his efforts to a selection of parts of his outfit that manifestly he meant to turn over to Adam. At length having made the selection to his satisfaction, he went out to wake up the burro Jinny. As he led Jinny into camp all the other burros trooped along.

"Watch me pack an' then you try your hand on Jinny," he said.

Adam was all eyes while the prospector placed in position the old ragged pads of skins and blankets, and the packsaddles over them, to be buckled carefully. It was all comparatively easy until it came to tying the pack on with a rope in what Dismukes called a hitch. However, after Dismukes had accomplished it on three of the

133

other burros, Adam believed he could make a respectable showing. To this end he began to pack Jinny, and did very well indeed till he got to the hitch, which was harder to tie than it looked. After several attempts he succeeded. During this procedure Jinny stood with one long ear up and the other down, as if nothing on earth mattered to her.

"Carry the canteen of water yourself," said Dismukes, as he led Adam out from under the tree and pointed west. "See where that long, low, sharp ridge comes down to the desert? . . . Well, that's fifty miles. Around that point lies a wide canyon. Indians live up that canyon. They are good people. Stay with them — work for them till you learn the desert. . . . Now as to gettin' there. Go slow. Rest often in the shade of ironwoods like this one. Take a good rest durin' the middle of the day. As long as you sweat you're in no danger. But if your skin gets dry you need to get out of the sun an' to drink. There are several springs along the base of this range. Chocolate Mountains, they're called. By keepin' a sharp eye for patches of bright-green brush you'll see where the water is. An' don't ever forget that water is the same as life blood."

Adam nodded solemnly as he realized how the mere thought of thirst constricted his throat and revived there a semblance of the pain he had endured.

"Go slow. Maybe you'll take two days or three

days to reach the Indians. By keepin' that ridge in sight you can't miss them."

The next move of the prospector was to take Adam around on the other side of the tree and wave his hand at the expanse of desert.

"Now follow me an' get these landmarks in your mind. Behind us lies the Chocolate range. You see it runs down almost southeast. That shiny black mountain standin' by itself is Pilot Knob. It's near Yuma, as of course you remember. Now straight across from us a few miles lies a line of sand dunes. They run same way as the Chocolates. But they're low — can't be seen far. Do you make out a dim, gray, strange-lookin' range just over the top of them?"

"Yes, I see that clearly. Looks like clouds," replied Adam.

"That's the Superstition Mountains. You will hear queer stories about them. Most prospectors are afraid to go there, though it's said Pegleg Smith's lost gold mine is somewhere in there. The Indians think the range is haunted. An' everyone who knows this desert will tell you how the Superstition range changes somehow from time to time. It does change. Those mountains are giant sand dunes an' they change their shape with the shiftin' of the winds. That's the fact, but I'm not gainsayin' how strange an' weird they are. An' I, for one, believe Pegleg Smith did find gold there. But there's no water. An' how can a man live without water? . . . Well, to go on, that dim, purple, high range beyond the Superstitions lies across the line in Mexico. . . . Now, lookin' round to the right of the Superstitions to the northwest, an' you see how the desert slopes down an' down on all sides to a pale, hazy valley that looks like a lake. It's the Salton Sink — below sea level — an' it's death for a man to try to cross there at this season. It looks obscured an' small, but it's really a whole desert in itself. In times gone by the Colorado River has broken its banks while in flood an' run back in there to fill that sink. Miles an' miles of fresh water which soon evaporated! Well, it's a queer old earth an' this desert teaches much. . . . Now look straight up the valley. The ragged high peak is San Jacinto an' the other high one farther north is San Gorgonio — two hundred miles from here. Prospectors call this one Grayback because it has the shape of a louse. These mountains are white with snow in the winter. Beyond them lies the Mohave Desert, an immense waste, which hides Death Valley in its iron- walled mountains. . . . Now comin' back down the valley on this side you see the Cottonwood range an' it runs down to meet the Chocolates. There's a break in the range. An' still farther down there's a break in the Chocolate range an' there's where your canyon comes out. You'll climb the pass some day, to get on top of the Chuckwalla Mountains, an' from there you will see north to the Mohave an' east to the Colorado — all stark naked desert that seems to hit a man in the face. . . . An', well, I guess I've done my best for you."

Adam could not for the moment safely trust himself to speak. The expanse of desert shown him, thus magnified into its true perspective, now stretched out with the nature of its distance and nudity strikingly clear. It did seem to glare a menace into Adam's face. It made him tremble. Yet there was fascination in the luring, deceitful Superstition range, and a sublimity in the measureless sweep of haze and purple slope leading north to the great peaks, and a compelling beckoning urge in the mystery and unknown that seemed to abide beyond the bronze ridge which marked Adam's objective point.

"I'll never forget your — your kindness," said Adam, finally turning to Dismukes.

The prospector shook hands with him, and his grip was something to endure.

"Kindness is nothin'. I owed you what a man owes to himself. But don't forget anythin' I told you."

"I never will," replied Adam. "Will you let me pay you for the — the burro and outfit?" Adam made this request hesitatingly, because he did not know the law of the desert, and he did not want to offer what might be an offense.

"Sure you got plenty of money?" queried Dismukes, gruffly.

"Indeed I have," rejoined Adam, eagerly.

"Then I'll take what the burro an' grub cost." He named a sum that appeared very small to Adam, and, receiving the money in his horny hands, he carefully deposited it in a greasy buckskin sack.

"Wansfell, may we meet again," he said in farewell. "Good luck an' good-by. . . . Don't forget."

"Good-by," returned Adam, unable to say more.

With a whoop at the four burros and a slap on the haunch of one of them, Dismukes started them southward. They trotted ahead with packs bobbing and wagging. What giant strides Dismukes took! He seemed the incarnation of dogged strength of manhood, yet something ludicrous clung about him in his powerful action as well as in his immense squat form. He did not look back.

Adam slapped Jinny on the haunch and started her westward.

The hour was still early morning. A rosy freshness of the sunrise still slanted along the bronze slopes of the range and here and there blossoms of *ocatilla* shone red. The desert appeared to be a gently rising floor of gravel, sparsely decked with ironwood and mesquite, and an occasional cactus, that, so far as Adam could see, did not harbor a living creature. The day did not seem to feel hot, but Adam knew from the rising heat veils that it was hot. Excitement governed his feelings. Actually he was on the move, with an outfit and every hope to escape possible pursuers, with the absolute surety of a hard yet wonderful existence staring him in the face.

Not until he felt a drag in his steps did he think of his weakened condition. Resting awhile in the shade of a tree, he let the burro graze on the scant brush, and then went on again. Thus he traveled on, with frequent rests, until the heat made it imperative for him to halt till afternoon. About the middle of the afternoon he packed and set forth again.

A direct line westward appeared to be bringing him closer to the slope of the mountain; and it was not long before he saw a thick patch of green brush that surely indicated a water hole. The very sight seemed to invigorate him. Nevertheless, the promised oasis was far away, and not before he had walked till he was weary and rested many times did he reach it. To find water and grass was like making a thrilling discovery. Adam unpacked Jinny and turned her loose, not, however, without some misgivings as to her staying there.

Though he suffered from an extreme fatigue and a weakness that seemed to be in both muscle and bone, a kind of cheer came to him with the camp-fire duties. Never had he been so famished! The sun set while he ate, and, despite his hunger, more than once he had to stop to gaze down across the measureless slope, smoky and red, that ended in purple obscurity. It struck him suddenly, as he was putting some sticks of dead ironwood on the fire, how he had ceased to look back over his shoulder toward the south.

The fire sputtered, the twilight deepened, the silence grew vast and vague. His eyelids were as heavy as lead, and all the nerves and veins of his body seemed to run together and to sink into an abyss the restfulness of which was unutterably sweet.

Some time during Adam's slumbers a nightmare possessed him. At the moment he was about to be captured he awakened, cold with clammy sweat and shaking in every limb. With violent start of consciousness, with fearful uncertainty, he raised himself to peer around. The desert night encompassed him. It was late, somewhere near the morning hour. Low down over the dark horizon line hung a wan distorted moon that shone with weird luster. Adam saw the black mountain wall above him apparently lifting to the stars, and the thick shadow of gloom filling the mouth of the canyon where he lay. He listened. And then he breathed a long sigh of relief and lay back in his blankets. The silence was that of a grave. There were no pursuers. He had only dreamed. And he closed his eyes again, feeling some blessed safeguard in the fact of his loneliness.

Dawn roused him to his tasks, stronger physically, eager and keen, but more watchful than he had been the preceding day and with less thrill than he had felt. He packed in half an hour and was traveling west when the sun rose. Gradually with the return of his habit of watchfulness came his former instinctive tendency to look back over his shoulder. He continually drove this away and it continually returned. The only sure banishment of it came through action, with its attendant exercise of his faculties. Therefore he rested less and walked more, taxing his strength to its utmost that morning, until the hot noon hour forced him to halt. Then while Jinny nibbled at the bitter desert plants Adam dozed in the thin shade of a mesquite. Close by grew a large *ocatilla* cactus covered with red flowers among which bees hummed. Adam never completely lost sense of this melodious hum, and it seemed to be trying to revive memories that he shunned.

The sun was still high and hot when Adam resumed travel, but it was westering and the slanting rays were bearable. After he got thoroughly warmed up and sweating freely he did not mind the heat, and was able to drive Jinny and keep up a strong stride for an hour at a time. His course now led along the base of the mountain wall, and that long low ridge which marked his destination began to seem less unattainable. The afternoon waned, the sun sank, the heat declined, and Jinny began to show signs of weariness. It bothered Adam to keep her headed straight. He searched the line where desert slope met the mountain wall for another green thicket of brush marking a water hole, but he could not see one. Darkness overtook him and he was compelled to make dry camp. This occasioned him some uneasiness, not that he did not have plenty of water for himself, but because he worried about the burro and the possibility of not finding water the next day. Nevertheless, he slept soundly.

On the following morning, when he had been tramping along for an hour or more, he espied far ahead the unmistakable green patch of thicket that heralded the presence of water. The sight stirred him. He walked well that morning, resting only a couple of hours at noon; but the green patch, after the manner of distant objects on the desert, seemed just as far away as when he saw it first. The time came, however, when there was no more illusion and he knew he was getting close to the place. At last he reached it, a large green thicket that choked the mouth of a narrow canyon. He found a spring welling from under the mountain base and sending a slender stream out to be swallowed by the sand.

Adam gave Jinny a drink before he unpacked her. There was a desirable camp site, except that it lacked dead firewood close at hand. Adam removed the pack, being careful to put boxes and bags together and to cover them with the canvas. Then he started out to look for some dead ironwood or mesquite to burn. All the desert growths, mostly greasewood and mesquite, were young and green. Adam searched in one direction and then in another, without so much as finding a stick. Next he walked west along the rocky wall, and had no better success until he came to a deep recession in the wall, full of brush; and here with considerable labor he collected a bundle of dry sticks. With this he trudged back toward camp.

Before long he imagined he saw smoke. "Queer how those smoke trees fool a fellow," be said. And even after he thought he smelled smoke, he was sure of deception. But upon nearing the green thicket that hid his camp he actually did see thin blue smoke low down against the background of rocky wall. The sight alarmed him. The only explanation which offered itself to his perplexity was the possibility that a prospector had arrived at the spring during his absence and had started a fire. Adam began to hurry. His alarm increased to dread.

When he ran around the corner of thicket to his camp site he did see a fire. It was about burned out. There was no prospector, no signs of packs or burros. And Jinny was gone!

"What — what?" stammered Adam, dropping his bundle of sticks. He was bewildered. A sense of calamity beset him. He ran forward.

"Where — where's my pack?" he cried.

The dying fire was but the smoldering remains of his pack. It had been burned. Blankets, boxes, bags had been consumed. Some blackened utensils lay on the ground near the charred remains of his canvas. Only then did the truth of this catastrophe burst upon him. All his food had been burned.

10

Some moments elapsed before the stunning effects of this loss had worn off enough to permit Adam's mind to connect the cause of it with the disappearance of Jinny.

After careful scrutiny of tracks near where the pack had lain, Adam became convinced that Jinny was to blame for his destitution. His proofs cumulated in a handful of unburnt matches that manifestly had been flung and scattered away from the pack. The tricky burro, taking advantage of Adam's absence, had pulled the canvas off the pack, and in tearing around in the boxes for morsels to eat she had bitten into the box of matches and set them on fire.

"I didn't think — I didn't think!" cried Adam, remembering the advice of Dismukes.

Overcome by the shock, he sank upon the ground and fell prey to gloomy and hopeless forebodings.

"I'll lie down and die," he muttered. But he could not so much as lie down. He seemed possessed by a devil who would not admit the idea of surrender or death. And this spirit likewise seemed to take him by the hair of his head and lift him up to scatter the tears from his eyes. "Why can't I cuss the luck like a man — then look round to see what's got to be done?"

Jinny had made good her escape. When Adam gave up all hope of finding the burro the hour was near sunset and it was high time that he should decide what to do.

"Go on — to the Indian camp," he declared, tersely.

He decided to start at once and walk in the cool of night, keeping close to the mountain wall so as not to lose his way. His spirits rallied. Going back to the camp scene, he carefully gathered up all the unburnt matches and placed them with others he carried in his pocket. He found his bag of salt only partly consumed, and he made haste to secure it. His canteen lay beside the spring.

The ruddy sunset and the stealing down of twilight and the encroaching blackness of night had no charms for Adam now. His weariness increased as the hours prolonged themselves. Short, frequent rests were more advisable than long ones. The canopy of stars seemed in procession westward; and many a bright one he watched sink behind the black slope of mountain toward which he was bound. There were times when his eyes closed involuntarily and all his body succumbed to sleep as he toiled on. These drowsy spells always came to a painful end, for he would walk into a thorny mesquite. Adam saw a weird, misshapen moon rise late over a dark range to blanch the desert with wan light. He walked all night, and when dawn showed him landmarks now grown familiar he had a moment of exhilaration. The long, low-reaching ridge of mountain loomed right before him. When he rounded the sharp, blunt corner his eyes were greeted by sight of a deep-mouthed canyon yawning out of the range, and full of palms and other green trees. He saw a white stream bed and the shine of water, and what he took to be the roofs of palm-thatched huts.

"I've got there. This is the Indian canyon — where Dismukes told me to stay," said Adam, with pride in his achievement. A first sight of what he took to be habitations cheered him. Again that gloomy companion of his mind was put to rout. It looked worth striving and suffering for — this haven. The barrenness of the desert all around made this green canyon mouth an oasis. It appeared well hidden, too. Few travelers passing along the valley would have suspected its presence. The long, low ridge had to be rounded before the canyon could be detected.

With steps that no longer dragged Adam began his descent of the canyon slope. It was a long, gradual incline, rough toward the bottom, and the bottom was a good deal farther down than it had seemed. At length he reached the wide bed of white boulders, strewn about in profusion, where some flood had rolled them. In the center of this bed trickled a tiny stream of water, slightly alkaline, Adam decided, judging from the white stain on the margin of sand. Following the stream bed, he made his way up into the zone of green growths, a most welcome change from the open glare of the desert. He plodded on perhaps a mile, without reaching the yellow thatch of palms.

"Will I — never — get there?" panted Adam, almost spent.

Finally Adam reached a well-defined trail leading up out of the stream bed. He followed it to a level flat covered with willows and cottonwoods, all full foliaged and luxuriantly green, and among which stately palms, swaddled in huge straw sheaths of their own making, towered with lofty tufted crowns. The dust in the trail showed no imprints of feet. Adam regarded that as strange. Still, he might be far from the camp or village that had looked so close from the slope above. Suddenly he emerged from the green covert into an open glade that contained palm-thatched huts, and he uttered a little cry of joy. But it took only a second glance to convince him that the huts were deserted, and his joy was short lived. Hastily he roamed from one hut to another. He found ollas, great, clay water jars, and pieces of broken pottery, and beds of palm leaves through which the lizards rustled, but no Indians, nor any signs of recent habitation.

"Gone! Gone!" he whispered, hoarsely. "Now

— I'll starve — to death!"

His accents of despair contained a note of hardness, of indifference born of his extreme fatigue. His eyes refused to stay open, and sleep glued them shut. When he opened them again it was to the light of another day. Stiff and lame, with a gnawing at the pit of his stomach and an oppressed mind, Adam found himself in sad plight. Limping down to the stream, he bathed his face and quenched his thirst, and then, removing his boots, he saw that his feet were badly blistered. He decided to go barefoot, to save his boots as well as to give the raw places a chance to heal.

Then without any more reflection he wrought himself into a supreme effort of will, and it was so passionate and strong that he believed it would hold as long as intelligence governed his actions.

"My one chance is to live here until the Indians come back," he decided. "There's water here and green growths. It's an oasis where animals, birds, living creatures come to drink. . . . I must eat."

His first move was to make slow and careful examination of the trails. One which led toward the mountain bore faint traces of footprints that a recent rain had mostly obliterated. He lost this trail on the smooth rock slope. The others petered out in the stones and sage. Then he searched along the sand bars of the stream for tracks of living creatures; and he found many,

148

from cat tracks to the delicate ones of tiny birds. After all, then, the desert was an abode for living things. The fact stimulated Adam, and he returned to the glade to exercise every faculty he possessed in the invention of instruments or traps or snares.

He had a knife and a pair of long leather boot strings. With these, and a bundle of arrowweed sticks, and a tough elastic bow of ironwood, and strips of bark, and sharp bits of flinty rock Adam set to work under the strong, inventive guiding spirit of necessity. As a boy he had been an adept at constructing figure-four traps. How marvelous the accuracy of memory! He had been the one to build traps for his brother Guerd, who had not patience or skill, but who loved to set traps in the brier patches for redbirds. Adam's nimble fingers slacked a little as his mind surveyed that best part of his life. To what extremity a man could be reduced! The dexterity of his idle youth to serve him thus in his terrible hour of need! He remembered then his skill at making slings; and following this came the inspired thought of the possibility of constructing one. He had a strong rubber band doubled round his pocketbook. Sight of it thrilled him. He immediately left off experimenting with the bow and went to making a sling. His difficulty was to find cords to make connections between the rubbers and a forked prong, and also between the rubbers and a carrier of some sort. For the latter he cut a triangular piece out of the top of his boot. Always in the old days he had utilized leather from cast-off shoes, and had even made a collection of old footgear for this purpose. But where to get the cords? Bark would not be pliable and strong enough. Somewhere from the clothes he wore he must extract cords. The problem proved easy. His suspenders were almost new and they were made of linen threads woven together. When he began to ravel them he made the discovery that there was enough rubber in them to serve for a second sling.

When the instrument was finished he surveyed it with satisfaction. He had no doubt that the deadly accuracy he had once been master of with this boyish engine of destruction would readily return to him. Then he went back to work on the other contrivances he had planned.

A failing of the daylight amazed him. For an instant he imagined a cloud had crossed the sun. But the sun had set and darkness was at hand.

"If days fly like this one, life will soon be over," he soliloquized, with a sigh.

In one of the thatched huts he made a comfortable bed of palm leaves. They seemed to retain the heat of the day. When Adam lay down to go to sleep he experienced a vague, inexplicable sense that the very strangeness of the present circumstance was familiar to him. But he could not hold the sensation, so did not understand it. He was very tired and very sleepy, and there was an uncomfortable empty feeling within him. He looked out and listened, slowly aware of a great, soft, silent black enveloping of his environment by the desert night. There seemed to be an aloofness in the immensity of this approach and insulation — a nature that, once comprehended, would be appalling. This thought just flashed by. His mind seemed concerned with something between worry and fear which persisted till he fell asleep.

In the dim, gray dawn he awoke and realized that it was hunger which had awakened him. And he stole out on his imperative quest. He did not see the sunrise nor the broadening day. His instinct was to hunt. Doves and blackbirds visited the stream, and a covey of desert quail seemed tame; but, owing to overeagerness and clumsiness, he did not succeed in killing a single one. He followed them from place to place, all over the oasis, until he lost sight of them. He baited his two traps with cactus fruit and set them, and he prowled into every nook and cranny of the canyon oasis. Lizards, rattlesnakes, rats, ground squirrels rustled from his stealthy steps. It amazed him how wary they were. He might have caught the rattlesnakes, but the idea of eating them was repugnant and impossible to him. The day passed more swiftly than had yesterday. Its close found him so tired he could scarcely stand, and with gnawing hunger growing worse. The moment he lay down sleep claimed him.

Next day he had more and better opportunities to secure meat, but he failed through haste and poor judgment and inaccuracy. His lessons were severe and they taught him the stern need of perfection. That day he saw a hawk poise high over a spot, dart down swiftly, to rise with a squealing rat in its claws. Again he saw a shrike, marked dull gray and black, sail down from a tree, fly very low along an open space of ground to avoid detection, and pounce upon a lizard. Likewise he saw a horned toad shoot out an extraordinarily long and almost invisible tongue, to snatch a bee from a flower. In these actions Adam divined his first proof of the perfection of desert hunters. They did not fail. But he was not thus equipped.

All during the hot period of the day, when birds and animals rested, Adam practiced with his crude weapons. His grave, serious eagerness began to give way to instinctive force, a something of fierceness that began to come out in him. It seemed every moment had its consciousness of self, of plight, of presaged agony, but only in flashes of thought, only fleeting ideas instantly repudiated by the physical. He had given a tremendous direction to his mind and it spent its force that way.

The following morning, just at sunrise, he located the covey of desert quail. They had sailed down from the sage slopes to alight among the willows bordering the stream. Adam crawled on the sand, noiseless as a snake, his sling held in readiness. He was breathless and hot. His blood gushed and beat in his veins. The very pursuit of meat made the saliva drip from his mouth and made his stomach roll with pangs of emptiness. Then the strain, the passion of the moment, were beyond his will to control, even if there had not been a strange, savage joy in them. He glided through the willows, never rustling a branch. The plaintive notes of the quail guided him. Then through an opening he saw them — gray, sleek, plump birds, some of them with tiny plumes. They were picking in the damp sand near the water. Adam, lying flat, stretched his sling and waited for a number of the quail to bunch. Then he shot. The heavy pebble sped true, making the gray feathers fly. One quail lay dead. Another fluttered wildly. The others ran off through the willows. Adam rushed upon the crippled quail, plunging down swift and hard; and catching it, he wrung its neck. Then he picked up the other.

"I got 'em! I got 'em!" he cried, elated, as he felt the warm plump bodies. It was a moment of strange sensation. Breathless, hot, wet with sweat, shaking all over, he seemed to have reverted to the triumph of the boy hunter. But there was more, and it had to do with the physical reactions inside his body. It had to do with hunger.

Picking the feathers off these birds required too much time. Adam skinned them and cleaned them, and then washed them in the stream. That done, he hurried back to his camp to make a fire and cook them. A quick method would be to broil them. He had learned how to do this with strips of meat. His hunger prevented him from waiting until the fire was right, and it also made him hurry the broiling. The salt that he had rescued from his pack now found its use, and it was not long before he had picked clean the bones of these two quail.

Adam found that this pound or so of meat augmented his hunger. It changed the gnawing sensations, in fact modified them, but it induced a greedy, hot hunger for more. An hour after he had eaten, as far as appetite was concerned, he seemed worse off. Then he set out again in quest of meat.

The hours flew, the day ended, night intervened, and another dawn broke. Success again crowned his hunt. He feasted on doves. Thereafter, day by day, he decimated the covey of tame quail and the flock of tame doves until the few that were left grew wary and finally departed. Then he hunted other birds. Quickly they learned the peril of the white man; and the day came when few birds visited the oasis.

Next to invite Adam's cunning, were the ground squirrels, the trade rats, and the kangaroo rats. He lived off them for days. But they grew so wary that he had to dig them out of the ground, and they finally disappeared. At this juncture a pair of burros wandered into the oasis. They were exceedingly wild. Adam failed to trap one of them. He watched for hours from a steep place where he might have killed one by throwing down a large rock. But it was in vain. At first, in desperation, holding his naked knife in hand, he chased them over stones and through the willows and under the thorny mesquites, all to no avail. He dropped from exhaustion and weakness, and lay where he had fallen till the next morning.

The pangs of hunger now were maddening. He had suffered them, more or less, and then alleviated them with meat, and then felt them grow keener and stronger until the edge wore off. After a few more meatless days the pains gradually subsided. It was a relief. He began to force himself to go out and hunt. Then an exceedingly good stroke of fortune befell him in that he killed a rabbit. His strength revived, but also his pains.

Then he lost track of days, but many passed, and each one of them took something from him in effort, in wakefulness, in spirit. His aggressiveness diminished daily and lasted only a short while. The time came when he fell to eating rattlesnakes and any living creatures in the oasis that he could kill with a club.

But at length pain left him, and hunger, and then his peril revealed itself. He realized it. The desire to kill diminished. With the cessation of activity there returned a mental state in which he could think back and remember all that he had done there, and also look forward to the inevitable prospect. Every morning he dragged his weary body, now merely skin and bones, out to the stream to drink, and then around and around in a futile hunt. He chewed leaves and bark; he ate mesquite beans and cactus fruit. After a certain number of hours the longer he went without meat the less he cared for it, or for living. But when, now and then, he did kill something to eat, then his instinct to survive flashed up with revived hunger. The process of detachment from passion to live was one of agony, infinitely worse than starvation. He had come to learn that starvation would be the easiest and most painless of deaths. It would have been infinitely welcome but for the thought that always followed resignation — that he had sworn to fight. That kept him alive.

His skin turned brown and shriveled up like dried parchment wrinkling around bones. He did not recognize his hands, and when he lay flat on the stones to drink from the stream, he saw reflected there a mummified mask with awful eyes.

Longer and longer grew the hours wherein he slept by night and lay idle by day, watching, listening, feeling. Something came back to him or was born in him during these hours. But the truth of his state eluded him. It had to do with peace, with dream, with effacement. He seemed no longer real. The hot sun, the pleasant wind, the murmur of bees, the tinkle of water, the everlasting processional march of the heat veils across the oasis — with all these things his mind seemed happily concerned. At dawn when he awoke his old instinct predominated and he searched for meat. But unless he had some success this questing mood did not last. It departed as weakness and lassitude over-balanced the night's rest. For the other hours of that day he lay in the sun, or the shade — it did not matter — and felt or dreamed as he starved.

As he watched thus one drowsy noon hour, seeing the honeybees darting to and fro, leaving the flowers to fly in straight line across the oasis, there occurred to him the significance of their toil. He watched these flying bees come and go; and suddenly it flashed over him that at the end of the bee line there must be a hive. Bees made nests in trees. If he could find the nest of the bees that were working here he would find honey. The idea stimulated him.

Adam had never heard how bee hunters lined bees to their hives, but in his dire necessity he instinctively adopted the correct method. He watched the bees fly away, keeping them in sight as long as possible, then he walked to the point he had marked as the last place he had seen them, and here he watched for others. In half an hour the straight bee flights led to a large dead cottonwood, hollow at top and bottom, a tree he had passed hundreds of times. The bees had a hive in the upper chamber of the trunk. Adam set fire to the tree and smoked the bees out. Then the problem consisted of felling the tree, for he had not the strength to climb it. The trunk was rotten inside and out. It burned easily, and he helped along the work by tearing out pieces of the soft wood. Nearly all the day was consumed in this toil, but at length the tree fell, splitting and breaking to pieces. The hollow chamber contained many pounds of honey.

Adam's struggle then was to listen to an intelligence that warned him that if he made a glutton of himself it would cause him great distress and perhaps kill him. How desperately hard it was to eat sparingly of the delicious honey! He tried, but did not succeed. That restraint was beyond human nature. Nevertheless, he stopped far short of what he wanted. He stored the honey away in ollas left there by the Indians.

All night and next day he paid in severe illness for the honey of which he had partaken. The renewed exercise of internal organs that had ceased to function produced convulsions and retching that made him roll on the ground as a man poisoned. Life was tenacious in him and he recovered; and thereafter, while the honey lasted, he slowly gained strength enough to hunt once more for meat. But the fertile oasis was now as barren of living creatures as was the naked desert outside. Adam's hope revived with his barely recovered strength. He pitied himself in his moments of deluded cheerfulness, of spirit that refused to die. Long ago his physical being had resigned itself, but his soul seemed beyond defeat. How strange the variations of his moods! His intelligence told him that sight of an animal would instantly revert him to the level of a beast of prey or a stalking, bloodthirsty savage.

During these days his eyes scanned the bronze slope of mountain where the tracks of the Indians had faded. They might return in time to save his life. He hoped in spite of himself. In the early time of his imprisonment there he had prayed for succor, but he had long since ceased that. The desert had locked him in. Every moment, every hour that had passed, the ceaseless hunts and then the dreaming spells, held their clear-cut niches in his memory. Looked back at, they seemed far away in the past, even those as close as yesterday; and every sensation was invested by a pang. At night he slept the slumber of weakness, and so the mockery of the dark hours did not make their terrible mark upon his mind. But the solemn days! They sped swiftly by, yet, remembered, they seemed eternities. Desert-bound days — immeasurably silent — periods of the dominance of the blasting sun; days of infinite space, beyond time, beyond life, as they might have been upon the burned-out moon! The stones that blistered unprotected flesh, the sand and the dust, the rock-ribbed ranges of bronze and rust — these tangible evidences of the earth seemed part of those endless days. There were sky and wind, the domain of the open and its master; but these existed for the eagles, and perhaps for the spirits that wailed down the naked shingles of the desert. A man was nothing. Nature filled this universe and had its inscrutable and ruthless laws.

How little the human body required to subsist on! Adam lived long on that honey; and he gained so much from it that after it was gone the hunger pangs revived a hundred times more fiercely than ever. They had been deadened, which fact left him peace; revived by a windfall of food, they brought him agony. It drove him out to hunt for meat. He became a stalking specter whose keen eye an insect could not have escaped. Hunger now beset him with all its terrors magnified. To starve was nothing, but to eat while starving was hell! The pangs were as if made by a serpent with teeth of fire tearing at his vitals. Tighter and tighter he buckled his belt until he could squeeze his waist in his long, skinny hands so that his fingers met. Whenever his pains began to subside, like worms growing quiet, then a rat or a stray bird or a lizard or a scaly little side-winder rattlesnake would fall to his cunning, as if in mockery of the death that ever eluded him; and next day the old starving pains would convulse his bowels again.

So that he was driven, a gaunt and ever gaunter shadow of a man, up and down the beaten trails of the oasis. Soon he would fall and die, be sun-dried and blow away like powdered leather on the desert wind. By his agonies he measured the inhospitableness and inevitableness of the wasteland. Every thought had some connection with his torture or some relation to his physical being in its fight for existence. In this desert oasis were living things, creatures grown too wary for him now, and willows, cacti, sages, that had conquered over the barrenness of the desert. On his brain had been etched by words of steel the fact that no power to fight was so great and unquenchable as that of man's. He lived on, he staggered on through the solemn, glaring days.

One morning huge columnar clouds, white as fleece, with dark-gray shades along their lower borders, blotted out the sun. How strangely they shaded the high lights! Usually when clouds formed on the desert they lodged round the peaks and hung there. But these were looming across the wasteland, promising rain. A fresh breeze blew the leaves.

Adam was making his weary round of the oasis, dragging one foot like a dead weight after the other. Once he thought he heard an unusual sound, and with lips wide and with bated breath he listened. Only the mocking, solemn silence! Often he was haunted by the memory of sounds. Seldom indeed did he hear his own voice any more. Then he plodded on again with the eyes of a ferret, roving everywhere.

He had proceeded a few rods when a distant but shrill whistle brought him to a startled and thrilling halt. It sounded like the neigh of a horse. Often he had heard the brays of wild burros. In the intense silence, as he strained his ears, he heard only the labored, muffled throbs of his heart. Gradually his hopes, so new and strange, subsided. Only another mockery of his memory! Or perhaps it was a whistle of the wind in a crevice, or of an eagle in flight.

Parting the willows before him as he walked, he went through the thicket out into the open where the stream flowed. It was very low, just a tiny rill of crystal-clear water. He was about to step forward toward the flat rock where he always knelt to drink, when another sound checked him. A loud, high buzz, somehow startling! It had life.

Suddenly he espied a huge rattlesnake coiled in the sand, with head erect and its rattles quivering like the wings of a poised humming bird. The snake had just shed an ugly, brown, scaly skin, and now shone forth resplendent, a beautiful clean gray with markings of black. It did not show any fear. The flat triangular head, sleek and cunning, with its deadly jewel-like eyes, was raised half a foot above the plump coils.

Adam's weary, hopeless hunting instinct sustained a vivifying, galvanizing shock. Like a flash he changed, beginning to tremble. He dropped his sling as an ineffective weapon against so large a snake. His staring eyes quivered like the vibrating point of a compass needle as he tried to keep them on the snake and at the same time sight a stone or club with which to attack his quarry. A bursting gush of blood, hot in its tearing pangs, flooded out all over his skin, starting the sweat. His heart lifted high in his breast, almost choking him. A terrible excitement animated him and it was paralleled by a cold and sickening dread that the snake would escape and pounds of meat be lost to him.

Never taking eyes off the snake, Adam stooped down to raise a large rock in his hand. He poised it aloft and, aiming with intense keenness, he flung the missile. It struck the rattlesnake a glancing blow, tearing its flesh and bringing blood. With the buzz of a huge bee caught in a trap the snake lunged at Adam, stretching its mutilated length on the sand.

It was long, thick, fat. Adam smelled the exuding blood and it inflamed him. Almost he became a beast. The savage urge in him then was to fall upon his prey and clutch it with his bare hands and choke and tear and kill. But reason still restrained such limit as that. Stone after stone he flung, missing every time. Then the rattlesnake began to drag itself over the sand. Its injury did not retard a swift progress. Adam tried to bound after it, but he was so weak that swift action seemed beyond him. Still, he headed off the snake and turned it back. Stones were of no avail. He could not hit with them, and every time he bent over to pick one up he got so dizzy that he could scarcely rise.

"Club, Club! Got — have club!" he panted,

hoarsely. And espying one along the edge of the stream, he plunged to secure it. This moment gave the rattlesnake time to get ahead. Wildly Adam rushed back, brandishing the club. His tall gaunt form, bent forward, grew over-balanced as he moved, and he made a long fall, halfway across the stream. He got up and reached the snake in time to prevent it from escaping under some brush.

Then he swung the club. It was not easy to hit the snake crawling between stones. And the club was of rotten wood. It broke. With the blunt end Adam managed to give his victim a blow that retarded its progress.

Adam let out a hoarse yell. Something burst in him — a consummation of the instinct to kill and the instinct to survive. There was no difference between them. Hot and mad and weak, he staggered after the crippled snake. The chase had transformed the whole internal order of him. He was starving to death, and he smelled the blood of fresh meat. The action infuriated him and the odor maddened him. Not far indeed was he then from the actual seizing of that deadly serpent in his bare hands.

But he tripped and fell again in a long forward plunge. It brought him to the sand almost on top of the snake. And here the rattlesnake stopped to coil, scarcely two feet from Adam's face.

Adam tried to rise on his hands. But his strength had left him. And simultaneously there left him the blood madness of that chase to kill and eat. He realized his peril. The rattlesnake would strike him. Adam had one flashing thought of the justice of it — one sight of the strange, cold, deadly jewel eyes, one swift sense of the beauty and magnificent spirit of this reptile of the desert, and then horror possessed him. He froze to his marrow. The icy mace of terror had stunned him. And with it had passed the flashing of his intelligence. He was only a fearful animal, fascinated by another, dreading death by instinct. And as he collapsed, sagging forward, the rattlesnake struck him in the face with the stinging blow of a red-hot iron. Then Adam fainted.

11

When Adam recovered consciousness he imagined he was in a dream.

But a dragging, throbbing pain in his face seemed actuality enough to discredit any illusions of slumber. It was shady where he lay or else his eyes were dimmed. Presently he made out that he reclined under one of the palm-thatched roofs.

"I've been moved!" he cried, with a start.

And that start, so full of pain and queer dragging sensations as if a weighted body, brought back memory to him. His mind whirled and darkened. The sickening horror of close proximity to the rattlesnake, its smell and color and deadly intent, all possessed Adam again. Then it cleared away. What had happened to him? His hand seemed to have no feeling; just barely could he move it to his face, where the touch of wet cloth bandages told a story of his rescue by some one. Probably the Indians had returned. It had been the whistle of a horse that had thrilled him.

"I've — been — saved!" whispered Adam, and he grew dizzy. His eyes closed. Dim shapes seemed to float over the surface of his mind; and there were other strange answerings of his being to this singular deliverance.

Then he heard voices — some low, and others deep and guttural. Voices of Indians! How strong the spirit of life in him! "I — I wasn't ready — to die," he whispered. Gleams of sunlight low down, slanting on the palm leaves, turning them to gold, gave him the idea that the time was near sunset. In the corner of the hut stood ollas and bags which had not been there before, and on the ground lay an Indian blanket. A shadow crossed the sunlit gleams. An Indian girl entered. She had very dark skin and straight hair as black as night. Upon seeing Adam staring at her with wide-open eyes she uttered a cry and ran out. A hubbub of low voices sounded outside the shack. Then a tall figure entered; it was that of an Indian, dressed in the ragged clothes of a white man. He was old, his dark bronze face like a hard, wrinkled mask.

"How?" he asked, gruffly, as he bent over Adam. He had piercing black eyes.

"All right — good," replied Adam, trying to smile. He sensed kindliness in this old Indian.

"White boy want dig gold — get lost — no grub — heap sick belly?" queried the Indian, putting a hand on Adam's flat abdomen.

"Yes — you bet," replied Adam.

"Hahh! Me Charley Jim — heap big medicine man. Me fix um. Snake bite no hurt. . . . White boy sick bad — no heap grub — long time."

"All right — Charley Jim," replied Adam.

"Hahh!" Evidently this exclamation was Charley Jim's expression for good. He arose and backed away to the opening that appeared blocked by dark-skinned, black-haired Indians. Then he pointed at one of them. Adam saw that he indicated the girl who had first come to him. She appeared very shy. Adam gathered the impression that she had been the one who had saved him.

"Charley Jim, who found me — who saved me from that rattlesnake?"

The old Indian understood Adam well enough. He grinned and pointed at the young girl, and pronounced a name that sounded to Adam like, "Oella."

167

"When? How long ago? How many days?" asked Adam.

Charley Jim held up three fingers, and with that he waved the other Indians from the opening and went out himself.

Adam was left to the bewildered thoughts of a tired and hazy mind. He had no strength at all, and the brief interview, with its excitement, and exercise of voice, brought him near the verge of unconsciousness. He wavered amid dim shadows of ideas and thoughts. When that condition passed, he awoke to dull, leaden pain in his head. And his body felt like an empty sack the two sides of which were pasted together flat.

The sunlit gleams vanished and the shades of evening made gloom around him. He smelled fragrant wood smoke, and some other odor, long unfamiliar, that brought a watery flow to his mouth and a prickling as of many needles. Then in the semidarkness one of the Indians entered and knelt beside him. Adam distinguished the face of the girl, Oella. She covered him with a blanket. Very gently she lifted his head, and moved her body so that it would support him. The lifting hurt Adam; he seemed to reel and sway, and a blackness covered his sight. The girl held him and put something warm and wet between his lips. She was trying to feed him with a stick or a wooden spoon. The act of swallowing made his throat feel as if it was sore. What a slow process! Adam rather repelled than assisted his nurse, but his antagonism was purely

168

physical and involuntary. Whatever the food was, it had no taste to him. The heat of it, however, and the soft, wet sensation, grew pleasant. He realized when hunger awakened again in him, for it was like a shot through his vitals.

Then the girl laid him back, spread the blanket high, and left him. The strange sensation of fullness, of movement inside Adam's breast, occupied his mind until drowsiness overcame him.

Another day awakened Adam to the torture of reviving hunger and its gnawing pains, so severe that life seemed unwelcome. The hours were weary and endless. But next day was not so severe, and thereafter gradually he grew better and was on the road to a slow recovery.

The Indians that had befriended Adam were of a family belonging to the Coahuila tribe. Charley Jim appeared to be a chief of some degree, friendly toward the whites, and nomadic in spirit, as he wandered from oasis to oasis. He knew Dismukes, and told Adam that the prospector and he had found gold up this canyon. Charley Jim's family consisted of several squaws, some young men, two girls, of whom Oella was the younger, and a troop of children, wild as desert rats.

Adam learned from Charley Jim that the head of this canyon contained a thicket of mesquite trees, the beans of which the Indians prized as food. Also there were abundant willows and arrowweeds, with which wood the Indians constructed their huge, round, basket granaries. The women of the family pounded the mesquite beans into meal or flour, which was dampened and put away for use. Good grass and water in this remote canyon were further reasons why Charley Jim frequented it. But he did not appear to be a poor Indian, for he had good horses, a drove of burros, pack outfits that were a mixture of Indian and prospector styles, and numerous tools, utensils, and accouterments that had been purchased at some freighting post.

Adam was so long weak, and dependent upon Oella, that when he did grow strong enough to help himself the Indian girl's habit of waiting upon him and caring for him was hard to break. She seemed to take it for granted that she was to go on looking after him; and the fineness and sensitiveness of her, with the strong sense of her delight in serving him, made it impossible for Adam to offend her. She was shy and reserved, seldom spoke, and always maintained before him a simplicity, almost a humility, as of servant to master. With acquaintance, too, the still, dark, impassive face of her had become attractive to look at, especially her large, black, inscrutable eyes, soft as desert midnight. They watched Adam at times when she imagined he was unaware of her scrutiny, and the light of them then pleased Adam, and perturbed him also, reminding him of what an old aunt had told him once, "Adam, my boy, women will always love you!" The prophecy had not been fulfilled, Adam reflected with sadness, and in Oella's case he concluded his fancies were groundless.

Still, he had to talk to somebody or grow into the desert habit of silence, and so he began to teach Oella his language and to learn hers. The girl was quick to learn and could twist her tongue round his words better than he could round hers. Moreover, she learned quickly anything he cared to teach her; and naturally even in the desert there were customs into which Adam preferred to introduce something of the white man's way. Indians were slovenly and dirty, and Adam changed this in Oella's case. The dusky desert maiden had little instinctive vanities that contact with him developed.

One day, when the summer was waning and Adam was getting about on his feet, still a gaunt and stalking shadow of his former self, but gaining faster, the old Indian chief said:

"White man heap strong — ride — go away soon?"

"No, Charley Jim, I want stay here," replied Adam.

"Hahh!" replied the Indian, nodding.

"Me live here — work with Indian. White man no home — no people. He like Indian. He work — hunt meat for Indian."

"Heap sheep," replied Charley Jim, with a

slow, expressive wave of his hand toward the mountain peaks.

"Charley Jim take white man's money, send to freight post for gun, shells, clothes, flour, bacon — many things white man need?"

"Hahh!" The chief held up four fingers and pointed west, indicating what Adam gathered was four days' ride to a freighting post.

"Charley Jim no tell white men about me."

The Indian took the money with grave comprehension, and also shook the hand Adam offered.

The Indian boys who rode away to the freighting post on the river were two weeks in returning. To celebrate the return of the boys Adam suggested a feast and that he would bake the bread and cook the bacon. Oella took as by right the seat of honor next to Adam, and her habitual shyness did not inhibit a rather hearty appetite. On this occasion Adam finally got the wild little half-naked dusky children to come to him. They could not resist sweets.

A shining new rifle, a Winchester .44, was the cynosure of all eyes in that Indian encampment. When Adam took it out to practice, the whole family crowded around to watch, with the intense interest of primitive people who marveled at the white man's weapon. Only the little children ran from the sharp reports of the rifle, and they soon lost their fear. Whenever Adam made a good shot it was Oella who showed pride where the others indicated only their wonder.

Thus the days of simplicity slipped by, every one of which now added to Adam's fast-returning strength. Flour and bacon quickly built up his reduced weight; and as for rice and dried fruits, they were so delicious to Adam that he feared it would not be a great while before he must needs send for more. He remembered the advice of Dismukes anent the value of his money.

The hot summer became a season of the past. The withering winds ceased to blow. In the early autumn days Adam began his hunting. Charley Jim led the way, keeping behind a fringe of mesquite, out to a gray expanse of desert, billowy and beautiful in the ruddy sunlight. They crawled through sage to the height of a low ridge, and from here the chief espied game. He pointed down a long gray slope, but Adam could see only a monotonous beauty, spotted by large tufts of sage and here and there a cactus. Then the Indian took Adam's sombrero, and the two scarfs he had, one red and one blue, and tied them round the hat, which he elevated upon a stick. After that he bent his falcon gaze on the slope. Adam likewise gazed, with infinite curiosity, thrill, and expectation.

"Hahh!" grunted Charley Jim, presently, and his sinewy dark hand clutched Adam. Far down vague gray spots seemed to move. Adam strained his eyes. It seemed a long time till they approached close enough to distinguish their species.

"Antelope, by jiminy!" ejaculated Adam, in excitement.

"Heap jiminy— you bet!" responded Charley Jim.

Adam was experiencing that thrill to its utmost, and also other sensations of wonder and amaze. Was it possible these wild-looking desert creatures were actually so curious about the brightly decked sombrero that they could not resist approaching it to see what it was? There they came, sleek, tawny-gray, alert, deerlike animals, with fine pointed heads, long ears, and white rumps. The bold leader never stopped at all. But some of his followers hesitated, trotted to and fro, then came on. How graceful they were! How suggestive of speed and wildness! Adam's finger itched to shoot off the gun and scare them to safety. "Fine hunter, I am!" he muttered. "This is murder. . . . Why on earth does a man have to eat meat?" The Indian beside him was all keen and strung with his instincts and perhaps they were truer to the needs of human life.

Soon, however, all of Adam's sensations were blended in a thrilling warmth of excitement. The antelope were already within range, and had it not been for Charley Jim's warning hand Adam would not have been able to resist the temptation to fire. Perhaps he would have missed then, for he certainly shook in every muscle, as a man with the ague. Adam forced himself to get the better of this spell of nerves.

"Heap soon!" whispered Charley Jim, relaxing the pressure of his hand on Adam. The leader approached to within fifty feet, with several other antelope close behind, when the Indian whistled. Like statues they became. Then Adam fired. The leader fell, and also one of those behind him. The others flashed into gray speeding shapes, with rumps darting white; and Adam could only stare in admiring wonder at their incomparable swiftness.

"Hahh!" ejaculated the chief, in admiration. "White man heap hunter — one shoot — two bucks. Him eye like eagle!"

Thus did a lucky shot by Adam, killing two antelope when he had aimed at only one, initiate him into his hunting on the desert and win for him the Indian sobriquet of Eagle.

And so began Adam's desert education. He had keen appreciation of his good fortune in his teacher. The Coahuila chief had been born on that desert and he must have been nearly sixty years old. As a hunter he had the eye of a mountain sheep, the ear of a deer, the nose of a wolf. He had been raised upon meat. He loved the stalking of game. Thus Adam, through this old Indian's senses and long experience and savage skill, began to see the life of the desert. It unfolded before his eyes, manifold in its abundance, infinitely strange and marvelous in its ferocity and ability to survive. Adam learned to see as the Indian, and had his own keen mind to analyze and weigh and ponder. But his knowledge came slowly, painfully, hard earned, in spite of its thrilling time-effacing quality.

In those wonderful autumn days Adam learned that the antelope could go long without water, that nature had endowed it with great speed to escape the wolves and cats of the desert, that from its prominent eyes it could see in any direction, that its coloring was the protective gray of the sage plains.

He learned that the lizard could change its color like the chameleon, adapting itself to the color of the rock upon which it basked in the sun, that it could dart across the sands almost too swiftly for the eye to follow.

He learned that the gray desert wolf was a king of wolves, living high in the mountains and coming down to the flats; and there, by reason of his wonderfully developed strength and speed, chasing and killing his prey in the open.

He learned that the coyote was an eater of carrion, of rabbits and rats, of bird's eggs, of mesquite beans, of anything that happened to come its way — a gray, skulking, cunning beast, cowardly as the wolf was brave, able, like the antelope and the jack rabbit, to live without water, and best adapted of all beasts to the desert.

He learned that the jack rabbit survived

through the abnormal development of his ears and legs — the first extraordinarily large organs built to catch sound, and the latter long, strong members that enable him to run with ease away from his foes. And he learned that the cottontail rabbit lived in thickets near holes into which he could pop, and that his fecundity in reproducing his kind saved his species from extinction.

Adam learned about the desert ants, the kangaroo rats, the trade rats, the horned toads, the lizards, the snakes, the spiders, the bees, the wasps — the way they lived and what they lived upon. How marvelously nature adapted them to their desert environment, each perfect, each in its place, each fierce and self-sufficient, each fulfilling its mysterious destiny of sacrificing its individual life to the survival of its species! How cruel nature was to the individual — how devoted to the species!

Adam learned that the same fierce life of all desert creatures was likewise manifested in the life of the plants. By thorns and poison sap and leafless branches, and by roots penetrating far and deep, and by organs developed to catch and store water, so the plants of the desert outwitted the beasts and endured the blasting sun and drought. How beyond human comprehension was the fact that a cactus developed a fluted structure less exposed to heat — that a tree developed a leaf that never presented its broad surface to the sun!

The days passed, with ruddy sunrises, white, glaring, solemn noons, and golden sunsets. The simplicity and violence of life on the desert passed into Adam's being. The greatness of stalking game came to him when the Indian chief took him to the heights after bighorn sheep; but it was not the hunting and killing of this wariest and finest of wild beasts, wonderful as it was, that constituted for Adam something great. It was the glory of the mountain heights. All his life he had dreamed of high places, those to which he could climb physically and those that he aspired to spirituallly. Lost indeed were hopes of the latter, but of the former he had all-satisfying fulfillment. Adam dated his changed soul from the day he first conquered the heights. There, on top of the Chocolate range, his keen sight, guided by the desert eyes of the old Indian, ranged afar over the gray valleys and red ranges to the Rio Colorado, down the dim wandering line of which he gazed, to see at last Picacho, a dark, purple mass above the horizon. From the moment Adam espied this mountain he suffered a return of memory and a sleepless and eternal remorse. The terrible past came back to him; never again, he divined, to fade while life lasted. His repentance, his promise to Dismukes, his vow to himself, began there on the heights with the winds sweet and strong in his face and the dark blue of the sky over his head, and beneath the vast desert, illimitable on all sides, lonely and grand, the abode of silence.

The days passed into months. Far to the north the dominating peaks of San Jacinto and San Gorgonio took on the pure white caps of snow, that slowly spread, as the days passed, down the rugged slopes. Winter abided up there. But on the tops of the Chocolate and Chuckwalla ranges no snow fell, although the winter wind sometimes blew cold and bleak. Adam loved the wind of the heights. How cold and pure, untainted by dust or life or use! He grew to have the stride of a mountaineer. And the days passed until that one came on which the old Indian chief let Adam hunt alone. "Go, Eagle!" he said, with sorrow for his years and pride in the youth of his white friend. "Go!" And the slow gestures of his long arms were as the sailing movement of the wings of an eagle.

The days passed, and few were they that did not see Adam go out in the sweet, cool dawn, when the east glowed like an opal, to climb the bronze slope, sure footed as a goat, up and up over the bare ridges and through the high ravines where the lichens grew and a strange, pale flower blossomed, on and on over the jumble of weathered rock to the heights. And there he would face the east with its glorious burst of golden fire, and spend the last of that poignant gaze on the sunrise-crowned glory of old Picacho. The look had the meaning of a prayer to Adam, yet it was like a blade in his heart.

In that look he remembered his home, his mother, his brother, and the vivid days of play and love and hope, his fateful journey west, his fall and his crime and his ruin. Alone on the heights, he forced that memory to be ever more vivid and torturing. Hours he consecrated to remorse, to regret, to suffering, to punishment. He lashed his soul with bitter thoughts, lest he forget and find peace. Life and health and strength had returned to him in splendid growing measure which he must use to pay his debt.

But there were other hours. He was young. Red blood throbbed in his veins, and action sent that blood in a flame over his eager body. To stride along the rocky heights was something splendid. How free — alone! It connected Adam's present hour with a remote past he could not comprehend. He loved it. He was proud that the Indians called him Eagle. For to watch the eagles in their magnificent flights became a passion with him. The great blue condors and the grisly vultures and the bow-winged eagles — all were one and the same to him, indistinguishable from one another as they sailed against the sky, sailing, sailing so wondrously, with never a movement of wings, or shooting across the heavens like thunderbolts, or circling around and upward to vanish in the deep blue. There were moments when he longed to change his life to that of an eagle, to find a mate and a nest on a lofty crag, and there, ringed by the azure world above and with the lonely barren below, live with the elements.

Here on the heights Adam was again visited by that strange sensation, inexplicable and illusive and fast fleeting, which had been born in him one lonely hour in the desert below. Dismukes had told him how men were lured by the desert and how they all had their convictions as to its cause, and how they missed the infinite truth.

"It will come to me!" cried Adam as he faced the cool winds.

Stalking mountain sheep upon the mighty slopes was work to make a man. It was a wild and perilous region of jagged ridges and bare slants and loose slopes of weathered rocks. The eyes of the sheep that lived at this height were like telescopes; they had the keenest sight of all wild beasts. The marvelous organ of vision stood out on the head as if it were the half of a pear, so that there was hardly an angle of the compass toward which a sheep could not see. Like the antelope, mountain sheep were curious and could be lured by a bright color and thereby killed. But Adam learned to abhor this method. He pitted his sight and his strength and endurance against those of the sheep. In this way he magnified the game of hunting. His exhaustion and pain and peril he welcomed as lessons to the end that his knowledge and achievement must be in a measure what Dismukes might have respected. Failure to Adam was nothing but a spur to renewed endeavor. The long climb, the crumbling ledge, the slipping rock, the deceitful distance, the crawl over sharp rocks, the hours of waiting — these too he welcomed as one who had set himself limitless tasks. Then when he killed a ram and threw it over his shoulder to carry it down the mountain, he found labor which was harder even than the toil of the gold mill at Picacho. To stride erect with a rifle in one hand, and a hold upon a heavy sheep with the other, down the slippery ledges, across the sliding banks, over the cracked and rotten lava, from the sunset-lighted heights to the gloomy slopes below — this was how in his own estimation he must earn and keep the respect of the Indians. They had come to look up to the white man they called Eagle. He taught them things to do with their hands, work of white men which bettered their existence, and he impressed them the more by his mastery of some of their achievements.

The days passed into months. Summer came again and the vast oval bowl of desert glowed in the rosy sunrise, glared in the white noon hours, and burned at sunset. The moving heat veils smoked in rippling clouds over the Salton Sink; the pale wavering line of the Superstition Mountains changed mysteriously with each day; the fog clouds from the Pacific rolled over to lodge against the fringed peaks. Time did not mean anything to the desert, though it worked so patiently and ceaselessly in its infinite details. The desert might have worked for eternity. Its moments were but the months that were growing into years of Adam's life. Again he saw San Jacinto and San Gorgonio crowned with snow that gleamed so white against the blue.

Once Charley Jim showed Adam a hole in the gravel and sand of a gulley, where Dismukes had dug out a pocket of gold. Adam gathered that the Indian had brought Dismukes here. "White man gold mad," said the chief. "No happy, little gold. Want dig all — heap hog — dam' fool!"

So Charley Jim characterized Dismukes. Evidently there had been some just cause, which he did not explain, for his bringing Dismukes into this hidden canyon. And also there was some significance in his bringing Adam there. Many had been the rewards of Charley Jim and his family for saving and succoring Adam.

"Indian show Eagle heap gold," said Charley Jim, and led him to another gully opening down into the canyon. In the dry sand and gravel of this wash Adam found gold. The discovery gave him a wonderful thrill. But it did not drive him mad. Adam divined in the dark, impassive face of his guide something of the Indian's contempt for a white man's frenzy over gold.

Then the chief said in his own tongue that the Indian paid his debt to friend and foe, good for good and evil for evil — that there were white men to whom he could trust the secret treasures of the desert.

The day came when something appeared to stimulate the wandering spirit of the Coahuila chief. Taking his family and Adam, he began a nomadic quest for change of scene and work and idleness. The life suited Adam, for he knew Charley Jim did not frequent the trails of white men.

No time so swiftly fleeting as days and nights out in new and strange places of the desert! Adam kept track of time by the coming and going of the white crowns of snow on the peaks, and by the green and gold and then barren gray of the cottonwoods.

Like coming home was it to get back to the oasis in the canyon of the Chocolate range. Adam loved the scene of his torture. Every stone, every tree, was a familiar friend, and seemed to whisper welcome to him. Here also had passed the long, long months of mental anguish. On this flat rock he had sat a whole day in hopeless pain. In this sandy-floored aisle of palms he had walked hour by hour, through many weary days, possessed by the demon of remorse.

Best of all, out there reached the gray, endless expanse of desert, so lonely and melancholy and familiar, extending away to the infinitude of purple distance; and there loomed the lofty, bare heights of rock which, when he scaled them as an Indian climbing to meet his spirits, seemed to welcome him with sweet, cold winds in his face. How he thrilled at sight of the winding gleam of the Rio Colorado! What a shudder, as keen and new a pang as ever, wrenched him at sight of Picacho! It did not change. Had he expected that? It towered there in the dim lilac colors of the desert horizon, colossal and commanding, immutable and everlasting, like the sin he had committed in its shadow.

Somewhere in the shadow of that doomed and turreted peak lay the grave of his brother Guerd.

"I'll go back some day!" whispered Adam, and the spoken words seemed the birth of a long-germinating idea. Picacho haunted him. It called him. It was the place that had given the gray color and life to his destiny. And suddenly into his memory flashed an image of Margarita. Poor, frail, dusky-eyed girl! She had been but the instrument of his doom. He held her guiltless — long ago he had forgiven her. But memory of her hurt. Had she not spoken so lightly of what he meant to hold sacred? "Ah, señor — so long ago and far away!" Faithless, mindless, soulless! Adam would never forget. Never a sight of a green *palo verde* but a pang struck through his breast!

At sunset the old chief came to Adam, somber and grave, but with dignity and kindness tempering the seriousness of his aspect. He spoke the language of his people.

"White man, you are of the brood of the eagle. Your heart is the heart of an Indian. Take my

185

daughter Oella as your wife."

Long had Adam feared this blow, and now it had fallen. He had tried to pay his debt, but it could not be paid.

"No, chief, the white man cannot marry Oella. He has blood upon his hands — a price on his head. Some day — he might have to hang for his crime. He cannot be dishonest with the Indian girl who saved him."

Perhaps the chief had expected that reply, but his inscrutable face showed no feeling. He made one of his slow, impressive gestures — a wave of his hand, indicating great distance and time; and it meant that Adam was to go.

Adam dropped his head. That decree was irrevocable and he knew it was just. While he packed for a long journey twilight stole down upon the Indian encampment. Adam knew, when he faced Oella in the shadow of the palms, that she had been told. Was this the Indian maiden who had been so shy, so strange? No, this seemed a woman of full, heaving breast, whose strong, dark face grew strained, whose magnificent eyes level and piercing, searched his soul. How blind he had been! All about her seemed eloquent of woman's love. His heart beat with quick, heavy throbs.

"Oella, your father has ordered me away," said Adam. "I am an outcast. I am hunted. If I made you my wife it might be to your shame and sorrow."

"Stay. Oella is not afraid. We will hide in

the canyons," she said.

"No. I have sinned. I have blood on my hands. But, Oella, I am not dishonorable. I will not cheat you."

"Take me," she cried, and the soft, deep-toned, passionate voice shook Adam's heart. She would share his wanderings.

"Good-by, Oella," he said, huskily. And he strode forth to drive his burro out into the lonely, melancholy desert night.

12

The second meeting between Adam and the prospector Dismukes occurred at Tecopah, a mining camp in the Mohave Desert.

The mining camp lay in a picturesque valley where green and gray growths marked the course of the gravel-lined creek, and sandy benches spread out to dark, rocky slopes, like lava, that heaved away in the bleak ranges.

It was in March, the most colorful season in the Mohave, that Adam arrived at Tecopah to halt on a grassy bench at the outskirts of the camp. A little spring welled up here and trickled down to the creek. It was drinking water celebrated among desert men, who had been known to go out of their way to drink there. The telltale ears of Adam's burros advised him of the approach of some one, and he looked up from his camp tasks to find a familiar figure approaching him. He rubbed his eyes. Was that strange figure the same as the one so vividly limned on his memory? Squat, huge, grotesque, the man coming toward him was Dismukes! His motley, patched garb, his old slouch hat, his boots yellow with clay and alkali, appeared the same he had worn on the memorable day Adam's eyes had unclosed to see them.

Dismukes drove his burros up to the edge of the bench, evidently having in mind the camp site Adam occupied. When he espied Adam he hesitated and, gruffly calling to the burros, he turned away.

"Hello, Dismukes!" called Adam. "Come on. Plenty room to camp here."

The prospector halted stolidly and slowly turned back. "You know me?" he asked, gruffly, as he came up.

"Yes, I know you, Dismukes," replied Adam, offering his hand.

"You've got the best of me," said Dismukes, shaking hands. He did not seem a day older, but perhaps there might have been a little more gray in the scant beard. His great ox eyes, rolling and dark, bent a strange, curious glance over Adam's lofty figure.

"Look close. See if you can recognize a man you befriended once," returned Adam. The moment was fraught with keen pain and a melancholy assurance of the changes time had made. Strong emotion of gladness, too, was stirring deep in him. This was the man who had saved him and who had put into his mind the inspiration and passion to conquer the desert.

Dismukes was perplexed, and a little ashamed. His piercing gaze was that of one who had befriended many men and could not remember.

"Stranger, I give it up. I don't know you."

"Wansfell," said Adam, his voice full.

Dismukes stared. His expression changed, but it was not with recognition.

"Wansfell! Wansfell!" he ejaculated. "I know that name. . . . Hell, yes! I've heard of you all over the Mohave! . . . I'm sure glad to meet you. . . . But, I never met you before."

The poignancy of that meeting for Adam reached a climax in the absolute failure of Dismukes to recognize him. Last and certain proof of change! The desert years had transformed Adam Larey, the youth, into the man Wansfell. For the first moment in all that time did Adam feel an absolute sense of safety. He would never be recognized, never be apprehended for his crime. He seemed born again.

"Dismukes, how near are you to getting all your five hundred thousand?" queried Adam, with a smile. There seemed to be a sad pleasure in thus baffling the old prospector.

189

"By Gad! how'd you know about that?" exclaimed Dismukes.

"You told me."

"Say, Wansfell! Am I drunk or are you a mind reader?" demanded the prospector, bewildered. "Comin' along here I was thinkin' about that five hundred thousand. But I never told anyone — except a boy once — an' he's dead."

"How about your white-faced burro Jinny — the one that used to steal things out of your pack?" asked Adam, slowly.

"Jinny! Jinny!" ejaculated Dismukes, with a start. His great ox eyes dilated and something of shock ran through his huge frame. "That burro I never forgot. I gave her away to a boy who starved on the desert. She came back to me. Tracked me to Yuma. . . . An' you — you — how'd you know Jinny? . . . Man, who are you?"

"Dismukes, I was the boy you saved — down under the Chocolates — ninety miles from Yuma. Remember . . . it was Jinny saw me wandering in a circle, mad with thirst. You saved me — gave me Jinny and a pack — told me how to learn the desert — sent me to the Indians. . . . Dismukes, I was that boy. I am now — Wansfell."

The prospector seemed to expand with the increased strain of his gaze into Adam's eyes, until the instant of recognition.

"By God! I know you now!" he boomed, and locked his horny hands on Adam in a gladness that was beyond the moment and had to do, perhaps, with a far-past faith in things. "I thought you died on the desert. Jinny's comin' back seemed proof of that. . . . But you lived! You — that boy, tall as a mescal plant — with eyes of agony. . . . I never forgot. . . . An' now you're Wansfell!"

"Yes, my friend. Life is strange on the desert," replied Adam. "And now unpack your burros. Make camp with me here. We'll eat and talk together."

A sunset, rare on the Mohave, glowed over the simple camp tasks of these men who in their wanderings had met again. Clouds hung along the mountain tops, colored into deeper glory as the sun sank. The dark purples had an edge of silver, and the fleecy whites turned to pink and rose, while golden rays shot up from behind the red-hazed peaks. Over the valley fell a beautiful and transparent light, blending and deepening until a shadow as blue as the sea lay on Tecopah.

While the men ate their frugal repast they talked, each gradually growing used to a situation that broke the desert habit of silence. There was an unconscious deference of each man toward the other — Wansfell seeing in Dismukes the savior of his life and a teacher who had inspired him to scale the heights of human toil and strife; Dismukes finding in Wansfell a development of his idea, the divine spirit of man rising above the great primal beasts of the desert, self-preservation and ferocity.

"Wansfell, have you kept track of time?" asked Dismukes, reflectively, as he got out a black, stumpy pipe that Adam remembered.

"No. Days and weeks glide into years — that's all I can keep track of," replied Adam.

"I never could, either. What is time on the desert? Nothin'. . . . Well, it flies, that's sure. An' it must be years since I met you first down there in the Colorado. Let's see. Three times I went to Yuma — once to Riverside — an' twice to San Diego. Six trips inside. That's all I've made to bank my money since I met you. Six years. But, say, I missed a year or so."

"Dismukes, I've seen the snows white on the peaks eight times. Eight years, my friend, since Jinny cocked her ears that day and saved me. How little a thing life is in the desert!"

"Eight years!" echoed Dismukes, and wagged his huge shaggy head. "It can't be. . . . Well, well, time slips away. Wansfell, you're a young man, though I see gray over your temples. And you can't have any more fear because of that — that crime you confessed to me. Lord! man, no one would ever know you as that boy!"

"No fear that way any more. But fear of myself, Dismukes. If I went back to the haunts of men I would forget."

"Ah yes, yes!" sighed Dismukes. "I understand. I wonder how it'll be with me when my hour comes to leave the desert. I wonder."

"Will that be long?"

"You can never tell. I might strike it rich to-morrow. Always I dream I'm goin' to. It's the dream that keeps a prospector nailed to the lonely wastes."

Indeed, this strange man was a dreamer of dreams. Adam understood him now, all except that obsession for just so much gold. It seemed the only flaw in a great character. But the fidelity to that purpose was great as it was inexplicable.

"Dismukes, you had a third of your stake when we met years ago. How much now?"

"More than half, Wansfell, safe in banks an' some hid away," came the answer, rolling and strong. What understanding of endless effort abided in that voice!

"A quarter of a million! My friend, it is enough. Take it and go — fulfill your cherished dream. Go before it's too late."

"I've thought of that. Many times when I was sick an' worn out with the damned heat an' loneliness I've tempted myself with what you said. But, no. I'll never do that. It's the same to me now as if I had no money at all."

"Take care, Dismukes," warned Adam. "It's the gaining of gold — not what it might bring — that drives you."

"Ah! *Quien sabe,* as the Mexicans say? . . . Wansfell, have you learned the curse — or it may be the blessing — of the desert — what makes us wanderers of the wastelands?"

"No. I have not. Sometimes I feel it's close to me, like the feeling of a spirit out there on

193

the lonely desert at night. But it's a great thing, Dismukes. And it is linked to the very beginnings of us. Some day I'll know."

Dismukes smoked in silence, thoughtful and sad. The man's forceful assurance and doggedness seemed the same, yet Adam sensed a subtle difference in him, beyond power to define. The last gold faded from the bold domes of the mountains, the clouds turned gray, the twilight came on as a stealthy host. And from across the creek came discordant sounds of Tecopah awakening to the revelry of a gold diggings by night.

"How'd you happen along here?" queried Dismukes, presently.

"Tecopah was just a water hole for me," replied Adam.

"Me, too. An' I'm sure sayin' that I like to fill my canteens here. Last year I camped here, an' when I went on I kept one of my canteens so long the water spoiled. . . . Found some gold trace up in the Kingston range, but my supplies ran low an' I had to give up. My plan now is to go in there an' then on to the Funeral Mountains. They're full of mineral. But a dry, hard, poison country for a prospector. Do you know that country?"

"I've been on this side of the range."

"Bad enough, but the *other* side of the Funerals is Death Valley. That gash in summer is a blastin', roarin' hell. I've crossed it every month in the year. None but madmen ever tackle Death Valley in July, in the middle of the day.

194

I've seen the mercury go to one hundred and forty degrees. I've seen it one hundred and twenty-five at midnight, an', friend, when them furnace winds blow down the valley at night sleep or rest is impossible. You just gasp for life. . . . But strange to say, Wansfell, the fascination of the desert is stronger in Death Valley than at any other place."

"Yes, I can appreciate that," replied Adam, thoughtfully. "It must be the sublimity of death and desolation — the terrible loneliness and awfulness of the naked earth. I am going there."

"So I reckoned. An' see here, Wansfell, I'll get out my pencil an' draw you a little map of the valley, showin' my trails an' water holes. I know that country better than any other white man. It's a mineral country. The lower slope of the Funerals is all clay, borax, soda, alkali, salt, niter, an' when the weather's hot an' that stuff blows on the hot winds, my God! it's a horror! But you'll want to go through it all an' you'll go back again."

"Where do you advise me to go in?"

"Well, I'd follow the Amargosa. It's bad water, but better than none. Go across an' up into the Panamints, an' come back across again by Furnace Creek. I'll make you a little map. There's more bad water than good, an' some of it's arsenic. I found the skeletons of six men near an arsenic water hole. Reckon they'd come on this water when bad off for thirst an' didn't know enough to test it. An' they drank their fill an' died in their tracks. They had gold, too. But I never could find out anythin' about these men. No one ever heard of them an' I was the only man who knew of the tragedy. Well, well, it's common enough for me, though I never before run across so many dead men. Wansfell, I reckon you've found that common, too, in your wanderings — dried-up mummies, yellow as leather, or bleached bones an' grinnin' skull, white in the sun?"

"Yes, I've buried the remains of more than one poor devil," replied Adam.

"Is it best to bury them? I let them lay as warnin' to other poor devils. No one but a crazy man would drink at a water hole where there was a skeleton. . . . Well, to come back to your goin' to Death Valley. I'd go in by the Amargosa. It's a windin' stream an' long, but safe. An' there's firewood an' a little grass. Now when you get across the valley you'll run into prospectors an' miners an' wanderers at the water holes. An' like as not you'll meet some of the claim jumpers an' robbers that live in the Panamints. From what I hear about you, Wansfell, I reckon a meetin' with them would be a bad hour for them, an' somethin' of good fortune to honest miners. Hey?"

"Dismukes, I don't run from men of that stripe," replied Adam, grimly.

"Ahuh! I reckon not," said Dismukes, just as grimly. "Well, last time I was over there — let's see, it was in September, hotter n' hell, an' I run across two queer people up in a canyon I'd never prospected before. Didn't see any sign of any other prospectors ever bein' in there. . . . Two queer people — a man an' a woman livin' in a shack they'd built right under the damnedest roughest slope of weathered rock you ever saw in your life. Why, it was a plain case of suicide, an' so I tried to show them! Every hour you could hear the crack of a rollin' bowlder or the graty slip of an avalanche, gettin' oneasy an' wantin' to slide. But the woman was deathly afraid of her husband an' he was a skunk an' a wolf rolled into a man, if I ever saw one. I couldn't do anythin' for the poor woman, an' I couldn't learn any more than I'm tellin' you. That's not much. But, Wansfell, she wasn't a common sort. She'd been beautiful once. She had the saddest face I ever saw. I got two feelin's, one that she wasn't long for this earth, an' the other that the man hated her with a terrible hate. . . . I meet with queer people an' queer situations as I wander over this desert, but here's the beat of all my experience. An', Wansfell, I'd like to have you go see that couple. I reckon they'll be there, if alive yet. He chose a hidden spot, an' he has Shoshone Indians pack his supplies in from the ranches way on the other side of the Panamints. A queer deal, horrible for that poor woman, an' I've been haunted by her face ever since. I'd like you to go there."

"I'll go. But why do you say that, Dismukes?" asked Adam, curiously.

"Well — you ought to know what your name means to desert men," replied Dismukes, constrainedly, and he looked down at the camp fire, to push forward a piece of half-burnt wood.

"No, I never heard," said Adam. "I've lived 'most always alone. Of course I've had to go to freighting posts and camps. I've worked in gold diggings. I've guided wagon trains across the Mohave. Naturally, I've been among men. But I never heard that my name meant anything."

"Wansfell! I remember *now* that you called yourself Wansfell. I've heard that name. Some of your doings, Wansfell, have made camp-fire stories. See here, Wansfell, you won't take offense at me."

"No offense, friend Dismukes," replied Adam, strangely affected. Here was news that forced him to think of himself as a man somehow related to and responsible to his kind. He had gone to and fro over the trails of the desert, and many adventures had befallen him. He had lived them, with the force the desert seemed to have taught him, and then had gone his way down the lonely trails, absorbed in his secret. The years seemed less than the blowing sand. He had been an unfortunate boy burdened with a crime; he was now a matured man, still young in years, but old with the silence and loneliness and strife of the desert, gray at the temples, with that old burden still haunting him. How

198

good to learn that strange men spoke his name with wonder and respect! He had helped wanderers as Dismukes had helped him; he had meted out desert violence to evil men who crossed his trail; he had, doubtless, done many little unremembered deeds of kindness in a barren world where little deeds might be truly overappreciated; but the name Wansfell meant nothing to him, the reputation hinted by Dismukes amazed him, strangely thrilled him; the implication of nobility filled him with sadness and remorse. What had he done with the talents given him?

"Wansfell, you see — you're somethin' of the man I might have been," said Dismukes, hesitatingly.

"Oh no, Dismukes," protested Adam. "You are a prospector, honest and industrious, and wealthy now, almost ready to enjoy the fruits of your long labors. Your life has a great object. . . . But I — I am only a wanderer of the wasteland."

"Aye, an' therein lies your greatness!" boomed the prospector, his ox eyes dilating and flaring. "I am a selfish pig — a digger in the dirt for gold. My passion has made me pass by men, an' women, too, who needed help. Riches — dreams! . . . But you — you, Wansfell — out there in the loneliness an' silence of the wastelands — you have found God! . . . I said you would. I've met other men who had."

"No, no," replied Adam. "You're wrong. I

199

don't think I've found God. Not yet! . . . I have no religion, no belief. I can't find any hope out there in the desert. Nature is pitiless, indifferent. The desert is but one of her playgrounds. Man has no right there. No, Dismukes, I have not found God."

"You have, but you don't know it," responded Dismukes, with more composure, and he began to refill a neglected pipe. "Well, I didn't mean to fetch up such talk as that. You see, when I do fall in with a prospector once in a month of Sundays I never talk much. An' then it'd be to ask him if he'd seen any float lately or panned any color. But you're different. You make my mind work. An', Wansfell, sometimes I think my mind has been crowded with a million thoughts all cryin' to get free. That's the desert. A man's got to fight the desert with his intelligence or else become less than a man. An' I always did think a lot, if I didn't talk."

"I'm that way, too," replied Adam. "But a man should talk when he gets a chance. I talk to my burros, and to myself, just to hear the sound of my voice."

"Ah! Ah!" exclaimed Dismukes, with deep breath. He nodded his shaggy head. Adam's words had struck an answering chord in his heart.

"You've tried for gold here?" queried Adam.

"No. I was here first just after the strike, an' often since. Water's all that ever drew me. I'd starve before I'd dig for gold among a pack

200

of beasts. I may be a desert wolf, but I'm a lone one."

"They're coyotes and you're the gray wolf. I liken 'most every man I meet to some beast or creature of the desert."

"Aye, you're right. The desert stamps a man. An' Wansfell, it's stamped you with the look of a desert eagle. Ha-ha! I ain't flatterin' to either of us, am I? Me a starved gray wolf, huntin' alone, mean an' hard an' fierce! An' you a long, lean-headed eagle, with that look of you like you were about to strike — *pong!* . . . Well, well, there's no understandin' the work of the desert. The way it develops the livin' creatures! They all have to live, an' livin' on the desert is a thousand times harder than anywhere else. They all have to be perfect machines for destruction. Each seems so swift that he gets away, yet each is also so fierce an' sure that he catches his prey. They live on one another, but the species doesn't die out. That's what stumps me about the desert. Take the human creatures. They grow fiercer than animals. Maybe that's because nature did not intend man to live on the desert. An' it is no place for man. Nature intended these classes of plants an' these species of birds an' beasts to live, fight, thrive, an' reproduce their kind on the desert. But men can't thrive nor reproduce their kind here."

"How about the Indians who lived in the desert for hundreds of years?" asked Adam.

"What's a handful of Indians? An' what's a few years out of the millions of years that the desert's been here, just as it is now? Nothin' — nothin' at all! Wansfell, there will be men come into the desert, down there below the Salton Sink, an' in other places where the soil is productive, an' they'll build dams an' storage places for water. Maybe a lot of fools will even turn the Colorado River over the desert. They'll make it green an' rich an', like the Bible says, blossom as a rose. An' these men will build ditches for water, an' reservoirs an' towns an' cities, an' cross the desert with railroads. An' they'll grow rich an' proud. They'll think they've conquered it. But, poor fools! they don't know the desert! Only a man who has lived with the desert much of his life can ever know. Time will pass an' men will grow old, an' their sons an' grandsons after them. A hundred an' a thousand years might pass with fruitfulness still in the control of man. But all that is only a few grains of time in all the endless sands of eternity. The desert's work will have been retarded for a little while. But the desert works ceaselessly an' with infinite patience. The sun burns, the frost cracks, the avalanche rolls, the rain weathers. Slowly the earth crust heaves up into mountains an' slowly the mountains wear down, atom by atom, to be the sands of the desert. An' the winds — how they blow for ever an' ever! What can avail against the desert winds? They blow the sand an' sift an' seep an' bury. . . . Men will die an' the places that knew them will know them no more. An' the desert will come back to its own. That is well, for it is what God intended."

"God and nature, then, with you are one and the same?" queried Adam.

"Yes. Twenty years sleepin' on the sand with the stars in my face has taught me that. Is it the same with you?"

"No. I grant all that you contend for the desert and for nature. But I can't reconcile nature and God. Nature is cruel, inevitable, hopeless. But God must be immortality."

"Wansfell, there's somethin' divine in some men, but not in all, nor in many. So how can that divinity be God? The immortality you speak of — that is only your life projected into another life."

"You mean if I do not have a child I will not have immortality?"

"Exactly."

"But what of my soul?" demanded Adam, solemnly.

Dismukes drooped his shaggy head. "I don't know. I don't know. I've gone so deep, but I can't go any deeper. That always stumps me. I've never found my soul! Maybe findin' my soul would be findin' God. I don't know. . . . An' you, Wansfell — once I said you had the spirit an' mind to find God on the desert. Did you?"

Adam shook his head. "I'm no farther than you, Dismukes, though I think differently about life and death. . . . I've fought to live on this wasteland, but I've fought hardest to think. It seems that always nature strikes me with its terrible mace! I have endless hours to look at the desert and I see what you see — the strange ferocity of it all — the fierce purpose. No wonder you say the desert stamps a man!"

"Aye! An' woman, too! Take this she-devil who runs a place here in Tecopah — Mohave Jo is the name she bears. Have you seen her?"

"No, but I've heard of her. At Needles I met the wife of a miner, Clark, who'd been killed here at Tecopah."

"Never heard of Clark. But I don't doubt the story. It's common enough — miners bein' killed an' robbed. There's a gang over in the Panamints who live on miners."

"I'm curious to see Mohave Jo," said Adam.

"Well, speakin' of this one-eyed harridan reminds me of a man I met last trip across the Salton flats, down on the Colorado. Met him at Walters — a post on the stage line. He had only one eye, too. There was a terrible scar where his eye, the right one, had been. He was one of these Texans lookin' for a man. There seems to be possibilities of a railroad openin' up that part of the desert. An' this fellow quizzed me about water holes. Of course, if any one gets hold of water in that country he'll strike it rich as gold, if the country ever opens up.

It's likely to happen, too. Well, this man had an awful face. He'd been a sheriff in Texas, some one said, an' later at Ehrenberg. Hell on hangin' men! . . . Of course I never asked him how he lost his eye. But he told me — spoke of it more than once. The deformity had affected his mind. You meet men like that — sort of crazy on somethin'. He was always lookin' for the fellow who'd knocked out his eye. To kill him!"

"Do you — recall his — name?" asked Adam, his voice halting with a thick sensation in his throat. The past seemed as yesterday.

"Never was much on rememberin' names," responded Dismukes, scratching his shaggy head. "Let's see — why, yes, he called himself Collis— Collis— haw. That's it — Collishaw. Hard name to remember. But as a man he struck me easy to remember. . . . Well, friend Wansfell, I've had enough talkin' to do me for a spell. I'm goin' to bed."

While Adam sat beside the fire, motionless, pondering with slow, painful amaze over what he had just heard, Dismukes prepared for his night's rest. He unrolled a pack, spread a ragged old canvas, folded a blanket upon it, and arranged another blanket to pull up over him, together with the end of the canvas. For a pillow he utilized an old coat that lay on his pack. His sole concession to man's custom of undressing for bed was the removal of his old slouch hat. Then with slow, labored movement he lay down to stretch his huge body and pull the coverlets over him. From his cavernous breast heaved a long, deep sigh. His big eyes, dark and staring, gazed up at the brightening stars, and then they closed.

Adam felt tempted to pack and move on to a quiet and lonely place off in the desert, where he could think without annoyance. Keen and bitterly faithful as had been his memory, it had long ceased to revive thoughts of Collishaw, the relentless sheriff and ally of Guerd. How strange and poignant had been the shock of recollection! It had been the blow Adam had dealt — the savage fling of his gun in Collishaw's face — that had destroyed an eye and caused a hideous disfigurement. And the Texan, with that fatality characteristic of his kind, was ever on the look-out for the man who had ruined his eyesight. Perhaps that was only one reason for his thirst for revenge. Guerd! Had Collishaw not sworn to hang Adam? "You'll swing for this!" he had yelled in his cold, ringing voice of passion. And so Adam lived over again the old agony, new and strange in its bitter mockery, its vain hope of forgetfulness. Vast as the desert was, it seemed small now to Adam, for there wandered over it a relentless and bloodthirsty Texan, hunting to kill him. The past was not dead. The present and the future could not be wholly consecrated to atonement. A specter, weird and grotesque as a yucca tree, loomed out there in the shadows of the desert night. Death stalked on Adam's trail. The hatred of men was beyond power to understand. Work, fame, use, health, love, home, life itself, could be sacrificed by some men just to kill a rival or an enemy. Adam remembered that Collishaw had hated him and loved Guerd. Moreover, Collishaw had that strange instinct to kill men — a passion which grew by what it fed on — a morbid mental twist that drove him to rid himself of the terrible haunting ghost of his last victim by killing a new one. Added to that was a certain leaning toward the notorious.

"We'll meet some day," soliloquized Adam. "But he would never recognize me."

The comfort of that fact did not long abide in Adam's troubled mind. He would recognize Collishaw. And that seemed to hold something fatalistic and inevitable. "When I meet Collishaw I'll tell him who I am — and I'll kill him!" That fierce whisper was the desert voice in Adam — the desert spirit. He could no more help that sudden bursting flash of fire than he could help breathing. Nature in the desert did not teach men to meet a threat with forgiveness, nor to wait until they were struck. Instinct had precedence over intelligence and humanity. In the eternal strife to keep alive on the desert a man who conquered must have assimilated something of the terrible nature of the stinging *cholla* cactus, and the hard, grasping tenacity of the mesquite roots, and the ferocity of the wildcat, and the cruelty of the hawk — something of the nature of all that survived. It was a law. It forced a man to mete out violence in advance of that meant for him.

"To fight and to think were to be my blessings," soliloquized Adam, and he shook his head with a long-familiar doubt. Then he had to remember that no blessings of any kind whatsoever could be his. Stern and terrible duty to himself!

So he rolled in his blankets and stretched his long body to the composure of rest. Sleep did not drop with soft swiftness upon his eyes, as it had upon those of Dismukes. He had walked far, but he was not tired. He never tired any more. There seemed to be no task of a single day that could weary his strength. And for long he lay awake, listening to the deep breathing of his companion, and the howl of the coyotes, and the sounds of Tecopah, so unnatural in the quiet of the desert. A sadness weighed heavily upon Adam. At first he was glad to have met Dismukes, but now he was sorry. A tranquillity, a veil seemed to have been rent. The years had not really changed the relation of his crime, nor materially the nature of his sin. But they had gradually, almost imperceptibly, softened his ceaseless and eternal remorse. By this meeting with Dismukes he found that time effaced shocks, blows, stains, just as it wore away the face of the desert rock. That, too, was a law; and in this Adam divined a blessing that he could not deny. Dismukes had unleashed a specter out of the dim glow of the past. Eight years! So many, and yet they were as eight days! There were the bright stars, pitiless and cold, and the dark bold mountains that had seemed part of his strength. In the deep-blue sky above and in the black shadow below Adam saw a white face, floating, fading, reappearing, mournful and accusing and appalling — a face partaking of the old boyish light and joy and of the godlike beauty of perfect manhood — the haunting face of his brother Guerd. It haunted Adam, and the brand of Cain burned into his brain. The old resurging pangs in his breast, the long sighs, the oppressed heart, the salt tears, the sleepless hours — these were Adam's again, as keen as in the first days of his awakening down on the Colorado Desert, where from the peaks of the Chocolate Mountains he had gazed with piercing eyes far south to the purple peak — Picacho, the monument, towering above his brother's grave. "Some day I'll go back!" whispered Adam, as if answering to an imperative and mysterious call.

The long night wore on with the heavens star-fired by its golden train, and the sounds at last yielding to the desert silence. Adam could see Dismukes, a wide, prone figure, with dark face upturned to the sky, a man seemingly as strange and strong as the wastelands he talked so much about, yet now helpless in sleep, unguarded, unconscious, wrapped in his deep dreams of the joy and life his gold was to bring him. Adam felt a yearning pity for this dreamer. Did he really love gold or was his passion only a dream? Whatever that was and whatever the man was, there rested upon his ragged, dark face a shadow of tragedy. Adam wondered what his own visage would reflect when he lay asleep, no more master of a mind that never rested? The look of an eagle? So Dismukes had said, and that was not the first time Adam had heard such comparison. He had seen desert eagles, dead and alive. He tried to recall how they looked, but the images were not convincing. The piercing eye, clear as the desert air, with the power of distance in the gray depths; the lean, long lines; the wild poise of head, bitter and ruthless and fierce; the look of loneliness — these characters surely could not be likened to his face. What a strange coincidence that Dismukes should hit upon the likeness of an eagle — the winged thunderbolt of the heights — the lonely bird Adam loved above all desert creatures! And so Adam wandered in mind until at last he fell asleep.

13
●

When Adam awoke he saw that Dismukes had breakfast steaming on the fire.

"I'm on my way to-day," announced the prospector. "What'll you do?"

"Well, I'll hang around Tecopah as long as I can stand it," replied Adam.

"Humph! That won't be long, unless you got in mind somethin' like you did at the Donner Placers, down in the Providence Mountains."

"Friend, what do you know about that?" queried Adam.

"Nothin'. I only heard about it. . . . Wansfell, do you pan any gold?"

"Sometimes, when I happen to run across it," replied Adam, "but that isn't often."

"Do you work?"

"Yes, I've worked a good deal, taking it all together. In the mines, on the river at Needles, driving mule teams and guiding wagon trains. Never got paid much, though."

"How do you live?" asked Dismukes, evidently curious.

"Oh, I fare well enough to keep flesh on my bones."

"You've got flesh — or I reckon it's muscle. Wansfell, you're the best-built man I ever saw on the desert. Most men dry up an' blow away. . . . Will you let me give you — lend you some money?"

"Money! So that's why you're so curious?" responded Adam. "Thanks, my friend. I don't need money. I had some, you know, when you ran across me down in the Chocolates. I used about a thousand dollars while I lived with the Coahuila Indians. And I've got nine thousand left."

"Say, you don't pack all that money along with you?"

"Yes. Where else would I keep it?"

"Wansfell, some of these robbers will murder you."

"Not if I see them first. My friend, don't be concerned. Surely I don't look sick."

"Humph! Well, just the same, now that you're headin' up into this country, I advise you to be careful. Don't let anybody see you with money. I've been held up an' robbed three times."

"Didn't you make a fight for your gold?"

"No chance. I was waylaid — had to throw up my hands. . . . They tell me you are ready with a gun, Wansfell?"

"Dismukes, you seem to have heard much about me."

"But you didn't throw a gun on Baldy McKue," said Dismukes, with a dark flare from his rolling eyes.

"No — I did not," replied Adam.

"You killed McKue with your bare hands," flashed Dismukes. A red stain appeared to come up under his leathery skin. "Wansfell, will you tell me about it?"

"I'd rather not, Dismukes. There are *some* things I forget."

"Well, it meant a good deal to me," replied Dismukes. "McKue did me dirt. He jumped claims of mine down here near Soda Sink. An' he threatened to kill me — swore the claims were his — drove me off. I met him in Riverside, an' there he threatened me with arrest. He was a robber an' a murderer. I believe he ambushed prospectors. McKue was like most men who stick to the desert — he went down to the level of the beast. I hated him. . . . This stranger who told me — he swore there wasn't an un-cracked bone left in McKue's body. . . . Wansfell, if you did that to McKue you've squared accounts. Is it true?"

"Yes."

Dismukes rubbed his huge hands together and his ox eyes rolled and dilated. A fierce and savage grimness distorted his hard face for an instant and passed away.

"What'd you kill him for?"

"Because he'd have killed me."

"Didn't you look him up on purpose to kill him?"

"No. . . . A year before that time I went

213

to Goffs. Some one took me into an old tent where a woman lay dying. I could do little for her. She denounced McKue; she blamed him that she lay there, about to die. She did die and I buried her. Then I kept an eye open for McKue."

"I wondered — I wondered," said Dismukes. "It struck me deep. Lord knows fights are common out here. An' death — why, on the desert every way you turn you see death. It's the life of the desert. But the way this was told me struck me deep. It was what I'd like to have done myself. Wansfell, think of the wonderful meetin's of men on the desert — an', aye, meetin' of men with women, too! They happen different out here. Think of the first time we met! An' this time! Wansfell, we'll meet again. It's written in those trails of sand out there, wanderin' to an' fro across the desert."

"Dismukes, the desert is vast. Sometimes you will not meet a man in months of travel — and not in years will you meet a woman. But when you do meet them life seems intensified. The desert magnifies."

"Wansfell, I want you to go across into Death Valley," declared Dismukes, with the deep boom in his voice. "That woman in the shack! Her eyes haunt me. Somethin' terrible wrong! That man who keeps her there — if he's not crazy, he's worse than a gorilla. For a gorilla kills a woman quick. . . . Wansfell, I'd give a lot to see you handle this man like you handled McKue!"

"*Quien sabe,* as you say?" replied Adam. "Draw that map of your trails in Death Valley. I've got a little book here, and a pencil."

It was singular to see the gold digger labor with his great, stumpy, calloused fingers. He took long to draw a few lines, and make a few marks, and write a few names in the little book. But when he came to talk of distance and direction, of trails and springs, of flat valley and mountain range — then how swift and fluent he was! All that country lay clearly in his mind, as if he were a great desert condor gazing down from the heights upon the wasteland which was his home.

"Now, I'll be goin' down into the Funerals soon," concluded Dismukes. "You see here's Furnace Creek where it runs into Death Valley. You'll cross here an' come up Furnace Creek till you strike the yellow clay hills on the right. It's a hell of a jumble of hills — absolutely bare. I think there's gold. You'll find me somewhere."

It seemed settled then that Adam and Dismukes were to meet in some vague place at some vague time. The desert had no limitations. Time, distance, and place were thought of in relation to their adaptation to desert men.

"Well, it's gettin' late," said Dismukes, looking up at the white flare of sun. "I'll pack an' go on my way."

While Dismukes strode out to drive in his

burros Adam did the camp chores. In a short time his companion appeared with the burros trotting ahead of him. And the sight reminded Adam of the difference between prospectors. Dismukes was not slow, easy, careless, thoughtless. He had not suffered the strange deterioration so common to his class. He did not belong to the type who tracked his burros all day so that he might get started *mañana*. Adam helped him pack.

"Wansfell, may we meet again," said Dismukes, as they shook hands.

"All trails cross on the desert. I hope you strike it rich."

"Some day — some day. Good-by," returned Dismukes, and with vigorous slaps he started the burros.

Adam was left to his own devices. After Dismukes passed out of sight in the universal gray of the benches Adam spent a long while watching a lizard on a stone. It was a chuckwalla, a long, slim, greenish-bronze reptile, covered with wonderful spots of vivid color, and with eyes like jewels. Adam spent much time watching the living things of the desert, or listening to the silence. He had discovered that watching anything brought its reward — sometimes in a strange action or a phenomenon of nature or a new thought.

Later he walked down to the creek bottom where the smelter was in operation. Laborers were at a premium there, and he was offered

216

work. He said he would consider it. But unless there turned out to be some definite object to keep him in Tecopah, Adam would not have bartered his freedom to the dust-clouded mill for all the gold it mined. These clanging mills and hot shafts and dark holes oppressed him.

The long-deferred hour at last arrived in which Adam, on a ruddy-gold dawn in early April, drove his burros out into the lonesome desert toward the Amargosa. He did not look back. Tecopah would not soon forget Wansfell! That was his grim thought.

The long, drab reaches of desert, the undulating bronze slopes waving up to the dark mountains, called to him in a language that he felt. If Adam Larey — or Wansfell, wanderer of the wasteland, as he had come to believe himself — had any home, it was out in the vast open, under the great white flare of sunlight and the star-studded canopy of night.

This was a still morning in April, and the lurid sun, bursting above the black escarpment in the east, promised a rising temperature. Day by day the heat had been increasing, and now, at sunrise, the smoky heat veils were waving up from the desert floor. For Adam the most torrid weather had no terrors, and the warmth of a morning like this felt pleasant on his cheek. He had been confined to one place, without action, for so long that now, as he began to feel the slow sweat burn pleasantly on his body, there came a loosening of his muscles, a relaxing of tension, a marshaling, as it were, of his great forces of strength and endurance. The gray slopes beyond did not daunt him. His stride was that of a mountaineer, and his burros had to trot to keep ahead of him.

And as Adam's body gradually responded to this readjustment to the desert and its hard demands, so his mind seemed to slough off, layer by layer, the morbid, fierce, and ruthless moods that like lichens had fastened upon it. The dry, sweet desert air seemed to permeate his brain and clear it of miasmas and shadows. He was free. He was alone. He was self-sufficient. The desert called. From far beyond that upheaved black and forbidding range, the Funeral Mountains, something strange, new, thrilling awaited his coming. The strife of the desert had awakened in him a craving to find the unattainable. He had surmounted all physical obstacles. He would conquer Death Valley; he would see it in all its ghastliness; he would absorb all its mysteries; he would defy to the limit of endurance its most fatal menaces to life.

In the afternoon Adam rounded a corner of

a league-long sloping mesa and gazed down into the valley of the Amargosa. It looked the bitterness, the poison, and the acid suggested by its Spanish name. The narrow meandering stream gleamed like silver in the sunlight. Mesquite and other brush spotted its gravelly slopes and sandy banks. Adam headed down into the valley. The sun was already westering, and soon, as he descended, it hung over the ragged peaks. He reached the creek. The burros drank, but not with relish. Adam gazed at the water of the Amargosa with interest. It was not palatable, yet it would save life.

Adam set about the camp tasks long grown second nature with him, and which were always congenial and pleasant. He built a fire of dead mesquite. Then he scoured his oven with sand, and greased it. He had a heavy pan which did duty as a gold-pan, a dish-pan, and a wash-pan. This he half filled with flour, and, adding water, began to mix the two. He had gotten the dough to about the proper consistency when a rustling in the brush attracted his attention. He thought he caught a glimpse of a rabbit. Such opportunity for fresh meat was rare on the desert. Hastily wiping his hands, he caught up his gun and stole out into the aisle between the mesquites. As luck would have it, he did espy a young cottontail, and was fortunate enough to make a good shot. Returning to camp, he made sudden discovery of a catastrophe.

Jennie had come out of her nap, if, indeed,

she had not been shamming sleep, and she had her nose in the dish-pan. She was eating the dough.

"Hyar, you camp robber!" yelled Adam, making for her.

Jennie jerked up her head. The dough stuck to her nose and the pan stuck to the dough. She eluded Adam, for she was a quick and nimble burro. The pan fell off, but the ball of dough adhered to her mouth and nose, and as she ran around camp in a circle it was certain that she worked her jaws, eating dough as fast as she could. Manifestly for Jennie, here was opportunity of a lifetime. When finally Adam did catch her the dough was mostly eaten. He gave her a cuff and a kick which she accepted meekly, and, drooping her ears, she apparently fell asleep again.

While Adam was at his simple meal the sun set, filling the valley with red haze and tipping with gold the peaks in the distance. The heat had gone with the sun. He walked to and fro in the lonely twilight. Jennie had given up hope of any more opportunity to pilfer, and had gone to grazing somewhere down the stream. There was absolutely no sound. An infinite silence enfolded the solitude. It was such solitude as only men of Adam's life could bear. To him it was both a blessing and a curse. But to-night he had an all-pervading and all-satisfying power. He seemed to be growing at one with the desert and its elements. After a while the twilight shadows shaded into the blackness of night, and the stars blazed. Adam had been conscious all day of the gradual relaxing of strain, and now in the lonely solitude there fell away from him the feelings and thoughts engendered at Tecopah.

"Loneliness and silence and time!" he soliloquized, as he paced his sandy beat. "These will cure any trouble — any disease of mind — any agony of soul. Ah! I know. I never forget. But how different now to remember! . . . That must be the secret of the power of the desert over men. It is the abode of solitude and silence. It is like the beginning of creation. It is like an eternity of time."

By the slow healing of the long-raw wound in his heart Adam had come to think of time's relation to change. Memory was still as poignant as ever. But a change had begun in him — a change he divined only after long months of strife. Dismukes brought a regurgitation of the old pain; yet it was not quite the same. Eight years! How impossible to realize that, until confronted by physical proofs of the passing of time! Adam saw no clear and serene haven for his wandering spirit, but there seemed to be a nameless and divine promise in the future. His steps had not taken hold of hell. He had been driven down the naked shingles of the desert, through the storms of sand, under the infernal heat and bitter cold, like a man scourged naked, with screaming furies to whip the air at his ears.

And, lo! time had begun to ease his burden, soften the pain, dim the past, change his soul.

The moment was one of uplift. "I have my task," he cried, looking high to the stars. "Oh, stars — so serene and pitiless and inspiring — teach me to perform that task as you perform yours!"

He would go on as he had begun, fighting the desert and its barrenness, its blasting heat, its evil influences, wandering over these wastelands that must be his home; and he would stake the physical prowess of him to yet harder, fiercer tasks of toil, driving his spirit to an intenser, whiter flame. If the desert could develop invincible energy of strength in a man, he would earn it. If there were a divinity in man, infinitely beyond the beasts of the desert and the apes of the past, a something in mysterious affinity with that mighty being he sensed out there in the darkness, then he would learn it with a magnified and all-embracing consciousness.

Adam went to his bed on the warm sands complete in two characters — a sensing, watching, listening man like the savage in harmony with the nature of the elements around him, and a feeling, absorbed, and meditating priest who had begun to divine the secrets beyond the dark-shadowed, starlit desert waste.

Adam's first sight of Death Valley came at an early morning hour, as he turned a last curve in the yawning canyon he had descended.

He stood in awe.

222

"Oh, desolation!" he cried. And it seemed that, as the shock of the ghastliness beneath him passed, he remembered with flashing vividness all that had come to him in his long desert wanderings, which seemed now to cumulate its terrible silence, desolation, death, and decay in this forbidding valley.

He remembered the origin of that name — Death Valley. In 1849, when the California gold frenzy had the world in its grip, seventy Mormon gold seekers had wandered into this red-walled, white-floored valley, where sixty-eight of them perished. The two that escaped gave this narrow sink so many hundred feet below sea level the name Death Valley! Many and many another emigrant and prospector and wanderer, by his death from horrible thirst and blasting heat and poison-dusted wind and destroying avalanche and blood-freezing cold, had added to the significance of that name and its dreadful fame. On one side the valley was shadowed by the ragged Funeral range; on the other by the red and gloomy Panamints. Furnace Creek, the hot stream that came down from the burning slopes; and Ash Meadow, the valley floor, gray and dead, like the bed of a Dead Sea; and the Devil's Chair, a huge seat worn by the elements in the red mountain wall, where the death king of the valley watched over his fiends — these names were vivid in Adam's mind along with others given by prospectors in uncouth or eloquent speech. "She's a hummer in July," said one; and another, "Salty lid of hell"; and still another, "Valley of the white shadow of death."

Death Valley was more than sixty miles long and from seven to twelve wide. No two prospectors had ever agreed on these dimensions, although all had been in perfect harmony as to its hellish qualities. Death was the guardian of the valley and the specter that patrolled its beat. Mineral wealth was the irresistible allurement which dared men to defy its terrors. Gold! Dismukes himself had claimed there were ledges of gold quartz, and Dismukes was practical and accurate. Many fabulous stories of gold hung on the lips of wandering prospectors. The forbidding red rocks held jewels in their hard confines — garnets, opals, turquoises; there were cliffs of marble and walls of onyx. The valley floor was a white crust where for miles and miles there was nothing but salt and borax. Beds of soda, of gypsum, of niter, of sulphur, abounded in the vaster fields of other minerals. It was a valley where nature had been prodigal of her treasures and terrible in her hold upon them. But few springs and streams flowed down into this scoriac sink, and of these all were heavily impregnated with minerals, all unpalatable, many sour and sulphuric, some hot, a few of them deadly poison. In the summer months the heat sometimes went to one hundred and forty-five degrees. The furnace winds of midnight were withering to flesh and blood. And sometimes the air carried invisible death in shape of poison gas or dust. In winter, sudden changes of temperature, whirling icy winds down upon a prospector who had gone to sleep in warmth, would freeze him to death. Avalanches rolled down the ragged slopes and cloudbursts carried destruction.

Adam got his bearings, according to the map made by Dismukes, and set out from the mouth of the canyon to cross the valley. A long sandy slope dotted by dwarfed mesquites extended down to the bare, crinkly floor of the valley, from which the descent to a lower level was scarcely perceptible. When Adam's burros early in the day manifested uneasiness and weariness there was indeed rough going. The sand had given way to a hard crust of salt or borax, and little dimples and cones made it difficult to place a foot on a level. Some places the crust was fairly hard; in others it cracked and crunched under foot. The color was a mixture of a dirty white and yellow. Far ahead Adam could see a dazzling white plain that resembled frost on a frozen river.

Adam proceeded cautiously behind the burros. They did not like the travel, and, wary little beasts that they were, they stepped gingerly in places, as if trying their weight before trusting it upon the treacherous-looking crust. Adam felt the beat of the sun upon him, and the reflection of heat from the valley floor. He had been less oppressed upon hotter days than this. The sensations he began to have here were similar to

225

those he had experienced in the Salton Sink, where he had gone below sea level. The oppression seemed to be a blood pressure, as if the density of the air closed tighter and heavier around his body.

At last the burros halted. Adam looked up from the careful task of placing his feet to see that he had reached a perfectly smooth bed of salt, glistening as if it were powdered ice. This was the margin of the place that from afar had looked like a frozen stream. Stepping down upon it, Adam found that it trembled and heaved with his weight, but upheld him. There was absolutely no sign to tell whether the next yard of surface would hold him or not. Still, from what he had gone over he believed he could trust the rest. As he turned to retrace his steps he saw his tracks just as plainly in the salt as if they had been imprinted in snow. He led Jennie out, and found that, though her hoofs sank a little, she could make it by stepping quickly. She understood as well as he, and when released went on of her own accord, anxious to get the serious job over. Adam had to drive the other burro. The substance grew softer as Adam progressed, and in the middle of that glistening stream it became wet and sticky. The burros labored through this lowest level of the valley, which fortunately was narrow.

On the other side of it extended a wide flat of salt and mud, very rough, upheaved as if it had boiled and baked to a crust, then cracked and sunk in places. Full of holes and pitfalls, and rising in hummocks gnarled and whorled like huge sea shells, it was an exceedingly toilsome and dangerous place to travel. The crust continually crumpled under the hoofs of the burros, and gave forth hollow sounds, as if a bottomless cavern ran under the valley floor. As Adam neared the other side he encountered thin streams of water that resembled acid. It was necessary to find narrow places in these and leap across. Beyond these ruts in the crust began an almost imperceptible rise of the valley floor, which in the course of a couple of miles led out of the broken, choppy sea of salt to a sand-and-gravel level. How relieved Adam was to reach that! He had been more concerned for the safety of the burros than for his own.

It was now hot enough for Adam to imagine something of what a formidable place this valley would be in July or August. On all sides the mountains stood up dim and obscure and distant in a strange haze. Low down, the heat veils lifted in ripples, and any object at a distance seemed illusive. The last hour taxed Adam's endurance, though he could have gone perhaps as far again across the lavalike crust. When he reached the slope that led up to the base of the red mountains he halted the burros for a rest. The drink he took then was significant, for it was the fullest he had taken in years. He was hot and wet; his eyes smarted and his feet burned.

When Adam had rested he consulted the map, and found that he must travel up the slope and to the west to gain the black buttress of rock that was his objective point. And considering how dim it looked through the haze, he concluded he had better be starting. One moment, however, he gave to a look at the Funeral range which he had come through, and which now loomed above the valley, a magnificent and awe-inspiring upheaval of the earth. The lower and nearer heights were marked on Dismukes's map as the Calico Mountains, and indeed their many colors justified the name. Beyond and above them towered the Funerals, spiked and peaked, ragged as the edge of a saw, piercing the blue sky, a gloomy and black-zigzagged and drab-belted range of desolation and grandeur. Adam's gaze slowly shifted westward to the gulf, a hazy void, a vast valley with streaked and ridged and canyoned slopes inclosing the abyss into which veils of rain seemed dropping. Broken clouds had appeared in the west, pierced by gold and red rays, somewhat dulled by the haze. That scene up the valley of death was confounding. He gazed spellbound, and every second saw more and different aspects. How immense, unreal, weird!

He got up from the stone seat that had almost burned through his clothes, and bent his steps westward, driving the wearying burros ahead of him. Three miles toward the black buttressed corner he wanted to gain before dark — so his experienced desert eyes calculated the distance. But this was Death Valley. No traveler of the desert had ever correctly measured distance in this valley of shadows and hazes and illusions. He was making three miles an hour. Yet at the end of an hour he seemed just as far away as ever. Another hour was full of deceits and misjudgments. But at the end of the third he reached the black wall, and the line that had seemed a corner was the mouth of a canyon.

Adam halted, as if at the gateway of the unknown. The sun was setting behind the mountains that now overhung him, massive and mighty, a sheer, insurmountable world of rock which seemed to reach to the ruddy sky. Wonderful shadows were falling, purple and blue low down, rosy and gold above; and the canyon smoked with sunset haze.

The map of Dismukes marked the canyon, and a spring of water just beyond its threshold, and also the shack where the strange man and woman lived under the long slant of weathered rock. Adam decided not to try to find the location that night, so he made dry camp.

Darkness found him weary and oppressed. The day had seemed short, but the distance long. Tired and sleepy as he was, when he lay down in his bed he felt a striking dissimilarity of this place to any other he had known on the desert. How profound the silence! Had any sound ever pervaded it? All was gloom and shadow below, with black walls rising to star-fretted sky as

229

blue as indigo. The valley seemed to be alive. It breathed, yet invisibly and silently. Indeed, there was a mighty being awake out there in the black void. Adam could not believe any man and woman lived up this canyon. Dismukes had dreamed. Had not Adam heard from many prospectors how no white woman could live in Death Valley? He had been there only a day, yet he felt that he could understand why it must be fatal to women. But it was not so because of heat and poison wind and cataclysms of nature, for women could endure those as well as men. But no woman could stand the alterations of terror and sublimity, of beauty and horror. That which was feminine in Adam shuddered at a solitude that seemed fitting to a burned-out world. He was the last of his race, at the end of its existence, the strongest finally brought to his doom, and to-morrow the earth would be sterile — thus Adam's weary thoughts passed into dreams.

He awakened somewhat later than usual. Over the Funeral range the sun was rising, a coalescing globule of molten fire, enormous and red, surrounded by a sky-broad yellow flare. This sunrise seemed strangely closer to the earth and to him than any sunrise he had ever watched. The valley was clear, still, empty, a void that made all objects therein look small and far away. After breakfast Adam set out to find his burros.

This high-walled opening did not appear to be a canyon, but a space made by two mountain slopes running down to a wash where water flowed at some seasons. Beyond the corners there opened what seemed to be a gradually widening and sloping field, gray with rocks and sand and stunted brush, through the center of which straggled a line of gnarled mesquites, following the course of the wash. Adam found his burros here, Jennie asleep as usual, and Jack contentedly grazing.

The cracking of a rock rolling down a rough slope thrilled Adam. He remembered what Dismukes had said about the perilous location of the shack where the man and woman lived under the shadow of a weathering mountain. Adam turned to look across the space in the direction whence the sound had come.

There loomed a mighty mountain slope, absolutely destitute of plants, a gray, drab million-faceted ascent of rocks. Adam strode toward it, gradually getting higher and nearer through the rock-strewn field. It had looked so close as to seem magnified. But it was a goodly distance. Presently he espied a rude shack. He halted. That could not be what he was searching for. Still, it must be. Adam had not expected the place to be so close to Death Valley. It was not a quarter of a mile distant from the valley and not a hundred feet higher than the lowest sink hole, which was to say that this crude, small structure lay in Death Valley and below sea level.

Adam walked on, growing more curious and

doubtful. Surely this hut had been built and abandoned by some prospector. Yet any prospector could have built a better abode than this. None but a fool or a knave would have selected that perilous location. The ground began to slope a little and become bare of bush, and was dotted here and there with huge bowlders that looked as if they had rolled down there recently. No sign of smoke, no sign of life, no sign of labor — absence of these strengthened Adam's doubt of people living there. Suddenly he espied the deep track of a man's foot in the sand. Adam knelt to study it. "Made yesterday," he said.

He rose with certainty. Dismukes had been accurate as to direction, though his distances had been faulty. Adam gazed beyond the shack, to right, and then left. He espied a patch of green mesquite and hummocks of grass. There was the water Dismukes had marked. Then Adam looked up.

A broad belt of huge bowlders lay beyond the shack, the edge of the talus, the beginning of the base of a mountainside, wearing down, weathering away, cracking into millions of pieces, every one of which had both smooth and sharp surfaces. This belt was steep and fan shaped, spreading at the bottom. As it sloped up it grew steeper, and the rocks grew smaller. It had the flow of a glacier. It was an avalanche, perhaps sliding inch by inch and foot by foot, all the time. The curved base of the fan extended for a couple of miles, in the distance growing rounded and symmetrical in its lines. It led up to a stupendous mountain abutment, dull red in color, and so seamed and cracked and fissured that it had the crisscross appearance of a rock of net, or numberless stones of myriad shapes pieced together by some colossal hand, and now split and broken, ready to fall. Yet this rugged, bold, uneven surface of mountain wall shone in the sunlight. It looked as if it had been a solid mass of granite shattered by some cataclysm of nature. Above this perpendicular splintered ruin heaved up another slope of broken rocks, hanging there as if by magic, every one of the endless heaps of stones leaning ready to roll. Frost and heat had disintegrated this red mountain. What history of age was written there! How sinister that dull hue of red! No beauty shone here, though the sun gleamed on the millions of facets. The mountain of unstable rock towered dark and terrible and forbidding even in the broad light of day. What held that seamed and lined and sundered mass of rock together! For what was it waiting? Only time, and the law of the desert! Even as Adam gazed a weathered fragment loosened from the heights, rolled off the upper wall, pitched clear into the air, and cracked ringingly below, to bound and hurtle down the lower slope, clapping less and less until it ceased with a little hollow report. That was the story of the mountain. By atom and by mass it was in motion, working down to a level. Bowlders twice as large as the shack, weighing thousands of tons, had rolled down and far out on the field. Any moment another might topple off the rampart and come hurtling down to find the shack in its path. Some day the whole slope of loose rock, standing almost on end, would slide down in avalanche.

"Well," muttered Adam, darkly, "any man who made a woman live there was either crazy or meant her to have an awful death."

Adam strode on to the shack. It might afford shelter from sun, but not from rain or dust. Packsaddles and boxes were stacked on one side; empty cans lay scattered everywhere; a pile of mesquite, recently cut, stood in front of the aperture that evidently was a door; and on the sand lay blackened stones and blackened utensils, near the remains of a still smoldering fire.

"Hello, inside," called Adam, as he halted at the door. No sound answered. He stooped to look in, and saw bare sand floor, a rude, low table made of box boards, flat stones for seats, utensils and dishes, shelves littered with cans and bags. A flimsy partition of poles and canvas, with a door, separated this room from another and larger one. Adam saw a narrow bed of blankets raised on poles, an old valise on the sandy floor, woman's garments hanging on the brush walls. He called again, louder this time. He saw a flash of something gray through the torn canvas, then heard a low cry — a woman's voice. Adam raised his head and stepped back.

"Elliot! . . . You've come back!" came the

voice, quick, low, and tremulous, betokening relief from dread.

"No. It's a stranger," replied Adam.

"Oh!" The hurried exclamation was followed by soft footfalls. A woman in gray appeared in the doorway — a woman whose proportions were noble, but frail. She had a white face and large, deep eyes, strained and sad. "Oh — who are you?"

"Ma'am, my name's Wansfell. I'm a friend of Dismukes, the prospector who was here. I'm crossing Death Valley and I thought I'd call upon you."

"Dismukes? The little miner, huge, like a frog?" she queried, quickly, with dilating eyes. "I remember. He was kind, but — And you're his friend?"

"Yes, at your service, ma'am."

"Thank — God!" she cried, brokenly, and she leaned back against the door. "I'm in trouble. I've been alone — all — all night. My husband left yesterday. He took only a canteen. He said he'd be back for supper. . . . But — he didn't come. Oh, something has happened to him."

"Many things happen in the desert," said Adam. "I'll find your husband. I saw his tracks out here in the sand."

"Oh, can you find him?"

"Ma'am, I can track a rabbit to its burrow. Don't worry any more. I will track your husband and find him."

The woman suddenly seemed to be struck

235

with Adam's tone, or the appearance of him. It was as if she had not particularly noticed him at first. "Once he got lost — was gone two days. Another time he was overcome by heat — or something in the air."

"You've been alone before?" queried Adam, quick to read the pain of the past in her voice.

"Alone? . . . Many — many lonely nights," she said. "He's left me — alone — often — purposely — for me to torture my soul here in the blackness. . . . And those rolling rocks — cracking in the dead of night — and —" Then the flash of her died out, as if she had realized she was revealing a shameful secret to a stranger.

"Ma'am, is your husband just right in his mind?" asked Adam.

She hesitated, giving Adam the impression that she wished to have him think her husband irrational, but could not truthfully say so.

"Men do strange things in the desert," said Adam. "May I ask, ma'am, have you food and water?"

"Yes. We've plenty. But Elliot makes me cook — and I never learned how. So we've fared poorly. But he eats little and I less!"

"Will you tell me how he came to build your hut here where, sooner or later, it'll be crushed by rolling stones?"

A tragic shadow darkened in the large, dark-blue eyes that Adam now realized were singularly beautiful.

236

"I — He — This place was near the water. He cut the brush here — he didn't see — wouldn't believe the danger," she faltered. She was telling a lie, and did not do it well. The fine, sensitive, delicate lips, curved and soft, sad with pain, had not been fashioned for falsehood.

"Perhaps I can make him see," replied Adam. "I'll go find him. Probably he's lost. The heat is not strong enough to be dangerous. And he's not been gone long. Don't worry. My camp is just below. I'll fetch him back to-day — or to-morrow at farthest."

She murmured some incoherent thanks. Adam was again aware of her penetrating glance, staring, wondering even in her trouble. He strode away with bowed head, searching the sand for the man's tracks. Presently he struck them and saw that they led down toward the valley.

To follow such a plain trail was child's play for Adam's desert sight, that had received its early training in the preservation of his life. He who had trailed lizards to their holes, and snakes to their rocks, to find them and eat or die — he was as keen as a wolf on the scent. This man's trail led straight down to the open valley, out along the western bulge of slope, to a dry water hole.

From there the footprints led down to the parapet of a wide bench, under which the white crust began its level monotony toward the other side of the valley. Different here was it from the place miles below where Adam had crossed.

It was lower — the bottom of the bowl. Adam found difficulty in breathing, and had sensations like intermittent rushes of blood to his head. The leaden air weighed down, and, though his keen scent could not detect any odor, he knew there was impurity of some kind on the slow wind. It reminded him that this was Death Valley. He considered a moment. If the man's tracks went on across the valley, Adam would return to camp for a canteen, then take up the trail again. But the tracks led off westward once more, straggling and aimless. Adam's stride made three of one of these steps. He did not care about the heat. That faint hint of gas, however, caused him concern. For miles he followed the straggling tracks, westward to a heave of valley slope that, according to the map of Dismukes, separated Death Valley from its mate adjoining — Lost Valley. On the left of this ridge the tracks wandered up the slope to the base of the mountain and followed it in wide scallops. The footmarks now showed the dragging of boots, and little by little they appeared fresher in the sand. This wanderer had not rested during the night.

The tracks grew deeper, more dragging, wavering from side to side. Here the man had fallen. Adam saw the imprints of his hands and a smooth furrow where evidently he had dragged a canteen across the sand. Then came the telltale signs of where he had again fallen and had begun to crawl.

"Looks like the old story," muttered Adam. "I'll just about find him dying or dead. . . . Better so — for that woman who called him husband! . . . I wonder — I wonder."

Adam's year of wandering had led him far from the haunts of men, along the lonely desert trails and roads where only a few solitary humans like himself dared the elements, or herded in sordid and hard camps; but, nevertheless, by some virtue growing out of his strife and adversity, he had come to sense something nameless, to feel the mighty beat of the heart of the desert, to hear a mourning music over the silent wastes — a still, sad music of humanity. It was there, even in the gray wastelands.

He strode on with contracted eyes, peering through the hot sunlight. At last he espied a moving object. A huge land turtle toiling along! No, it was a man crawling on hands and knees.

15
●

Adam ran with the strides of a giant. And he came up to a man, ragged and dirty, crawling wearily along, dragging a canteen through the sand.

"Say, hold on!" called Adam, loudly.

The man halted, but did not lift his head. Adam bent down to peer at him.

"What ails you?" queried Adam, sharply.

"Huh!" ejaculated the man, stupidly. Adam's repeated question, accompanied by a shake, brought only a grunt.

Adam lifted the man to his feet and, supporting him, began to lead him over the sand. His equilibrium had been upset, and, like all men overcome on the desert, he wanted to plunge off a straight line. Adam persevered, but the labor of holding him was greater than that of supporting him.

At length Adam released the straining fellow, as much out of curiosity to see what he would do as from a realization that time could not be wasted in this manner. He did not fall, but swayed and staggered around in a circle, like an animal that had been struck on the head. The texture of his ragged garments, the cut of them, the look of the man, despite his soiled and unkempt appearance, marked him as one not commonly met with in the desert.

The coppery sun stood straight overhead and poured down a strong and leaden heat. Adam calculated that they were miles from camp and would never reach it at this rate. He pondered. He must carry the man. Suiting action to thought, he picked him up and, throwing him over his shoulder, started to plod on. The weight was little to one of Adam's strength, but the squirming and wrestling of the fellow to get down made Adam flounder in the sand.

"You poor devil!" muttered Adam, at last brought to a standstill. "Maybe I can't save your life, anyway."

With that he set the man down and, swinging a powerful blow, laid him stunned upon the sand. Whereupon it was easy to lift him and throw him over a shoulder like an empty sack. Not for a long distance over the sand did that task become prodigious. But at length the burden of a heavy weight and the dragging sand and the hot sun brought Adam to a pass where rest was imperative. He laid the unconscious man down while he recovered breath and strength. Then he picked him up and went on.

After that he plodded slower, rested oftener, weakened more perceptibly. Meanwhile the hours passed, and when he reached the huge gateway in the red iron mountain wall the sun was gone and purple shadows were mustering in the valley. When he reached the more level field where the thick-strewn bowlders lay, all before his eyes seemed red. A million needles were stinging his nerves, running like spears of light into his darkened sight.

The limit that he had put upon his endurance was to reach the shack. He did so, and he was nearly blind when the woman's poignant call thrilled his throbbing ears. He saw her — a white shape through ruddy haze. Then he deposited his burden on the sand.

"Oh!" the woman moaned. "He's dead!"

Adam shook his head. Pity, fear, and even terror rang in her poignant cry, but not love.

"Ah! . . . You've saved him, then. . . . He's injured — there's a great bruise — he breathes so heavily."

While Adam sat panting, unable to speak, the woman wiped her husband's face and worked over him.

"He came back once — and fell into a stupor like this, but not so deep. What can it be?"

"Poison — air," choked Adam.

"Oh, this terrible Death Valley!" she cried.

Adam's sight cleared and he saw the woman, clad in a white robe over her gray dress, a garment clean and rich, falling in thick folds — strange to Adam's sight, recalling the past. The afterglow of sunset shone down into the valley, lighting her face. Once she must have been beautiful. The perfect lines, the noble brow, the curved lips, were there, but her face was thin, strained, tragic. Only the eyes held beauty still.

"You saved him?" she queried, with quick-drawn breath.

"Found him — miles and miles — up the — valley — crawling on — his hands and knees," panted Adam. "I had — to carry him."

"You carried him!" she exclaimed, incredulously. Then the large eyes blazed. "So that's why you were so livid — why you fell? . . . Oh, you splendid man! You giant! . . . He'd have died out there — alone. I thank you with all my heart."

She reached a white worn hand to touch Adam's with an exquisite eloquence of gratitude.

"Get water — bathe him," said Adam. "Have you ammonia or whisky?" And while he laboriously got to his knees the woman ran into the shack. He rose, feeling giddy and weak. All his muscles seemed beaten and bruised, and his heart pained. Soon the woman came hurrying out, with basin and towel and a little black satchel that evidently contained medicines. Adam helped her work over her husband, but, though they revived him, they could not bring him back to intelligent consciousness.

"Help me carry him in," said Adam.

Inside the little shack it was almost too dark to see plainly.

"Have you a light?" he added.

"No," she replied.

"I'll fetch a candle. You watch over him while I move my camp up here. You might change his shirt, if he's got another. I'll be back right away, and I'll start a fire — get some supper for us."

By the time Adam had packed and moved his effects darkness had settled down between the slopes of the mountains. After he had unpacked near the shack, his first move was to light a candle and take it to the door.

"Here's a light, ma'am," he called.

She glided silently out of the gloom, her gar-

243

ments gleaming ghostlike and her white face with its luminous eyes, dark and strange as midnight, looking like a woman's face in tragic dreams. As she took the candle her hand touched Adam's.

"Thank you," she said. "Please don't call me ma'am. My name is Magdalene Virey."

"I'll try to remember. . . . Has your husband come to yet?"

"No. He seems to have fallen into a stupor. Won't you look at him?"

Adam followed her inside and saw that she marked his lofty height. The shack had not been built for anyone of his stature.

"How tall you are!" she murmured.

The candle did not throw a bright light, yet by its aid Adam made out the features of the man whose life he had saved. It seemed to Adam to be the face of a Lucifer whose fiendish passions were now restrained by sleep. Whoever this man was, he had suffered a broken heart and ruined life.

"He's asleep," said Adam. "That's not a trance or stupor. He's worn out. I believe it'd be better not to wake him."

"You think so?" she replied, with quick relief.

"I'm not sure. Perhaps if you watch him awhile you can tell. . . . I'll get some supper and call you."

Adam's habitual dexterity over camp tasks failed him this evening. Presently, however, the supper was ready, and he threw brush on the fire to make a light.

"Mrs. Virey," he called at the door, "come and eat now."

When had the camp fire of his greeted such a vision, except in his vague dreams? Tall, white-gowned, slender, and graceful, with the poise of a woman aloof and proud and the sad face of a Madonna — what a woman to sit at Adam's camp fire in Death Valley! The shadowed and thick light hid the ravages that had by day impaired her beauty. Adam placed a canvas pack for her to sit upon, and then he served her, with something that was not wholly unconscious satisfaction. Of all men, he of the desert could tell the signs of hunger; and the impression had come to him that she was half starved. The way she ate brought home to Adam with a pang the memorable days when he was starving. This woman sitting in the warm, enhancing glow of the camp fire had an exquisitely spiritual face. She had seemed all spirit. But self-preservation was the first instinct and the first law of human nature, or any nature.

"When have I eaten so heartily!" she exclaimed at last. "But, oh! it all tasted so good. . . . Sir, you are a capital cook."

"Thank you," replied Adam, much gratified.

"Do you always fare so well?"

"No. I'm bound to confess I somewhat outdid myself to-night. You see, I seldom have such opportunity to serve a woman."

She rested her elbows on her knees, with her hands under her chin, and looked at him with intense interest. In the night her eyes seemed very full and large, supernaturally bright and tragic. They were the eyes of a woman who still preserved in her something of inherent faith in mankind. Adam divined that she had scarcely looked at him before as an individual with a personality, and that some accent or word of his had struck her singularly.

"It was that miner, Dis— Dis—"

"Dismukes," added Adam.

"Yes. It was he who sent you here. You are a miner, too?"

"No. I care little for gold."

"Ah! . . . What are you, then?"

"Just a wanderer. Wansfell, the Wanderer, they call me."

"They? Who are they?"

"Why, I suppose they are the other wanderers. Men who tramp over the desert — men who seek gold or forgetfulness or peace or solitude — men who are driven — or who hide. These are few, but, taken by the years, they seem many."

"Men of the desert have passed by here, but none like you," she replied, with gravity, and her eyes pierced him. "*Why* did you come?"

"Years ago my life was ruined," said Adam slowly. "I chose to fight the desert. And in all the years the thing that helped me most was not to pass by anyone in trouble. The desert

246

sees strange visitors. Life is naked here, like those stark mountain-sides. . . . Dismukes is my friend — he saved me from death once. He is a man who knows this wasteland. He told me about your being here. He said no white woman could live in Death Valley. . . . I wondered — if I might — at least advise you, turn you back — and so I came."

His earnestness deeply affected her.

"Sir, your kind words warm a cold and forlorn heart," she said. "But I cannot be turned back. It's too late."

"No hour is ever too late. . . . Mrs. Virey, I'll not distress you with advice or importunities. I know too well the need and the meaning of peace. But the fact of your being here — a woman of your evident quality — a woman of your sensitiveness and delicate health — why, it is a terrible thing! This is Death Valley. The month is April. Soon it will be May — then June. When mid-summer comes you cannot survive here. I know nothing of *why* you are here — I don't seek to know. But you cannot stay. It would be a miracle for your husband to find gold here, if that is what he seeks. Surely he has discovered that."

"Virey does not seek gold," the woman said.

"Does he know that a white woman absolutely cannot live here in Death Valley? Even the Indians abandon it in summer."

"He knows. There are Shoshone Indians up on the mountains now. They pack supplies to us. They have warned him."

Adam could ask no more, yet how impossible not to feel an absorbing interest in this woman's fate. As he sat with bowed head, watching the glowing and paling of the red embers, he felt her gaze upon him.

"Wansfell, you must have a great heart — like your body," she said, presently. "It is blessed to meet such a man. Your kindness, your interest, soften my harsh and bitter doubt of men. We are utter strangers. But there's something in this desert that bridges time — that bids me open my lips to you . . . a man who traveled this ghastly valley to serve me! . . . My husband, Virey, knows that Death Valley is a hell on earth. So do I. That is why he brought me . . . that is why I came!"

"My God!" breathed Adam, staring incredulously at her. Dismukes had prepared him for tragedy; the desert had shown him many dark and terrible calamities, misfortunes, mysteries; he had imagined he could no longer be thrown off his balance by amaze. But that a sad-eyed, sweet-voiced woman, whose every tone and gesture and look spoke of refinement and education, of a life infinitely removed from the wild ruggedness of the desert West — that she could intimate what seemed in one breath both murder and suicide — this staggered Adam's credulity.

Yet, as he stared at her, realizing the tremendous passion of will, of spirit, of something more that emanated from her, divining how in her case intellect and culture had been added to the eternal feminine of her nature, he knew she spoke the truth. Adam had met women on the desert, and all of them were riddles. Yet what a vast range between Margarita Arallanes and Magdalene Virey!

"Won't your husband leave — take you away from here?" asked Adam, slowly.

"No."

"We — I have a way of forcing men to see things. I suppose I —"

"Useless! We have traveled three thousand miles to get to Death Valley. Years ago Elliot Virey read about this awful place. He was always interested. He learned that it was the most arid, ghastly, desolate, and terrible place of death in all the world. . . . Then, when he got me to Sacramento — and to Placerville — he would talk with miners, prospectors, Indians — anyone who could tell him about Death Valley. . . . Virey had a reason for finding a hell on earth. We crossed the mountains, range after range — and here we are. . . . Sir, the hell of which we read — even in its bottommost pit — cannot be worse than Death Valley."

"You will let me take you home — at least out of the desert?" queried Adam, with passionate sharpness.

"Sir, I thank you again," she replied, her voice thrilling richly. "But no — no! You do not understand — you cannot — and it's impossible to explain."

"Ah! Yes, some things are. . . . Suppose you let me move your camp higher up, out of this thick, dead air and heat — where there are trees and good water?"

"But it is not a beautiful and a comfortable camp that Virey — that we want," she said, bitterly.

"Then let me move your shack across the wash out of danger. This spot is the most forbidding I ever saw. That mountain above us is on the move. The whole cracked slope is sliding like a glacier. It is an avalanche waiting for a jar — a slip — something to start it. The rocks are rolling down all the time."

"Have I not heard the rocks — cracking, ringing — in the dead of night!" she cried, shuddering. Her slender form seemed to draw within itself and the white, slim hands clenched her gown. "Rocks! How I've learned to hate them! These rolling rocks are living things. I've heard them slide and crack, roll and ring — hit the sand with a thump, and then with whistle and thud go by where I lay in the dark. . . . People who live as I have lived know nothing of the elements. I had no fear of the desert — nor of Death Valley. I dared it. I laughed to scorn the idea that any barren wild valley, any maelstrom of the sea, any Sodom of a city could be worse than the chaos of my soul. . . . But I didn't know. I am human. I'm a woman. A woman is meant to bear children. Nothing else! . . . I learned that I was afraid of the

250

dark — that such fear had been born in me. These rolling rocks got on my nerves. I wait — I listen for them. And I pray. . . . Then the silence — that became so dreadful. It is insupportable. Worse than all is the loneliness. . . . Oh, this God-forsaken, lonely Death Valley! It will drive me mad."

As Adam had anticipated, no matter what strength of will, what sense of secrecy bound this woman's lips, she had been victim to the sound of her own voice, which, liberated by his sympathy, had spoken, and a word, as it were, had led to a full, deep, passionate utterance.

"True. All too terribly true," replied Adam. "And for a woman — for you — these feelings will grow more intense. I beg of you, at least let me move your camp back out of danger."

"No! Not a single foot!" she blazed, as if confronted with something beyond his words. After that she hid her face in her hands. A long silence ensued. Adam, watching her, saw when the tremble and heave of her breast subsided. At length she looked up again, apparently composed. "Perhaps I talked more than I should have. But no matter. It was necessary to tell you something. For you came here to help an unknown woman. Not to anyone else have I breathed a word of the true state of my feelings. My husband watches me like a hawk, but not yet does he know my fears. I'll thank you, when you speak to him, if you stay here so long, not to tell him anything I've said."

"Mrs. Virey, I'll stay as long as you are here," said Adam, simply.

The simplicity of his speech, coupled with the tremendous suggestion in the fact of his physical presence, his strength and knowledge to serve her despite her bitter repudiation, seemed again to knock at the heart of her femininity. In the beginning of human life on the earth, and through its primal development, there was always a man to protect a woman. But subtly and inevitably there had been in Adam's words an intimation that Magdalene Virey stood absolutely alone. More, for with spirit, if not with body, she was fighting Death Valley, and also some terrible relation her husband bore to her.

"Sir — you would stay here — on a possible chance of serving me?" she whispered.

"Yes," replied Adam.

"Virey will not like that."

"I'm not sure, but I suspect it'll not make any difference to me what he likes."

"If you are kind to me he will drive you away," she went on, with agitation.

"Well, as he's your husband he may prevent me from being kind, but he can't drive me away."

"But suppose I ask you to go?"

"If that's the greatest kindness I can do you — well, I'll go. . . . But do you ask me?"

"I — I don't know. I may be forced to — not by *him*, but by my pride," she said, desperately. "Oh, I'm unstrung! I don't know what to say. . . . After all, just the sound of a kind voice makes me a coward. O God! if people in the world only knew the value of kindness! I never did know. . . . This desert of horrors teaches the truth of life. . . . Once I had the world at my feet! . . . Now I break and bow at the sympathy of a stranger!"

"Never mind your pride," said Adam, in his slow, cool way. "I understand. I've a good deal of woman in me. Whatever brought you to Death Valley, whatever nails you here, is nothing to me. Even if I learn it, what need that be to you? If you do not want me to stay to work for you, watch over your husband — why, let me stay for my own sake."

She rose and faced him, with soul-searching eyes. She could not escape her nature. Emotion governed her.

"Sir, you speak nobly," she replied, with lips that trembled. "But I don't understand you. Stay here — where I am — for your sake! Explain, please."

"I have my burden. Once it was even more terrible than yours. Through that I can feel as you feel now. I have lived the loneliness — the insupportable loneliness — of the desert — the silence, the heat, the hell. But my burden still weighs on my soul. If I might somehow help your husband, who is going wrong, blindly following some road of passion — change him or stop him, why that would ease my burden.

If I might save you weariness, or physical pain, or hunger, or thirst, or terror — it would be doing more for myself than for you. . . . We are in Death Valley. You refuse to leave. We are, right here, two hundred feet below sea level. When the furnace heat comes — when the blasting midnight wind comes — it means either madness or death."

"Stay — Sir Knight," she said, with a hollow, ringing gayety. "Who shall say that chivalry is dead? . . . Stay! and know this. I fear no man. I scorn death. . . . But, ah, the woman of me! I hate dirt and vermin. I'm afraid of pain. I suffer agonies even before I'm hurt. I miss so unforgettably the luxuries of life. And lastly, I have a mortal terror of going mad. Spare me that and you will have my prayers in this world — and beyond . . . . Good night."

"Good night," replied Adam.

She left him to the deepening gloom and the dying camp fire. Adam soon grew conscious of extreme fatigue in mind and body. Spreading his blankets on the sands, he stretched his weary, aching body without even an upward glance at the stars, and fell asleep.

Daylight again, as if by the opening of eyelids! The rose color was vying with the blue of the sky and a noble gold crowned the line of eastern range which Adam could see through the V-shaped split that opened into the valley. He pulled on his boots, and gave his face an unusual and detrimental luxury in the desert. Water was bad for exposed flesh in arid country. The usual spring and buoyancy of his physical being was lacking this day. Such overstrain as yesterday's would require time to be remedied. So Adam moved slowly and with caution.

First Adam went to the spring. He found a bubbling gush of velvet-looking water pouring out of a hole and running a few rods to sink into the sand. The color of it seemed inviting — so clear and soft and somehow rich. The music of its murmur, too, was melodious. Adam was a connoisseur of waters. What desert wanderer of years was not? Before he tasted this water, despite its promise, he knew it was not good. Yet it did not have exactly an unpleasant taste. Dismukes had said this water was all right, yet he seldom stayed long enough in one locality to learn the ill effects of the water. Adam knew he too could live on this water. But he was thinking of the delicate woman lost here in Death Valley with an idiot or a knave of a husband.

The spring was located some two hundred yards or more from the shack and just out of line of the rock-strewn slope. Spreading like a fan, this weathered slant of stones extended its long, curved length in the opposite direction. Adam decided to pitch his permanent camp, or at least sleeping place, here on the grass. Here he erected a brush-and-canvas shelter to make shade, and deposited his effects under it. That done, he returned to the shack to cook breakfast.

There appeared to be no life in the rude little misshapen hut. Had the man who built it ever been a boy? There were men so utterly helpless and useless out in the wilds, where existence depended upon labor of hands, that they seemed foreign to the descendants of Americans. Adam could not but wonder about the man lying in there, though he tried hard to confine his reflections to the woman. He did not like the situation. Of what avail the strong arm, the desert-taught fierceness to survive? If this man and woman had ever possessed instincts to live, to fight, to reproduce their kind, to be of use in the world, they had subverted them to the debasements of sophisticated and selfish existence. The woman loomed big to Adam, and he believed she had been dragged down by a weak and vicious man.

Leisurely Adam attended to the preparation of breakfast, prolonging tasks that always passed swiftly through his hands.

"Good morning, Sir Wansfell," called a voice with something of mockery in it, yet rich and wistful — a low-pitched contralto voice full of music and pathos and a pervading bitterness.

It stirred Adam's blood, so sluggish this morning. It seemed to carry an echo from his distant past. Turning, he saw the woman, clad in gray, with a girdle of cord twisted around her slender waist. Soft and clean and fleecy, that gray gar-

256

ment, so out of place there, so utterly incongruous against the background of crude shack and wild slope, somehow fitted her voice as it did her fragile shape, somehow set her infinitely apart from the women Adam had met in his desert wanderings. She came from the great world outside, a delicate spark from the solid flint of class, a thoroughbred whom years before the desert might have saved.

"Good morning, Mrs. Virey," returned Adam. "How are you — and did your husband awake?"

"I slept better than for long," she replied, "and I think I know why. . . . Yes, Virey came to. He's conscious, and asked for water. But he's weak — strange. I'd like you to look at him presently."

"Yes, I will."

"And how are you after your tremendous exertions of yesterday?" she inquired.

"Not so spry," said Adam, with a smile. "But I'll be myself in a day or so. I believe the air down in the valley affected me a little. My lungs are sore. . . . I think it would be more comfortable for you if we had breakfast in your kitchen. The sun is hot."

"Indeed yes. So you mean to — to do this — this camp work for me — in spite of —"

"Yes. I always oppose women," he said. "And that is about once every two or three years. You see, women are scarce on the desert."

"Last night I was upset. I am sorry that I was ungracious. I thank you, and I am only too glad to accept your kind service," she said, earnestly.

"That is well. Now, will you help me carry in the breakfast?"

Unreality was not unusual to Adam. The desert had as many unrealities, illusions, and specters as it had natural and tangible things. But while he sat opposite to this fascinating woman, whose garments exuded some subtle fragrance of perfume, whose shadowed, beautiful face shone like a cameo against the drab wall of the brush shack, he was hard put to it to convince himself of actuality. She ate daintily, but she was hungry. The gray gown fell in graceful folds around the low stone seat. The rude table between them was a box, narrow and uneven.

"Shall I try to get Virey to eat?" she asked, presently.

"That depends. On the desert, after a collapse, we are careful with food and water."

"Will you look at him?"

Adam followed her as she swept aside a flap of the canvas partition. This room was larger and lighter. It had an aperture for a window. Adam's quick glance took this in, and then the two narrow beds of blankets raised on brush cots. Virey lay on the one farther from the door. His pallid brow and unshaven face appeared drawn into terrible lines, which, of course, Adam could not be sure were permanent or the result of the collapse in the valley. He inclined, however, to the conviction that Virey's face was the distorted reflection of a tortured soul. Surely he had been handsome once. He had deep-set black eyes, a straight nose, and a mouth that betrayed him, despite its being half hidden under a mustache. Adam, keen and strung in that moment as he received his impressions of Virey, felt the woman's intensity as if he had been studying her instead of her husband. How singular women were! How could it matter to her what opinion he formed of her husband? Adam knew he had been powerfully prejudiced against this man, but he had held in stern abeyance all judgment until he could look at him. For long years Adam had gazed into the face of the desert. Outward appearance could not deceive him. As the cactus revealed its ruthless nature, as the tiny inch-high flower bloomed in its perishable but imperative proof of beauty as well as life, as the long flowing sands of the desert betrayed the destructive design of the universe — so the face of any man was the image of his soul. And Adam recoiled instinctively, if not outwardly, at what he read in Virey's face.

"You're in pain?" queried Adam.

"Yes," came the husky whisper, and Virey put a hand on his breast.

"It's sore here," said Adam, feeling Virey. "You've breathed poisoned air down in the valley. It acts like ether. . . . You just lie quiet for a while. I'll do the work around camp."

"Thank you," whispered Virey.

The woman followed Adam outside and gazed earnestly up at him, unconscious of herself, with her face closer than it had ever been to him and full in the sunlight. It struck Adam that the difference between desert flowers and the faces of beautiful women was one of emotion. How much better to have the brief hour of an unconscious flower, wasting its fragrance on the desert air!

"He's ill, don't you think?" queried the woman.

"No. But he recovers slowly. A man must have a perfect heart and powerful lungs to battle against the many perils in this country. But Virey will get over this all right."

"You never give up, do you?" she inquired.

"Come to think of that, I guess I never do," replied Adam.

"Such spirit is worthy of a better cause. You are doomed here to failure."

"Well, I'm not infallible, that's certain. But you can never tell. The fact of my standing here is proof of the overcoming of almost impossible things. I can't make Death Valley habitable for you, but I can lessen the hardships. How long have you been here?"

"Several months. But it's years to me."

"Who brought you down? How did you get here?"

"We've had different guides. The last were Shoshone Indians, who accompanied us across a range of mountains, then a valley, and last over the Panamints. They left us here. I rode a horse. Virey walked the last stages of this journey to Death Valley — from which there will be no return. We turned horse and burros loose. I have not seen them since."

"Are these Shoshones supposed to visit you occasionally?"

"Yes. Virey made a deal with them to come every full moon. We've had more supplies than we need. The trouble is that Virey has the inclination to eat, but I have not the skill to prepare food wholesomely under these rough conditions. So we almost starved."

"Well, let me take charge of camp duties. You nurse your husband and don't neglect yourself. It's the least you can do. You'll have hardship and suffering enough, even at best. You've suffered, I can see, but not physically. And you never knew what hardship meant until you got into the desert. If you *live*, these things will cure you of any trouble. They'll hardly cure Virey, for he has retrograded. Most men in the desert follow the line of least resistance. They sink. But *you* will not. . . . And let me tell you. There are elemental pangs of hunger, of thirst, of pain that are blessings in disguise. You'll learn what rest is and sleep and loneliness. People who live as you have lived are lopsided. What do they know of life close to the earth? Any other life is false. Cities, swarms of men and women, riches, luxury, poverty — these

261

were not in nature's scheme of life. . . . Mrs. Virey, if anything *can* change your soul it will be the desert."

"Ah, Sir Wansfell, so you have philosophy as well as chivalry," she replied, with the faint accent that seemed to be mockery of herself. "Change my soul if you can, wanderer of the desert! I am a woman, and a woman is symbolical of change. Teach me to cook, to work, to grow strong, to endure, to fight, to look up at those dark hills whence cometh your strength. . . . I am here in Death Valley. I will never leave it in body. My bones will mingle with the sands and molder to dust. . . . But my soul — ah! that black gulf of doubt, of agony, of terror, of hate — change *that* if you can."

These tragic, eloquent words chained Adam to Death Valley as if they had been links of steel; and thus began his long sojourn there.

Work or action was always necessary to Adam. They had become second nature. He planned a brush shelter from the sun, a sort of outside room adjoining the shack, a stone fireplace and table and seats, a low stone wall to keep out blowing sand, and a thick, heavy stone fence between the shack and the slope of sliding rocks. When these tasks were finished there would be others, and always there would be the slopes to climb, the valley to explore. Idleness in Death Valley was a forerunner of madness. There must be a reserve fund of long work and exercise, so that when the blazing, leaden-hazed middays of August came, with idleness imperative, there would be both physical force and unclouded mind to endure them. The men who succumbed to madness in this valley were those who had not understood how to combat it.

That day passed swiftly, and the twilight hour seemed to have less of gloom and forbidding intimations. That might well have been due to his eternal hope. Mrs. Virey showed less gravity and melancholy, and not once did she speak with bitterness or passion. She informed Adam that Virey had improved.

Two more days slipped by, and on the third Virey got up and came forth into the sunlight. Adam happened to be at work near by. He saw Virey gaze around at the improvements that had been made and say something about them to his wife. He looked a man who should have been in the prime of life. Approaching with slow gait and haggard face, he addressed Adam.

"You expect pay for this puttering around?"

"No," replied Adam, shortly.

"How's that?"

"Well, when men are used to the desert, as I am, they lend a hand where it is needed. That's not often."

"But I didn't want any such work done round my camp."

"I know, and I excuse you because you're ignorant of desert ways and needs."

"The question of excuse for me is offensive."

263

Adam, rising abreast of the stone wall he was building, fixed his piercing eyes upon this man. Mrs. Virey stood a little to one side, but not out of range of Adam's gaze. Did a mocking light show in her shadowy eyes? The doubt, the curiosity in her expression must have related to Adam. That slight, subtle something about her revealed to Adam the inevitableness of disappointment in store for him if he still entertained any hopes of amenable relations with Virey.

"We all have to be excused sometimes," said Adam, deliberately. "Now I had to excuse you on the score of ignorance of the desert. You chose this place as a camp. It happens to be the most dangerous spot I ever saw. Any moment a stone may roll down that slope to kill you. Any moment the whole avalanche may start. That slope is an avalanche."

"It's my business where I camp," rejoined Virey.

"Were you aware of the danger here?"

"I am indifferent to danger."

"But you are not alone. You have a woman with you."

Manifestly, Virey had been speaking without weighing words and looking at Adam without really seeing him. The brooding shade passed out of his eyes, and in its place grew a light of interest that leaped to the crystal-cold clearness of a lens.

"You're a prospector," he asserted.

"No. I pan a little gold dust once in a while for fun, because I happen across it."

"You're no miner, then — nor hunter, nor teamster."

"I've been a little of all you name, but I can't be called any one of them."

"You might be one of the robbers that infest these hills."

"I might be, only I'm not," declared Adam, dryly. The fire in his depths stirred restlessly, but he kept a cool, smothering control over it. He felt disposed to be lenient and kind toward this unfortunate man. If only the woman had not stood there with that half-veiled mocking shadow of doubt in her eyes!

"You're an educated man!" ejaculated Virey, incredulously.

"I might claim to be specially educated in the ways of the desert."

"And the ways of women, are *they* mysteries to you?" queried Virey, with scorn. His interrogation seemed like a bitter doubt flung out of an immeasurable depth of passion.

"I confess that they are," replied Adam. "I've lived a lonely life. Few women have crossed my trail."

"You don't realize your good fortune — if you tell the truth."

"I would not lie to any man," returned Adam, bluntly.

"Bah! Men are all liars, and women make them so. . . . You're hanging round my camp,

265

making a bluff of work."

"I deny that. Heaving these stones is work. *You* lift a few of them in this hot sun. . . . And my packing you on my back for ten miles over the floor of Death Valley — was that bluff?"

"You saved my life!" exclaimed the man, stung to passion. There seemed to be contending tides within him — a fight of old habits of thought, fineness of feeling, against an all-absorbing and dominating malignancy. "Man, I can't thank you for that. . . . You've done me no service."

"I don't want or expect thanks. I was thinking of the effort it cost me."

"As a man who was once a gentleman, I do thank you — which is a courtesy due my past. But now that you have put me in debt for a service I didn't want, why do you linger here?"

"I wish to help your wife."

"Ah! that's frank of you. That frankness is something for which I really thank you. But you'll pardon me if I'm inclined to doubt the idealistic nature of your motive to help her."

Adam pondered over this speech without reply. Words always came fluently when he was ready to speak. And he seemed more concerned over Virey's caustic bitterness than over his meaning. Then, as he met the magnificent flash in Magdalene Virey's eyes, he was inspired into revelation of Virey's veiled hint and into a serenity he divined would be kindest to her pride.

"Go ahead and help her," Virey went on.

"You have my sincere felicitations. My charming wife is helpless enough. I never knew how helpless till we were thrown upon our own resources. She cannot even cook a potato. And as for baking bread in one of those miserable black ovens, stranger, if you eat some of it I will not be long annoyed by your attentions to her."

"Well, I'll teach her," said Adam.

His practical response irritated Virey excessively. It was as if he wished to insult and inflame, and had not considered a literal application to his words.

"Who are you? What's your name?" he queried, yielding to a roused curiosity.

"Wansfell," replied Adam.

"Wansfell?" echoed Virey. The name struck a chord of memory — a discordant one. He bent forward, a little, at a point between curiosity and excitement. "Wansfell? . . . I know that name. Are you the man who in this desert country is called Wansfell the Wanderer?"

"Yes, I'm that Wansfell."

"I heard a prospector tell about you," went on Virey, his haggard face now quickened by thought. "It was at a camp near a gold mine over here somewhere — I forget where. But the prospector said he had seen you kill a man named Mc something— McKin — no, McKue. That's the name. . . . Did he tell the truth?"

"Yes, I'm sorry to say. I killed Baldy McKue — or rather, to speak as I feel, I was the means

267

by which the desert dealt McKue the death justly due him."

Virey now glowed with excitement, changing the man.

"Somehow that story haunted me," he said. "I never heard one like it. . . . This prospector told how you confronted McKue in the street of a mining camp. In front of a gambling hell, or maybe it was a hotel. You yelled like a demon at McKue. He turned white as a sheet. He jerked his gun, began to shoot. But you bore a charmed life. His bullets did not hit you, or, if they did, to no purpose. You leaped upon him. His gun flew one way, his hat another. . . . Then — then you killed him with your hands! . . . Is that true?"

Adam nodded gloomily. The tale, told vividly by this seemingly galvanized Virey, was not pleasant. And the woman stood there, transfixed, with white face and tragic eyes.

"My God! You killed McKue by sheer strength — with your bare hands! . . . I had not looked at your hands. I see them now. . . . So McKue was your enemy?"

"No. I never saw him before that day," replied Adam.

Virey slowly drew back wonderingly, yet with instinctive shrinking. Certain it was that his lips stiffened.

"Then why did you kill him?"

"He ill-treated a woman."

Adam turned away as he replied. He did not

268

choose then to show in his eyes the leaping thought that had been born of the memory and of Virey's strange reaction. But he heard him draw a quick, sharp breath and step back. Then a silence ensued. Adam gazed up at the endless slope, at the millions of rocks, all apparently resting lightly in their pockets, ready to plunge down.

"So that was it," spoke up Virey, evidently with effort. "I always wondered. Wild West sort of story, you know. Strange I should meet you. . . . Thanks for telling me. I gather it wasn't pleasant for you."

"It's sickening to recall, but I have no regrets," replied Adam.

"Quite so. I understand. Man of the desert — ruthless — inhuman sort of thing."

"Inhuman?" queried Adam, and he looked at Virey, at last stung. Behind Virey's pale, working face and averted eyes Adam read a conscience in tumult, a spirit for the moment terrorized. "Virey, you and I'd never agree on meanings of words. . . . I broke McKue's arms and ribs and legs, and while I cracked them I told him what an inhuman dastard he had been — to ruin a girl, to beat her, to abandon her and her baby — to leave them to die. I told him how I had watched them die . . . then I broke his neck! . . . McKue was the inhuman man — not I."

Virey turned away, swaying a little, and his white hand, like a woman's, sought the stone wall for support, until he reached the shack, which he entered.

"I'm sorry, Mrs. Virey, that story had to come up," said Adam, confronting her with reluctance. But she surprised him again. He expected to find her sickened, shrinking from him as a bloody monster, perhaps half fainting; he found, however, that she seemed serene, controlling deep emotions which manifested themselves only in the marble whiteness of her cheek, the strained darkness of her eye.

"The story was beautiful. I had not heard it," she said, and the rich tremor of her voice thrilled Adam: "What woman would not revel in such a story? . . . Wansfell the Wanderer. It should be Sir Wansfell, Knight of the Desert! . . . Don't look at me so. Have you not learned that the grandest act on earth is when a man fights for the honor or love or happiness or life of a woman? . . . I am a woman. Many men have loved me. Virey's love is so strong that it is hate. But no man ever yet thought of *me* — no man ever yet heard the little songs that echoed through my soul — no man ever fought to save *me!* . . . My friend, I dare speak as you speak, with the nakedness of the desert. And so I tell you that just now I watched my husband — I listened to the words which told his nature, as if that was new to me. I watched you stand there — I listened to you. . . . And so I dare to tell you — if you come to fight my battles I shall have added to my life of shocks

270

and woes a trouble that will dwarf all the others
. . . the awakening of a woman who has been
blind! . . . The facing of my soul — perhaps
its salvation! A crowning agony — a glory come
too late!"

16
●

At sunset Adam cooked supper for the Vireys,
satisfying his own needs after they had finished.
Virey talked lightly, even joked about the first
good meal he had sat down to on the desert.
His wife, too, talked serenely, sometimes with
the faintly subtle mockery, as if she had never
intimated that a dividing spear threatened her
heart. That was their way to hide the truth
and emotion when they willed. But Adam was
silent.

Alone, out under the shadow of the towering
gate to the valley, he strode to and fro, absorbed
in a maze of thoughts that gradually cleared,
as if by the light of the solemn stars and virtue
of the speaking silence. He had chanced upon
the strangest and most fatal situation in all his
desert years. Yes, but was it by chance? Straight
as an arrow he had come across the barrens
to meet a wonderful woman who was going to

love him, and a despicable man whom he was going to kill. That seemed the fatality which rang in his ears, shone in the accusing stars, hid in the heavy shadows. It was a matter of feeling. His intelligence could not grasp it. Had he been in Death Valley four days or four months? Was he walking in his sleep, victim of a nightmare? The desert, faithful always, answered him. This was nothing but the flux and reflux of human passion, contending tides between man and woman, the littleness, the curse, the terror, and yet the joy of life. Death Valley yawned at his feet, changeless and shadowy, awful in its locked solemnity of solitude, its voicelessness, its desolation that had been desolation in past ages. He could doubt nothing there. His thoughts seemed almost above human error. A spirit spoke for him.

Virey had dragged his wife to this lonely and dismal hell hole on earth to share his misery, to isolate her from men, to hide her glory of charm, to gloat over her loneliness, to revenge himself for a wrong, to feed his need of possession, his terrible love that had become hate, to watch the slow torture of her fading, wilting, drooping in this ghastly valley, to curse her living, to burn endlessly in torment because her soul would elude him forever, to drive her to death and die with her.

Death Valley seemed a harmonious setting for this tragedy and a fitting grave for its actors. The worst in nature calling to the darkest in mankind! What a pity Virey could not divine his littleness — that he had been a crawling maggot in the peopled ulcer of the world — that in the great spaces where the sun beat down was a fiery cleansing!

But Magdalene Virey was a riddle beyond solving. Nevertheless, Adam pondered every thought that would stay before his consciousness. Any woman was a riddle. Did not the image of Margarita Arallanes flash up before him — that dusky-eyed, mindless, soulless little animal, victim of nature born in her? Adam's thought halted with the seeming sacrilege of associating Magdalene Virey with memory of the Mexican girl. This Virey woman had complexity — she had mind, passion, nobility, soul. What had she done to earn her husband's hate? She had never loved him — that was as fixed in Adam's sight as the North Star. Nor had she loved another man, at least not with the passion and spirit of her wonderful womanhood. Adam divined that with the intensity of feeling which the desert loneliness and solitude had taught him. He could have felt the current of any woman's great passion, whether it was in torrent, full charged and devastating, or at its lowering ebb. But, as inevitable as was life itself, there was the mysterious certainty that Magdalene Virey had terribly wronged her husband. How? Adam had repudiated any interest in what had driven them here; not until this moment had he permitted his doubt to insult the woman. Yet how helpless he was! His heart was full of unutterable pity. He could never have loved Magdalene Virey as a man, but as a brother he was yearning to change her, save her. What else in life was worth living for, except only the dreams on the heights, the walks along the lonely trails? By his own agony he had a strange affinity for anyone in trouble, especially a woman, and how terribly he saw the tragedy of Magdalene Virey! And it was not only her death that he saw. Death in a land where death reigned was nothing. For her he hated the certainty of physical pain, the turgid pulse, the redhot iron band at the temples, the bearing down of weighted air, the drying up of flesh and blood. More than all he hated the thought of death of her spirit while her body lived. There would be a bloodless murder long before her blood stained Virey's hands.

But this thought gave Adam pause. Was he not dealing with a personality beyond his power to divine? What did he know of this strange woman? He knew naught, but felt all. She was beautiful, compelling, secretive, aloof, and proud, magnificent as a living flame. She was mocking because knowledge of the world, of the frailty of women and falsity of men, had been as an open page. She had lived in sight of the crowded mart, the show places where men and women passed, knowing no more of earth than that it was a place for graves. She was bitter because she had drunk bitterness to the dregs. But the sudden up-flashing warmth of her, forced out of her reserve, came from a heart of golden fire. Adam constituted himself an omniscient judge, answerable only to his conscience. By all the gods he would be true to the truth of this woman!

Never had she been forced into this desert of desolation. That thought of Adam's seemed far back in the past. She had dared to come. Had Death Valley and the death it was famed for any terrors for her? By the side of her husband she had willingly come, unutterably despising him, infinitely brave where he was cowardly, scornfully and magnificently prepared to meet any punishment that might satisfy him. Adam saw how, in this, Magdalene Virey was answering to some strange need in itself. Let the blind, weak, egoist Virey demand the tortures of the damned! She would pay. But she was paying also a debt to herself. Adam's final conception of Magdalene Virey was that she had been hideously wronged by life, by men; that in younger days of passionate revolt she had transgressed the selfish law of husbands; that in maturer years, with the storm and defeat and disillusion of womanhood, she had risen to the heights, she had been true to herself; and with mockery of the man who could so underestimate her, who dared believe he could make her a craven, whimpering, guilty wretch, she had faced the desert with him. She had seen the great love that was not love change to terrible

275

hate. She had divined the hidden motive. She let him revel in his hellish secret joy. She welcomed Death Valley.

Adam marveled at this unquenchable spirit, this sublime effrontery of a woman. And he hesitated to dare to turn that spirit from its superb indifference. But this vacillation in him was weak. What a wonderful experience it would be to embody in Magdalene Virey the instinct, the strife, the nature of the desert! With her mind, if he had the power to teach, she would grasp the lesson in a single day.

And lastly, her unforgettable implication, "the crowning agony," of what he might bring upon her. There could be only one interpretation of that — love. The idea thrilled him, but only with wonder and pity. It took possession of Adam's imagination. Well, such love might come to pass! The desert storms bridged canyons with sand in one day. It was a place of violence. The elements waited not upon time or circumstance. The few women Adam had come in contact with on the desert had loved him. Even the one-eyed Mohave Jo, that hideous, unsexed, monstrous deformity of a woman, whom he had met and left groveling in the sand at his feet, shamed at last before a crowd of idle, gaping, vile men — even she had awakened to this strange madness of love. But Adam had not wanted that of any woman, since the poignant moment of his youth on the desert, when the dusky-eyed Margarita had murmured of love so fresh and sweet to him, "Ah, so long ago and far away!"

Least of all did Adam want the love of Magdalene Virey. "If she were young and I were young! Or if she had never . . . !" Ah! even possibilities, like might-have-beens, were useless dreams. But the die was cast. Serve Magdalene Virey he would, and teach her the secret of the strength of the sand wastes and the lonely hills, and that the victory of life was not to yield. Fight for her, too, he would. In all the multiplicity of ways he had learned, he would fight the solitude and loneliness of Death Valley, the ghastliness so inimical to the creative life of a woman, the heat, the thirst, the starvation, poison air, the furnace wind, storm and flood and avalanche. Just as naturally, if need be, if it fatefully fell out so, he would lay his slaying hands in all their ruthless might upon the man who had made her dare her doom.

When, next morning at sunrise hour, Adam presented himself at the Virey camp, he was greeted by Mrs. Virey, seemingly a transformed woman. She wore a riding suit, the worn condition of which attested to the rough ride across the mountain. What remarkable difference it made in her appearance! It detracted from her height. And the slenderness of her, revealed rather than suggested by her gowns, showed much of grace and symmetry. She had braided her hair and let it hang. When the sun had tanned her white face and hands Magdalene Virey would really be transformed.

Adam tried not to stare, but his effort was futile.

"Good morning," she said, with a bright smile.

"Why, Mrs. Virey, I — I hardly knew you!" he stammered.

"Thanks. I feel complimented. It is the first time you've looked at *me*. Shorn of my dignity — no, my worldliness, do I begin well, desert man? . . . No more stuffy dresses clogging my feet! No more veils to protect my face! Let the sun burn! I want to work. I want to help. I want to learn. If madness must be mine, let it be a madness to learn what in this God-forsaken land ever made you the man you are. There, Sir Wansfell, I have flung down the gage."

"Very well," replied Adam, soberly.

"And now," she continued, "I am eager to work. If I blunder, be patient. If I am stupid, make me see. And if I faint in the sun or fall beside the trail, remember it is my poor body that fails, and not my will."

So, in the light of her keen interest, Adam found the humdrum mixing of dough and the baking of bread a pleasure and a lesson to him, rather than a task.

"Ah, how important are the homely things of life!" she said. "A poet said 'we live too much in the world.' . . . I wonder did he mean just this. We grow away from or never learn the simple things. I remember my grandfather's farm — the plowed fields, the green corn, the yellow wheat, the chickens in the garden, the mice in the barn, the smell of hay, the smell of burning leaves, the smell of the rich brown earth. . . . Wansfell, not for years have I remembered them. Something about you, the way you work over that bread, like a nice old country lady, made me remember. . . . Oh, I wonder what I have missed!"

"We all miss something. It can't be helped. But there are compensations, and it's never too late."

"You are a child, with all your bigness. You have the mind of a child."

"That's one of my few blessings. . . . Now you try your hand at mixing the second batch of dough."

She made a picture on her knees, with her sleeves rolled up, her beautiful hands white with flour, her face beginning to flush. Adam wanted to laugh at her absolute failure to mix dough, and at the same moment he had it in him to weep over the earnestness, the sadness, the pathetic meaning of her.

Eventually they prepared the meal, and she carried Virey's breakfast in to him. Then she returned to eat with Adam.

"I shall wash the dishes," she announced.

"No," he protested.

Then came a clash. It ended with a compromise. And from that clash Adam realized he might dominate her in little things, but in a great conflict of wills she would be the stronger. It was a step in his own slow education. There was a constitutional difference between men and women.

Upon Adam's resumption of the work around the shack Mrs. Virey helped him as much as he would permit, which by midday was somewhat beyond her strength. Her face sunburned rosily and her hands showed the contact with dirt and her boots were dusty.

"You mustn't overdo it," he advised. "Rest and sleep during the noon hours."

She retired within the shack and did not reappear till the middle of the afternoon. Meanwhile, Adam had worked at his tasks, trying at the same time to keep an eye on Virey, who wandered around aimlessly over the rock-strewn field, idling here and plodding there. Adam saw how Virey watched the shack; and when Magdalene came out again he saw her and grew as motionless as the stone where he leaned. Every thought of Virey's must have been dominated by this woman's presence, the meaning of her, the possibilities of her, the tragedy of her.

"Oh, how I slept!" she exclaimed. "Is it work that makes you sleep?"

"Indeed yes."

"Ah! I see my noble husband standing like Mephistopheles, smiling at grief. . . . What's he doing over there?"

"I don't know, unless it's watching for you. He's been around like that for hours."

"Poor man!" she said, with both compassion and mockery. "Watching me? What loss of precious time — and so futile! It is a habit he contracted some years ago. . . . Wansfell, take me down to the opening in the mountain there, so that I can look into Death Valley."

"Shall I ask Virey?" queried Adam, in slight uncertainty.

"No. Let him watch or follow or do as he likes. I am here in Death Valley. It was his cherished plan to bury me here. I shall not leave until he takes me — which will be never. For the rest, he is nothing to me. We are as far apart as the poles."

On the way down the gentle slope Adam halted amid sun-blasted shrubs, scarcely recognizable as greasewood. Here he knelt in the gravel to pluck some flowers so tiny that only a trained eye could ever have espied them. One was a little pink flower with sage color and sage odor; another a white daisy, very frail, and without any visible leaves; and a third was a purple-red flower, half the size of the tiniest buttercup, and this had small dark-green leaves.

"Flowers in Death Valley!" exclaimed Mrs. Virey, in utter amaze.

"Yes. Flowers of a day! They sprang up yesterday; to-day they bloom, to-morrow they will die. I don't know their names. To me their blossoming is one of the wonders of the desert.

I think sometimes that it is a promise. A whole year the tiny seeds lie in the hot sands. Then comes a mysterious call and the green plant shoots its inch-long stalk to the sun. Another day beauty unfolds and there is fragrance on the desert air. Another day sees them wither and die."

"Beauty and fragrance indeed they have," mused the woman. "Such tiny flowers to look and smell so sweet! I never saw their like. Flowers of a day! . . . They indeed give rise to thoughts too deep for tears!"

Adam led his companion to the base of the mountain wall, and around the corner of the opening, so that they came suddenly and unexpectedly into full view of Death Valley. He did not look at her. He wanted to wait a little before doing that. The soft gasp which escaped her lips and the quick grasping of his hand were significant of the shock she sustained.

Their position faced mostly down the valley. It seemed a vast level, gently sloping up to the borders where specks of mesquite dotted the sand. Dull gray and flat, these league-wide wastes of speckled sand bordered a dazzling-white sunlit belt, the winding bottom of the long bowl, the salty dead stream of Death Valley. Miles and miles below, two mountain ranges blended in a purple blaze, and endless slanting lines of slopes ran down to merge in the valley floor. The ranges sent down offshoots of mountains that slanted and lengthened into the valley.

One bright-green oasis, that, lost in the vastness, was comparable to one of the tiny flowers Adam had plucked out of the sand, shone wonderfully and illusively out of the glare of gray and white. A dim, mystic scene!

"O God! . . . It is my grave!" cried Magdalene Virey.

"We all are destined for graves," replied Adam, solemnly. "Could any grave elsewhere be so grand — so lonely — so peaceful? . . . Now let us walk out a little way, to the edge of that ridge, and sit there while the sun sets."

On this vantage point they were out some distance in the valley, so that they could see even the western end of the Panamint range, where a glaring sun had begun to change its color over the bold black peaks. A broad shadow lengthened across the valley and crept up the yellow foothills to the red Funeral Mountains. This shadow marvelously changed to purple, and as the radiance of light continued to shade, the purple deepened. Over all the valley at the western end appeared a haze the color of which was nameless. Adam felt the lessening heat of the sinking sun. Half that blaze was gone. It had been gold and was now silver. He swept his gaze around jealously, not to miss the transformations; and his companion, silent and absorbed, instinctively turned with him. Across the valley the Funerals towered, ragged and sharp, with rosy crowns; and one, the only dome-shaped peak, showed its strata of gray and drab through the rose. Another peak, farther back, lifted a pink shaft into the blue sky. What a contrast to the lower hills and slopes, so beautifully pearl gray in tint! And now, almost the instant Adam had marked the exquisite colors, they began to fade. On that illimitable horizon line there were soon no bright tones left. Far to the south, peaks that had been dim now stood out clear and sharp against the sky. One, gold capped and radiant, shadowed as if a cloud had come between it and the sun. Adam turned again to the west, in time to see the last vestige of silver fire vanish. Sunset!

A somber smoky sunset it was now, as if this Death Valley was the gateway of hell and its sinister shades were upflung from fire. Adam saw a vulture sail across the clear space of sky, breasting the wind. It lent life to the desolation.

The desert day was done and the desert shades began to descend. The moment was tranquil and sad. It had little to do with the destiny of man — nothing except that by some inscrutable design of God or an accident of evolution man happened to be imprisoned where nature never intended man to be. Death Valley was only a ragged rent of the old earth, where men wandered wild, brooding, lost, or where others sought with folly and passion to dig forth golden treasure. The mysterious lights changed. A long pale radiance appeared over the western range and lengthened along its bold horizon. The only red color left was way to the south, and that

284

shone dim. The air held a solemn stillness.

"Magdalene Virey," said Adam, "what you see there resembles death — it may be death — but it is peace. Does it not rest your troubled soul? A woman must be herself here."

She, whose words could pour out in such torrent of eloquence, was silent now. Adam looked at her then, into the shadowed eyes. What he saw there awed him. The abyss seen through those beautiful, unguarded windows of her soul was like the gray scored valley beneath, but lighting, quickening with thought, with hope, with life. Death Valley was a part of the earth dying, and it would become like a canyon on the burned-out moon; but this woman's spirit seemed everlasting. If her soul had been a whited sepulcher, it was in the way of transfiguration. Adam experienced a singular exaltation in the moment, a gladness beyond his comprehension, a sense that the present strange communion there between this woman's awakening and the terrible lessons of his life was creating for him a far-distant interest, baffling, but great in its inspiration.

In the gathering twilight he led her back to camp, content that it seemed still impossible for her to speak. But the touch of her hand at parting was more eloquent than any words.

Then alone, in his blankets, with gaze up at the inscrutable, promising stars, Adam gave himself over to insistent and crowding thoughts, back of which throbbed a dominating, divine hope in his power to save this woman's life and soul, and perhaps even her happiness.

Next day Adam's natural aggressiveness asserted itself, controlled now by an imperturbable spirit that nothing could daunt. He approached Virey relentlessly, though with kindness, even good nature, and he began to talk about Death Valley, the perilous nature of the camping spot, the blasting heat of midsummer and the horror of the midnight furnace winds, the possibility of the water drying up. Virey was cold, then impatient, then intolerant, and finally furious. First he was deaf to Adam's persuasion, then he tried to get out of listening, then he repudiated all Adam had said, and finally he raved and cursed. Adam persisted in his arguments until Virey strode off.

Mrs. Virey heard some of this clash. Apparently Adam's idea of changing her husband amused her. But when Virey returned for supper he was glad enough to eat, and when Adam again launched his argument it appeared that Mrs. Virey lost the last little trace of mockery. She listened intently while Adam told her husband why he would have to take his wife away from Death Valley before midsummer. Virey might as well have been stone deaf. It was not Virey, however, who interested the woman, but something about Adam that made her look and listen thoughtfully.

Thus began a singular time for Adam, unmatched in all his desert experience. He gave his whole heart to the task of teaching Magdalene Virey and to the wearing down of Virey's will. All the lighter tasks that his hands had learned he taught her. Then to climb to the heights, to pick the ledges for signs of gold or pan the sandy washes, to know the rocks and the few species of vegetation, to recognize the illusion of distance and color, to watch the sunsets and the stars became daily experiences. Hard as work was for her delicate hands and muscles, he urged her to their limit. During the first days she suffered sunburn, scalds, skinned fingers, bruised knees, and extreme fatigue. When she grew tanned and stronger he led her out on walks and climbs so hard that he had to help her back to camp. She learned the meaning of physical pain, and to endure it. She learned the blessing it was to eat when she was famished, to rest when she was utterly weary, to sleep when sleep was peace.

Through these brief, full days Adam attacked Virey at every opportunity, which time came to be, at length, only during meals. Virey would leave camp, often to go up the slope of weathered rocks, a dangerous climb that manifestly fascinated him. Reaching a large rock that became his favorite place, he would perch there for long hours, watching, gazing down like a vulture waiting for time to strike its prey. All about him seemed to suggest a brooding wait. He slept during the midday hours and through the long nights. At dusk, which was usually bedtime for all, Adam often heard him talking to Mrs. Virey in a low, hard, passionate voice. Sometimes her melodious tones, with the mockery always present when she spoke to her husband, thrilled Adam, while at the same moment it filled him with despair. But Adam never despaired of driving Virey to leave the valley. The man was weak in all ways except that side which pertained to revenge. Notwithstanding the real and growing obstacle of this passion, Adam clung to his conviction that in the end Virey would collapse. When, however, one day the Indians came, and Virey sent them away with a large order for supplies, Adam gave vent to a grim thought, "Well, I can always kill him."

All the disgust and loathing Adam felt for this waster of life vanished in the presence of Magdalene Virey. If that long-passed sunset hour over Death Valley had awakened the woman, what had been the transformation of the weeks? Adam had no thoughts that adequately expressed his feeling for the change in her. It gave him further reverence for desert sun and heat and thirst and violence and solitude. It gave him strange new insight into the mystery of life. Was any healing of disease or agony impossible — any change of spirit — any renewal of life? Nothing in relation to human life was impossible. Magnificently the desert magnified and multiplied time, thought, effort, pain, health, hope

— all that could be felt.

It seemed to Adam that through the physical relation to the desert he was changing Magdalene Virey's body and heart and soul. Brown her face and hands had grown; and slowly the graceful, thin lines of her slender body had begun to round out. She was gaining. If it had not been for her shadowed eyes, and the permanent sadness and mockery in the beautiful lips, she would have been like a girl of eighteen. Her voice, too, with its contralto richness, its mellow depth, its subtle shades of tone, proclaimed the woman. Adam at first had imagined her to be about thirty years old, but as time passed by, and she grew younger with renewed strength, he changed his mind. Looking at her to guess her age was like looking at the desert illusions. Absolute certainty he had, however, of the reward and result of her inflexible will, of splendid spirit, of sincere gladness. She had endured physical toil and pain to the limit of her frail strength, until she was no longer frail. This spirit revived what had probably been early childish love of natural things; and action and knowledge developed it until her heart was wholly absorbed in all that it was possible to do there in that lonesome fastness. With the genius and intuition of a woman she had grasped at the one solace left her — the possibility of learning Adam's lesson of the desert. What had taken him years to acquire she learned from him or divined in days.

She had a wonderful mind.

Once, while they were resting upon a promontory that overhung the valley, Adam spoke to her. She did not hear him. Her eyes reflected the wonder and immensity of the waste beneath her. Indeed, she did not appear to be brooding or thinking. And when he spoke again, breaking in upon her abstraction, she was startled. He forgot what he had intended to say, substituting a query as to her thoughts.

"How strange!" she murmured. "I didn't have a thought. I forgot where I was. Your voice seemed to come from far off."

"I spoke to you before, but you didn't hear," said Adam. "You looked sort of, well — watchful, I'd call it."

"Watchful? Yes, I was. I feel I was, but I don't remember. This is indeed a strange state for Magdalene Virey. It behooves her to cultivate it. But what kind of a state was it? . . . Wansfell, could it have been happiness?"

She asked that in a whisper, serious, and with pathos, yet with a smile.

"It's always happiness for me to watch from the heights. Surely you are finding happy moments?"

"Yes, many, thanks to you, my friend. But they are conscious happy moments, just sheer joy of movement, or sight of beauty, or a thrill of hope, or perhaps a vague dream of old, far-off, unhappy things. And it *is* happiness to remember them. . . . But this was different. It was unconscious. I tell you, Wansfell, I did not have a thought in my mind! I saw — I watched. Oh, how illusive it is!"

"Try to recall it," he suggested, much interested.

"I try — I try," she said, presently, "but the spell is broken."

"Well, then, let me put a thought into your mind," went on Adam. "Dismukes and I once had a long talk about the desert. Why does it fascinate all men? What is the secret? Dismukes didn't rate himself high as a thinker. But he is a thinker. He knows the desert. To me he's great. And he and I agreed that the commonly accepted idea of the desert's lure is wrong. Men seek gold, solitude, forgetfulness. Some wander for the love of wandering. Others seek to hide from the world. Criminals are driven to the desert. Besides these, all travelers crossing the desert talk of its enchantments. They all have different reasons. Loneliness, peace, silence, beauty, wonder, sublimity — a thousand reasons! Indeed, they are all proofs of the strange call of the desert. But these men do not go deep enough."

"Have you solved the secret?" she asked, wonderingly.

"No, not yet," he replied, a little sadly. "It eludes me. It's like finding the water of the mirage."

"It's like the secret of a woman's heart, Wansfell."

291

"Then if that is so — tell me."

"Ah! no woman ever tells that secret."

"Have you come to love the desert?"

"You ask me that often," she replied, in perplexity. "I don't know. I — I reverence — I fear — I thrill. But love — I can't say that I love the desert. Not yet. Love comes slowly and seldom to me. I loved my mother. . . . Once I loved a horse."

"Have you loved men?" he queried.

"No!" she flashed, in sudden passion, and her eyes burned dark on his. "Do *you* imagine that of me? . . . I was eighteen when I — when they married me to Virey. I despised him. I learned to loathe him. . . . Wansfell, I never really loved any man. Once I was mad — driven!"

How easily could Adam strike the chords of her emotion and rouse her to impassioned speech! His power to do this haunted him, and sometimes he could not resist it until wistfulness or trouble in her eyes made him ashamed.

"Some day I'll tell you how *I* was driven once — ruined," he said.

"Ruined! You? Why, Wansfell, you are a man! Sometimes I think you're a god of the desert! . . . But tell me — what ruined you, as you mean it?"

"No, not now. I'm interested in your — what is it? — your lack of power to love."

"Lack! How little you know me! I am *all* power to love. I am a quivering mass of exquisitely delicate, sensitive nerves. I am a seething torrent of hot blood. I am an empty heart, deep and terrible as this valley, hungry for love as it is hungry for precious rain or dew. I am an illimitable emotion, heaving like the tides of the sea. I am all love."

"And I — only a stupid blunderer," said Adam.

"You use a knife relentlessly, sometimes. . . . Wansfell, listen. . . . I have a child — a lovely girl. She is fourteen years old — the sweetest . . . Ah! Before she was born I did not love her — I did not *want* her. But afterward! . . . Wansfell, a mother's love is divine. But I had more than that. All — all my heart went out to Ruth. . . . *Love!* Oh, my God! does any man know the torture of love? . . . Oh, *I* know! I had to leave her — I had to give her up . . . and I'll never — never see — her — again!"

The woman bowed with hands to her face and all her slender body shook.

"Forgive me!" whispered Adam, huskily, in distress. It was all he could say for a moment. She had stunned him. Never had he imagined her as a mother. "Yet — yet I'm glad I know now. You should have told me. I am your friend. I've tried to be a — a brother. Tell me, Magdalene. You'll be the less troubled. I will help you. I think I understand — just a little. You seemed to me only a very young woman — and you're a mother! Always I say I'll never

293

be surprised again. Why, the future is all surprise! . . . And your little girl's name is Ruth? Ruth Virey. What a pretty name!"

Adam had rambled on, full of contrition, hating himself, trying somehow to convey sympathy. Perhaps his words, his touch on her bowed shoulder, helped her somewhat, for presently she sat up, flung back her hair, and turned a tear-stained face to him. How changed, how softened, how beautiful! Slowly her eyes were veiling an emotion, a glimpse of which uplifted him.

"Wansfell, I'm thirty-eight years old," she said.

"No! I can't believe that!" he ejaculated.

"It's true."

"Well, well! I guess I'll go back to figuring the desert. But speaking of age — you guess mine. I'll bet you can't come any nearer to mine."

Gravely she studied him, and in the look and action once more grew composed.

"You're a masculine Sphinx. Those terrible lines from cheek to jaw — they speak of agony, but not of age. But you're gray at the temples. Wansfell, you are thirty-seven — perhaps forty."

"Magdalene Virey!" cried Adam, aghast. "Do I look so old? Alas for vanished youth! . . . I am only twenty-six."

It was her turn to be amazed. "We had better confine ourselves to other riddles than love and age. They are treacherous. . . . Come, let us be going."

17
●

The hour came when Magdalene Virey stirred Adam to his depths.

"Wansfell," she said, with a rare and wonderful tremor in her voice, "I love the silence, the loneliness, the serenity — even the tragedy of this valley of shadows. Ah! It is one place that will never be popular with men — where few women will ever come. Nature has set it apart for wanderers of the wastelands, men like you, unquenchable souls who endure, as you said, to fight, to strive, to seek, to find. . . . And surely for lost souls like me! Most men and all women must find death here, if they stay. But there is death in life. I've faced my soul here, in the black, lonely watches of the desert nights. And I would endure any agony to change that soul, to make it as high and clear and noble as the white cone of the mountain yonder."

Mysterious and inscrutable, the desert influence had worked upon Magdalene Virey. On the other hand, forces destructive to her physical being had attacked her. It was as if an invisible withering wind had blown upon

295

a flower in the night. Adam saw this with distress. But she laughed at the truth of it — laughed without mockery. Something triumphant rang like a bell in her laugh. Always, in the subtlety of character she had brought with her and the mystery she had absorbed from the desert, she stayed beyond Adam's understanding. It seemed that she liked to listen to his ceaseless importunities; but merciless to herself and aloof from Virey, she refused to leave Death Valley.

"Suppose I pack the burros and tuck you under my arm and take you, anyway?" he queried, stubbornly.

"I fancy I'd like you to tuck me under your arm," she replied, with the low laugh that came readily now, "but if you did — it would be as far as you'd get."

"How so?" he demanded, curiously.

"Why, I'd exercise the prerogative of the eternal feminine and command that time should stand still right there."

A sweetness and charm, perhaps of other days, a memory of power, haunted face and voice then.

"Time — stand still!" echoed Adam, ponderingly. "Magdalene, you are beyond me."

"So it seems. I'm a little beyond myself sometimes. You will never see in me the woman who has been courted, loved, spoiled by men."

"Well, I grasp that, I guess. But I don't care to see you as such a woman. I might not —"

296

"Ah! you might not respect me," she interrupted. "Alas! . . . But, Wansfell, if I had met *you* when I was eighteen I would never have been courted and loved and ruined by men. . . . You don't grasp that, either."

Adam had long ceased to curse his density. The simplicity of him antagonized her complexity. His had been the blessed victory over her bitterness, her mockery, her consciousness of despair. His had been the gladness of seeing her grow brown and strong and well, until these early June days had begun to weaken her. That fact had augmented his earnestness to get her to leave the valley. But she was adamant. And all his importunities and arguments and threats she parried with some subtle femininity of action or look or speech that left him bewildered.

The time came when only early in the mornings or late in the afternoons could they walk to their accustomed seat near the gateway of the valley and climb to the promontories. Nature moved on remorselessly with her seasons, and the sun had begun to assume its fiery authority during most of the daylight hours.

One morning before sunrise they climbed, much against Adam's advice, to a high point where Mrs. Virey loved to face the east at that hour. It was a hard climb, too hard for her to attempt in the heat and oppression that had come of late. Nevertheless, she prevailed upon

297

Adam to take her, and she had just about strength enough to get there.

They saw the east luminous and rosy, ethereal and beautiful, momentarily brightening with a rayed effulgence that spread from a golden center behind the dark bold domes of the Funeral Mountains. They saw the sun rise and change the luminous dawn to lurid day. One moment, and the beauty, the glory, the promise were as if they had never been. The light over Death Valley at that height was too fierce for the gaze of man.

On the way down, at a narrow ledge, where loose stones made precarious footing, Adam cautioned his companion and offered to help her. Waving him on, she followed him with her lithe free step. Then she slipped off the more solid trail to a little declivity of loose rocks that began to slide with her toward a slope where, if she went over it, she must meet serious injury. She did not scream. Adam plunged after her and, reaching her with a long arm just as she was about to fall, he swung her up as if she had only the weight of a child. Then, holding her in his arms, he essayed to wade out of the little stream of sliding rocks. It was difficult only because he feared he might slip and fall with her. Presently he reached the solid ledge and was about to set her upon her feet.

"Time — stand still here!" she exclaimed, her voice full of the old mockery of herself, with an added regret for what might have been, but could never be, with pathos, with the eternal charm of woman who could never separate her personality, her consciousness of her sex, from their old relation to man.

Adam halted his action as if suddenly chained, and he gazed down upon her, where she rested with her head on the bend of his left elbow. There was a smile on the brown face that had once been so pale. Her large eyes, wide open, exposed to the sky, seemed to reflect its dark blue color and something of its mystery of light. Adam saw wonder there, and reverence that must have been for him, but seemed incredible, and the shading of unutterable thoughts.

"Put me down," she said.

"Why did you say, 'Time — stand still here'?" he asked, as he placed her upon her feet.

"Do you remember the time when I told you how words and lines and verses of the poets I used to love come to mind so vividly out here? Sometimes I speak them, that is all."

"I understand. All I ever read has come back to me here on the desert, as clear as the print on the page — seen so many years ago. I used to hate Sunday school when I was a boy. But now, often, words of the Bible come before my mind. . . . But are you telling me the whole truth? Why did you say, 'Time — stand still here,' when I held you in my arms?"

"What a boy you are!" she murmured, and her eyes held a gladness for the sight of him. "Confess, now, wouldn't that moment have been a beautiful one for time to stop — for life to stand still — for the world to be naught — for thought and memory to cease?"

"Yes, it would," he replied, "but no more beautiful than this moment while you stand there so. When you look like that you make me hope."

"For what?" she queried, softly.

"For you."

"Wansfell, you are the only man I've ever known who could have held me in his arms and have been blind and dead to the nature of a woman. . . . Listen. You've done me the honor to say I have splendid thoughts and noble emotions. I hope I have. I know you have inspired many. I know this valley of death has changed my soul. . . . But, Wansfell, I am a woman, and a woman is more than her high and lofty thoughts — her wandering inspirations. A woman is a creature of feeling, somehow doomed. . . . When I said, 'Time — stand still here,' I was false to the woman in me that you idealize. A thousand thoughts, emotions, memories, desires, sorrows, vanities prompted the words of which you have made me ashamed. But to spare myself a little, let me say that it would indeed be beautiful for me to have you take me up into your arms — and then for time to stand still forever."

"Do you mean that — so — you'd feel safe, protected, at rest?" he asked, with emotion.

"Yes, and infinitely more. Wansfell, it is a woman's fate that the only safe and happy and desired place for her this side of the grave is in the arms of the man she loves. A real man — with strength and gentleness — for her and her alone! . . . It is a terrible thing in woman, the need to be loved. As a baby I had the need — as a girl — and as a woman it became a passion. Looking back now, through the revelation that has come to me here in this valley of silence — when thought is clairvoyant and all-pervading — I can see how the need of love, the passion to be loved, is the strongest instinct in any woman. It is an instinct. She can no more change it than she can change the shape of her hand. Poor fated women! Education, freedom, career may blind them to their real nature. But it is a man, the right man, that means life to a woman. Otherwise the best in her dies. . . . That instinct in me — for which I confess shame — has been unsatisfied despite all the men who have loved me. When you saved me — perhaps from injury — and took me into your arms, the instinct over which I have no control flashed up. While it lasted, until you looked at me, I wanted that moment to last forever. I wanted to be held that way — in your great, strong arms — until the last trumpet sounded. I wanted you to see only me, feel only me, hold only me, live for only me, love *me* beyond all else on earth and in heaven!"

As she paused, her slender brown hands at her heaving breast, her eyes strained as if peering through obscurity at a distant light, Adam could only stare at her in helpless fascination. In such moods as this she taught him as much of the mystery of life as he had taught her of the nature of the desert.

"Now the instinct is gone," she continued. "Chilled by your aloofness! I am looking at it with intelligence. And, Wansfell, I'm filled with pity for women. I pity myself, despite the fact that my mind is free. I can control my acts, if not my instincts and emotions. I am bound. I am a woman. I am a she-creature. I am little different from the fierce she-cats, the she-lions — any of the she-animals that you've told me fight to survive down on your wild Colorado Desert. . . . That seems to me the sex, the fate, the doom of women. Ah! no wonder they fight for men — spit and hiss and squall and scratch and rend! It's a sad thing, seen from a woman's mind. That great mass of women who cannot reason about their instincts, or understand the springs of their emotions — they are the happier. Too much knowledge is bad for my sex. Perhaps we are wrongly educated. *I* am the happier for what you have taught me. I can see myself now with pity instead of loathing. I am not to blame for what life has made me. There are no wicked women. They must be loved or they are lost. . . . My friend, the divinity in human life is seen best in some lost woman like me."

"Magdalene Virey," protested Adam, "I can't

follow you. . . . But to say *you* are a lost woman — that I won't listen to."

"I *was* a lost woman," interrupted Mrs. Virey, her voice rising out of the strong, sweet melody. "I had my pride, and I defied the husband whose heart I broke and whose life I ruined. I scorned the punishment, the exile he meted out to me. That was because I was thoroughbred. But all the same I was lost. Lost to happiness, to hope, to effort, to repentance, to spiritual uplift. Death Valley will be my tomb, but there will be resurrection for me. . . . It is you, Wansfell, you have been my salvation. . . . *You* have the power. It has come from your strife and agony on the desert. It is beyond riches, beyond honor. It is the divine in you that seeks and finds the divine in unfortunates who cross your wandering trail."

Adam, rendered mute, could only offer his hand; and in silence he led her down the slope.

That afternoon, near the close of the hot hours, Adam lay in the shade of the brush shelter he had erected near the Virey shack. He was absorbed in watching a tribe of red ants, and his posture was so unusual that it gave pause to Virey, who had come down from the slope. The man approached and curiously gazed at Adam, to see what he was doing.

"Looking for grains of gold?" inquired Virey, with sarcasm. "I'll lend you my magnifying glass."

"I'm watching these red ants," replied Adam, without looking up.

Virey bent over and, having seen, he slowly straightened up.

"Go to the ant, thou sluggard!" he ejaculated, and this time without sarcasm.

"Virey, I'm no sluggard," returned Adam. "It's you who are that. I'm a worker."

"Wansfell, I was not meaning you," said Virey. "There are things I hate you for, but laziness is certainly not included in them. . . . I never worked in my life. I had money left me. It was a curse. I thought I could buy everything. I bought a wife — the big-eyed woman to whom you devote your services — and your attentions. . . . And I bought for myself the sweetness of the deadly nightshade flower — a statue of marble, chiseled in the beautiful curves of mocking love — a woman of chain lightning and hate. . . . If I had lived by industry, as live those red ants you're watching, I might not now have one foot in my grave in Death Valley."

Thus there were rare instances when Virey appeared a man with the human virtues of regret, of comprehension, of intolerance, but never a word issued from his lips that was not tinged with bitterness. Had the divinity in him been blasted forever? Or was it a submerged spark that could quicken only to a touch of the woman lost to him? Adam wondered. Sometimes a feeling of pity for Virey stole over him, but it never

304

lasted long. Adam had more respect for these red ants than for some men, despite the alleged divinity. He abhorred the drones of life. The desert taught how useless were the idlers — how nature ruthlessly cut them off.

The red ants had a hill some few paces from the shelter where Adam lay. One train of ants, empty handed, as it were, traveled rapidly from the ant hill toward the camp litter; and another train staggered under tremendous burdens in the other direction. At first Adam thought these last were carrying bits of bread, then he thought they were carrying grains of gravel, and then he discovered, by moving closer to watch, that they were carrying round black-and-white globules, several times as large as their own bodies. Presently he concluded that these round objects were ant eggs which the tribe was moving from one hill to another. It was exceedingly interesting to watch them. He recognized them as the species of desert ant that could bite almost as fiercely as a scorpion. Their labor was prodigious. The great difficulty appeared to be in keeping the eggs in their jaws. These burdens were continually falling out and rolling away. Some ants tried many times and in many ways to grasp the hard little globules. Then, when this was accomplished, came the work compared with which the labor of man seemed insignificant. After getting a start the loaded ants made fair progress over smooth, hard ground, but when they ran into a crust of earth or a pebble or a chip they began the toil of a giant. The ant never essayed to go round the obstacle. He surmounted it. He pushed and lifted and heaved, and sometimes backed over, dragging his precious burden behind him. Others would meet a little pitfall and, instead of circling it to get to the ant hill, they would roll down, over and over, with their eggs, until they reached the bottom. Then it was uphill work on the other side, indefatigable, ceaseless, patient, wonderful.

Adam presently had to forego his little sentiment about the toil of the ants over their eggs. The black-and-white globules were seeds of maize. On the night before, Adam's burro Jennie had persisted around camp until he gave her the last of some maize left in one of his packs. Jennie had spilled generous quantities of the maize in the sand, and the ants were carrying home the seeds.

How powerful they were! How endowed with tireless endurance and a persistence beyond human understanding! The thing that struck Adam so singularly was that these ants did not recognize defeat. They could not give up. Failure was a state unknown to their instincts. And so they performed marvelous feats. What was the spirit that actuated them? The mighty life of nature was infinitely strong in them. It was the same as the tenacity of the lichen that lived on the desert rocks, or the eyesight of the condor that could see its prey from the invisible heights of the sky, or the age-long destructive movements of the mountain tops wearing down to the valleys.

When Adam got up from his pleasant task and meditation he was surprised to find Mrs. Virey standing near with eyes intent on him. Then it became incumbent upon him to show her the toils of the red ants. She watched them attentively for a while.

"Wonderful little creatures!" she exclaimed. "So this watching is one of the secrets of your desert knowledge. Wansfell, I can't compare these ants to men. They are far superior. They have order, purpose. They are passionless, perfect organizations to carry on their lives. They will work and live — the descendants of this very tribe of ants — long after the race of men has disappeared off the face of the earth. . . . But wonderful as they are, and interesting as are their labors, I'd prefer to watch you chop wood, or, better, to climb the slope with your giant stride."

That night, some time later, Adam was awakened by a gale that swooped up through the gateway from the valley. It blew away the cool mountain air which had settled down from the heights. It was a warmer wind than any Adam had ever before experienced at night. It worried him. Forerunner, it must be, of the midnight furnace winds that had added to the frame of Death Valley! It brought a strange, low, hollow roar, unlike any other sound in nature. It was a voice. Adam harkened to the warning. On the morrow he would again talk to Virey. Soon it might be too late to save Magdalene Virey. She had obstructed his will. She would not leave without her husband. She had bidden Adam stay there in Death Valley to serve her, but she seemed to have placed her husband beyond Adam's reach. The ferocity in Adam had never found itself in relation to Virey. Adam had persuaded and argued with the persistence of the toiling ant, but to work his way with Virey seemed to demand the swoop of the desert hawk.

This strange warm wind, on its first occurrence during Adam's stay in the valley, rose to a gale and then gradually subsided until it moaned away mournfully. Its advent had robbed Adam of sleep; its going seemed to leave a deader silence, fraught with the meaning of its visit.

Adam could sleep no more. This silence belied the blinking of the stars. It proved the solidarity of the universe. Nothing lived, except his soul, that seemingly had departed from his body in a dream, and now with his vague thoughts and vaguer feelings wandered over the wastelands, a phantom in the night. Silence of utter solitude — most intense, dead, dreaming, waiting, sepulcher-like, awful! Where was the rustle of the wings of the bats? The air moved soundlessly, and it seemed to have the substance of shadows. A dead solitude — a terrible silence! A man and the earth! The wide spaces, the wild places of the earth as it was in the beginning! Here could be the last lesson to a thinking man — the last development of a man into savage or god.

There! Was that a throb of his heart or a ring in his ear? Crack of a stone, faint, far away, high on the heights, a lonely sound making real the lonely night. It relieved Adam. The tension of him relaxed. And he listened, hopefully, longing to hear another break in the silence that would be so insupportable.

As he listened, the desert moon, oval in shape, orange hued and weird, sailed over the black brow of the mountain and illumined the valley in a radiance that did not seem of land or sea. The darkness of midnight gave way to orange shadows, mustering and shading, stranger than the fantastic shapes of dreams.

Another ring of rock on rock, and sharp rattle, and roll on roll, assured Adam that the weathering gods of the mountain were not daunted by the silence and the loneliness of Death Valley. They were working as ever. Their task was to level the mountain down to the level of the sea. The stern, immutable purpose seemed to vibrate in the ringing cracks and in the hollow reports. These sounds in their evenness and perfect rhythm and lonely tone established once more in Adam's disturbed consciousness the nature of the place. Death Valley! The rolling of rocks dispelled phantasms.

Then came a low, grating roar. The avalanche of endless broken rocks had slipped an inch.

It left an ominous silence. Adam stirred restlessly in his blankets. There was a woman in the lee of that tremendous sliding slope — a woman of delicate frame, of magnificent spirit, of a heart of living flame. Every hour she slept or lay wide eyed in the path of that impending cataclysm was one of exceeding peril. Adam chafed under the invisible bonds of her will. Because she chose to lie there, fearless, beyond the mind of man to comprehend, was that any reason why he should let her perish? Adam vowed that he would end this dread situation before another nightfall. Yet when he thought of Magdalene Virey his heart contracted. Only through the fierce spirit of the desert could he defy her and beat down the jailer who chained her there. But that fierce spirit of his seemed obstructed by hers, an aloof thing, greater than ferocity, beyond physical life.

And so Adam lay sleepless, listening to the lonely fall of sliding rocks, the rattle and clash, and then the hollow settling. Then he listened to the silence.

It was broken by a different note, louder, harsher — the rattle and bang of a stone displaced and falling from a momentum other than its own. It did not settle. Heavy and large, it cracked down to thud into the sand and bump out through the brush. Scarcely had it quieted when another was set in motion, and it brought a low, sliding crash of many small rocks. Adam sat up, turning his ear toward the slope. Another large stone banged down to the sands. Adam heard the whiz of it, evidently hurtling through the air between his camp and the Vireys'. If that stone had struck their shack!

Adam got up and, pulling on his boots, walked out a little way from his camp. What an opaque orange gloom! Nevertheless, it had radiance. He could see almost as well as when the full moon soared in silver effulgence. More cracking and rolling of little rocks, and then the dislodgment of a heavy one, convinced Adam that a burro was climbing the slope or a panther had come down to prowl around camp. At any rate the displacement of stones jarred unnaturally on Adam's sensitive ear.

Hurrying across to the Virey shack, he approached the side farther from the slope and called through the brush wall, "Mrs. Virey!"

"Yes. What do you want, Wansfell?" she replied, instantly. She had been wide awake.

"Have you heard the sliding rocks?"

"Indeed I have! All through that strange roar of wind — and later."

"You and Virey better get up and take your blankets out a ways, where you will not be in danger. I think there's a burro or a panther up on the slope. You know how loose the stones are — how at the slightest touch they come sliding and rolling. I'll go up and scare the beast away."

"Wansfell, you're wrong," came the reply, with that old mockery which always hurt Adam.

311

"You should not insult a burro — not to speak of a panther."

"What?" queried Adam, blankly.

"It is another kind of an animal."

But for that subtle mockery of voice Adam would have been persuaded the woman was out of her head, or at least answering him in her sleep.

"Mrs. Virey, please —"

"Wansfell, it's a sneaking coyote," she called, piercingly, and then she actually uttered a low laugh.

Adam was absolutely dumfounded. "Coyote!" he ejaculated.

"Yes. It's my husband. It's Virey. He found out the rolling rocks frightened me at night. So he climbs up there and rolls them. . . . Sees how close he can come to hitting the shack! . . . Oh, he's done that often!"

An instant Adam leaned there with his head bent to the brush wall, as if turned to stone. Then like a man stung he leaped up and bounded round the shack toward the slope.

In the orange radiance on that strange, moon-blanched slope he dimly saw a moving object. It stood upright. Indeed, no burro or panther! Adam drew a deep and mighty breath for the yell that must jar the very stones from their sockets.

"HYAR!" he yelled in stentorian roar. Like thunder the great sound pealed up the slope. "COME DOWN OR I'LL WRING YOUR NECK!"

312

Only the clapping, rolling, immeasurable echoes answered him. The last hollow clap and roll died away, leaving the silence deader than before.

Adam spent the remainder of that night pacing to and fro in the orange-hued shadows, fighting the fierce, grim violence that at last had burst its barrier. Adam could have wrung the life out of this Virey with less compunction than he would have in stamping on the head of a venomous reptile. Yet it was as if a spirit kept in the shadow of his form, as he strode the bare shingle, gazing up at the solemn black mountains and at the wan stars.

Adam went down to the gateway between the huge walls. A light was kindling over the faraway Funeral range, and soon a glorious star swept up, as if by magic, above the dark rim of the world. The morning star shining down into Death Valley! No dream — no illusion — no desert mirage! Like the Star of Bethlehem beckoning the Wise Men to the East, it seemed to blaze a radiant path for Adam down across the valley of dim, mystic shadows. What could be the meaning of such a wonderful light? Was that blue-white lilac-haloed star only another earth upon which the sun was shining? Adam lifted his drawn face to its light and wrestled with the baser side of his nature. He seemed to be dominated by the spirit that kept close to his side. Magdalene Virey kept vigil with him on that lonely beat. It was her agony which swayed and wore down his elemental passion. Would not he fail her if he killed this man? Virey's brutality seemed not the great question at issue for him.

"I'll not kill him — yet!"

Thus Adam eased the terrible contention within him.

When he returned to camp the sun had risen red and hot, with a thin, leaden haze dulling its brightness. No wind stirred. Not a sound broke the stillness. Magdalene Virey sat on the stone bench under the brush shelter, waiting for him. She rose as he drew near. Never had he seen her like this, smiling a welcome that was as true as her presence, yet facing him with darkened eyes and tremulous lips and fear. Adam read her. Not fear of him, but of what he might do!

"Is Virey back yet?" he asked.

"Yes. He just returned. He's inside — going to sleep."

"I want to see him — to get something off my mind," said Adam.

"Wait — Adam!" she cried, and reached for him as he wheeled to go toward the shack.

One glance at her brought Adam to a standstill, and then to a slow settling down upon the stone seat, where he bowed his head. Life had held few more poignant moments than this, in his pity for others. Yet he thrilled with admiration for this woman. She came close to him, leaned against him, and the quiver of her body showed she needed the support. She put a shaking hand on his shoulder.

"My friend — brother," she whispered, "if you kill him — it will undo — all the good you've done — for me."

"You told me once that the grandest act of a man was to fight for the happiness — the life of a woman," he replied.

"True! And haven't you fought for my happiness, and my life, too? I would have died long ago. As for happiness — it has come out of my fight, my work, my effort to meet you on your heights — more happiness than I deserve — than I ever hoped to attain. . . . But if you kill Virey — all will have been in vain."

"Why?" he asked.

"Because it is I who ruined him," she replied, in low, deep voice, significant of the force behind it. "As men go in the world he was a gentleman, a man of affairs, happy and carefree. When he met me his life changed. He worshiped me. It was not his fault that I could not love him. I hated him because they forced me to marry him. For years he idolized me. . . . Then — then came the shock — his despair, his agony. It made him mad. There is a very thin line between great love and great hate."

"What — what ruined him?" demanded Adam.

"Adam, it will be harder to confess than any other ordeal of my whole life. Because — because *you* are the one man I should have met years ago. . . . Do you understand? And I — who yearn for your respect — for your — Oh, spare me! . . . I who need your faith — your strange, incomprehensible faith in me — I, who hug to my hungry bosom the beautiful hopes you have in me — I must confess my shame to save my husband's worthless life."

"No. I'll not have you — you humiliating yourself to save him anything. I give my word. I'll never kill Virey unless he harms you."

"Ah! But he has harmed me. He has struck me. . . . Wansfell! don't leap like that. Listen. Virey will harm me, sooner or later. He is obsessed with his one idea — to see me suffer. That is why he has let you and me wander around together so much. He hoped in his narrow soul to see you come to love me, and me to love you — so through that I should fall *again* — to suffer more anguish — to offer more meat for his hellish revenge. . . . But, lo! I am uplifted — forever beyond his reach — never to be rent by his fiendish glee . . . . unless you kill him — which would stain my hands with his blood — bring back the doom of soul from which you rescued me!"

"Magdalene, I swear I'll never kill Virey unless he kills you," declared Adam, as if forced beyond endurance.

"Ah, I ask no more!" she whispered, in passionate gratitude. "My God! how I feared you — yet somehow gloried in your look! . . . And

316

now listen, friend, brother — man who should have been my lover — I hurry to my abasement. I kill the she-thing in me and go on to my atonement. I fight the instincts of a woman. I sacrifice a possible paradise, for I am young and life is sweet."

She circled his head with her arm and drew it against her heaving breast. The throbs of that tortured heart beat, beat, beat all through Adam's blood, to the core of his body.

"My daughter Ruth was not Virey's child," she went on, her voice low, yet clear as a bell. "I was only nineteen — a fool — mad — driven. I thought I was in love, but it was only one of those insane spells that so often ruin women. . . . For years I kept the secret. Then I could not keep it any longer. At the height of Virey's goodness to me, and his adoration, and his wonderful love for Ruth, I told him the truth. I *had* to tell it. . . . That killed his soul. He lived only to make me suffer. The sword he held over my head was the threat to tell my secret to Ruth. I could not bear that. A thousand deaths would have been preferable to that. . . . So in the frenzy of our trouble we started west for the desert. My father and Ruth followed us — caught up with us at Sacramento. Virey hated Ruth as passionately as he had loved her. I dared not risk him near her in one of his terrible moods. So I sent Ruth away with my father, somewhere to southern California. She did not know it was parting forever. But, O

God in heaven — how I knew it! . . . Then, in my desperation, I dared Virey to do his worst. I had ruined him and I would pay to the last drop of blood in my bitter heart. We came to Death Valley, as I told you, because the terror and desolation seemed to Virey to be as close to a hell on earth as he could find to hide me. Here he began indeed to make me suffer — dirt and vermin and thirst and hunger and pain! Oh! the horror of it all comes back to me! . . . But even Death Valley cheated him. You came, Wansfell, and now — at last — I believe in God!"

Adam wrapped a long arm around her trembling body and held her close. At last she had confessed her secret. It called to the un-plumbed depths of him. And the cry in his heart was for the endless agony of woman. And it was a bitter cry of doubt. If Magdalene Virey had at last found faith in God, it was more than Adam had found, though she called him the instrument of her salvation. A fierce and terrible rage flamed in him for the ruin of her. Like a lion he longed to rise up to slay. Blood and death were the elements that equalized wrong. Yet through his helpless fury whispered a still voice into his consciousness — she had been miserable and now she was at peace; she had been lost and now she was saved. He could not get around that. His desert passion halted there. He must go on alone into the waste places and ponder over the wonder of this woman and

what had transformed her. He must remember
her soul-moving words and, away somewhere
in the solitude and silence, learn if the love she
intimated was a terrible truth. It could not be
true now, yet the shaking of her slender form
communicated itself to his, and there was inward
tumult, strange, new, a convulsive birth of a
sensation dead these many years — dead since
that dusky-eyed Margarita Arallanes had tilted
her black head to say, "Ah, so long ago and
far away!"

Memory surged up in Adam, moving him to
speak aloud his own deeply hidden secret, by
the revelation of which he might share the shame
and remorse and agony of Magdalene Virey.

"I will tell you my story," he said, and the
words were as cruel blades at the closed portals
of his heart. Huskily he began, halting often,
breathing hard, while the clammy sweat beaded
upon his brow. What was this life — these years
that deceived with forgetfulness? His trouble was
there as keen as on the day it culminated. He
told Magdalene of his boyhood, of his love for
his brother Guerd, and of their life in the old
home, where all, even friendships of the girls,
was for Guerd and nothing for him. As he progressed, Magdalene Virey's own agony was forgotten. The quiver of her body changed to
strung intensity, the heaving of her bosom was
no longer the long-drawn breath to relieve oppression. Remorselessly as she had bared her
great secret, Adam confessed his little, tawdry,

319

miserable romance — his wild response to the lure of a vain Mexican girl, and his fall, and the words that had disillusioned him.

"Ah, so long ago and far away!" echoed Magdalene Virey, all the richness of her wonderful voice gathering in a might of woman's fury. "Oh, such a thing for a girl to say! . . . And Adam — *she,* this Margarita, was the only woman you ever loved — ever knew that way?"

"Yes."

"And she was the cause of your ruin?"

"Indeed she was, poor child!"

"The damned hussy!" cried Magdalene, passionately. "And you — only eighteen years old? How I hate her! . . . And what of the man who won her fickle heart?"

Adam bowed as a tree in a storm. "He — he was my brother."

"Oh *no!*" she burst out. "The boy you loved — the *brother!* Oh, it can't be true!"

"It was true. . . . And, Magdalene — I killed him."

Then with a gasp she enveloped him, in a fierce, protective frenzy of tenderness, arms around him, pressing his face to her breast, hanging over him as a mother over her child.

"Oh, my God! Oh, my God! How terrible! . . . Your *brother!* . . . And I thought my secret, my sin, my burden so terrible! Oh, my heart bleeds for you. . . . Wansfell, poor unhappy wanderer!"

320

18
●

July! At last the endlessly long, increasingly
hot June days brought the leaden-hazed month
of July, when no sane man ever attempted to
cross Death Valley while the sun was high.

In all hours, even in the darkness, the bold,
rugged slopes of the Panamints reflected sinister
shades of red. And the valley was one of gray
swirling shadows and waving veils of heat like
transparent smoke. Beyond that vast, strange,
dim valley rose the drab and ocher slopes of
the Funeral Mountains, sweeping up to the
bronze battlements and on to the lilac and purple
peaks blurred in the leaden-hued haze that obscured the sky. The sun was sky-broad, an
illimitable flare, with a lurid white heart into
which no man could look.

Adam was compelled to curtail his activities.
He did not suffer greatly from the heat, but
he felt its weakening power. Ever his blood
seemed at fever heat. Early in the mornings
and late in the evenings he prepared simple
meals, which, as the days dragged on, were less
and ever less partaken of by his companions

and himself. During the midday hours, through the terrible heat, he lay in the shade, sweltering and oppressed, in a stupor of sleep. The nights were the only relief from the immense and merciless glare, the bearing down of invisible bars of red-hot iron. Most of these long hours of darkness Adam lay awake or walked in the gloom or sat in the awful stillness, waiting for he knew not what. But that he waited for something he knew with augmenting dread.

When the full blast of this summer heat came, Virey changed physically and mentally. He grew thin. He walked with bowed shoulders. His tongue protruded slightly and he always panted. Every day he ate less and slept less than on the day before. He obeyed no demands from Adam and took no precautions. His sufferings would have been less and his strength would have been greater had he refrained from exposing himself to the sun. But he reveled in proofs of the nature of Death Valley.

And if Virey had ever worn a mask in front of Adam he now dropped it. Indeed he ignored Adam, no longer with scorn or indifference, but as if unaware of his presence. Whenever Adam wanted to be heard by Virey, which desire diminished daily, he had to block his path, confront him forcefully. Virey was given over wholly to his obsession. His hate possessed him body and soul. And if it had ever been a primitive hate to destroy, it had been restrained, and therefore rendered infinitely cruel, by the slow, measured process of thought, of premeditation.

Often when Adam absented himself from camp, Virey had a trick of climbing the weathered slope to roll down rocks. He seemed mad to do this. Yet when Adam returned he would come clambering down, wet and spent, a haggard, sweating wretch not yet quite beyond fear. In vain had Adam argued, pleaded, talked with him; in vain had been the strident scorn of a man and the curses of rage. Virey, however, had a dread of Adam's huge hands. Something about them fascinated him. When one of these, clenched in an enormous fist, was shoved under his nose with a last threat, then Virey would retire sullenly to the shack. In every way that was possible he kept before Magdalene Virey the spectacle of his ruin and the consciousness that it was her doing. These midsummer days soon made him a gaunt, unshaven, hollow-eyed wretch. Miserable and unkempt he presented himself at meals, and sat there, a haggard ghost, to mouth a little food and to stare at his wife with accusing eyes. He reminded her of cool, shaded rooms, of exquisite linen and china, of dainty morsels, of carved-glass pitchers full of refreshing drink and clinking ice. Always he kept before her the heat, the squalor, the dirt, the horror of Death Valley. When he could present himself before her with his thin, torn garments clinging wet to his emaciated body, his nerves gone from useless exertions, his hands bloody and shaking as if with palsy, his tongue hanging out — when he could surprise her thus and see her shrink, then he experienced rapture. He seemed to cry out: Woman! behold the wreck of Virey!

But if that was rapture for him, to gloat over the doom of her seemed his glory. Day by day Death Valley wrought by invisible lines and shades a havoc in Magdalene Virey's beauty. To look at her was to have sinking proof that Death Valley had never been intended for a woman, no matter how magnificent her spirit. The only spirit that could prevail here was the one which had lost its earthly habiliments. Like a cat playing with a mouse, Virey watched his wife. Like Mephistopheles gloating over the soul of a lost woman, Virey attended to the slow manifestations of his wife's failing strength. He meant to squeeze every drop of blood out of her heart and still keep, if possible, life lingering in her. His most terrible bitterness seemed to consist of his failure to hide her utterly and forever from the gaze of any man save himself. Here he had hidden her in the most desolate place in the world, yet another man had come, and, like all the others, had been ready to lay down his life for her. Virey writhed under this circumstance over which he had no control. It was really the only truth about the whole situation that he was able to grasp. The terrible tragedy of his hate was that it was not hate, but love. Like a cannibal, he would have eaten his wife raw, not from hunger, but from his passion to consume her, incorporate her heart and blood and flesh into his, make her body his forever. Thought of her soul, her mind, her spirit, never occurred to Virey. So he never realized how she escaped him, never understood her mocking scorn.

But through his thick and heat-hazed brain there must have pierced some divination of his failing powers to torture her. The time came when he ceased to confront her like a scarecrow, he ceased accusing her, he ceased to hold before her the past and its contrast with the present, he gave up his refinement of cruelty. This marked in Virey a further change, a greater abasement. He reverted to instinct. He retrograded to a savage in his hate, and that hate found its outlet altogether in primitive ways.

Adam's keen eye saw all this, and the slow boil in his blood was not all owing to the torrid heat of Death Valley. His great hands, so efficient and ruthless, seemed fettered. A thousand times he had muttered to the silence of the night, to the solemn, hazed daylight, to the rocks that had souls, and to the invisible presence ever beside him: "How long must I stand this? How long — how long?"

One afternoon as he awoke late from the sweltering siesta he heard Mrs. Virey scream. The cry startled him, because she had never done that before. He ran.

Adam found her lying at the foot of the stone

bench in a dead faint. The brown had left her skin. How white the wasted face! What dark shadows under the hollow eyes! His heart smote him remorselessly.

As he knelt and was about to lift her head he espied a huge, black, hairy spider crawling out of the folds of her gray gown. It was a tarantula, one of the ugliest of the species. Adam flipped it off with his hand and killed it under his boot.

Then with basin of water and wetted scarf he essayed to bring Mrs. Virey back to consciousness. She did not come to quickly, but at last she stirred, and opened her eyes with a flutter. She seemed to be awakening from a nightmare of fear, loathing, and horror. For that instant her sight did not take in Adam, but was a dark, humid, dilated vision of memory.

"Magdalene, I killed the tarantula," said he. "It can't harm you now. . . . Wake up! Why, you're stiff and you look like — like I don't know what! . . . You fainted and I've had a time bringing you to."

"Oh!" she cried. "It's you." And then she clung to him while he lifted her, steadying her upon her feet, and placed her on the stone bench. "So I fainted? . . . Ugh! That loathsome spider! Where is it?"

"I covered it with sand," he replied.

"Would it have — bitten me?"

"No. Not unless you grasped it."

Slowly she recovered and, letting go of him,

leaned back in the seat. Crystal beads of sweat stood out upon her white brow. Her hair was wet. Her sensitive lips quivered.

"I've a perfect horror of mice, bugs, snakes, spiders — anything that crawls," she said. "I can't restrain it. I inherited it from my mother. . . . And what has mind got to do with most of a woman's feelings? Virey has finally found that out."

"Virey! . . . What do you mean?" rejoined Adam.

"I was leaning back here on the bench when suddenly I heard Virey slipping up behind me. I knew he was up to something. But I wouldn't turn to see what. Then with two sticks he held the tarantula out over me — almost in my face. I screamed. I seemed to freeze inside. He dropped the tarantula in my lap. . . . Then all went black."

"Where — is he now?" asked Adam, finding it difficult to speak.

"He's in the shack."

Adam made a giant stride in that direction, only to be caught and detained by her clinging hands. Earnestly she gazed up at him, with melancholy, searching eyes.

He uttered a loud laugh, mirthless, a mere explosion of surcharged breath. "No! . . . I can't get angry. I can't be a man any more. This Death Valley and the sun — and you — have worked on my mind. . . . But I'll tell you what — nothing can stop me from beating

327

Virey — so he'll never do that again."

"Ah! . . . So I've worked on your mind? Then it's the only great deed I ever did. . . . Wansfell, I told you Virey has threatened to shoot you. He's meant to more than once, but when you have come he has been afraid. But he might."

"I wish to heaven he'd try it," responded Adam, and, loosing the woman's hold upon his hands, he strode toward the shack.

"Virey, come out!" he called, loudly, though without any particular feeling. There was no reply, and he repeated the call, this time louder. Still Virey remained silent. Waiting a moment longer, Adam finally spoke again, with deliberate, cold voice. "Virey, I don't want to mess up that room, with all your wife's belongings in there. So come outside."

At that Adam heard a quick, panting breath. Then Virey appeared — came to the door of the shack. Adam could not have told what the man's distorted face resembled. He carried a gun, and his heart was ferocious if his will was weak.

"Don't you — lay one of your — bloody hands on me," he panted.

Adam took two long strides and halted before Virey, not six feet distant.

"So you've got your little gun, eh?" he queried, without any particular force. Adam had been compelled to smother all that mighty passion within him, or he could not have answered for his actions. "What are you going to do with it?"

"If you make a — move at me — I'll kill you," came the husky, panting response,

"Virey, I'm going to beat you within an inch of your worthless life," declared Adam, monotonously, as if he had learned this speech by rote. "But I've got to talk first. I'm full of a million things to call you."

"Damn you, I'll not listen," replied Virey, beginning to shake with excitement. The idea of using the gun had become an intent and was acting powerfully upon him. "You leave my — camp — you get out — of this valley!"

"Virey, are you crazy?" queried Adam. The use of his voice had changed that deadlock of his feelings. He must not trust himself to bandy speech with Virey. The beating must be administered quickly or there would be something worse. Yet how desperately hard not to try to awaken conscience or sense in this man!

"No, I'm not crazy," yelled Virey.

"If you're not crazy, then that trick of throwing a tarantula on your wife was damnable — mean — hellish — monstrous. . . . My God! man, can't you see what a coward you are? To torture her — as if you were a heathen! That delicate woman — all quivering nerves! To pick on a weakness, like that of a child! Virey, if you're not crazy you're the worst brute I've ever met on the desert. You've sunk lower than men whom the desert

329

has made beasts. You —"

"Beast I am — thanks to my delicate wife," cried Virey, with exceeding bitter passion. "Delicate? Ha-ha! The last lover of Magdalene Virey can't see she's strong as steel — alive as red fire! How she clings to memory! How she has nine lives of a cat — and hangs on to them — just to remember! . . . And you — meddler! You desert rat of a preacher! Get out — or I'll kill you!"

"Shoot and be damned!" flashed Adam, as with leap as swift as his voice he reached a sweeping arm.

Virey's face turned ashen. He raised the gun. Adam knocked it up just as it exploded. The powder burned his forehead, but the bullet sped high. Another blow sent the gun flying to the sand. Then Adam, fastening a powerful grip on Virey, clutching shirt and collar and throat at once, dragged him before the stone bench where Mrs. Virey sat, wide eyed and pale. Here Adam tripped the man and threw him heavily upon the sand. Before he could rise Adam straddled him, bearing him down. Then Adam's big right hand swept and dug in the sand to uncover the dead tarantula.

"Ah! here's your spider!" he shouted. And he rubbed the hairy, half-crushed tarantula in Virey's face. The man screamed and wrestled. "Good! you open your mouth. Now we'll see. . . . Eat it — eat it, damn your cowardly soul!" Then Adam essayed to thrust the spider between

330

Virey's open lips. He succeeded only partly. Virey let out a strangling, spitting yell, then closed his teeth as a vise. Adam smeared what was left of the crushed tarantula all over Virey's face.

"Now get up," he ordered, and, rising himself, he kicked Virey. Adam, in the liberation of his emotions by action, was now safe from himself. He would not kill Virey. He could even hold in his enormous strength. He could even think of the joy of violence that was rioting inside him, of the ruthless fierceness with which he could have rent this man limb from limb.

Virey, hissing and panting in a frenzy, scrambled to his feet. Fight was in him now. He leaped at Adam, only to meet a blow that laid him on the sand. It had not stunned him. Up he sprang, bloody, livid, and was at Adam again. His frenzy lent him strength and in that moment he had no fear of man or devil. The desert rage was on him. He swung his fists, beat wildly at Adam, tore and clawed. Adam slapped him with great broad hands that clapped like boards, and then, when Virey lunged close, he closed his fist and smashed it into Virey's face. The man of the cities went plowing in the sand. Then on his hands and knees he crawled like a dog, and, finding a stone, he jumped up to fling it. Adam dodged the missile. Wildly Virey clutched for more, throwing one after another. Adam caught one and threw it back, to crack hard on his opponent's shin. Virey yelled no more. His rage took complete possession of him. Grasping up a large rock, he held it as a mace and rushed upon Adam to brain him. That action and intent to kill was the only big response he had made to this wild environment. He beat at Adam. He lunged up to meet his foe's lofty head. He had no fear. But he was mad. No dawning came to him that he was being toyed with. Strong and furious at the moment, he might have succeeded in killing a lesser man. But before Adam he was powerless to do murder. Then the time came when Adam knocked the rock out of his hand and began to beat him, blow on blow to face and body, with violence, but with checked strength, so that Virey staggered here and there, upheld by fists. At last, whipped out of rage and power to retaliate, Virey fell to the sands. Adam dragged him into the shack and left him prostrate and moaning, an abject beaten wretch who realized his condition.

Most difficult of all for Adam then was to face Mrs. Virey. Yet the instant he did he realized that his ignorance of women was infinite.

"Did the bullet — when he fired — did it hit you?" she queried, her large eyes, intense and glowing, wonderfully dark with emotion, flashing over him.

"No — it missed — me," panted Adam, as with heavy breaths he sank upon the stone bench.

"I picked up the gun. I was afraid he'd find

it. You'd better keep it now," she said, and slipped it into his pocket.

"What a — dis— gusting — sight for you — to have — to watch!" exclaimed Adam, trying to speak and breathe at once.

"It was frightful — terrible at first," she returned. "But after the gun went flying — and you had stopped trying to make him eat the — the spider — uggh! how sickening! . . . After that it got to be — Well, Wansfell, it was the first time in the years I've known my husband that I respected him. He meant to kill you. It amazed me. I admired him. . . . And as for you — to see you tower over him — and parry his blows — and hit him when you liked — and knock him and drag him — oh, that roused a terrible something in me! I never felt so before in my whole life. I was some other woman. I watched the blood flow, I heard the thuds and heavy breaths, I actually smelled the heat of you, I was so close — and it all inflamed me, made me strung with savage excitement — I had almost said joy. . . . God knows, Wansfell, we have hidden natures within our breasts."

"If only it's a lesson to him!" sighed Adam.

"Then it were well done," she replied, "but I doubt — I doubt. Virey is hopeless. Let us forget. . . . And now will you please help me search in the sand here for something I dropped. It fell from my lap when I fainted, I suppose. It's a small ivory case with a miniature I think all the world of. Last and best of my treasures!"

Adam raked in the sand along the base of the bench, and presently found the lost treasure. How passionately, with what eloquent cry of rapture, did she clutch it!

"Look!" she exclaimed, with wonderful thrill in her voice, and held the little case open before Adam's eyes.

He saw a miniature painting of a girl's face, oval, pure as a flower, with beautiful curls of dark bronze, and magnificent eyes. In these last Adam recognized the mother of this girl. The look of them, the pride and fire, if not the color, were the same as Magdalene Virey's.

"A sweet and lovely face," said Adam.

"Ruth!" she whispered. "My daughter — my only child — my baby that I abandoned to save her happiness! . . . Oh, mockery of life that I was given such a heart to love — that I was given such a perfect child!"

The midsummer midnight furnace winds began to blow.

They did not blow every night or many nights consecutively; otherwise all life in the valley would soon have become extinct. Adam found the hot winds heretofore, that he had imagined were those for which the valley was famed, were really comfortable compared with these terrible furnace blasts. In trying to understand their nature, Adam concluded they were caused by a displacement of higher currents of cool air.

Sometime during the middle of the night there began a downward current of cool air from the mountain heights; and this caused a disturbance of the vast area of hot air in the burning valley below sea level. The tremendous pressure drove the hot air to find an outlet so it could rise to let the cool air down, and thus there came gusts and gales of furnace winds, rushing down the valley, roaring up the canyons.

The camp of the Vireys, almost in the center of one of these outlets and scarcely a quarter of a mile from the main valley, lay open to the full fury of these winds.

The 1st of August was a hazy, blistering day in which the valley smoked. Veils of transparent black heat — shrouds of moving white transparent heat! The mountains' tops were invisible, as if obscured in thin, leaden-hued fog; their bases showed dull, sinister red through the haze. Nothing moved except the strange veils and the terrible heaven-wide sun that seemed to have burst. It was a day when, if a man touched an unshaded stone with his naked hand, he would be burned as by a hot iron. A solemn, silent, sulphurous, smoky, deadly day, inimical to life!

But at last the sunset of red hell ended that day and merciful darkness intervened. The fore part of the night was hot, yet endurable, and a relief compared to the sunlit hours. Adam marked, however, or imagined, a singular, ominous, reddish hue of the dim stars, a vast still veil between him and the sky, a waiting hush. He walked out into the open, peering through the dimness, trying to comprehend. The color of the stars and heavens, and of the dull black slopes, and of the night itself, seemed that of a world burned out. Immense, dim, mysterious, empty, desolate! Had this Death Valley finally unhinged his mind? But he convinced himself that it was normal. The unreality, the terror, the forbidding hush of all the elements, the imminence of catastrophe — these were all actually present. Anything could happen here. Exaggeration of sense was impossible. This Death Valley was only a niche of the universe and the universe only a part of the infinite. He felt his intelligence and emotion, and at the same time the conviction that only a step away was death. The old wonder arose — was death the end? Not possible! Yet the cruelty, the impassivity of nature, letting the iron consequences fall — this seemed to crush him. For the sake of a woman who suffered agony of body and mind, Adam was at war with nature and the spirit of creation. Why? The eternal query had no answer. It never would be answered.

As the hours wore away the air grew hotter, denser. Like a blanket it seemed to lie heavily on Adam. It was the hottest, stillest, most oppressive, strangest night of all his desert experience. Sleep was impossible. Rest was impossible. Inaction was impossible. Every breath seemed impossible of fulfillment. A pressure constricted Adam's lungs. The slow, gentle walk that he drove himself to take, which it was impossible to keep from taking, brought out a hot flood of sweat on his body, and the drops burned as they trickled down his flesh.

"If the winds blow to-night!" he muttered, in irresistible dread.

Something told him they would blow. To-night they would blow harder and hotter than ever before. The day of leaden fire had promised that. Nature had her midnight change to make in the elements. Time would not stand still. The universe prevailed on its inscrutable course; the planets burned; the suns blazed upon their earths; and this ball of rock on which Adam clung, groaning with the other pygmies of his kind, whirled and hurtled through space, now dark and then light, now hot and then cold, slave to a blaring master ninety million miles away. It was all so inconceivable, inscrutable, unbelievable.

There came a movement of air fanning his cheek, emphasizing the warmth. He smelled anew the dry alkali dust, the smoky odor, almost like brimstone. The hour was near midnight and the deathlike silence brooded no more. A low moan, as of a lost soul, moved somewhere on the still air. Weird, dismal, uncanny, it fitted the spectral shadows and shapes around him, and the night with its mystery. No human sound, though it resembled the mourn of humanity!

A puff of hot wind struck Adam in the face, rushed by, rustling the dead and withered brush, passed on to lull and die away. It seemed to leave a slow movement in the still air, a soft, restless, uneasy shifting, as of an immense volume becoming unsettled. Adam knew. Behind that sudden birth of life of dead air pressed the furious blasts of hell — the midnight furnace wind of Death Valley.

Adam listened. How strange, low, sad the moan! His keen ears, attuned to all varieties of desert sound, seemed to fill and expand. The moan swelled to a low roar, lulling now, then rising. Like no sound he had ever heard before, it had strange affinity with the abyss of shadows. Suddenly the air around Adam began a steady movement northward. Its density increased, or else the movement, or pressure behind, made it appear so. And it grew swift, until it rustled the brush. Down in the valley the roar swelled like the movement of a mighty storm through a forest. When the gale reached the gateway below Adam it gave a hollow bellow.

The last of the warm, still air was pressed beyond Adam, apparently leaving a vacuum, for there did not appear to be air enough to breathe. The roar of wind sounded still quite distant, though now loud. Then the hot blast struck Adam — a burning, withering wind. It was as if he had suddenly faced an open furnace from which flames and sparks leaped out upon him. That he could breathe, that he lived a moment, seemed a marvel. Wind and roar filled the wide space between the slopes and rushed on, carrying sand and dust and even shadows with it. That blast softened in volume and had almost died away when another whooped up through the gateway, louder and stronger and hotter than its predecessor. It blew down Adam's sun shelter of brush and carried the branches rustling away. Then stormed contending tides of winds until, what with burning blasts and whirling dust devils and air thick with powdered salt and alkali, life became indeed a torment for Adam, man of the desert as he was.

In the face of these furnace winds, tenacity of life had new meaning for Adam. The struggle to breathe was the struggle of a dying man to live. But Adam found that he could survive. It took labor, greater even than toiling through a sandstorm, or across a sun-scorched waste to a distant water hole. And it was involuntary labor. His great lungs were not a bellows for him to open when he chose. They were compelled to work. But the process, in addition to the burn and sting, the incessant thirst, the dust-laden air, the hot skullbone like an iron lid that must fly off, and the strange, dim, red starlight, the somber red varying shadow, the weird rush and roar and lull — all these created heroic fortitude if a man was to endure. Adam understood why no human being could long exist in Death Valley.

"She will not live through the night," muttered Adam. "But if she does, I think I'll take her away."

While in the unearthly starlit gloom, so dimly red, Adam slowly plodded across to the Virey camp, that idea grew in his mind. It had augmented before this hour, only to faint at the strength of her spirit, but tonight was different. It marked a climax. If Magdalene Virey showed any weakening, any change of spirit, Adam knew he would have reached the end of his endurance.

She would be lying or sitting on the stone bench. It was not possible to breathe inside the shack. Terrible as were the furnace winds, they had to be breasted — they had to be fought for the very air of life. She had not the strength to walk up and down, to and fro, through those endless hours.

Adam's keen eyes, peering through the red-tinged obscurity, made out the dark shape of Virey staggering along back and forth like an old man driven and bewildered, hounded by the death he feared. The sight gave Adam a moment of fierce satisfaction. Strong as was the influence of Magdalene Virey, it could not keep down hate for this selfish and fallen man. Selfish beyond all other frailty of human nature! The narrow mind obsessed with self — the I and me and mine — the miserable littleness that could not forgive, that could not understand! Adam had pity even in his hate.

He found the woman on the bench, lying

prone, a white, limp, fragile shape, motionless as stone. Sitting down, he bent over to look into her face. Her unfathomable eyes, wide and dark and strained, stirred his heart as never before. They were eyes to which sleep was a stranger — haunted eyes, like the strange midnight at which they gazed out, supernaturally bright, mirroring the dim stars, beautiful as the walking dreams never to come true — eyes of melancholy, of unutterable passion, of deathless spirit. They were the eyes of woman and of love.

Adam took her wasted hand and held it while waiting for the wind to lull so that she could hear him speak. At length the hot blast moved on, like the receding of a fire.

"Magdalene, I can't stand this any longer," he said.

"You mean — these winds — of hell?" she panted, in a whisper.

"No. I mean your suffering. I might have stood your spiritual ordeal. Your remorse — your agony of loss of the daughter Ruth — your brave spirit defying Virey's hate. . . . But I can't stand your physical torment. You're wasting away. You're withering — burning up. This hand is hot as fire — and dry as a leaf. You must drink more water. . . . Magdalene, lift your head."

"I — cannot," she whispered, with wan smile. "No — strength left."

Adam lifted her head and gave her water to

drink. Then as he laid her back another blast of wind came roaring through the strange opaque night. How it moaned and wailed around the huge bowlders and through the brush! It was a dance of wind fiends, hounding the lost spirits of this valley of horrors. Adam felt the slow, tight tide of his blood called stingingly to his skin and his extremities, and there it burned. It was not only his heart and his lungs that were oppressed, but the very life of his body seemed to be pressing to escape through the pores of his skin — pressed from inward by the terrible struggle to survive and pressed back from outside by the tremendous blast of wind! The wind roared by and lulled to a moan. The wave of invisible fire passed on. Out there in the dim starlight Virey staggered back and forth under the too great burden of his fate. He made no sound. He was a specter. Beyond the gray level of gloom with its strange shadows rose the immense slope of loose stones, all shining with dim, pale-red glow, all seemingly alive, waiting for the slide of the avalanche. And on the instant a rock cracked with faint ring, rolled with little hollow reports, mockingly, full of terrible and latent power. It had ominous answer in a slight jar of the earth under Adam's feet, perhaps an earthquake settling of the crust, and then the whole vast slope moved with a low, grating sound, neither roar nor crash, nor rattle. The avalanche had slipped a foot. Adam could have pealed out a cry of dread for this woman.

What a ghastly fantasy the struggle for life in Death Valley! What mockery of wind and desert and avalanche!

"Wansfell — listen," whispered the woman. "Do you hear — it passing on?"

"Yes," replied Adam, bending lower to see her eyes. Did she mean that the roar of wind was dying away?

"The stormy blast of hell — with restless fury — drives the spirits onward!" she said, her voice rising.

"I know — I understand. But you mustn't speak such thoughts. You must not give up to the wandering of your mind. You must fight," implored Adam.

"My friend — the fight is over — the victory is mine. . . . I shall escape Virey. He possessed my body — poor weak thing of flesh! . . . but he wanted my love — my soul. . . . My soul to kill! He'll never have either. . . . Wansfell, I'll not live — through the night. . . . I am dying now."

"No — no!" cried Adam, huskily. "You only imagine that. It's only the oppression of these winds — and the terror of the night — this awful, unearthly valley of death. You'll live. The winds will wear out soon. If only you fight you'll live. . . . And tomorrow — Magdalene, so help me God — I'll take you away!"

He expected the inflexible and magnetic opposition of her will, the resistless power of her spirit to uplift and transform. And this time

343

he was adamant. At last the desert force within him had arisen above all spiritual obstacles. The thing that called was life — life as it had been in the beginning of time. But no mockery or eloquence of refusal was forthcoming from Magdalene Virey. Instead, she placed the little ivory case, containing the miniature painting of her daughter Ruth, in Adam's hand and softly pressed it there.

"But — if I should die — I want you to have this picture of Ruth," she said. "I've had to hide it from Virey — to gaze upon it in his absence. Take it, my friend, and keep it, and look at it until it draws you to her. . . . Wansfell, I'll not bewilder you by mystic prophecies. But I tell you solemnly — with the clairvoyant truth given to a woman who feels the presence of death — that my daughter Ruth will cross your wanderer's trail — come into your life — and love you. . . . Remember what I tell you. I see! . . . You are a young man still. She is a budding girl. You two will meet, perhaps in your own wastelands. Ruth is all of me — magnified a thousand times. More — she is as lovely as an unfolding rose at dawn. She will be a white, living flame. . . . It will be as if I had met you long ago— when I was a girl — and gave you what by the nature of life was yours. . . . Wansfell, you wakened my heart — saved my soul — taught me peace. . . . I wonder how you did it. You were just a man. . . . There's a falseness of life — the

344

scales fell from my eyes one by one. It is the heart, the flesh, the bursting stream of red blood that count with nature. All this strife, this travail, makes toward a perfection never to be attained. But effort and pain, agony of flesh, and victory over mind make strength, virility. . . . Nature loves barbarian women who nurse their children. I — with all my love — could not nurse my baby Ruth. It's a mystery no longer. Death Valley and a primitive man have opened my eyes. Nature did not intend people to live in cities, but in forests, as lived the Aryans of India, or like the savages of Brazilian jungles. Like the desert beasts, self-sufficient, bringing forth few of their kind, but better, stronger species. The weak perish. So should the weak among men. . . . Ah! hear the roar! Another wind of death! . . . But I've said all. . . . Wansfell, go find Ruth — find me in her — and — remember!"

The rich voice, growing faint at the last, failed as another furnace blast came swooping up with its dust and heat. Adam bowed his head and endured. It passed and another came. The woman lay with closed eyes and limp body and nerveless hands. Hours passed and the terrible winds subsided. The shadow of a man that was Virey swaying to and fro, like a drunken specter, vanished in the shack. The woman slept. Adam watched by her side till dawn, and when the gray light came he could no more have been changed than could the night have been recalled. He would find the burros and pack them and saddle one for Magdalene Virey to ride; he would start to climb out of Death Valley and when another night fell he would have her safe on the cool mountain heights. If Virey tried to prevent this, it would mean the terrible end he merited. Adam gazed down upon the sleeping woman. How transparent, how frail a creature! She mystified Adam. She represented the creative force in life. She possessed that unintelligible and fatal thing in nature — the greatest, the most irresistible, the purest expression of truth, of what nature strove so desperately for — and it was beauty. Her youth, her error, her mocking acceptance of life, her magnificent spirit, her mother longing, her agony and her physical pangs, her awakening and repentance and victory — all were written on the pale face and with the indestructible charm of line and curve and classic feature constituted its infinite loveliness. She was a sleeping woman, yet she was close to the angels.

Adam looked from her to the ivory case in his hand.

"Her daughter Ruth — for me!" he said, wonderingly. "How strange if we met! If — if — But that's impossible. She was wandering in mind."

He carried the little case to his camp, searched in his pack for an old silk scarf, and, tearing this, he carefully wrapped the gift and deposited it inside the leather money belt he wore hidden round his waist.

346

"Now to get ready to leave Death Valley!" he exclaimed, in grim exultance.

Adam's burros seldom strayed far from camp. This morning, however, he did not find them near the spring nor down in the notches of the mountain wall. So he bent his steps in the other direction. At last, round a corner of slope, out of sight of camp, he espied them, and soon had them trotting ahead of him.

He had traversed probably half the distance he had come when the burro Jennie halted to shoot up her long ears. Something moving had attracted her attention, but Adam could not see it. He drove her on. Again she stopped. Adam could now see the shack, and as he peered sharply there seemed to cross his vision a bounding gray object. He rubbed his eyes and muttered. Perhaps the heat had affected his sight. Then between him and the shack flashed a rough object, gray-white in color, and it had the bounding motion of a jack rabbit. But it could not have been a rabbit, because it was too large, and, besides, there were none in the valley. A wild cat, perhaps? Adam urged Jennie on, and it struck him that she was acting queerly. This burro never grew contrary without cause. When she squealed and sheared off to one side Adam knew something was amiss. That vague shock returned to his consciousness, stronger, more certain and bewildering. Halting so as to hear better, he held his breath and listened. Crack and roll of rock — slow sliding rattle — crack!

The mystery of the bounding gray objects was solved. Virey had again taken to rolling rocks down the slope.

Adam broke into a run. He was quite a distance from the shack, though now he could see it plainly. No person was in sight. More than once, as he looked, he saw rocks bound high above the brush and fall to puff up dust. Virey was industrious this morning, making up for lost time, taking sure advantage of Adam's absence. Adam ran faster. He reached a point opposite the fanlike edge of the great slant of loose stones, and here he seemed to get into a zone of concatenated sounds. The wind, created by his run, filled his ears. And his sight, too, seemed not to be trusted. Did it not magnify a bounding rock and puff of dust into many rocks and puffs? Streaks were running low down in the brush, raising little dusty streams. He saw clumps of brush shake and bend. If something queer, such as had affected Jennie, did not possess his sight and mind, then it surely possessed Death Valley. For something was wrong.

Suddenly Adam's ears were deafened by a splitting shock. He plunged in his giant stride, slowed and halted. He heard the last of a sliding roar. The avalanche had slipped. But it had stopped. Bounding rocks hurtled in front of Adam, behind him, and puffs and streaks of dust were everywhere. He heard the whiz and thud of a rolling rock passing close behind him. As he gazed a large stone bounded from the ground and seemed to pass right through the shack. The shack collapsed. Adam's heart leaped to his throat. He was riveted to the spot. Then, mercifully it seemed, a white form glided out from the sun shelter. It was the woman, still unharmed. The sight unclamped Adam's voice and muscle.

"Go across! Hurry!" yelled Adam, with all the power of his lungs. He measured the distance between him and her. Two hundred yards! Rocks were hurtling and pounding across that space.

The woman heard him. She waved her white hand and it seemed she was waving him back out of peril. Then she pointed up the slope. Adam wheeled. What a thrilling sight! Rocks were streaking down, hurtling into the air, falling to crack powder from other rocks, that likewise were set in motion. Far up the long gray slope, with its million facets of stones shining in the sunlight, appeared Virey, working frantically. No longer did he seek to frighten his wife. He meant to kill her. His insane genius had read the secret of the slope, and in an instant he would have the avalanche in motion. The cracking clamor increased. Adam opened his lips to yell a terrible threat up at Virey, but a whizzing bowlder, large as a bucket, flashing within a foot of his head, awakened him to his own peril. He saw other rocks bounding down in line with him, and, changing his position, stepping, leaping, dodging, he managed to evade them. He had no fear for himself, but terror for the woman, and for Virey deadly rage possessed his heart.

Then a piercing split, as of rocks rent asunder, a rattling crash, and the lower half of the great gray slope was in motion The avalanche! Adam leaped at the startling sound, and, bounding a few yards to a huge bowlder, high as his head and higher, he mounted it. There, unmindful of himself, he wheeled to look for Magdalene Virey. Too late to reach her! She faced that avalanche, arms spread aloft, every line of her body instinct with the magnificent spirit which had been her doom.

"Run! Run! Run!" shrieked Adam, wildly.

Lost was his piercing shriek in the swallowing, gathering might of the crashing roar of the avalanche. A pall of dust, a gray tumbling mass, moved down ponderously, majestically, to hide from Adam's sight the white form of Magdalene Virey. It spread to where Adam stood, enveloped him, and then, in boom and thunder and crash as of falling worlds, the bowlder was lifted and carried along with the avalanche.

19
●

Adam was thrown prostrate. In the thick, smothering dust he all but lost his senses. Adam felt what seemed a stream of stones rolling over his feet. The thundering, deafening roar rolled on, spread and thinned to a rattling crash, deadened and ceased. Then from the hollows of the hills boomed a mighty echo, a lifting and throwing of measureless sound, that thumped from battlement to battlement and rumbled away like muttering thunder.

The silence then was terrible by contrast. As horror relaxed its grim clutch Adam began to realize that miraculously he had been spared. In the hot, dusty pall he fought for breath like a drowning man. The heavy dust settled and the lighter drifted away.

Adam clambered to his feet. The huge bowlder that had been his ship of safety appeared to be surrounded by a sea of small rocks, level with where he stood. The avalanche had spread a deep layer of rocks all over and beyond the space adjacent to the camp. Not a vestige of the shack remained. Magdalene Virey had been buried forever beneath a mass of stone. Adam's great frame shuddered with the convulsions of his emotion. He bent and bowed under the inevitable. "Oh, too late! too late! . . . Yet I knew all the time!" was the mournful cry he sent out into the silence. Dazed, sick, horror-stricken, he bowed there above Magdalene Virey's sepulcher and salt tears burned his eyes and splashed down upon the dusty stones. He suffered, dully at first, and then acutely, as his stunned consciousness began to recover. Tragic this situation had been from the beginning, and it could have had but one end.

Suddenly he remembered Virey. The thought transformed him.

"He must have slid with the avalanche," muttered Adam. "Buried under here somewhere. One sepulcher for him and wife! . . . So he wanted it — alive or dead!"

The lower part of the great slope was now solid rock, dusty and earthy in places, in others the gray color of live granite. It led his eye upward, half a mile, to the wide, riblike ridge that marked the lower margin of another slope of weathered rocks. It shone in the hot sunlight. Dark veils of heat rose, resembling smoke against the sky. The very air seemed trembling, and over that mountain-side hovered the shadow of catastrophe.

A moving white object caught Adam's roving sight. His desert eyes magnified that white object. A man! He was toiling over the loose stones.

"*Virey!*" burst out Adam, and with the explosion of the word all of the desert stormed in him and his nature was no different from the cataclysm that had shorn and scarred the slope.

Like a wide-lunged primordial giant, Adam lifted his roar of rage toward the heights — a yell that clapped fierce echoes from the cliffs. Virey heard. He began to clamber faster over the rocks and sheered off toward the right, where, under the beetling, steep slopes, every rod was more fraught with peril.

Adam bounded like a huge soft-footed cat over and up the hummocky spread of the avalanche. Virey's only avenue of escape lay upward and to the left. Once Adam cut him off there, he was in a trap.

To the right over the ridge small stones began to show, rolling and bouncing, then shooting like bullets off the bare slant below. Virey was out of Adam's sight now, but evidently still headed in the fatal direction. Like a mountain sheep, surest-footed of beasts, Adam bounded from loose rock to sharp corner, across the wide holes, on and upward.

Another low, vast slope spread out and sheered gradually up before him, breaking its uniformity far to the right, and waving gracefully to steep slants of loose rock perilous to behold. Adam heard the faint cracking of stones. He hurried on, working away from the left, until he was climbing straight toward the splintered, toppling mass of mountain peak, a mile above him. All now, in every direction, was broken rock, round, sharp, flat, octagonal, every shape, but mostly round, showing how in the process of ages the rolling and grinding had worn off the edges. Here the heat smoked up. When Adam laid a hurried hand on a stone he did not leave it there long.

At length he again espied Virey, far to the right and half a mile farther up, climbing like a weary beast on hands and feet. By choice or by mistake he had gone upward to the most hazardous zone of all that treacherous, unstable mountain-side. Even now the little dusty slides rolled from under him. Adam strode on. He made short cuts. He avoided the looser slides. He zigzagged the steeper places. He would attend to safe stepping stones for a few rods, then halt to lift his gaze toward that white-shirted man toiling up like a crippled ape. The mountain slope, though huge and wide under the glaring sun, seemed to lose something of its openness. The red battlements and ramparts of the heights were frowning down upon it, casting a shadow of menace, if not of shade. The terrible forces of nature became manifest. Here the thunderbolts boomed and the storms battled, and in past ages the earthquake and volcanic fire had fretted the once noble peak. It was ruined. It had disintegrated. Ready to spread its million cracks and crumble, it lowered gloomily.

Red, sinister, bare, ghastly, this smoky slope under the pitiless sun was a fitting place for

Wansfell to get his hands on Virey — murderer of a woman. Adam thought of it that way because he remembered how Virey had been fascinated at the story of Baldy McKue. But mostly Adam's mind worked like the cunning instinct of a wolf to circumvent its prey. Thoughts were but flashes. The red tinge in Adam's sight did not all come from the color or the rock. And it was when he halted to look or rest that he thought at all.

But the time came when he halted for more than that. Placing his hands around his mouth, he expanded his deep lungs and burst into trumpetlike yell:

"VIREY!" The fugitive heard, turned from his toiling, slid to a seat on the precarious slope, and waited. "I'LL BREAK YOUR BONES!"

A wild cry peeled down to ring in Adam's ears. He had struck terror to the heart of the murderer. And Adam beat down his savage eagerness, so as to lengthen the time till Virey's doom. Not thus did the desert in Adam speak, but what the desert had made him. Agony, blood, death! They were almost as old as the rocks. Other animate shapes, in another age, had met in strife there, under the silent, beetling peak. Life was the only uttermost precious thing. All else, all suffering, all possession, was nothing. To kill a man was elemental, as to save him was divine.

Virey's progress became a haunting and all-satisfying spectacle to behold, and Adam's pursuit became studied, calculated, retarded — a thing as cruel as the poised beak of a vulture.

Virey got halfway up a gray, desolate, weathered slant, immense in its spread, another fan-shaped, waiting avalanche. The red ragged heights loomed above; below hung a mountainside as unstable as water, restrained, perhaps, by a mere pebble. Here Virey halted. Farther he could not climb. Like a spent and cornered rat he meant to show fight.

Adam soon reached a point directly below Virey, some hundreds of yards — a long, hard climb. He paused to catch his breath.

"Bad slope for me if he begins to roll stones!" muttered Adam, grimly.

But neither rolling stones nor avalanches could stop Adam. The end of this tragedy was fixed. It had been set for all the years of Virey's life and back into the past. The very stones cried out. Glaring sun, smoking heat, shining slope, and the nameless shadow — all were tinged with a hue inimical to Virey's life. The lonely, solemn, silent desert day, at full noon-tide heat, bespoke the culmination of something Virey had long ago ordained. Far below, over the lower hills of the Panamints, yawned Death Valley, ghastly gray through the leaden haze, an abyss of ashes, iron walled and sun blasted, hateful and horrible as the portal of hell. High up and beyond, faintly red against an obscure space of sky, towered the Funerals, grand and desolate.

Adam began to climb the weathered slope,

taking a zigzag course. Sliding stones only slightly retarded his ascent. He stepped too quickly. Usually when a stone slipped his weight had left it.

Virey set loose a bowlder. It slid, rolled, leaped, fell with a crack, and then took to hurtling bounds, starting a multitude of smaller stones. Adam kept keen eye on the bowlder and paid no attention to the others. Then he stepped aside out of its course. As it whizzed past him Virey slid another loose upon the slope. Adam climbed even as the rock bounded down, and a few strides took him to one side. Virey ran over, directly in line with Adam, and started another huge rock. Thus by keeping on a zigzag ascent Adam kept climbing most of the time, and managed to avoid the larger missiles. The smaller ones, however, could not all be avoided. And their contact was no slight matter. Virey tugged upon a large rock, deeply embedded, and rolled it down. Huge, bounding, crashing, it started a rattling slide that would have swept Adam to destruction had it caught him. But he leaped out of line just in the nick of time. Virey began to work harder, to set loose smaller stones and more of them, so that soon he had the slope a perilous ascent for Adam. They cracked and banged down, and the debris rattled after them. Adam swerved and leaped and ran. He smelled the brimstone powder and the granite dust. Fortunately, no cloud of dust collected to obscure his watchful sight. He climbed on, swiftly when advantage offered, cautiously when he must take time to leap and dodge. Then a big rock started a multitude of small ones, and all clattered and spread. Adam dashed forward and backward. The heavier stones bounced high, and as many came at one time, he could not watch all. As he dodged one, another waved the hair of his head, and then another, striking his shoulder, knocked him down. The instant he lay there, other stones rolled over him. Adam scrambled up. Even pain could not change his fierce, cold implacability, but it accelerated his action. He played no longer with Virey. He yelled again what he meant to do with his hands, and he spread them aloft, great, clawlike members, the sight of which inflamed Virey to desperation. Frantically he plowed up the stones and rolled them, until he had a deluge plunging down the slope. But it was not written that Adam should be disabled. Narrow shaves he had, and exceeding risks he took, yet closer and closer he climbed. Only a hundred yards now separated the men. Adam could plainly see Virey's ragged shirt, flying in shreds, his ashen face, his wet hair matted over his eyes.

Suddenly above the cracks and rattling clash rose a heavy, penetrating sound. Mighty rasp of a loose body against one of solidity! Startled to a halt, Adam gazed down at his feet. The rocks seemed to be heaving. Then a dreadful yell broke sharply. Virey! Adam flashed his gaze upward in time to see the whole slope move.

And that move was accompanied by a rattling crash, growing louder and more prolonged. Virey stood stricken by mortal terror in the midst of an avalanche.

Wheeling swiftly, Adam bounded away and down, his giant strides reaching farther and faster, his quivering body light and supple, his eye guiding his flying feet to surfaces that were safe. Behind, beyond, above him the mountain slope roared until sound no longer meant anything. His ears were useless. The slope under him heaved and waved. Running for his life, he was at the same time riding an avalanche. The accelerating motion under him was strange and terrifying. It endowed him with wings. His feet scarcely touched the stones and in a few seconds he had bounded off the moving section of slope.

Then he halted to turn and see, irresistibly called to watch Virey go to what must soon be a just punishment. The avalanche, waving like swells of the sea, seemed slowing its motion. Thin dust clouds of powdered rock hung over it. Adam again became aware of sound — a long-drawn, rattling roar, decreasing, deadening, dying. Suddenly as the avalanche had started it halted. But it gave forth grating, ominous warnings. Only an upper layer of the loose rock had slid down, and the under layer appeared precisely like what the surface had been — rocks and rocks of all sizes, just as loose, just as ready to roll.

Adam dared to stride back upon that exposed under layer, the better to see straight down the steep slope. Grim and grisly it shone beneath the gloomy sun. Perhaps the powdered dust created an obscurity high in the air, but low down all was clear.

Virey could be plainly seen, embedded to his hips in the loose stones. Writhing, squirming, wrestling, he sought to free himself from that grip of granite. In vain! He was caught in a vise of his own making. Prisoner of the mountain-side that he had used to betray his wife! He had turned toward Adam, face upward. There seemed a change in him, but in the racking excitement of that moment Adam could not tell what.

Then that desert instinct, like the bursting of a flood, moved Adam to the violence of strife, the ruthlessness of nature, the blood-spilling of men. Madness of hate seized him. The torrid heat of that desert sun boiled in his blood, the granite of the slope hardened in his heart, the red veils of smoky shadows colored his sight. Loneliness and solitude were terrible forces of nature — primitive as the beginnings of life. For years the contending strife of the desert had been his. For months desolation, death, decay of Death Valley!

"MY TURN!" he yelled, in voice of thunder, and, bristling haired, supple, and long armed, with strength and laugh and face of a savage, he heaved a huge rock.

It rolled, it cracked, it banged, it hurtled high, to crash and smash, and then, leaping aloft, instinct as if with mockery, it went over Virey's head to go on down over the precipice, whence it sent up a sliding roar. Adam heaved another stone and watched it. Virey grew motionless as a statue. He could not dance and dodge away from rolling rocks as Adam had done. How strangely that second rock rolled! Starting in line with Virey, it swerved to the right, then hit the slope and swerved back in line, then, hitting again, swerved once more, missing the miserable victim by a small margin.

"AHA THERE, VIREY!" yelled Adam, waving his hands. "ALL DAY AND ALL NIGHT I'LL ROLL STONES!"

Virey was mute. He was chained. He was helpless. He could not move or faint or die. Retribution had overtaken him. The nature of it was to be the nature of the slow torture and merciless death he had inflicted upon his wife. As he had chosen the most deadly and lonely and awful spot on earth to hide her and kill her, so the nature that he had embraced now chose to turn upon him. There was law here — law of the unknown forces in life and in the elements. At that very moment a vulture streaked down from the hazed heights and sailed, a black shadow of wide-spread wings, across the slope. What had given this grisly-omened bird sight and scent illimitable?

Adam braced his brawny shoulder under the

361

bulge of a rock weighing tons. Purple grew his face. His muscles split his shirt. His bones cracked. But there was a nameless joy in this exercise of his enormous strength. They were two men — one was weak, the other was strong. And nature could not abide both. The huge rock grated, groaned, stirred, moved — and turned over, slowly to roll, to crunch, to pound, and then to gather speed, growing a thing of power, ponderous, active, changing, at last to hurtle into the air, to plunge down with thunderous crash, then to roll straight as a bee line at Virey. But a few yards in front of him it rose aloft, with something of grace, airily, and, sailing over Virey's head, it banged and boomed out of sight below. Long the echoes clapped, and at last the silence, the speaking silence of that place, closed on the slope. It awoke again to Adam's rolling of a stone and another and another and then two together. All these rocks rolled differently. They were playthings of the god of the mountain. The mover of thunderbolts might have been aiming his colossal missiles at an invisible target. All these rolling stones seemed to head straight for Virey, but they were at the last instant deflected by chance. They hit the slope and passed wide or high. They were in league with the evil spirit that had dominated Virey. They were instruments of torture. They were of the nature of the desert. They belonged to Death Valley.

Adam did not soon tire at his gigantic task.

The rolling stones fascinated him. From dead things they leaped to life. How they hurtled through space! Some shot aloft a hundred feet. Others split, and rolled, like wheels, down and down, the halves passing on either side of the doomed Virey. A multitude of rocks Adam turned loose, and then another multitude. Into the heaving of every one went his intent to kill. But Virey bore a charmed life.

A time came when Adam rolled his last stone. Like the very first one, it sped straight for Virey, and just as it appeared about to crush him it veered to one side. Adam stared grim and aghast. Could he never kill Virey as Virey had murdered his wife and tried to kill him?

"She — said I'd — never kill — you!" panted Adam, and the doubt in him was a strange, struggling thing, soon beaten down by his insatiable rage. Then he took a stride downward, meaning to descend and finish Virey with his hands.

As he stepped down the avalanche below grated with strange, harsh sound. It seemed to warn him. Halting, he gazed with clearer eyes. What was this change in Virey? Adam bent and peered. Had the man's hair turned snow white?

Adam made another and a longer stride downward. And that instant the slope trembled. Virey flung up his arms as if to ward off another rolling stone. A rending, as of the rockbound fastness of the slope yielding its hold — then the avalanche, with Virey in the center, moved downward, slowly heaving like a swell of weighted waves, and started to roll with angry roar. It gathered a ponderous momentum. It would never stop again on that slope. A shining, red-tinged dust cloud shrouded Virey. And then the avalanche, spilling over the declivity below, shocked the whole mountain slope and lifted to the heavens a thick-crashing, rolling roar of thunder. Death Valley engulfed the hollow echo and boomed thunder across to the battlements of the Funeral Mountains. And when the last rumble wore away, silence and solitude reigned there, pervasive and peaceful, as they had in the ages before man, with his passions, had evolved to vex nature.

20
●

Adam's return to camp was as vague as one of his desert nightmares. But as thought gained something of ascendency over agitation he became aware of blood and dust and sweat caked with his clothes upon his person, proving the effect of his supreme exertions. He had heaved an endless number of rocks; he had heaved the mountain-side down upon Virey, all to no avail. A higher power had claimed him. And the spirit of Magdalene Virey, like her living presence, had inscrutably come between Adam and revenge.

When Adam had packed his burros, twilight in the clefts of the hills had deepened to purple. He filled his canteens, and started the burros down toward the gateway. The place behind him was as silent as a grave. Adam did not look back. He felt the gray obscurity close over the scene.

Down at the gateway he saw that the valley was still light with the afterglow of sunset. Diagonally and far across the ashen waste he descried the little dark patch which he knew to be an oasis, where the waters of Furnace Creek sank into the sands.

The intense heat, the vast stillness, the strange radiation from the sand, the peculiar gray light of the valley, told Adam that the midnight furnace winds would blow long before he reached his destination. But he welcomed any physical ordeal. He saw how a great strife with the elements, a strain to the uttermost of his strength and his passion to fight, would save his faith, his hope, perhaps his mind.

So gradual was the change from twilight to darkness that he would scarcely have noted it but for the dimming of the notched peak. Out there in the open valley it was not dark. It was really the color of moonlight on marble. Wan, opaque, mystic, it made distance false.

The mountains seemed far away and the stars close. Like the bottom of the Dead Sea, drained of its bitter waters, was this Death Valley. Action, strong and steady use of muscle, always had served to drive subjective broodings and wonderings and imaginings from Adam's mind. But not here, in this sink, at night! He seemed continually and immensely confronted with the unreality of a fact — a live man alone on the salt dead waste of Death Valley. Measureless and unbreakable solitude! The waste hole into which drained the bitter dregs of the desert!

He plodded on, driving the burros ahead of him. Jennie was contrary. Every few steps she edged off a straight line, and the angle of her ears and head showed that she was watching her master. She did not want to cross the valley. Instinct taught her the wisdom of opposition. Many a burro had saved its master's life by stubborn refusal to travel the wrong way. Adam was patient, even kind, but he relentlessly drove her on in the direction he had chosen.

At length the ashen level plain changed its hue and its surface. The salt crust became hummocky and a dirty gray. The color caused false steps on his part, and the burros groped at fault, weary and discouraged. Adam would mount a slow heave, only to find it a hollow crust that broke with his weight. Some months before — or, was it years? — when he had crossed the valley, far below this line, the layer of salt crust had been softer and under it ran murky waters, heavy as vitriol. Dry now as sunbaked clay! It made travel more difficult, although less dangerous. Adam broke through once. It reminded him that Dismukes had said the floor of Death Valley was "Forty feet from hell!" Not for a long while had he thought of Dismukes, yet this hazardous direction he was taking now appeared to be the outcome of long-made plans to meet the old prospector.

Long hours and slow miles passed behind him. When the burros broke through Adam had a task for all his strength. Once he could not pull Jennie out of a pitfall without unpacking her. And the time came when he had the added task of leading the way and dragging the burros with ropes. Burros did not lead well on good ground, let alone over this scored and burst salt crust.

The heat and oppressiveness and dense silence increased toward midnight; and then began a soft and steady movement of air down the valley. Adam felt a prickling of his skin and a drying of the sweat upon him. An immense and mournful moan breathed over the wasteland, like that of a mighty soul in travail. Adam got out of the hummocky zone upon the dry, crisp, white level of salt, soda, borax, alkali, where thin, pale sheets of powder moved with the silken rustle of seeping and shifting sands. Most fortunate was the fact that the rising wind was at his back. He strode on, again driving the burros ahead, holding straight for the dim notched peak. The rising wind changed the silence, the night, the stars, the valley — changed all in some unearthly manner. It seemed to muster all together, to move all, to insulate even the loneliness, and clothe them in transforming, drifting, shrouds of white, formless bodies impelled by nameless domination. Phantasmagoria of white winds, weird and wild! Midnight furnace blasts of Death Valley! Nature's equilibrium — nature's eternal and perfect balance of the elements!

Out here in the open, the hollow roar that had swelled and lulled through the canyons was absent. An incessant moaning, now rising, now falling, attended the winds on their march down the valley. Other difference there was here, and it was in the more intense heat. And the blowing of white shrouds into the opaque gloom, the sweeping of sheets of powdery dust along the level floor, the thick air that bore taste of bitter salt and odor of poison gas — these indeed seemed not phenomena of normal earth. The wind increased to a gale. Then suddenly it lulled and died, leaving the valley to a pale, silent deadness; and again, preceded by a mournful wail, it rose harder and fiercer till it was blowing seventy miles an hour. These winds were the blasts of fury. They held heated substance. The power behind them was the illimitable upper air, high as the sky and wide as the desert, relentlessly bearing down to drive way the day's torrid heat.

The gales accelerated Adam's progress, so that

sometimes he was almost running. Often he was thrown to his knees. And when the midnight storm reached its height the light of the stars failed, the outline of mountains faded in a white, whirling chaos, dim and moaning and terrible. Adam felt as if blood and flesh were burning up, drying out, shriveling and cracking. He lost his direction and clung to the burros, knowing their instinct to be surer guide than his. There came a time when pain left him, when sense of physical contacts and motions began to fade, when his brain seemed to reel. The burros dragged him on, and lower he swayed; oftener he plunged to his knees, plowing his big hands in the salt and lowering his face into the flying sheets of powder. He gasped and coughed and choked, and fought to breathe through his smothering scarf. And at last, as he fell exhausted, blind and almost asphyxiated, the hot gales died away. The change of air saved Adam from unconsciousness. He lay there, gradually recovering, until he gained feeling enough to know the burros were pulling on the rope which tied them and him together. They were squealing. They were trying to drag him, to warn him, to frighten him into the action that would save his life. Thus goaded, Adam essayed to get upon his feet, and the effort seemed a vague, interminable lifting of colossal weights, and a climbing up dragging stairs of sand. But for the burros he would have plunged in a circle.

Then followed a black and horrible interval

in which he seemed hauled across a pale shingle of naked earth, peopled with specters, a wandering, lost man, still alive but half dead, leashed to the spirits of burros he had driven to their death. Uphill, always uphill they pulled him, with his feet clogged by the clutching sands. A gray dawn broke, and his entrance into the light resembled climbing out of somber depths to the open world. Another drab wall of iron rock seemed to loom over him. The valley of the white shadows of death had been crossed. A green patch of mesquites and cottonwoods gleamed cool and dark out of the gray sands. The burros ran, with bobbing packs, straight to the water they had scented. Staggering on after them, Adam managed to remove their burdens; and that took the remnant of his strength. Yielding to a dead darkness of sense, he fell under the trees.

When he came to the day had far advanced and the sun, sloping to the west, was sinking behind the Panamints. Adam stumbled up, his muscles numb, as if contracted and robbed of their elasticity. His thirst told the story of that day's heat, which had parched him, even while he lay asleep in the shade. Hunger did not trouble him. Either he was weak from exertion or had suffered from breathing poisoned air or had lost something of his equilibrium. Whatever was wrong, it surely behooved him to get out of the lower part of the valley, up above sea level to a place where he could regain his strength.

To that end he hunted for his burros. They were close by, and he soon packed them, though with much less than his usual dexterity. Then he started, following the course of the running water.

This Furnace Creek ran down out of a deep-mouthed canyon, with yellow walls of gravel. The water looked like vinegar, and it was hot and had a bad taste. Yet it would sustain life of man and beast. Adam followed the lines of mesquites that marked its course up the gradually ascending floor of the canyon. He soon felt a loosening of the weight upon his lungs, and lessening of air pressure. Twilight caught him a couple of miles up the canyon, where a wide, long thicket of weeds and grass and mesquites marked the turning of Furnace Creek into the drab hills, and where springs and little streams trickled down from the *arroyos*.

Up one of these *arroyos*, in the midst of some gnarled mesquites, Adam made camp. Darkness soon set in, and he ate by the light of a camp fire. After he had partaken of food he discovered that he was hungry. Also, his eyelids drooped heavily. Despite these healthy reactions and a deeper interest in his surroundings, Adam knew he was not entirely well. He endeavored to sit up awhile, and tried to think. There were intervals when a deadlock occurred between thoughts. The old pleasure, the old watchful listening, the old intimate sense of loneliness, had gone from him. His mind did not seem to be on physical things at hand, or on the present moment. And when he actually discovered that all the time he looked down toward Death Valley he exclaimed, aghast: "I'm not here; I'm down there!"

Gloomy and depressed, he rolled in his blankets. And he slept twelve hours. Next day he felt better in body, but no different in mind. He set to work making a comfortable camp in spite of the fact that he did not seem to want to stay there. Hard work and plenty of food improved his condition. His strength of limb soon rallied to rest and nourishment. But the strange state of mind persisted, and began to encroach upon every moment. It took effort of will to attend to any action. Dismukes must be in this locality somewhere, according to the little map, but, though Adam remembered this, and reflected how it accounted for his own presence there, he could not dwell seriously upon the fact. Dismukes seemed relegated to the vague future. There was an impondering present imperative something that haunted Adam, yet eluded his grasp. At night he walked under the stars and could not shake off the spell; and next day, when in an idle hour he found himself walking again and again down the gravel-bedded canyon toward Death Valley, then he divined that what he had attributed to absent-mindedness was a far more serious aberration.

The discovery brought about a shock that quickened his mental processes. What ailed him?

He was well and strong again. What was wrong with his mind? Where had gone the old dreaming content, the self-sufficient communion with all visible forms of nature, and the half-conscious affinity with all the invisible spirit of the wilderness? How strangely he had been warped out of his orbit! Something nameless and dreadful and calling had come between him and his consciousness. Why did he face the west, at dawn, in the solemn white-hot noon, at the red sunset hour, and in the silent lonely watches of the night? Why did not the stars of the east lure his dreamy gaze as those in the west? He made the astounding discovery that there were moments, and moments increasing in number, when he did not feel alone. Some one walked in his shadow at noontide. At twilight a spirit seemed in keeping with his wandering westward steps. The world and natural objects and old habits seemed far off. He found himself whispering vagrant fancies, the substance of which, once realized, was baffling and disheartening. And at last he divined that a longing to return to Death Valley consumed him.

"Ah! So that's it!" he muttered, in consternation. "But why?"

It came to Adam then — the secret of the mystery. Death Valley called him. All that it was, all that it contained, all he had lived there, sent out insidious and enchanting voices of terrible silent power. The long shadow of that valley of purple shadows still enveloped him. Death, desolation, and decay; the appalling nudity of the racked bowels of the earth; the abode of solitude and silence, where shrieked the furies of the midnight winds; the grave of Magdalene Virey — these haunted Adam and lured him back with resistless and insupportable claim.

"Death Valley again — for me. I shall go mad," soliloquized Adam.

At last his mind was slowly being unhinged by the forces of the desert. Some places of the earth were too strong, too inhuman, too old, and too wasted for any man. Adam realized his peril, and that the worst of his case consisted in an indifference which he did not want to combat. Unless something happened — a great, intervening, destructive agent to counteract the all-enfolding, trancelike spell of Death Valley — Adam would return to the valley of avalanches and there he would go mad.

And the very instant he resigned himself, a cry pierced his dull ear. Sharply he sat up. The hour was near the middle of the forenoon. The day was hot and still. Adam's pulses slowly quieted down. He had been mistaken. The water babbled by his camp, bees flew over with droning hum. Then as he relaxed he was again startled by a cry, faint and far off. It appeared to come from up the canyon, round the low yellow corner of wall. He listened intently, but the sound was not repeated. Was not the desert full of silent voices? About this cry there was a tangible reality that stirred Adam out of his dreams, his glooms.

Adam went on, and climbed up the gravel bank on the left side, to a bare slope, and from that to the top of a ridge. His sluggish blood quickened. The old exploring instinct awoke. He had heard a distant cry. What next? There was something in the air.

Then Adam gazed around him to a distance. Adam shuddered and thrilled at the beetling, rugged, broken walls that marked the gateway where so often he had stood with Magdalene Virey to watch the transformations of shadowed dawn and sunset in Death Valley.

He descended to a level, and strode on, looking everywhere, halting now and then to listen, every moment gaining some hold on his old self. He went on and on, slow and sure, missing not a rod of ground, as if the very stones might speak to him. He welcomed his growing intensity of sensation, because it meant that he had either received a premonition or had reverted to his old self, or perhaps both.

Adam plodded along this wide gravel wash, with the high bronze saw-toothed peaks of the Funerals on the left, and some yellow-clay dunes showing their tips over the bank on the right. At length he came to a place that suggested a possible sloping of these colored clay dunes down into a basin or canyon. Climbing up the bank, he took a few steps across the narrow top, there to be halted as if he had been struck.

He had been confronted by a tremendous amphitheater, a yellow gulf, a labyrinthine maze so astounding that he discredited his sight.

Before him and on each side the earth was as bare as the bareness of rock — a mystic region of steps and slopes and slants, of channels and dunes and mounds, of cone-shaped and fan-shaped ridges, all of denuded crinkly clay with tiny tracery of erosion as graceful as the veins of a leaf, all merging their marvelous hues in a mosaic of golden amber, of cream yellow, of mauve, of bronze cinnamon. How bleak and ghastly, yet how beautiful in their stark purity of denudation! Endless was the number of smooth, scalloped, and ribbed surfaces, all curving with exquisite line and grace down into the dry channels under the dunes. At the base of the lower circle of the amphitheater the golds and yellows and russets were strongest, but along the wide wings moving away toward the abyss below were more vividly wonderful hues — a dark, beautiful mouse color on the left contrasting with a strange pearly cream on the other. These were striking bands of color, sweeping the eye away as far as they extended, and jealously drawing it back again. Between these great corners of the curve climbed ridges of gray and heliotrope to meet streaks of green — the mineral green of copper, like the color of the sea in sunlight — and snowy traceries of white that were narrow veins of outcropping borax. High up above the rim of the amphitheater, along the battlements of the mountain, stood out a zigzag belt of rusty red, from which the iron stain had run downward to tinge the lower hues. Above all this wondrous coloration upheaved the bare breast of the mountain, growing darker with earthy browns until the bold ramparts of the peak, gray like rock, gleamed pale against the leaden-blue sky. Low down through the opening of the amphitheater gleamed a void, a distant bottom of the bowl, dim and purple and ghastly, with shining white streaks like silver streams — and this was Death Valley.

And then Adam, with breast oppressed by feelings too deep for utterance, retracted his far-seeing gaze, once more to look over the whole amazing spectacle, from the crinkly buff clay under his feet to the dim white bottom of the valley. And at this keen instant he again heard a cry. Human it was, or else he had lost his mind, and all which he saw here was disordered imagination.

Turning back, he ran in the direction whence he believed the sound had come, passing by some rods the point where he had climbed out of the wash. And at the apex of the great curve, toward which tended all the multitude of wrinkles of the denuded slopes, he found a trail coming up out of the amphitheater and leading down into the wash. The dust bore unmistakable signs of fresh moccasin tracks, of hobnailed boots, and of traces where water had been spilled. The boot impressions led down and the moccasin tracks up; and, as these latter were the fresher, Adam, after a pause of astonishment and a keen glance all around, began to follow them.

The trail led across the wash and turned west toward where the walls commenced to take on the dignity of a canyon. Bunches of sage and greasewood began to dot the sand, and beyond showed the thickets of mesquite. Some prospector was packing water from the creek up the canyon and down into that amphitheater. Suddenly Adam thought of Dismukes. He examined the next hobnailed boot track he descried in the dust with minute care. The foot that had made it did not belong to Dismukes. Adam hurried on.

He came upon a spot where the man he was trailing surely an Indian — had fallen in the sand. A dark splotch, sticky and wet, had never been made by spilled water. Adam recognized blood when he touched it, but if he had not known it by the feel, he surely would have by the smell. Probably at that instant Adam became fully himself again. He was on the track of events, he sensed some human being in trouble; and the encroaching spell of Death Valley lost its power.

The trail led into the mesquites, to a wet glade rank with sedge and dank with the damp odor of soapy water.

A few more hurried strides brought Adam upon the body of an Indian, lying face down at the edge of the trickling little stream. His black matted hair was bloody. A ragged, torn, and stained shirt bore further evidence of violence. Adam turned him over, seeing at a glance that he had been terribly beaten about the head with a blunt instrument. He was gasping. Swiftly Adam scooped up water in his hat. He had heard that kind of a gasp before. Lifting the Indian's head, Adam poured water into the open mouth. Then he bathed the blood-stained face.

The Indian was of the tribe that had packed supplies for the Vireys. He was apparently fatally hurt. It was evident that he wanted to speak. And from the incoherent mixture of language which these Indians used in conversation with white men Adam gathered significant details of gold, of robbers, of something being driven round and round, grinding stone like maize.

"Arrastra!" queried Adam.

The Indian nodded and made a weak motion of his hand toward the trail that led to the yellow wilderness of clay, and then further gestures, which, with a few more gutturally whispered words, gave Adam the impression that a man of huge bulk, wide of shoulder, was working the old Spanish treadmill — *arrastra* — grinding for gold. Then the Indian uttered, with a last flash of spirit, the warning he could not speak, and, falling back, he gasped and faded into unconsciousness.

Adam stood up, thinking hard, muttering aloud some of his thoughts.

"Arrastra! . . . That was the way of Dismukes

— to grind for gold. . . . He's here — somewhere — down in that yellow hole. . . . Robbers have jumped his claim — probably are holding him — torturing him to tell of hidden gold . . . and they beat this poor Indian to death."

There was necessity for quick thought and quick action. The Indian was not dead, but he soon would be. Adam could do nothing for him. It was imperative to decide whether to wait here for the return of the water carrier or at once follow the trail to the yellow clay slopes. Adam wore a gun, but it held only two unused shells, and there was no more ammunition in his pack. The Indian had no weapon. Perhaps the water carrier would be armed. If Dismukes were dead, there need be no rash hurry to avenge him; if he lived as prisoner a little time more or less would not greatly matter. Adam speedily decided to wait a reasonable time for the man who packed water, and, if he came, to kill him and then hurry up the trail. There was, in this way, less danger of being discovered, and, besides, one of the robbers dispatched would render the band just so much weaker. Adam especially favored this course because of the possibility of getting a weapon.

"And more," muttered Adam, "if he happens to be a tall man I can pretend to be him — packing water back."

Therefore Adam screened himself behind a thick clump of mesquite near the trail and waited in ambush like a panther ready to spring.

As he crouched there, keen eyes up the canyon, ears like those of a listening deer, there flashed into Adam's mind one of Magdalene Virey's unforgettable remarks. "The power of the desert over me lies somewhere in my strange faculty of forgetting self. I watch, I hear, I feel, I smell, but I don't think. Just a gleam — a fleeting moment — then the state of consciousness or lack of consciousness is gone! But in that moment lies the secret lure of the desert. Its power over men!"

Swiftly as it had come the memory passed, and Adam became for fleeting moments at a time the embodiment of Magdalene Virey's philosophy, all unconscious when thought was absent from feeling. The hour was approaching midday and the wind began to rustle the mesquites and seep the sand. Adam smelled a dry dust somewhat tangy, and tasted the bitterness of it as he licked his lips. Flies had begun to buzz around the dead Indian. Instinctively Adam gazed aloft, and, yes, there far above him circled a vulture, and above that another, sweeping down from the invisible depths of blue, magically ringing a flight around the heavens, with never a movement of wings. They sailed round and round, always down. Where did they come from? What power poised them so surely in the air?

Adam waited. All at once his whole body vibrated with the leap of his heart. A tall, hulking man hove in sight, balancing a bar across his shoulders, from each end of which hung a large bucket. These buckets swung to and fro with the fellow's steps. Like a lazy man, he advanced leisurely. Adam saw a little puff of smoke lift from the red, indistinct patch that was this water carrier's face. He had cigarette or pipe. As he approached nearer and nearer, Adam received steadily growing and changing impressions of the man he was about to kill, until they fixed in the image of a long, loosely jointed body, a soiled shirt open at the neck, bare brown arms, and cruel red face. Just outside the mesquites, the robber halted to peer at the spot where the Indian had fallen, and then ahead as if he expected to see a body lying in the trail.

"Ho! Ho! if thet durned Injin I beat didn't crawl way down hyar! An' his brains oozin' out!" he ejaculated hoarsely, as he strode between the scratching mesquites, swinging the crossbar and buckets sidewise. "Takes a hell of a lot to kill some critters!"

Like a released spring Adam shot up. His big hands flashed to cut off a startled yell.

"Not so much!" he called, grimly, and next instant his giant frame strung to the expenditure of mighty effort.

At noon the wind was blowing a gusty gale and the sun shone a deep, weird, magenta color through the pall of yellow dust. The sky was not visible. Down on the ridges and in the washes dust sheets were whipped up at intervals. Clouds of flying sand rustled through the air, and sometimes the wind had force enough to carry grains of gravel. These intermittent blasts resembled the midnight furnace winds, except for the strange fact that they were not so hot, so withering. Every few minutes the canyon would be obscured in sweeping, curling streaks and sheets of dust. Then, as the gale roared away, the dust settled and the air again cleared. But high up, the dull, yellow pall hung, apparently motionless, with that weird sun, like a red-orange moon seen through haze, growing darker.

The fury of the elements seemed to favor Adam. Heat and gale and obscurity could tend only to relax the vigilance of men. Adam counted upon surprising the gang. To his regret, he had found no weapon on the robber he had overcome. Wearing the man's slouch sombrero pulled down, and carrying the water buckets suspended from the bar across his shoulders, Adam believed that in the thick of the duststorm he might approach near the gang, perhaps get right among them.

When he got to the top of the amphitheater and found it a weird and terrible abyss of flying yellow shadows and full of shriek of wind and moan and roar, he decided he would go down as far as might seem advisable, then try to slip up on the robbers, wherever they were, and get a look at them and their surroundings before rushing to the attack.

Down, and yet farther, Adam plodded, amazed at the depth of the pit, the bottom of which he had not seen. The plainly defined trail led him on, and in one place huge boot tracks, familiar to him, acted as a spur. The tracks were not many days old and had been made by Dismukes. Adam now expected to find his old friend dead or in some terrible situation. The place, the day, the heat, the wind — all presaged terror, violence, gold, and blood. No human beings would endure this nude and ghastly and burning hell hole of flying dust for anything except gold.

At last Adam got so far down, so deep into the yellow depths, that pall and roar of dust-storm appeared above him. He walked in a strange yellow twilight. And here the sun showed a darker magenta. Fine siftings of dust floated and fell all around him, dry, choking, and, when they touched his face, like invisible sparks of fire.

Interminably the yellow-walled wash wound this way and that, widening out to the dimensions of a canyon. At length Adam smelled smoke. He was close to a camp of some kind. Depositing the buckets in the trail, he sheered off and went up an intersecting wash.

When out of sight of the trail, he climbed up a soft clay slope and, lying flat at the top, he peeped over. More yellow ridges like the ribs of a washboard! They seemed to run out on all sides, in a circling maze, soft and curved and colorful, and shaded by what seemed unnatural shadows. But they were almost level. Here indeed was the pit of the amphitheater. With slow, desert-trained gaze Adam swept the graceful dunes. All bare! The twilight of changing yellow shadow hindered sure sight at considerable distance, and the sweeping rush of wind above, and then a low hollow roar, made listening useless.

At length Adam noticed how all the clay ridges or ends of slopes to his right ran about a hundred yards and then sheered down abruptly. Here, then, was the main canyon through which the trail ran. The line of it, a vague break in the yellow color, turned toward Adam's left. Adam deliberated a moment. Would he go on or return to the trail? Then he rose, crossed the top of the clay ridge, plunged down its soft bank, leaped the sandy and gravelly wash at the bottom, and started up the next ridge. This was exactly like the one he had surmounted. Adam kept on, down and up, down and up, until the yellow twilight in front of him appeared separated by a lazy column of blue. Adam's nostrils made sure of that. It was smoke. Cautiously crawling now, down and up, Adam gained the ridge from behind which rose the smoke. Here he crouched against the soft clay, breathing hard from his exertions, listening and peering.

The ridges about him began to show streaks of brown earth and ledges of rock. As he looked about he was startled by a rumbling, grating sound. It was continuous, but it had louder rumbles, almost bumps. The sound was rock grating on rock. Adam thought he knew what made it. With all his might he listened, pressing his ear down on the clay. The rumble kept on, but Adam could not hear any other sound until there came a lull in the wind above. Then he heard a squeaking creak — a sound of wood moved tight against wood; then sharp cracks, but of soft substances; then the ring of a shovel on stone; and at last harsh voices.

So far, so good, thought Adam. Only a few yards of clay separated him from mining operations, and he must see how many men were there and what was the lay of the land, and how best he could proceed. The old animal instinct to rush animated him, requiring severe control. While waiting for the wind to begin again, Adam wondered if he was to see Dismukes. He did not expect to.

The elements seemed to await Adam's wishes. At that very moment the yellow light shaded a little dimmer and the sinister-hued sun cloaked its ruddy face. The gale above howled, and the circling winds, lower down, gathered up sheets of dust and swept them across the shrouded amphitheater. And a wave of intenser heat moved down into the pit.

Adam sank his fingers into the soft clay and crawled up this last slope. The rattle of loosened clay and gravel rolling down was swallowed up in the roar of wind. Reaching the last foot of ascent, Adam cautiously peeped over. He saw a wider space, a sort of round pocket between two yellow ridges, that ran out and widened from a ledge of crumbling rock. He crawled a few inches farther, raised himself a little higher. Then he saw brush roofs of structures, evidently erected for shade. The rumble began again. Higher Adam raised himself. Then he espied a coat hanging on a corner post of one of the structures. Dismukes's coat! Adam could have picked it out of a thousand coats. Excitement now began to encroach upon his cool patience and determination. The gale seemed howling with rage at the truth here, still hidden from Adam's eyes. Higher he raised himself.

The brush-covered structure farther from him was a sun shelter, and under it lay piles of camp duffle. A camp fire smoked. Adam's swift eyes caught the gleam of guns. The day was too torrid for these campers to pack guns. The nearer structure was large, octagonal shape, built of mesquite posts and brush. From under it came the rumble of rocks and the metallic clink of shovels, and then the creak and crack and the heavy voice.

Still higher Adam pulled himself so that he might see under the brush shelter. A wide rent in the roof — a huge brown flash across this space — then lower down a movement of men to and fro — rumble of rocks, clink of shovel, thud of earth, creak and crack — a red undershirt — blue jeans — boots, and then passing, bending men nude to the waist — circle and sweep of long dark streak — then again the huge brown flash; it all bewildered Adam, so that one of his usually distinguishing glances failed to convey clear meaning of this scene. Then he looked and looked, and when he had looked a long, breathless moment he fell flat on the soft clay, digging his big hands deep, trembling and straining with the might of his passion to rush like a mad bull down upon the ruffians. It took another moment, that battling restraint. Then he raised to look with clearer, more calculating gaze.

The brush roof was a shelter for an *arrastra*. The octagonal shape of this sun shade filled the pocket that nestled between the slopes. Its back stood close to the ledge of crumbling rock from which the gold-bearing ore was being extracted. Its front faced the open gully. Under it an *arrastra* was in operation. As many of these Spanish devices as Adam had seen, no one of them had ever resembled this.

In the center of the octagon a round pit had been dug into the ground, and lined and floored with flat stones. An upright beam was set in the middle of this, and was fastened above to the roof. Crossbeams were attached to the upright, and from these crossbeams dragged huge rocks held by chains. A long pole, like the tongue of a wagon, extended from the upright and reached far out, at a height of about four feet from the ground. The principle of operation was to revolve the crossbeams and upright post, dragging the heavy rocks around and around the pit, thus crushing the ore. Adam knew that mercury was then used to absorb the gold from the crevices.

The motive power sometimes was a horse, and usually it was a mule. But in this instance the motive power was furnished by a man. A huge, broad, squat man naked to the waist! He was bound to the end of the long bar or tongue, and as he pushed it round and round his body was bent almost double. What wonderful brawny arms on which the muscles rippled and strung like ropes! The breast of this giant was covered with grizzled hair. Like a tired ox he bowed his huge head, wagging it from side to side. As he heaved around he exposed his broad back — the huge brown flash that had mystified Adam — and this mighty muscled back showed streaks and spots of blood.

A gaunt man, rawboned and dark, with a face like a ghoul, stood just outside the circle described by the long bar. He held a mesquite branch with forked and thorny end, which he used as a goad. Whenever the hairy, half-naked giant passed around this gaunt man would swing the whip. It cracked on the brown back — spattered the drops of blood.

There were three other men shoveling, carrying, and dumping ore into the pit. One was slight of build and hard of face. A red-undershirted fellow looked tough and wiry, of middle age, a seasoned desert rat, villainous as a reptile. The third man had a small, closely cropped head like a bullet, and a jaw that stood out beyond his brow, a hard visage smeared with sweat and dust. His big, naked shoulders proclaimed him young.

And the grizzled giant, whom the others were goading and working to death there in the terrible heat, was Adam's old savior and friend, Dismukes.

Cautiously Adam backed and slid down the clay slope, and hurried up and down another. When he had crossed several he turned to the left and ran down to the trail, and followed along that until he reached the spot where he had left the buckets of water.

There he drank deeply, and tried to restrain his hurry. But he was not tired or out of breath. And his mind seemed at a deadlock. A weapon, a shovel, a sledge to crush their skulls! To keep between them and their guns; thus Adam's thoughts had riveted themselves on a few actions. There was, on the surface of his body, a cold, hard, tingling stretch of skin over rippling muscles; and deep internally, the mysterious and manifold life of blood and nerve and bone awoke and flamed under the instinct of the ages. Adam's body then belonged to the past and to what the desert had made it.

Swinging the crossbar over his shoulders and lifting the buckets, he took the trail down toward the camp! He bowed his head and his shoulders more than the weight of the buckets made necessary. The perverse gale blew more fiercely than ever, and the hollow roar resounded louder, and the yellow gloom of dust descended closer, and a weird, dim light streamed through the pall, down upon the moving shadows. All was somber, naked, earthy in this thickening, lowering pall. Odor of smoke and dust! A fiercely burning heat that had the weight of hotly pressing lead! Bellow and shriek and moan of gale that died away! It was the portal to an inferno, and Adam was a man descended in age-long successions from simian beasts, and he strode in the image of God, with love his motive, rage his passion, and the wild years of the desert at his back, driving him on.

He rounded the last corner. There was the camp, fifty yards away. He now could almost straddle the only avenue of escape.

The wind lulled. A yellow shadow drifted away from the sun, and again it shone with sinister magenta hue. All the air seemed to wait, as if the appalling forces of nature, aghast at the strange lives of men, had halted to watch.

"Thar's Bill with the water!" yelled the red-shirted man.

Work and action ceased. The giant Dismukes looked, then heaved erect with head poised like that of a hawk.

"Aw, Bill, you son-of-a-gun!" called another robber, in welcome. "We damn near died, waitin' fer thet water!"

"Ho! Ho! . . . Bill, ye musta run ag'in' another Injun."

Adam walked on, shortening himself a little more, quickening his stride. When he reached and passed the shelter under which lay packs and coats and guns he suddenly quivered, as if released from dragging restraint.

The robber of slight frame and hard face had walked out from under the shelter. He alone had been silent. He had peered keenly, bending a little.

"Hey, is thet you, Bill?" he queried, with hard voice which suited his face.

The gaunt robber cracked his whip. "Fellars, air we locoed by this hyar dust? Damn the deceivin' light! . . . Too big fer Bill — er I'm blind with heat!"

"It ain't Bill!" screeched the little man, and he bounded toward where lay the guns.

Adam dropped the buckets. Down they thudded with a splash. Two of his great leaps intercepted the little man, who veered aside, dodged, and then tried to run by. Adam, with a lunge and a swing, hit him squarely on the side of the head. The blow rang soddenly. Its tremendous power propelled the man off his feet, turning him sidewise as he went through the air, and carried him with terrific force against one of the shelter posts, round which his limp body seemed to wrap itself. Crash! the post gave way, letting the roof sag. Then the smitten man rolled to lodge against a pack, and lay inert.

Whirling swiftly, Adam drew his gun, and paused a second, ready to rush.

The robbers stood stock-still.

"My Gawd!" hoarsely yelled the red-shirted one. 'Who's thet? . . . Did you see him soak Robbins?"

Dismukes let out a stentorian roar of joy, of hate, of triumph. Like a chained elephant he plunged to escape. Failing that, he surged down to yell: "Aha, you bloody claim jumpers! Now you're done! It's Wansfell!"

"*Wansfell!*" flashed the gaunt-faced villain, and that gaunt face turned ashen. "Grab a shovel! Run fer a gun!"

Then the red-shirted robber swung aloft his shovel and rushed at Adam, bawling fierce curses. Adam shot him through. The man seemed blocked, as if by heavy impact, then, more fiercely, he rushed again. Adam's second and last shot, fired at point-blank, staggered him. But the shovel descended on Adam's head, a hard blow, fortunately from the flat side. Clubbing his gun, Adam beat down the man, who went falling with his shovel under the shelter. Both of the other men charged Adam and the three met at the opening. They leaped so swiftly upon him and were so heavy bodied that they bore him to the ground. Adam's grim intention was to hang on to both of them so neither could run to get a weapon. To that end he locked a hold on each. Then began a whirling, wrestling, thudding battle. To make sure of them Adam had handicapped himself. He could not swing his mallet-like fists and he had not been fortunate enough to grip their throats. So, rolling over and over with them, he took the rain of blows, swinging them back, heaving his weight upon them. Foot by foot he won his way farther and farther from where the guns lay. If one yelling robber surged half erect, Adam swung the other to trip him. And once inside the wide doorway of that octagon structure, Adam rose with the struggling men, an iron hand clutching each, and, swinging them wide apart, by giant effort he brought them back into solid and staggering impact. He had hoped to bring their heads together. But only their bodies collided and the force of the collision broke Adam's hold on one. The young man of hulking frame went down, right on the shovel, and, quick to grasp it, he bounded up, fierce and strong. But as he swung aloft the weapon, Adam let go of the gaunt-faced man and hit him, knocking him against the other. They staggered back, almost falling.

Swift on that advantage, Adam swung a fist to the bulging jaw of the man with the shovel. As if struck by a catapult, he went down over the wooden beam and the shovel flew far. Then Adam blocked the doorway. The other fellow charged him, only to be knocked back. As he reeled, his comrade, panting loud, straddled the long beam. Just then Dismukes with quick wits heaved forward on the beam, to which he was bound, and the claim jumper went sprawling in the dirt. Dismukes celebrated his entrance into the fray with another stentorian yell.

Adam awoke now to a different and more intense sense of the fight. He had his antagonists cornered. They could never get by him to secure a gun. And the fierce test of violent strife, the ruthless law of the desert, the survival of the strongest, the blood lust, would have made him refuse any weapon save his hands. He stood on his feet and his hands were enough. Like a wolf he snapped his teeth, then locked his jaw. As he swung and battled and threw these foes backward a strange, wild joy accelerated his actions. When he struck, the sodden blow felt good. He avoided no return blows. He breasted them. The smell of sweat and blood, the heat of panting breaths in his face, the feel of hot, rippling muscle, all tended to make him the fiercer. His sight stayed keen, though tinged with red. He saw the beady, evil eyes of the big robber, like hot green fire, and the bruised and bleeding face with its snarling mouth; and as he saw, he struck out hard with savage thrill. He saw the gaunt and sallow visage of the other, bloody mouthed, with malignant gaze of frenzied hate, of glinting intent to kill, and as he saw he beat him down.

Then into his pulsing senses burst a terrible yell from Dismukes. The gaunt-faced man had fallen into the pit of the *arrastra*, and Dismukes had suddenly started ahead, shoving the beam over him. The big rocks dragging by chains from the crossbeam began to pound around on the ore. Jar and rumble! Then a piercing scream issued from the man who had been caught under the rocks, who was being dragged around the *arrastra*.

Adam saw, even as he knocked back another rush of the other man.

"GRINDIN' GOLD, WANSFELL!" roared Dismukes. "MORE ORE, PARD! . . . WE'RE GRINDIN' GOLD!"

The huge prospector bent to his task. Supreme was his tremendous effort. Strength of ten men! Blood gushed from the cuts on his brawny back. Faster he shoved until he was running. And as he came around, the ferocity of his bristling face and the swelling of the great chest with its mats of hair seemed to prove him half man, half beast, a gorilla in a death grapple.

Again the big robber lunged up, to lower his head and charge at Adam. He was past yelling. He did not seek to escape. He would have given his life to kill.

"MORE ORE, PARD WANSFELL!" yelled Dismukes, as with whistling breath he shoved round the terrible mill of rumbling rocks. A horrible, long-drawn cry issued from under them.

Then the sweep of the long beam caught the man who was charging Adam. Down to his knees it forced him, and, catching under his chin, was dragging him, when the upright post gave way with a crash. The released beam, under the tremendous momentum of Dismukes's massive weight and strength, seemed to flash across the half circle, lifting and carrying the man. A low wall of rock caught his body, and the beam, swinging free from its fastening, cracked his head as if it had been a ripe melon.

21

Sunset of that momentous and tragic day found Adam and Dismukes camped beyond the mouth of a wide pass that bisected the Funeral range.

It was a dry camp, but water from a pure spring some miles down had been packed out. Greasewood grew abundantly on the wide flat, and there were bunches of dry gray sage.

Adam felt well-nigh exhausted, and he would have been gloomy and silent but for his comrade. Dismukes might never have been harnessed to the beam of an *arrastra* and driven like a mule, and his awful treadmill toil in the terrible heat under the lacerating lash was as if it had never been. Dismukes was elated, he was exultant, he was strangely young again.

Always, to Adam, this giant prospector, Dismukes, had been beyond understanding. But now he was enigmatic. He transcended his old self. In the excitement following his rescue he had not mentioned the fact that Adam had saved his life. Adam thought greatly of this squaring of his old debt. But Dismukes seemed not to consider it. He never mentioned that but for Adam's intervention he would have been goaded like a mule, kicked and flayed and driven in the stifling heat, until he fell down to die. All Dismukes thought of was the gold he had mined, the gold the claim jumpers had mined — the bags of heavy gold that were his, and the possession of which ended forever his life-long toil for a fortune. A hundred times that afternoon, as the men had packed and climbed out of the valley, Dismukes had tried to force upon Adam a half of the gold, a quarter of it, a share. But Adam refused.

"Why, for Lord's sake?" Dismukes at last exploded, his great ox eyes rolling. "It's gold. Most of it I mined before those devils came. It's clean an' honest. You deserve a share. An' the half of it will more than make up the sum I've slaved an' saved to get. Why, man — why won't you take it?"

"Well, friend, I guess the only reason I've got is that it's too heavy to pack," replied Adam. He smiled as he spoke, but the fact was he had no other reason for refusal.

Dismukes stared with wide eyes and open mouth. Adam, apparently, was beyond his comprehension just the same as Dismukes was beyond Adam's. Finally he swore his astonishment, grunted his disapproval, and then, resigning himself to Adam's strange apathy, he straightway glowed again.

Adam, despite his amusement and something of sadness, could not help but respond in a measure to the intense rapture of his friend. Dismukes's great work had ended. His long quest for the Golden Fleece had been rewarded. His thirty-five years of wandering and enduring and toiling were over, and life had suddenly loomed beautiful and enchanting. The dream of boyhood had come true. The fortune had been made. And now to look forward to ease, rest, travel, joy — all that he had slaved for. Marvelous past — magnificent prospect of future!

Adam listened kindly, and went slowly, with tired limbs, about the camp tasks; and now he gazed at Dismukes, and again had an eye for his surroundings. Often he gazed up at the exceedingly high, blunt break in the Funeral range. What cataclysm of nature had made that rent? It was a zigzagged saw-toothed wall, with strata slanted at an angle of forty-five degrees. Zigzag veins of black and red bronze ran through the vast drab mass.

The long purple shadows that Adam loved had begun to fall. Several huge bats with white heads darted in irregular flight over the camp. Adam's hands, and his jaw, too, were swollen and painful as a result of the fight, and he served himself and ate with difficulty. And as for speech, he had little chance for that. Dismukes's words flowed like a desert flood. The man was bewitched. He would consume moments in eloquent description of what he was going to do, then suddenly switch to an irrelevant subject.

"Once, years ago, I was lost on the desert," he said, reminiscently. "First an' only time I ever got lost for sure. Got out of grub. Began to starve. Was goin' to kill an' eat my burro, when he up an' run off. Finally got out of water. That's the last straw, you know. . . . I walked all day an' all night an' all day, only to find myself more lost than ever. I thought I had been travelin' toward the west to some place I'd heard of water an' a ranch. Then I made sure I'd gone the wrong way. Staggerin' an' fallin' an' crawlin' till near daylight, at last I gave up an' stretched out to die. Me! I gave up — was glad to die. . . . I can remember the look of the pale stars — the gray mornin' light — the awful silence an' loneliness. Yes, I wanted to die quick. . . . An' all at once I heard a rooster crow!"

"Well! You'd lain down to die near a ranch. That was funny," declared Adam. Life did play queer pranks on men.

"Funny! Say, pard Wansfell, there's nothin' funny about death. An' as for life, I never dreamed how glorious it is, until I heard that rooster crow. I'll buy a farm of green an' grassy an' shady land somewhere in the East — land with runnin' water everywhere — an' I'll raise a thousand roosters just to hear them crow."

"Thought you meant to travel," said Adam.

"Sure. But I'll settle down sometime, I suppose," replied Dismukes, reflectively.

"Friend, will you marry?" inquired Adam, gravely. How intensely interesting was this man about to go out into the world!

"Marry! — What?" ejaculated the prospector.

"A woman, of course."

"My God!" rolled out Dismukes. The thought had startled him. His great ox eyes reflected changes of amazing thought, shadows of old emotions long submerged. "That's somethin' I never *did* think of. Me marry a woman! . . . No woman would ever have me."

"Dismukes, you're not so old. And you'll be rich. When you wear off the desert roughness you can find a wife. The world is full of good women who need husbands."

"Wansfell, you ain't serious?" queried Dismukes, puzzled and stirred. He ran a broad hand through his shock of grizzled hair. His eyes were beautiful then. "I never had wife or sweetheart. . . . No girl ever looked at me — when I was a boy. An' these years on the desert, women have been scarce, an' not one was ever anythin' to me."

"Well, when you get among a lot of pretty girls, just squeeze one for me," said Adam, with the smile that was sad.

Plain it was how Adam's attempt at pleasantry, despite its undercurrent, had opened up a vista of bewildering and entrancing prospects for Dismukes. This prospector had grown grizzled on the desert; his long years had been years of loneliness; and now the forgotten dreams and desires of youth thronged thick and sweet in his imagination. Adam left him to that engrossing fancy, hoping it would keep him content and silent for a while.

A golden flare brightened over the Panamint range, silhouetting the long, tapering lines of the peaks. Far to the west, when the sun had set, floated gray and silver-edged clouds, and under them a whorl of rosy, dusky, ruddy haze. All the slopes below were beginning to be enshrouded in purple, and even while Adam watched they grew cold and dark. The heat veils were still rising, but they were from the ridges of dark-brown and pale-gray earth far this side of the mountains. Death Valley was hidden, and for that Adam was glad. The winds had ceased, the clouds of dust had long settled. It was a bold and desolate scene, of wide scope and tremendous dimensions, a big country. The afterglow of sunset transformed the clouds. Then the golden flare faded fast, the clouds paled, the purple gloom deepened. Vast black ridges of mountains stood out like ragged islands in a desolate sea.

"Wansfell," spoke up Dismukes, "you need your hair cut."

"Maybe. But I'm glad it was long to-day when I got hit with the shovel."

"You sure did come near gettin' it cut then," replied Dismukes, with a hard laugh. "I'll tell you what your long hair reminds me of. Years ago I met a big fellow on the desert. Six feet three he was, an' 'most as big as you. An' a darn good pard on the trail. Well, he wore his hair very long. It hid his ears. An' in the hottest weather he never let me cut it. Well, the funny part all came out one day. Not so funny for him, to think of it! . . . We met men on the trail. They shot him an' were nigh to doin' for me. . . . My big pardner was a horse thief. He'd had his ears cut off for stealin' horses. An' so he wore his hair long like yours to hide the fact he had no ears."

"Friend Dismukes, *I* have ears, if my long hair is worrying you," replied Adam. "And if I had not had mighty keen ears you'd still be grinding gold for your claim jumpers."

At dusk, while the big bats darted overhead with soft swishing of wings, and the camp fire burned down to red and glowing embers, Dismukes talked and talked. And always he returned to the subject of gold and of his future.

"Pard, I wish you were goin' with me," he said, and the slow, sweeping gesture of the great horny hand had something of sublimity. He waved it away toward the east, and it signified the far places across the desert. "I'm rich. The years of lonely hell an' never-endin' toil are over. No more sour dough! No more thirst an' heat an' dust! No more hoardin' of gold! The time has come for me to spend. I'll bank my gold an' draw my checks. At Frisco I'll boil the alkali out of my carcass, an' shaved an' clipped an' dressed, I'll take again the name of my youth an' fare forth for adventure. I'll pay for the years of hard grub. I'll eat the best an' drink wine — wine — the sweetest an' oldest of wine! Wine in thin glasses. . . . I'll wear silk next my skin an' sleep on feathers. I'll travel like a prince. I can see the big niggers roll their eyes. 'Yas, sah, yas sah, the best for you, sah!' An' I'll tip them in gold. . . . I'll go to my old home. Some of my people will be livin'. An' when they see me they'll see their ship come in. They'll be rich. I'll not forget the friends of my youth. That little village will have a church or a park as my gift. I'll travel. I'll see the sights an' the cities. New York! Ha! if I like that place, I'll buy it! I'll see all there is to see, buy all there is to buy. I'll be merry, I'll be joyful. I'll live. I'll make up for all the lost years. But I'll never forget the poor an' the miserable. I can spend an' give a hundred dollars a day for the rest of my life. I'll cross the ocean. London! I've met Englishmen in the Southwest. Queer, cold sort of men! I'll see how they live. I'll go all over England. Then Paris! Never was I drunk, but I'll get drunk in Paris. I want to see the wonderful hotels an' shops an' theaters. I'll look at the beautiful French actresses. I'll go to hear the prima donnas sing. I'll throw gold double-eagles on the stage. An'

I'll take a fly at Monte Carlo. An' travel on an' on. To Rome, that great city where the thrones of the emperors still stand. I'll go spend a long hour high up in the ruins of the Coliseum. An' dreamin' of the days of the Cæsars — seein' the gladiators in the arena — I'll think of you, Wansfell. For there never lived on the old earth a greater fighter than you! . . . Egypt, the land of sun an' sand! I'll see the grand Sahara. An' I'll travel on an' on, all over the world. When I've seen it I'll come back to my native land. An' then, that green farm, with wooded hills an' runnin' streams! It must be near a city. Horses I'll have an' a man to drive, an' a house of comfort. . . . Mebbe there'll come a woman into my life. Mebbe children! The thought you planted in me, pard, somehow makes me yearn. After all, every man should have a son. I see that now. What blunders we make! But I'm rich, I'm not so old, I'll drink life to the very lees. . . . I see the lights, I hear the voices of laughter an' music, I feel the comfortin' walls of a home. A roof over my head! An' a bed as soft as downy feathers! . . . Mebbe, O my pard, mebbe the sweet smile of a woman — the touch of a lovin' hand — the good-night kiss of a child! . . . My God! how the thoughts of life can burn an' thrill!"

Twenty miles a day, resting several hours through the fierce noon heat, the travelers made down across the Mohave Desert. To them, who had conquered the terrible elements and desolation of Death Valley, this waste of the Mohave presented comparatively little to contend with. Still, hardened and daring as they were, they did not incur unnecessary risks.

The time was September, at the end of a fierce, dry summer. Cloudless sky, fervid and quivering air, burning downward rays of sun and rising veils of reflected heat from sand and rock — these were not to be trifled with. Dismukes's little thermometer registered one hundred and thirty degrees in the shade; that is, whenever there was any shade to rest in. They did not burden themselves with the worry of knowing the degrees of heat while they were on the march.

Water holes well known to Dismukes, though out of the beaten track, were found to be dry; and so the travelers had to go out of a direct line to replenish their supply. Under that burning sun even Dismukes and Adam suffered terribly after several hours without water. A very fine penetrating alkali dust irritated throat and nostrils and augmented the pain of thirst. Once they went a whole day without water, and at sundown reached a well kept by a man who made a living by selling water to prospectors and freighters and drivers of borax wagons. His prices were exorbitant. On this occasion, surlily surveying the parched travelers and the thirsty burros, he said his well was almost dry and he would not sell any water. Dismukes had told

Adam that the well-owner bore him a grudge. They expostulated and pleaded with him to no avail. Adam went to the well and, lifting a trapdoor, he peered down, to see quite a goodly supply of water. Then he returned to the little shack where the bushy-whiskered hoarder of precious water sat on a box with a rifle across his knees. Adam always appeared mild and serene, except when he was angry, at which time a man would have had to be blind not to see his mood. The well-owner probably expected Adam to plead again. But he reckoned falsely. Adam jerked the rifle from him and with a single movement of his hands he broke off the stock. Then he laid those big, hard hands on the man, who seemed to shrink under them.

"Friend, you've plenty of water. It's a live well. You can spare enough to save us. We'll double your pay. Come."

Adam loosened his right hand and doubled up the enormous malletlike fist and swung it back. The well-owner suddenly changed his front and became animated, and the travelers got all the water they needed. But they did not annoy him further by pitching camp near his place.

This country was crisscrossed by trails, and, arid desert though it was, every few miles showed an abandoned mine, or a prospector working a claim, or a shack containing a desert dweller. Adam and Dismukes were approaching the highway that bisected the Mohave Desert.

It grew to be more of a sandy country, and anywhere in sand, water was always scarce. Another of Dismukes's water holes was dry. It had not been visited for months. The one wanderer who had stopped there lay there half buried in the sand, a shrunken mummy of a man, with a dark and horrible mockery in the eyeless sockets of his skull. His skin was drawn like light-brown parchment over his face. Adam looked, and then again, and gave a sudden start. He turned the sun-dried visage more to the light. He recognized that face, set in its iron mask of death, with its grin that would grin forever until the brown skull went to dust.

"Regan!" he exclaimed.

"You know him?" queried Dismukes.

"Yes. He was an Irishman I knew years ago. A talky, cheerful fellow. Hard drinker. He loved the desert, but drink kept him in the mining camps. The last time I saw him was at Tecopah, after you left."

"Poor devil! He died of thirst. I know that cast of face. . . . Let's give him decent burial."

"Yes. Poor Regan! He was the man who named me Wansfell. Why he called me that I never knew — never will know."

Deep in the sand they buried the remains of Regan and erected a rude cross to mark his lonely grave.

Dismukes led Adam off the well-beaten trail one day, up a narrow sandy wash to a closed pocket that smelled old and musty. Here a green spring bubbled from under a bank of sand. Water clear as crystal, slightly green in tinge, sparkled and murmured. A whitish sediment bordered the tiny stream of running water.

"Arsenic!" exclaimed Adam.

"Yes. An' here's where I found a whole caravan of people dead. It was six years ago. Place hasn't changed much. Guess it's filled up a little with blowin' sand. . . . Aha! Look Here!"

Dismukes put the toe of his boot against a round white object protruding from the sand. It was a bleached skull.

"Men mad with desert thirst never stop to read," replied Adam, sadly.

In silence Adam and Dismukes gazed down at the glistening white skull. Ghastly as it was, it yet had beauty. Once it had been full of thought, of emotion; and now it was tenanted by desert sand.

Adam and Dismukes spent half a day at that arsenic spring, under the burning sun, suffering the thirst they dared not slake there, and they erected a rude cross that would stand for many and many a day. Deep in the crosspiece Adam cut the words: "DEATH! ARSENIC SPRING! DON'T DRINK! GOOD WATER FIVE MILES. FOLLOW DRY STREAM BED."

Dismukes appeared to get deep satisfaction and even happiness out of this accomplished task. It was a monument to the end of his desert experience. Good will toward his fellow men!

At last the day came when Adam watched Dismukes drive his burros out on the lonely trail, striding along with his rolling gait, a huge, short, broad-backed man, like a misshapen giant. What a stride he had! The thousands of desert miles it had mastered had not yet taken its force and spring. It was the stride of one who imagined he left nothing of life behind and saw its most calling adventures to the fore. He had tired of the desert. He had used it. He had glutted it of the riches he craved. And now he was heading down the trail toward the glittering haunts of men and the green pastures. Adam watched him with grief and yet with gladness, and still with something of awe. Dismukes's going forever was incomprehensible. Adam felt what he could not analyze. The rolling voice of Dismukes, sonorous and splendid, still rang in Adam's ears: "Pard, we're square! . . . Good-by!" Adam understood now why a noble Indian, unspoiled by white men, reverenced a debt which involved life. The paying of that debt was all of unity and brotherhood there existed in the world. If it was great to feel gratitude for the saving of his life, it was far greater to remember he had saved the life of his savior. Adam, deeply agitated, watched Dismukes stride down the barren trail, behind his bobbing burros, watched him stride on into the lonely, glaring desert, so solemn and limitless and mysterious, until he vanished in the gray monotony.

22
●

When the following March came, Adam had been a week plodding southward over the yucca plateaus of the Mohave.

The desert had changed its face. Left behind were the rare calico-veined ranges of mountains, the royal-purple porphyries, the wonderful white granites, the green-blue coppers, the yellow sulphurs, and the ruddy red irons. This desert had color, but not so vivid, not so striking. And it had become more hospitable to the survival of plant life. The sandy floor was no longer monotonously gray.

Adam loved the grotesque yucca trees. They were really trees that afforded shade and firewood, and they brought back no bittersweet memories like the *palo verdes*. The yuccas were fresh and green, renewed in the spring from the dusty gray sunburnt trees they had been in the autumn. Many of them bore great cone-shaped buds about to open, and on others had blossomed large white flowers with streaks of pink. A yucca forest presented a strange sight. These desert trees were deformed, weird, bristling, shaggy trunked, with grotesque shapes like

411

specters in torture.

Adam traveled leisurely, although a nameless and invisible hand seemed to beckon him from the beyond. His wandering steps were again guided, and something awaited him far down toward the Rio Colorado. He was completing a vast circle of the desert, and he could not resist that call, that wandering quest down toward the place which had given the color and direction to his life. But the way must be long, and as there were the thorns and rocks for his feet, so must there be bruises to his spirit.

At night on the moon-blanched desert, under the weird, spectral-armed yuccas, Adam had revelation of the clearness of teaching that was to become his. The years had been preparing him. When would come his supreme trial? What would it be? And there came a whisper out of the lonely darkness, on the cool night wind, that some day he would go back to find the grave of his brother and to meet the punishment that was his due. Then all that was physical, all that was fierce, enduring, natural, thrust the thought from him. But though the savage desert life in him burned strong and resistless, yet he began to hear a new, a different, a higher voice of conscience. He imagined he stifled it with fiercely repudiating gestures, but all the wonderful strength of his brawny hands, magnified a thousand times, could not thrust a thought from him.

412

Toward sunset one day Adam was down on the level desert floor, plodding along a sandy trail around the western wall of San Jacinto. The first *bisnagi* cacti he saw seemed to greet him as old friends. They were small, only a foot or so high, and sparsely scattered over the long rocky slope that led to the base of the mountain wall. The tops of these cacti were as pink as wild roses. Adam was sweeping his gaze along to see how far they grew out on the desert when he discovered that his burro Jennie had espied moving objects.

Coming toward Adam, still a goodly distance off, were two men and two burros, one of which appeared to have a rider. Presently they appeared to see Adam, for they halted, burros and all, for a moment. It struck Adam that when they started on again they sheered a little off a straight following of the trail. Whereupon Adam, too, sheered a little off, so as to pass near them. When they got fairly close he saw two rough-looking men, one driving a packed burro, and the other leading a burro upon which was a ragged slip of a girl. The sunlight caught a brown flash of her face. When nearly abreast, Adam hailed them.

"Howdy, stranger!" they replied, halting. "Come from inside?"

"No. I'm down from the Mohave," replied Adam. "How's the water? Reckon you came by the cottonwoods?"

"Nope. There ain't none there," replied one

413

of the men, shortly. "Plenty an' fine water down the trail."

"Thanks. Where you headed for?"

"Riverside. My gal hyar is sick an' pinin' fer home."

Adam had been aware of the rather sharp scrutiny of these travelers and that they had exchanged whispers. Such procedures were natural on the desert, only in this case they struck Adam as peculiar. Then he shifted his gaze to the girl on the burro. He could not see her face, as it was bowed. Apparently she was weeping. She made a coarse, drab little figure. But her hair shone in the light of the setting sun — rather short and curly, a rich dark brown with glints of gold.

Adam replied to the curt good-by of the men, and after another glance at them, as they went on, he faced ahead to his own course. Then he heard low sharp words, *"Shet up!"* Wheeling, he was in time to see one of these men roughly shake the girl, and speak further words too low for Adam to distinguish. Adam's natural conclusion was that the father had impatiently admonished the child for crying. Something made Adam hesitate and wonder; and presently, as he proceeded on his way, the same subtle something turned him round to watch the receding figures. Again he caught a gleam of sunlight from that girl's glossy head.

"Humph! Somehow I don't like the looks of those fellows," muttered Adam. He was annoyed with himself, first for being so inquisitive, and secondly for not having gone over to take a closer look at them. Shaking his head, dissatisfied with himself, Adam trudged on.

"They said no water at the cottonwoods," went on Adam. "No water when the peak is still white with snow. Either they lied or didn't know."

Adam turned again to gaze after the little party. He had nothing tangible upon which to hang suspicions. He went on, then wheeled about once more, realizing that the farther on he traveled the stronger grew his desire to look back. Suddenly the feeling cleared of its vagueness — no longer curiosity. It had been his thoughts that had inhibited him.

"I'll go back," said Adam. Tying his burros to greasewood bushes near the trail, he started to stride back over the ground he had covered. After a while he caught a glimmer of firelight through the darkness. They had made dry camp hardly five miles beyond the place where Adam had passed them.

It developed that these travelers had gone off the trail to camp in a wide, deep wash. Adam lost sight of the camp-fire glimmer, and had to hunt round until he came to the edge of the wash. A good-sized fire of greasewood and sage had been started, so that it would burn down to hot embers for cooking purposes. As Adam stalked out of the gloom into the camp he saw both men busy with preparations for the meal. The girl sat in a disconsolate attitude. She espied Adam before either of the men heard him. Adam saw her quiver and start erect. Not fright, indeed, was it that animated her. Suddenly one of the men rose, with his hand going to his hip.

"Who goes thar?" he demanded, warningly.

Adam halted inside the circle of light. "Say, I lost my coat. Must have fallen off my pack. Did you fellows find it?"

"No, we didn't find no coat," replied the man, slowly. He straightened up, with his hand dropping to his side. The other fellow was on his knees mixing dough in a pan.

Adam advanced with natural manner, but his eyes, hidden under the shadow of his wide hat brim, took swift stock of that camp.

"Pshaw! I was sure hoping you'd found it," he said, as he reached the fire. "I had a time locating your camp. Funny you'd come way off the trail, down in here."

"Funny or not, stranger, it's our bizness," gruffly replied the man standing. He peered keenly at Adam.

"Sure," replied Adam, with slow and apparent good nature. He was close to the man now, as close as he ever needed to get to any man who might make a threatening move. And he looked past him at the girl. She had a pale little face, too small for a pair of wonderful dark eyes that seemed full of woe and terror. She held out thin brown hands to Adam.

416

"Reckon you'd better go an' hunt fer yer coat," returned the man, significantly.

In one stride Adam loomed over him, his leisurely, casual manner suddenly transformed to an attitude of menace. He stood fully a foot and a half over this stockily built man, who also suddenly underwent a change. He stiffened. Warily he peered up, just a second behind Adam in decision. His mind worked too slowly to get the advantage in this situation.

"Say, I'm curious about this girl you've got with you," said Adam, deliberately.

The man gave a start. "Aw, you are, hey?" he rasped out, "Wall, see hyar, stranger, curious fellars sometimes die sudden, with their boots on."

Adam's force gathered for swift action. Keeping a sharp gaze riveted on this man, he addressed the girl: "Little girl, what's wrong? Are you —"

"Shet up! If you blab out I'll slit your tongue," yelled the fellow, whirling fiercely. No father ever spoke that way to his child. And no child ever showed such terror of her father.

"Girl, don't be afraid. Speak!" called Adam, in a voice that rang.

"Oh, save me — save me!" she cried, wildly.

Then the man, hissing like a snake, was reaching for his gun when Adam struck him. He fell clear across the fire and, rolling over some packs, lay still. The other one, cursing, started to crawl, to reach with flour-whitened hand for

417

a gun lying in a belt upon the sand. Adam kicked the gun away and pounced upon the man. Fiercely he yelled and struggled. Adam bore him down, burrowing his face in the sand. Then placing a ponderous knee on the back of the man's neck, he knelt there, holding him down.

"Girl, throw me that piece of rope," said Adam, pointing.

She shakily got up, her bare feet sinking in the sand, and, picking up the rope, she threw it to Adam. In short order he bound the man's arms behind his back.

"Now, little girl, you can tell me what's wrong," said Adam, rising.

"Oh, they took me away — from mother!" she whispered.

"Your mother? Where?"

"She's at the cottonwoods. We live there."

Adam could not see her plainly. The fire had burned down. He threw on more greasewood and some sage, that flared up with sparkling smoke. Then he drew the girl to the light. What a thin arm she had! And in the small face and staring eyes he read more than the fear that seemed now losing its intensity. Starvation! No man so quick as Adam to see that!

"You live there? Then he lied about the water?" asked Adam.

"Oh yes — he lied."

"Who are these men?"

"I don't know. They camped at the water. I — I was out — gathering firewood. One of

418

them — the one you hit — grabbed me — carried me off. He put his hand — on my mouth. Then the other man came — with the burros. . . . My mother's sick. She didn't know what happened. She'll be terribly frightened. . . . Oh, please take me — home!"

"Indeed I will," replied Adam, heartily. "Don't worry any more. Come now. Walk right behind me."

Adam led the way out of camp without another glance at the two men, one of whom was groaning. The girl kept close at Adam's heels. Away from the circle of camp-fire glow, he could see the gray aisles of clean sand between the clumps of greasewood, and he wound in and out between these until he found the trail. Suddenly he remembered the girl had no shoes.

"You'll stick your feet full of cactus," he said. "You should have on your shoes."

"I have no shoes," she replied. "But cactus doesn't hurt me — except the *cholla*. Do you know *cholla?* Even the Indians think *cholla* bad."

"Guess I do, little girl. Let me carry you."

"I can walk."

So they set off on the starlit trail, and here she walked beside him. Adam noted that she was taller than he would have taken her to be, her small head coming up to his elbow. She had the free stride of an Indian. He gazed out across the level gray and drab desert. Whatever way he directed his wandering steps over this land of waste, he was always gravitating toward new adventure. For him the lonely reaches and rock-ribbed canyons were sure to harbor, sooner or later, some humanity that drew him like a magnet. Everywhere the desert had its evil, its suffering, its youth and age. The heat of Adam's anger subsided with the thought that somehow he had let the ruffians off easily; and the presence of this girl, a mere child, apparently, for all her height, brought home to him the mystery, the sorrow, the marvel of life on the desert. A sick woman with a child living in the lonely shadow of San Jacinto! Adam felt in this girl's presence, as he had seen starvation in her face, a cruelty of life, of fate. But how infinitely grateful he felt for the random wandering steps which had led him down that trail!

All at once a slim, rough little hand slipped into his. Instinctively Adam closed his own great hand over it. That touch gave him such a thrill as he had never before felt in all his life. It seemed to link his strength and this child's trust. The rough little fingers and calloused little palm might have belonged to a hard-laboring boy, but the touch was feminine. Adam, desert trained by years that had dominated even the habits ingrained in his youth, and answering mostly to instinct, received here an unintelligible shock that stirred to the touch of a trusting hand, but was nothing physical. His body, his mind, his soul seemed but an exhaustive instrument of creation over which the desert played masterfully.

"It was lucky you happened along," said the girl.

"Yes," replied Adam, as if startled.

"They were bad men. And, oh, I was so glad to see them — at first. It's so lonely. No one ever comes except the Indians — and they come to *beg* things to eat — never to *give*. I thought those white men were prospectors and would give me a little flour or coffee — or something mother would like. We've had so little to eat."

"That so? Well, I have a full pack," replied Adam. "Plenty of flour, coffee, sugar, bacon, canned milk, dried fruit."

"And you'll give us some?" she asked, eagerly, in a whisper.

"All you need."

"Oh, you're good — good as those men were bad!" she exclaimed, with a throb of joy. "Mother has just starved herself for me. You see, the Indian who packed supplies to us hasn't come for long. Nobody has come — except those bad men. And our food gave out little by little. Mother starved herself for me. . . . Oh, I couldn't make her eat. She'd say she didn't want what I'd cook. Then I'd have to eat it."

"Isn't your mother able to get about?" asked Adam, turning to peer down into the dark little face.

"Oh no! She's dying of consumption," was the low, sad reply.

"And your father?" asked Adam, a little huskily.

"He died two years ago. I guess it's two, for the peak has been white twice."

"Died? — here in the desert?"

"Yes. We buried him by the running water where he loved to sit."

"Tell me — how did your parents and you come to be here."

"They both had consumption long before I was born," replied the girl. "Father had it — but mother didn't — when they were married. That was back in Iowa. Mother caught it from him. And they both were going to die. They had tried every way to get well, but the doctors said they couldn't. . . . So father and mother started West in a prairie schooner. I was born in it, somewhere in Kansas. They tried place after place, trying to find a climate that would cure them. I remember as far back as Arizona. But father never improved till we got to this valley. Here he was getting strong again. Then my uncle came and he found gold over in the mountains. That made father mad to get rich — to have gold for me. He worked too hard — and then he died. Mother has been slowly failing ever since."

"It's a sad story, little girl," replied Adam. "The desert is full of sad stories. . . . But your uncle — what became of him?"

"He went off prospecting for gold. But he came back several times. And the last was just before father died. Then he said he would come back again for me some day and take me out of the desert. Mother lives on that hope. But I don't want him to come. All I pray for is that she gets well. I would never leave her."

"So you've lived all your life on the desert?"

"Yes. Mother says I never slept under a real roof."

"And how old are you?"

"Nearly fourteen."

"So old as that? Well! I thought you were younger. And, little girl — may I ask how you learned to talk so — as if you had been to school?"

"My mother was a school-teacher. She taught me."

"What's your name?"

"It's Eugenie Linwood. But I don't like Eugenie. Father and mother always called me Genie. . . . What's your name?"

"Mine is Wansfell."

"You're the biggest man I ever saw. I thought the Yuma Indians were giants, but you're bigger. My poor father was not big or strong."

Presently Adam saw the dark-gray forms of his burros along the trail. Jennie appeared to be more contrary than usual, and kicked spitefully at Adam as he untied her. And as Adam drove her ahead with the other burro she often lagged to take a nip at the sage. During the several miles farther down the trail Adam was hard put to it to keep her going steadily. The girl began to tire, a circumstance which Adam had expected. She refused to be assisted, or to be put on one of the burros. The trail began to circle round the black bulge of the mountain, finally running into the shadow, where objects were hard to see. The murmur of flowing water soon reached Adam's ears — most welcome and beautiful sound to desert man. And then big cottonwoods loomed up, and beyond them the gleam of starlight on stately palm trees. Adam, peering low down through the shadows, distinguished a thatch-roofed hut.

"We'll not tell mother about the bad men," whispered the girl. "It'll only scare her."

"All right, Genie," said Adam, and he permitted himself to be led to a door of the hut. Dark as pitch was it inside.

"Mother, are you awake?" called Genie.

"Oh, child, where have you been?" rejoined a voice, faint and weak, with a note of relief. "I woke up in the dark. . . . I called. You didn't come."

Then followed a cough that had a shuddering significance for Adam.

"Mother, I'm sorry. I — I met a man on the trail. A Mr. Wansfell. We talked. And he came with me. He has a new pack of good things to eat. And, oh, mother! he's — he's different from those men who were here; he'll help us."

"Madam, I'll be happy to do anything I can for you and your little girl," said Adam, in his deep, kindly tones.

"Sir, your voice startled me," replied the woman, with a gasp. "But it's a voice I trust. The looks of men in this hard country deceive me sometimes — but never their voices. . . . Sir, if you will help us in our extremity, you will have the gratitude of a dying woman — of a mother."

The darkness was intense inside the hut, and Adam, leaning at the door, could see nothing. The girl touched his arm timidly, almost appealingly, as Adam hesitated over his reply. "You can — trust me," he said, presently. "My name is Wansfell. I'm just a desert wanderer. If I may — I'll stay here — look after your little girl till her uncle comes."

"At last — God has answered my — prayer!" exclaimed the woman, pantingly.

Adam unpacked his burros a half dozen rods from the hut, under a spreading cottonwood and near the juncture of two little streams of water that flowed down out of the gloom, one on each side of the great corner of mountain. And Adam's big hands made short shift of camp well made, with upright poles and thatch, covered by a thatched roof of palm leaves. The girl came out and watched him, and Adam had never seen hungrier eyes even in an Indian.

"It'd be fun to watch you — you're so quick — if I wasn't starved," said Genie.

What a slender, almost flat slip of a girl. Her dress was in tatters, showing bare brown flesh in places. The pinched little face further stirred Adam's pity. And there waved over him a strange pride in his immense strength, his wonderful hands, his desert knowledge that now could be put to the greatest good ever offered him in his wanderings.

"Genie, when you're starved you must eat very slowly — and only a little."

"I know. I've known all about people starving and thirsting. But I'm not that badly off. I've had a *little* to eat."

"Honest Injun?" he queried.

She had never heard that expression, so he changed it to another of like meaning.

"I wouldn't lie," she replied, with direct simplicity that indeed reminded Adam of an Indian.

Never had Adam prepared so good a camp dinner in such short time. And then, hungry as Genie was, she insisted that her mother should be served first. She took a lighted candle Adam gave her and led the way into the hut, while he followed, carrying food and drink that he believed best for a woman so weak and starved. The hut had two rooms, the first being a kitchen with stone floor and well furnished with camp utensils. The second room contained two rude cots made of poles and palm leaves, upon one of which Adam saw a pale shadow of a woman whose eyes verified the tragic words she had spoken.

Despite the way Adam stooped as he entered, his lofty head brushed the palm-leafed roof.

Genie laughed when he bumped against a cross-beam.

"Mother, he's the tallest man!" exclaimed the girl. "He could never live in our hut. . . . Now sit up, mother dear. Doesn't it all smell good. Oooooo! The Indian fairy has come."

"Genie, will you hold the candle so I can see the face of this kind man?" asked the woman, when she had been propped up in bed.

The girl complied, with another little laugh. Adam had not before been subjected to a scrutiny like the one he bore then. It seemed to come from beyond this place and time.

"Sir, you are a man such as I have never seen," she said, at length.

Plain it was to Adam that the sincerity, or whatever she saw in him, meant more to her than the precious food of which she stood in such dire need. Her hair was straggly and gray, her brow lined by pain and care, her burning eyes were sunk deep in dark hollows, and the rest of her features seemed mere pale shadows.

"I'm glad for your confidence," he said. "But never mind me. Try to eat some now."

"Mother, there's plenty," added Genie, with soft eagerness. "You can't fib to me about *this*. Oh, smell that soup! And there's rice — clean white rice with sugar and milk!"

"Child, if there's plenty, go and eat. . . . Thank you, sir, I can help myself."

Adam followed Genie out, and presently the look of her, as she sat on the sand, in ravenous bewilderment of what to eat first, brought back poignantly to him the starvation days of his earlier experience. How blessed to appreciate food! Indeed, Genie would have made a little glutton of herself had not Adam wisely obviated that danger for her.

Later, when she and her mother were asleep, he strolled under the cottonwoods along the murmuring stream where the bright stars shone reflected in the dark water. The place had the fragrance of spring, of fresh snow water, of green growths and blossoming flowers. Frogs were trilling from the gloom, a sweet, melodious music seldom heard by Adam. A faint, soft night breeze rustled in the palm leaves. The ragged mountain-side rose precipitously, a slanted mass of huge rocks, their shining surfaces alternating with the dark blank spaces. Above spread the sky, a wonderful deep blue, velvety, intense, from which blazed magnificent white stars, and countless trains and groups of smaller stars.

Rest and thought came to him then. Destiny had dealt him many parts to play on the desert. So many violent, harsh, and bitter tasks! But this was to be different. Not upon evil days had he fallen! Nor had his wandering steps here taken hold of hell! The fragrance under the shadow of this looming mountain was the fragrance of an oasis. And in that silent shadow slept a child who would soon be an orphan. Adam had his chance to live awhile in one of the desert's fruitful and blossoming spots. Only a desert man could appreciate the rest, the ease, the joy, the contrast of that opportunity. He could befriend an unfortunate child. But as refreshing and splendid as were these things, they were as naught compared to the blessing that would be breathed upon his head by a dying mother. Adam, lifting up his face to the starlight, felt that all his intense and passionate soul could only faintly divine what the agony of that mother had been, what now would be her relief. She knew. Her prayer had been answered. And Adam pondered and pondered over the meaning of her prayer and the significance of his wandering steps. He seemed to feel the low beat of a mighty heart, the encompassing embrace of a mighty and invisible spirit.

23

Daylight showed to Adam the cottonwood oasis as he had it pictured in memory, except for the palm-thatched hut.

He was hard at camp duties when Genie came out. The sun was rising, silver and ruddy and gold, and it shone upon her, played around her glossy head as she knelt on the grass beside the running water. While she bathed there, splashing diamond drops of water in the sunshine, she seemed all brightness and youth. But in the merciless light of day her face was too small, too thin, too pinched to have any comeliness. Her shining hair caught all the beauty of the morning. In one light it was auburn and in another a dark brown, and in any light it had glints and gleams of gold. It waved and curled rebelliously, a rich, thick, rippling mass falling to her shoulders. When, presently, she came over to Adam, to greet him and offer to help, then he had his first look at her eyes by day. Gazing into them, Adam hardly saw the small, unattractive, starved face. Like her hair, her eyes shone dark brown, and the lighter gleams were amber. The expression was of a straightforward soul, unconscious of unutterable sadness, gazing out at incomprehensible life, that should have been beautiful for her, but was not.

"Good morning, Genie," said Adam, cheerily. "Of course you can help me. There's heaps of work. And when you help me with that I'll play with you."

"Play!" she murmured, dreamily. She had never had a playmate.

Thus began the business of the day for Adam. When breakfast was over and done with he set to work to improve that camp, and especially with an eye to the comfort of the invalid. Adam knew the wonderful curative qualities of desert air, if it was wholly trusted and lived in. On the shady side of the hut he erected a wide

430

porch with palm-thatched roof that cut off the glare of the sky. With his own canvases, and others he found at the camp, he put up curtains that could be rolled up or let down as occasion required. Then he constructed two beds, one at each end of the porch, and instead of palm leaves he used thick layers of fragrant sage and greasewood. Mrs. Linwood, with the aid of Genie, managed to get out to her new quarters. Her pleasure at the change showed in her wan face. The porch was shady, cool, fragrant. She could look right out upon the clean, brown, beautiful streams where they met, and at the camp fire where Adam and Genie would be engaged, and at night she could see it blaze and glow, and burn down red. The low-branching cottonwoods were full of humming birds and singing birds, and always the innumerable bees. The clean white sand, the mesquites bursting into green, the nodding flowers in the grassy nooks under the great iron-rusted stones, the rugged, upheaved slope of mountain, and to the east an open vista between the trees where the desert stretched away gray and speckled and monotonous, down to the dim mountains over which the sun would rise; these could not but be pleasant and helpful. Love of life could not be separated from such things.

"Mrs. Linwood, sleeping outdoors is the most wonderful experience," said Adam, earnestly. "You feel the night wind. The darkness folds around you. You look up through the leaves to the dark-blue sky and shining stars. You smell the dry sand and the fresh water and the flowers and the spicy desert plants. Every breath you draw is new, untainted. Living outdoors, by day and night, is the secret of my strength."

"Alas! We always feared the chill night air," sighed Mrs. Linwood. "Life teaches so many lessons — too late."

"It is never too late," returned Adam.

Then he set himself to further tasks, and soon that day was ended. Other days like it passed swiftly, and each one brought more hope of prolonging Mrs. Linwood's life. Adam feared she could not live, yet he worked and hoped for a miracle. Mrs. Linwood improved in some mysterious way that seemed of spirit rather than of flesh. As day after day went by and Adam talked with her, an hour here, an hour there, she manifestly grew stronger. But was it not only in mind? The sadness of her changed. The unhappiness of her vanished. The tragic cast and pallor of her face remained the same but the spirit that shone from her eyes and trembled in her voice was one of love, gratitude, hope. Adam came at length to understand that the improvement was only a result of the inception of faith she had in him. With terrible tenacity she had clung to life, even while starving herself to give food to her child; and now that succor had come, her spirit in its exaltation triumphed over her body. Happiness was more powerful than the ravages of disease. But if that condition, if that mastery of mind over body, had continued, it would have been superhuman. The day came at last in which Mrs. Linwood sank back into the natural and inevitable state where the fatality of life ordered the eminence of death.

When she was convulsed with the spasms of coughing, which grew worse every day, Adam felt that if he could pray to the God she believed in, he would pray for her sufferings to be ended. He hated this mystery of disease, this cruelty of nature. It was one of the things that operated against his acceptance of her God. Why was life so cruel? Was life only nature? Nature was indeed cruel. But if life was conflict, if life was an endless progress toward unattainable perfection, toward greater heights of mind and soul, then was life God, and in eternal conflict with nature? How hopelessly and impotently he pondered these distressing questions! Pain he could endure himself, and he had divined that in enduring it he had enlarged his character. But to suffer as this poor woman was suffering — to be devoured by millions of infinitesimal and rapacious animals feasting on blood and tissue — how insupportably horrible! What man could endure that — what man of huge frame and physical might — of intense and pulsing life? Only a man in whom intellect was supreme, who could look upon life resignedly as not the ultimate end, who knew not the delights of sensation, who had no absorbing passion for the gray old desert or the heaving sea, or the windy heights and the long purple shadows, who never burned and beat with red blood running free — only a martyr living for the future, or a man steeped in religion, could endure this blight of consumption. When Adam considered life in nature, he could understand this disease. It was merely a matter of animals fighting to survive. Let the fittest win! That was how nature worked toward higher and stronger life. But when he tried to consider the God this stricken woman worshiped, Adam could not reconcile himself to her agony. Why? The eternal Why was flung at him. She was a good woman. She had lived a life of sacrifice. She had always been a Christian. Yet she was not spared this horrible torture. Why?

What hurt Adam more than anything else was the terror in Genie's mute lips and the anguish in her speaking eyes.

One day, during an hour when Mrs. Linwood rested somewhat easily, she called Adam to her. It happened to be while Genie was absent, listening to the bees or watching the flow of water.

"Will you stay here — take care of Genie — until her uncle comes back?" queried the woman, with her low, panting breaths.

"I promised you. But I think you should not want me to keep her here too long," replied Adam, earnestly. "Suppose he does not come back in a year or two?"

"Ah! I hadn't thought of that. What, then, is your idea?"

"Well, I'd wait here a good long time," said Adam, soberly. "Then if Genie's uncle didn't come, I'd find a home for her."

"A home — for Genie! . . . Wansfell, have you considered? That would take money — to travel — to buy Genie — what she ought to — have."

"Yes, I suppose so. That part need not worry you. I have money. I'll look out for Genie. I'll find a home for her."

"You'd do — all that?" whispered the woman.

"I promise you. Now, Mrs. Linwood, please don't distress yourself. It'll be all right."

"It *is* all right. I'm not — in distress," she replied, with something tremulous and new in her voice. "Oh, thank God — my faith — never failed!"

Adam was not sure what she meant by this, but as he revolved it in his mind, hearing again the strange ring of joy which had been in her voice, he began to feel that somehow he represented a fulfillment and a reward to her.

"Wansfell — listen," she whispered, with more force. "I — I should have told you. . . . Genie is not poor. No! . . . She's rich! . . . Her father found gold — over in the mountains . . . He slaved at digging. . . . That killed him. But he found gold. It's hidden inside the hut — under the floor — where I used to lie. . . . Bags of gold! Wansfell, my child will be rich!"

"Well! . . . Oh, but I'm glad!" exclaimed Adam.

"Yes. It sustains me. . . . But I've worried so. . . . My husband expected me — to take Genie out of the desert. . . . I've worried about that money. Genie's uncle — John Shaver is his name — he's a good man. He loved her. He used to drink — but I hope the desert cured him of that. I think — he'll be a father to Genie."

"Does he know about the gold that will be Genie's?"

"No. We never told him. My husband didn't trust John — in money matters. . . . Wansfell, if you'll say you'll go with Genie — when her uncle comes — and invest the money — until she's of age — I will have no other prayer except for her happiness. . . . I will die in peace."

"I promise. I'll do my best," he declared.

The next time she spoke to him was that evening at dusk. Frogs were trilling, and a belated mocking bird was singing low, full-throated melodies. Yet these beautiful sounds only accentuated the solemn desert stillness.

"Wansfell — you remember — once we talked of God," she said, very low.

"Yes, I remember," replied Adam.

"Are you just where you were — then?"

"About the same, I guess."

"Are you sure you understand yourself?"

"Sure? Oh no. I change every day."

"Wansfell, what do you call the thing in you

436

— the will to tarry here? The manhood that I trusted? . . . The forgetfulness of self? . . . What do you call this strength of yours that fulfilled my faith — that gave me to God utterly — that enables me to die happy — that will be the salvation of my child?"

"Manhood? Strength?" echoed Adam, in troubled perplexity. "I'm just sorry for you — for the little girl."

"Ah yes, sorry! Indeed you are! But you don't know yourself. . . . Wansfell, there was a presence beside my bed — just a moment before I called you. Something neither light nor shadow in substance — something neither life nor death. . . . It is gone now. But when I am dead it will come to you. *I* will come to you — like that. . . . Somewhere out in the solitude and loneliness of your desert — at night when it is dark and still — and the heavens look down — there you will face your soul. . . . You'll see the divine in man. . . . You'll realize that the individual dies, but the race lives. . . . You'll have thundered at you from the silence, the vast, lonely land you love, from the stars and the infinite beyond — that your soul is immortal. . . . That this *Thing* in you is God!"

When the voice ceased, so vibrant and full at the close, so more than physical, Adam bowed his head and plodded over the soft sand out to the open desert where mustering shadows inclosed him, and he toiled to and fro in the silence — a man bent under the Atlantean doubt and agony and mystery of the world.

The next day Genie's mother died.

Long before sunrise of a later day Adam climbed to the first bulge of the mountain wall. On lofty heights his mind worked more slowly — sometimes not at all. The eye of an eagle suffced him. Down below, on the level, during these last few days, while Genie sat mute, rigid, stricken, Adam had been distracted. The greatest problem of his desert experience confronted him. Always a greater problem — always a greater ordeal — that was his history of the years. Perhaps on the heights might come inspiration. The eastern sky was rosy. The desert glowed soft and gray and beautiful. Gray lanes wound immeasurably among bronze and green spots, like islands in a monotonous sea. The long range of the Bernardinos was veiled in the rare lilac haze of the dawn, and the opposite range speared the deep blue of sky with clear black-fringed and snowy peaks. Far down the vast valley, over the dim ridge of the Chocolates, there concentrated a bright rose and yellow and silver. This marvelous light intensified, while below the wondrous shadows deepened. Then the sun rose like liquid silver, bursting to flood the desert world.

The sunrise solved Adam's problem. His kindness, his pity, his patience and unswerving interest, his argument and reason and entreaty, had all failed to stir Genie out of her mute misery. Nothing spiritual could save her. But Genie had another mother — nature — to whom Adam meant to appeal as a last hope.

He descended the slope to the oasis. There, near a new-made grave that ran parallel with an old one, mossy and gray, sat Genie, clamped in her wretchedness.

"Genie," he called, sharply, intending to startle her. He did startle her. "I'm getting sick. I don't have exercise enough. I used to walk miles every day. I must begin again."

"Then go," she replied.

"But I can't leave you alone here," he protested. "Some other bad men might come. I'm sorry. You *must* come with me."

At least she was obedient. Heavily she rose, ready to accompany him, a thin shadow of a girl, hallowed eyed and wan, failing every hour. Adam offered his hand at the stream to help her across. But for that she would have fallen. She left her hand in his. And they set out upon the strangest walk Adam had ever undertaken. It was not long, and before it ended he had to drag her, and finally carry her. That evening she was so exhausted she could not repel the food he gave her, and afterward she soon fell asleep.

Next day he took her out again, and thereafter every morning and every afternoon, relentless in his determination, though his cruelty wrung his heart. Gentle and kind as he was, he yet saw that she fell into the stream, that she pricked her bare feet on cactus, that she grew frightened on the steep slopes, that she walked farther and harder every day. Nature was as relentless as Adam. Soon Genie's insensibility to pain and hunger was as if it had never been. Whenever she pricked or bruised the poor little feet Adam always claimed it an accident; and whenever her starved little body cried out in hunger he fed her. Thus by action, and the forcing of her senses, which were involuntary, he turned her mind from her black despair. This took days and weeks. Many and many a time Adam's heart misgave him, but just as often something else in him remained implacable. He had seen the training of Indian children. He knew how the mother fox always threw from her litter the black cub that was repugnant to her. The poor little black offspring was an outcast. He was soon weaned, and kicked out of the nest to die or survive. But if he did survive the cruel, harsh bitterness of strife and heat and thirst and starvation — his contact with his environment — he would grow superior to all the carefully mothered and nourished cubs. Adam expected this singular law of nature, as regarded action and contact and suffering, to be Genie's salvation, provided it did not kill her; and if she had to die he considered it better for her to die of travail, of effort beyond her strength, than of a miserable pining away.

One morning, as he finished his camp tasks, he missed her. Upon searching, he found her flat on the grassy bank of the stream, face downward, with her thin brown feet in the air. He wondered what she could be doing, and his heart sank, for she had often said it would be so easy and sweet to lie down and sleep in the water.

"Genie, child, what are you doing?" he asked.

"Look the bees — the honey bees! They're washing themselves in the water. First I thought they were drinking. But no! . . . They're washing. It's so funny."

When she looked up, Adam thrilled at sight of her eyes. If they had always been beautiful in shape and color, what were they now, with youth returned, and a light of the birth of wonder and joy in life? Youth had won over tragedy. Nature hid deep at the heart of all creation. The moment also had a birth for Adam — an exquisite birth of the first really happy moment of his long desert years.

"Let me see," he said, and he lowered his ponderous length and stretched it beside her on the grassy bank. "Genie, you're right about the bees being funny, but wrong about what they're doing. They are diluting their honey. Well, I'm not sure, but I think bees on the desert dilute their honey with water. Watch! . . . Maybe they drink at the same time. But you see — some of them have their heads turned away from the water, as if they meant to back down. . . . Bees are hard to understand."

"By the great horn spoon!" ejaculated Genie, and then she laughed.

Adam echoed her laugh. He could have shouted or sung to the skies. Never before, indeed, had he heard Genie use such an expression, but the content of it was precious to him. It revealed hitherto unsuspected depths in her, as the interest in bees hinted of an undeveloped love of nature.

"Genie, do you care about bees, birds, flowers — what they do — how they live and grow?"

"Love them," she answered, simply.

"You do! Ah, that's fine! So do I. Why, Genie, I've lived so long on the desert, so many years! What would I have done without love of everything that flies and crawls and grows?"

"You're not old," she said.

"It's good you think that. We'll be great pards now. . . . Look, Genie! Look at that humming bird! There, he darts over the water. Well! What's he doing?"

Adam's quick ear had caught the metallic hum of tiny, swift wings. Then he had seen a humming bird poised over the water. As he called Genie's attention it hummed away. Then, swift as a glancing ray, it returned. Adam could see the blur of its almost invisible wings. As it quivered there, golden throat shining like live fire, with bronze and green and amber tints so vivid in the sunlight, it surely was worthy reason for a worship of nature. Not only had it beauty, but it had singular action. It poised, then darted down, swift as light, to disturb the smooth water, either with piercing bill or flying wings. Time and again the tiny bird performed this antic. Was the diminutive-winged creature playing, or drinking, or performing gyrations for the edification of a female of his species, hidden somewhere in the overhanging foliage? Adam knew that some courting male birds cooed, paraded, strutted, fought before the females they hoped to make consorts. Why not a humming bird?

"By your great horn spoon, Genie!" exclaimed Adam. "I wonder if that's the way he drinks."

But all that Adam could be sure of was the beautiful opal body of the tiny bird, the marvelous poise as it hung suspended in air, the incredibly swift darts up and down, and the little widening, circling ripples on the water. No, there was more Adam could be sure of, and Genie's delight proved the truth of it — and that was how sure the harvest of thought, how sure the joy of life which was the reward for watching!

One morning when Adam arose to greet the sunrise he looked through the gap between the trees, and low down along the desert floor he saw a burst of yellow. At first he imagined it to be a freak of sunlight or reflection, but he soon decided that it was a *palo verde* in blossom. Beautiful, vivid, yellow gold, a fresh hue of the desert spring. May had come. Adam had forgotten the flight of time. What bittersweet stinging memory had that flushing *palo verde* brought back to him! He had returned to the desert land he loved best, and which haunted him.

Genie responded slowly to the Spartan training. She had been frail, at best, and when grief clamped her soul and body she had sunk to the verge. The effort she was driven to, and the exertion needful, wore her down until she appeared merely skin and bones. Then came the dividing line between waste and repair. She began to mend. Little by little her appetite improved until at last hunger seized upon her. From that time she grew like a weed. Thus the forced use of bone and muscle drove her blood as Adam had driven her, and the result was a natural functioning of physical life. Hard upon that change, and equally as natural, came the quickening of her mind. Healthy pulsing blood did not harbor morbid grief. Action was constructive; grief was destructive.

Adam, giving himself wholly to this task of rehabilitation, added to his relentless developing of Genie's body a thoughtful and interesting appeal to her mind. At once he made two discoveries — first, that Genie would give herself absorbingly to any story whatsoever, and secondly, that his mind seemed to be a full treasure house from which to draw. He who had spoken with so few men and women on the desert now was inspired by a child.

He told Genie the beautiful Indian legend of Taquitch as it had been told to him by Oella, the Coahuila maiden who had taught him her language.

When he finished Genie cried out: "Oh, I

444

know. Taquitch is up on the mountain yet! In summer he hurls the lightning and thunder. In winter he lets loose the storm winds. And always, by day and night, he rolls the rocks."

"Yes, Genie, he's there," replied Adam.

"Why did he steal the Indian maidens?" she asked, wonderingly.

Genie evolved a question now and then that Adam found difficult to answer. She had the simplicity of an Indian, and the inevitableness, and a like ignorance of the so-called civilization of the white people.

"Well, I suppose Taquitch fell in love with the Indian maidens," replied Adam, slowly.

"Fell in love. What's that?"

"Didn't your mother ever tell you why she married your father?"

"No."

"Why do you think she married him?"

"I suppose they wanted to be together — to work — and go places, like they came West when they were sick. To help each other."

"Exactly. Well, Genie, they wanted to be together because they loved each other. They married because they fell in love with each other. Didn't you ever have Indians camp here, and learn from them?"

"Oh yes, different tribes have been here. But I didn't see any Indians falling in love. If a chief wanted a wife he took any maiden or squaw he wanted. Some chiefs had lots of wives. And if a brave wanted a wife he bought her."

"Not much falling in love there," confessed Adam, with a laugh. "But, Genie, you mustn't think Indians can't love each other. For they can."

"I believe I've seen birds falling in love," went on Genie, seriously. "I've watched them when they come to drink and wash. Quail and road runners, now — they often come in pairs, and they act funny. At least one of each pair acted funny. But it was the pretty one — the one with a topknot — that did all the falling in love. Why?"

"Well, Genie, the male, or the man-bird, so to speak, always has brighter colors and crests and the like, and he — he sort of shines up to the other, the female, and shows off before her."

"Why doesn't she do the same thing?" queried Genie. "That's not fair. It's all one-sided."

"Child, how you talk! Of course love isn't one-sided," declared Adam, getting bewildered.

"Yes, it is. She ought to show off before him. But I'll tell you what — after they began to build a nest I never saw any more falling in love. It's a shame. It ought to last always. I've heard mother say things to father I couldn't understand. But now I believe she meant that after he got her — married her — he wasn't like he was before."

Adam had to laugh. The old discontent of life, the old mystery of the sexes, the old still, sad music of humanity spoken by the innocent and unknowing lips of this child. How feminine! The walls of the inclosing desert, like those of an immense cloister, might hide a woman all her days from the illuminating world, but they could never change her nature.

"Genie, I must be honest with you," replied Adam. "I've got to be parents, brother, sister, friend, everybody to you. And I'll fall short sometimes in spite of my intentions. But I'll be honest. . . . And the fact is, it seems to be a sad truth that men and man-birds, and man-creatures generally, are all very much alike. If they want anything, they want it badly. And when they fall in love they do act funny. They will do anything. They show off, beg, bully, quarrel, are as nice and sweet as — as sugar; and they'll fight, too, until they get their particular wives. Then they become natural — like they were before. It's my idea, Genie, that all wives of creation should demand always the same deportment which won their love. Don't you agree with me?"

"I do, you bet. That's what *I'll* have. . . . But will *I* ever be falling in love?"

The eyes that looked into Adam's then were to him as the wonder of the world.

"Of course you will. Some day, when you grow up."

"With you?" she asked, in dreamy speculation.

"Oh, Genie! Not me. Why — I — I'm too old!" he ejaculated. "I'm old enough to be your daddy."

"You're not old," she replied, with a finality that admitted of no question. "But if you were — and still like you are — what difference would it make?"

"Like I am! Well, Genie, how's that?" he queried, curiously.

"Oh, so big and strong! You can do so much with those hands. And your voice sort of — of quiets something inside me. When I lie down to sleep, knowing you're there under the cottonwood, I'm not afraid of the dark. . . . And your eyes are just like an eagle's. Oh, you needn't laugh! I've seen eagles. An Indian here once had two. I used to love to watch them look. But then their eyes were never kind like yours. . . . I think when I get big I'll go falling in love with you."

"Well, little girl, that's a long way off," said Adam, divided between humor and pathos. "But let's get back to natural history. A while ago you mentioned a bird called a road runner. That's not as well-known a name among desert men as chaparral cock. You know out in the desert there are no roads. This name road runner comes from a habit — and it's a friendly habit — of the bird running along the road ahead of a man or wagon. Now the road runner is the most wonderful bird of the desert. That is saying a great deal. Genie, tell me all you know about him."

"Oh, I know all about him," declared Genie, brightly. "There's one lives in the mesquite there. I see him every day, lots of times. Before you came he was very tame. I guess now he's afraid. But not so afraid as he was. . . . Well, he's a long bird, with several very long feathers for a tail. It's a funny tail, for when he walks he bobs it up and down. His color is speckled — gray and brown and white. I've seen dots of purple on him, too. He has a topknot that he can put up and lay down, as he has a mind to. When it's up it shows some gold color, almost red underneath. And when it's up he's mad. He snaps his big bill like — like — oh, I don't know what like, but it makes you shiver. I've never seen him in the water, but I know he goes in, because he shakes out his feathers, picks himself, and sits in the sun. He can fly, only he doesn't fly much. But, oh, how he can run! Like a streak! I see him chase lizards across the sand. You know how a lizard can run! Well, no lizard ever gets away from a road runner. There's a race — a fierce little tussle in the sand — a snap! snap! — and then old killer road runner walks proudly back, carrying the lizard in his bill. If it wasn't for the way he kills and struts I could love him. For he was very tame. He used to come right up to me. But I never cared for him as I do for other birds."

"Genie, you've watched a road runner, all right. I didn't imagine you knew so much. Yes, he's a killer, a murderer. But no worse than other desert birds. They all kill. They're all fierce. And if they weren't they'd die. . . . Now I want to tell you the most wonderful thing a road runner does. He'll fight and kill and eat a rattlesnake!"

"No! Honest Injun?" cried Genie.

"Yes. I've watched many a battle between a road runner and a rattlesnake, and nearly all of those battles were won by the birds. But *that* is not the most wonderful thing a road runner does. I'll tell you. I've never seen this thing myself, but a friend of mine, an old prospector named Dismukes, swears it's true. He knows more about the desert than any man I ever met, and he wouldn't tell a lie. Well, here's what it is. He says he saw a road runner come upon a sleeping rattlesnake. But he didn't pounce upon the snake. It happened to be that the snake slept on the sand near some bushes of *cholla* cactus. You know how the dead cones fall off and lie around. This wonderful bird dragged these loose pieces of cactus and laid them close together in a circle, all around the rattlesnake. Built a fence around him! Penned him in! Now I can vouch for how a rattlesnake hates cactus. . . . Then the fierce bird flew up and pounced down upon the snake. Woke him up! The rattlesnake tried to slip away, but everywhere he turned was a cactus which stuck into him, and over him the darting, picking bird. So round and round he went, striking as best he could. But he was unable to hit the bird, and every pounce upon him drew the blood.

You've heard the snap of that big long beak. Well, the rattlesnake grew desperate and began to bite himself. And what with his own bites and those of his enemy he was soon dead. . . . And then the beautiful, graceful, speckled bird proceeded to tear and devour him."

"I'll bet it's true!" ejaculated Genie. "A road runner could and would do just that."

"Very likely. It's strange, and perhaps true. Indeed, the desert is the place for things impossible anywhere else."

"Why do birds and beasts kill and eat each other?" asked Genie.

"It is nature, Genie."

"Nature could have done better. Why don't people eat each other? They do *kill* each other. And they eat animals. But isn't that all?"

"Genie, some kinds of people — cannibals in the South Seas — and savages — do kill and eat men. It is horrible to believe. Dismukes told me that he came upon a tribe of Indians on the west coast of Sonora in Mexico. That's not more than four hundred miles from here. He went down there prospecting for gold. He thought these savages — the Seri Indians, they're called — were descended from cannibals and sometimes ate man flesh themselves. No one knows but that they do it often. I've met prospectors and travelers who scouted the idea of the Seris being cannibals. But I've heard some bad stories about them. Dismukes absolutely believed that in a poor season for meat, if chance offered, they would kill and eat a white man. Prospectors have gone into that country never to return."

"Ughh! I've near starved, but I'd never get that hungry. I'd die. Wouldn't you?"

"Indeed I would, child."

And so, during the leisure hours, that grew more and longer as the hot summer season advanced, Adam led Genie nearer to nature, always striving with his observations to teach the truth, however stern, and to instruct and stimulate her growing mind. All was not music of birds and perfume of flowers and serene summer content at the rosy dawns and the golden sunsets. The desert life was at work. How hard to reconcile the killing with the living! But when Adam espied an eagle swooping down from the mountain heights, its wings bowed, and its dark body shooting so wondrously, then he spoke of the freedom of the lonely king of birds, and the grace of his flight, and the noble spirit of his life.

Likewise when Adam heard the honk of wild geese he made haste to have Genie see them winging wide and triangular flight across the blue sky, to the north. He told her how they lived all the winter in the warm south, and when spring came a wonderful instinct bade them rise and fly far northward, to the reedy banks of some lonely lake, and there gobble and honk and feed and raise their young.

On another day, and this was in drowsy June

when all the air seemed still, he was roused from his siesta by cries of delight from Genie. She knelt before him on the sand, and in one hand she held a beautiful horned toad, and the other hand she stretched out to Adam.

"Look! Oh, look!" she cried, ecstatically, and her eyes then rivaled the jeweled eyes of the desert reptile. Some dark-red drops of bright liquid showed against the brown of Genie's hand. "There! It's blood! I picked him up as I had all the others, so many hundreds of times. Only this time I felt something warm and wet. I looked at my hand. There! He had squirted the drops of blood! And, oh, I was quick to look at his eyes! One was still wet, bloody. I know he squirted the drops of blood from his eyes!"

Thus Adam had confirmed for him one of the mysteries of the desert. Dismukes had been the first to tell Adam about the strange habit of horned toads ejecting blood from their eyes. One other desert man, at least, had corroborated Dismukes. But Adam, who had seldom passed a horned toad without picking it up to gaze at the wondrous coloration, and to see it swell and puff, had never come upon the phenomenon. And horned toads on his trails had been many. To interest Genie, he built her a corral of flat stones in the sand, and he scoured the surrounding desert for horned toads. What a miscellaneous collection he gathered! They all had the same general scalloped outlines and tiny horns, but the color and design seemed to partake of the physical characteristics of the spot where each was found. If they squatted in the sand and lay still, it was almost impossible to see them, so remarkable was their protective coloration. Adam turned the assortment over to Genie with instruction to feed them, and play with them, and tease them in the hope that one might sometime effect drops of blood from his eyes. When it actually happened, Genie's patience was rewarded.

Adam's theory that the reward of the faithful desert watcher would always come was exemplified in more than one way. Genie had never seen or heard of a tarantula wasp. She had noticed big and little tarantulas, but of the fierce, winged, dragon-fly hawk of the desert — the tarantula wasp — she had no knowledge. Adam, therefore, had always kept a keen lookout for one.

They were up in the canyon on a hot June day, resting in the shade of the rustling palms. A stream babbled and splashed over the stones, and that was the only sound to break the dreaming silence of the canyon. All at once Adam heard a low whir like the hum of tiny wings. As he turned his head the sound became a buzz. Then he espied a huge tarantula wasp. Quickly he called to Genie, and they watched. It flew around and around about a foot from the ground, a fierce-looking, yet beautiful creature, with yellow body and blue gauzy wings. It was fully two inches and more long.

"He sees a tarantula. Now watch!" whispered Adam.

Suddenly the wasp darted down to the edge of a low bush, into some coarse grass that grew there. Instantly came a fierce whiz of wings, like the buzz of a captured bumblebee, only much louder and more vibrant. Adam saw the blades of grass tumble. A struggle to the death was going on there. Adam crawled over a few yards, drawing Genie with him; and they saw the finish of a terrific battle between the wasp and a big hairy tarantula.

"There! It's over, and the tarantula is dead," said Adam. "Genie, I used to watch this kind of a desert fight, and not think much more about it. But one day I made a discovery. I had a camp over here, and I watched a tarantula wasp kill a tarantula. I didn't know it then, but this wasp was a female, ready to lay her eggs. Well, she rolled the big spider around until she found a place that suited her. Then she dug a hole, rolled him into it, covered him over, and flew away. I wondered then why she did that. I went away from that camp, and after a while I came back. Then one day I remembered about the wasp burying the tarantula. And so, just for fun and curiosity, I found the grave — it was near the end of a stone — and I opened it up. What do you think I discovered?"

"Tell me!" exclaimed Genie, breathlessly.

"I found the tarantula almost eaten up by a lot of tiny wasps, as much like worms as wasps!

Then I understood. That tarantula wasp had killed the tarantula, laid her eggs inside his body, tumbled him into his grave, and covered him over. By and by those eggs hatched, and the little wasps ate the tarantula — lived and grew, and after a while came out full-fledged tarantula wasps like their mother."

24
●

Time passed. The days slipped by to make weeks, and weeks merged into months. Summer with its hot midday hours, when man and beast rested or slept, seemed to shorten its season by half. No human creature even entered a desert oasis without joy, nor left it without regret. As time went fleeting by Adam now and then remembered Dismukes, and these memories were full of both gladness and pathos. He tried to visualize the old prospector in the new role of traveler, absorber of life, spendthrift and idler. Nevertheless, Adam could never be sure in his heart that Dismukes would find what he sought.

But for the most part of the still, hot, waking hours, Adam, when he was not working or sleeping, devoted himself to Genie. The girl changed every day — how, he was unable to tell. Most wondrous of all in nature was human life, and beyond all sublimity was the human soul!

Every morning at sunrise Genie knelt by her mother's grave with bowed head and clasped hands, and every evening at sunset or in the golden dusk of twilight she again knelt in prayer.

"Genie, why do you kneel there — now?" asked Adam once, unable to contain his curiosity. "You did not use to do it. Only the last few weeks or month."

"I forgot I'd promised mother," she replied. "Besides, could I pray when I wanted to die?"

"No, I suppose not. It would be hard," replied Adam, gravely. "Please don't think me curious. Tell me, Genie, what do you pray for?"

"I used to pray, 'Now I lay me down to sleep,' as mother taught me when I was little. But now I make up my own prayers. I ask God to keep the souls of mother and father in heaven. I pray I may be good and happy, so when they look down and see me they will be glad. I pray for you, and then for every one in the world."

Slow, strong unrest, the endless moving of contending tides, heaved in Adam's breast.

"So you pray for me, Genie? . . . Well, it is good of you. I hope I'm worthy. . . . But, *why* do you pray?"

She pondered the question. Thought was developing in Genie. "Before mother died I prayed because she taught me. Since then — lately — it — it lifts me up — it takes away the sorrow here." And she put a hand over her heart.

"Genie, then you believe in God — the God who is supposed to answer your prayers?"

"Yes. And he is not a god like Taquitch — or the beasts and rocks that the Indians worship. My God is all around me, in the sunshine, in the air, in the humming bees and whispering leaves and murmuring water. I feel him everywhere, and in me, too!"

"Genie, tell me one prayer, just *one* of yours or your mother's that was truly answered," appealed Adam, with earnest feeling.

"We prayed for some one to come. I know mother prayed for some one to save me from being alone — from starving. And I prayed for some one to come and help her — to relieve her terrible dread about me. . . . And *you* came!"

Adam was silenced. What had he to contend with here? Faith and fact were beyond question, as Genie represented them. What little he knew! He could not even believe that a divine guidance had been the spirit of his wandering steps. But he was changing. Always the future — always the unknown calling — always the presentiment of sterner struggle, of larger growth, of ultimate fulfillment! His illusion, his fetish, his phantasmagoria rivaled the eternal and inexplicable faith of his friend Dismukes.

Andreas Canyon was far from the camp under the cottonwoods, but Adam and Genie, having once feasted their eyes upon its wildness and beauty and grandeur, went back again and again, so that presently the distance in the hot sun was no hindrance, and the wide area of white, glistening, terrible *cholla* cactus was no obstacle.

For that matter the cactus patch was endurable because of its singular beauty. Adam could not have told why *cholla* fascinated him, and, though Genie admitted she liked to look at the frosty silver-lighted cones and always had an impulse to prick her fingers on the cruel thorns, she could not explain why.

"Genie, the Yaqui Indians in Sonora love this *cholla*," said Adam. "Love it as they hate Mexicans. They will strip a Mexican naked, tear the skin off the soles of his feet, and drive him through the *cholla* until he's dead. It wouldn't take long! . . . All prospectors hate *cholla*. I hate it, yet I — I guess I'm a little like the Yaquis. I often prick my finger on *cholla* just to feel the sting, the burn, the throb. The only pain I could ever compare to that made by *cholla* is the sting of the sharp horn of a little catfish back in Ohio. Oh! I'll never forget that! A poison, burning sting! . . . But *cholla* is terrible because the thorns stick in your flesh. When you jerk to free yourself the thorns leave the cones. Each thorn has an invisible barb and it works deeper and deeper into flesh."

"Don't *I* know!" exclaimed Genie, emphatically. "I've spent whole hours digging them out of my feet and legs. But how pretty the *cholla* shines! Only it doesn't tell the truth, does it, Wanny?"

"Child, please don't call me Wanny. It's so — so silly," protested Adam.

"It's not. No sillier than your calling me child! I'm nearly fifteen. I'm growing right out of my clothes."

"Call me Adam."

"No, I don't like that name. And I can't call you mister or father or brother."

"But what's wrong with Adam?"

"I read in mother's Bible about Adam and Eve. I hated her when the devil got into her. And I didn't like Adam. And I don't like the *name* Adam. You'd never have been driven from heaven."

"I'm not so sure about that," said Adam, ruefully. "Genie, I was wicked when I was a — a young man."

"You were! Well, I don't care. *You'd* never be tempted to disobey the Lord — not by Eve with all her stolen apples!"

"All right, called me Wanny," returned Adam, and he made haste to change the subject. There were times when Genie, with her simplicity, her directness, her curiosity, and her innocence, caused Adam extreme perplexity, not to say embarrassment. He remembered his own bringing up. It seemed every year his childhood days came back closer. And thrown as he was in constant companionship with this child of nature, he began to wonder if the sophisticated education of children, especially girls, as it had

460

been in his youth, was as fine and simple and true to life as it might have been.

Andreas Canyon yawned with wide mouth and huge yellow cliffs. Just beyond the mouth of the canyon and across the wide space from cliff to slope bloomed the most verdant and beautiful oasis of that desert region. Huge gray bowlders, clean and old, and russet with lichen, made barricade for a clear stream of green water, as if to protect it from blowing desert sand. Yet there were little beaches of white sand, lined by colored pebbles. Green rushes and flags grew in the water. Beyond the stream, on the side of the flat-rocked slope, lay a many-acred thicket of mesquite, impenetrable except for birds and beasts. The green of the leaves seemed dominated by bronze colors of the mistletoe.

The oasis proper, however, was the grove of cottonwoods, sycamores, and palms. How bright green the foliage of cottonwoods — and smooth white the bark of sycamores! But verdant and cool as it was under their shade, Adam and Genie always sought the aloof and stately palms, wonderful trees not native there, planted years and years before by the Spanish padres.

"Oh, I love it here!" exclaimed Genie. "Listen to the palms whisper!"

They stood loftily, with spreading green fanlike leaves at the tops, and all the trunks swathed and bundled apparently in huge cases of straw. These yellow sheaths were no less than the leaves that had died. As the palms grew the new leaves kept bursting from the tufted tops, and those leaves lowest down died and turned yellow.

"Genie, your uncle seems a long time coming back for you," remarked Adam.

"I hope he never comes," she replied.

Adam was surprised and somewhat disconcerted at her reply, and yet strangely pleased.

"Why?" he asked.

"Oh, I never liked him and I don't want to go away with him."

"Your mother said he was a good man — that he loved you."

"Uncle Ed was good, and very kind to me. I — I ought to be ashamed," replied Genie. "But he drank, and when he drank he kissed me — he put his hands on me. I hated that."

"Did you ever tell your mother?" inquired Adam.

"Yes. I told her. I asked her why he did that. And she said not to mind — only to keep away from him when he drank."

"Genie, your uncle did wrong, and your mother did wrong not to tell you so," declared Adam, earnestly.

"Wrong? What do you mean — wrong? I only thought I didn't like him."

"Well, I'll tell you some day. . . . But now, to go back to what you said about leaving — you know I'm going with you when your uncle comes."

"Wanny, do *you* want that time to come

soon?" she asked, wistfully.

"Yes, of course, for your sake. You're getting to be a big girl. You must go to school. You must get out to civilization."

"Oh! I'm crazy to go!" she burst out, covering her face. "Yet I've a feeling I'll hate to leave here. . . . I've been so happy lately."

"Genie, it relieves me to hear you're anxious to go. And it pleases me to know you've been happy lately. You see I'm only a — a man, you know. How little I could do for you! I've tried. I've done my best. But at that best I'm only a poor old homeless outcast — a desert wanderer! I'm —"

"Hush up!" she cried, with quick, sweet warmth. Swiftly she enveloped him, hugged him close, and kissed his cheek. "Wanny, you're grand! . . . You're like Taquitch — you're *my* Taquitch with face like the sun! And I love you — love you as I never loved anyone except my mother! And I hope Uncle Ed never comes, so you'll have to take care of me always."

Adam gently disengaged himself from Genie's impulsive arms, yet, despite his embarrassment and confused sense of helplessness, he felt the better for her action. Natural, spontaneous, sincere, it warmed his heart. It proved more than all else what a child she was.

"Genie, let me make sure you understand," he said gravely. "I love you, too, as if you were my little sister. And if your uncle doesn't come I'll take you somewhere — find you a home.

But I never — much as I would like to — never can take care of you always."

"Why?" she flashed, with her terrible directness.

Adam had begun his development of Genie by telling the truth; he had always abided by it; and now, in these awakening days for her, he must never veer from the truth.

"If I tell you why — will you promise never to speak of it — so long as you live?" he asked, solemnly.

"Never! I promise. Never, Wanny!"

"Genie, I am an outcast. I am a hunted man. I can never go back to civilization and stay."

Then he told her the story of the ruin of his life. When he finished she fell weeping upon his shoulder and clung to him. For Adam the moment was sad and sweet — sad because a few words had opened up the dark, tragic gulf of his soul; and sweet because the passionate grief of a child assured him that even he, wanderer as he was, knew something of sympathy and love.

"But, Wanny, you — could — go and — be — pun— ished — and then — come back!" she cried, between sobs. "You'd — never — have to — hide — any more."

Out of her innocence and simplicity she had spoken confounding truth. What a terrible truth! Those words of child wisdom sowed in Adam the seed of a terrible revolt. Revolt — yea, revolt against this horrible need to hide — this fear and dread of punishment that always and forever so bitterly mocked his manhood! If he could find the strength to rise to the heights of Genie's wisdom — divine philosophy of a child! — he would no longer hate his shadowed wandering steps down the naked shingles and hidden trails of the lonely desert. But, alas! whence would come that strength? Not from the hills! Not from the nature that had made him so strong, so fierce, so sure to preserve his life! It could only come from the spirit that had stood in the dusky twilight beside a dying woman's side. It could come only from the spirit to whom a child prayed while kneeling at her mother's grave. And for Adam that spirit held aloof, illusive as the specters of the dead, beyond his grasp, an invisible medium, if indeed it was not a phantom, that seemed impossible of reality in the face of the fierce, ruthless, inevitable life and death and decay of the desert. Could God be nature — that thing, that terrible force, light, fire, water, pulse — that quickening of plant, flesh, stone, that dying of all only to renew — that endless purpose and progress, from the first whirling gas globe of the universe, throughout the ages down to the infinitesimal earth so fixed in its circling orbit, so pitiful in its present brief fertility? The answer was as unattainable as to pluck down the stars, as hopeless as to think of the fleeting of the years, as mysterious as the truth of where man came from and whence he was to go.

★ ★ ★

Snow on the gray old peak! It reminded Adam how, long ago, from far down the valley, he had watched the mountain crown itself in dazzling white. Snow on the heights meant winter that tempered the heat, let loose the storm winds; and therefore, down in the desert, comfort and swiftly flying days. Indeed, so swift were they that Adam, calling out sad and well-remembered words, "Oh, time, stand still here!" seemed to look at a few more golden sunsets and, lo! again it was spring. Time would not stand still nor would the budding, blossoming youth of Genie! Nor would the slow-mounting might of the tumult in Adam's soul!

Then swifter than the past, another year flew by. Genie's uncle did not come. And Adam began to doubt that he would ever come. And the hope of Genie's, that he never would come began insidiously to enter into Adam's thought. Again the loneliness, the solitude and silence, and something more he could not name, began to drag Adam from duty, from effort of mind. The desert never stopped its work, on plant, or rock, or man. Adam knew that he required another shock to quicken his brain, to stir again the spiritual need, to make him fight the subtle, all-pervading, ever-present influence of the desert.

In all that time Adam saw but two white men, prospectors passing by down the sandy trails.

Indians came that way but seldom. Across the valley there was an encampment, which he visited occasionally to buy baskets, skins, meat, and to send Indians out after supplies. The great problem was clothes for Genie. It was difficult to get materials, difficult for Genie to make dresses, and impossible to keep her from tearing or wearing or growing out of them. Adam found that Indian moccasins, and tough overalls such as prospectors wore, cut down to suit Genie, and woolen blouses she made herself, were the only things for her. Like a road runner she ran over the rocks and sand! For Genie, cactus was as if it were not! As for a hat, she would not wear one. Adam's responsibility weighed upon him. When he asked Genie what in the world she would wear when he took her out of the desert, to pass through villages and ranches and towns, where people lived, she naïvely replied, "What I've got on!" And what she wore at the moment was, of course, the boyish garb that was all Adam could keep on her, and which happened just then to be minus the moccasins. Genie loved to scoop up the warm white sand with her bare brown feet, and then to dabble them in the running water.

"Well, I give up!" exclaimed Adam, resignedly. "But when we do get to Riverside or San Diego, where there's a store, you've *got* to go with me to buy girl's dresses and things — and you've *got* to wear them."

"Oh, Wanny, that will be grand!" she cried,

dazzled at the prospect. "But — let's don't go — just yet!"

In the early fall — what month it was Adam could not be sure — he crossed the arm of the valley to the encampment of the Coahuilas. The cool nights and tempering days had made him hungry for meat. He found the Indian hunters at home, and, in fact, they had just packed fresh sheep meat down from the mountain. They were of the same tribe as the old chief, Charley Jim, who had taught Adam so much of the desert during those early hard years over in the Chocolates. Adam always asked for news of Charley Jim, usually to be disappointed. He was a nomad, this old chieftain, and his family had his wandering spirit. Adam shouldered his load of fresh meat and took his way down out of the canyon where the encampment lay, to the well-beaten trail that zigzagged along the irregular base of the mountain.

Adam rested at the dividing point of the trails. It was early in the day, clear and still. How gray and barren and monotonous the desert! All seemed dead A strange, soft, creeping apathy came over Adam, not a dreaminess, for in his dreams he lived the past and invented the future, but a state wherein he watched, listened, smelled, and felt, all unconscious that he was doing anything. Whenever he fell into this trance and was roused out of it, or came out of it naturally, then he experienced a wonderful sense of vague content. That feeling was evanescent. Always he longed to get it back, but could not.

In this instant his quick eye caught sight of something that was moving. A prospector with a brace of burros — common sight indeed it was to Adam, though not for the last few years.

The man was coming from the south, but outside of the main trail, for which, no doubt, he was heading. Adam decided to wait and exchange greetings with him. After watching awhile Adam was constrained to mutter, "Well, if that fellow isn't a great walker, my eyes are failing!" That interested him all the more. He watched burros and driver grow larger and clearer. Then they disappeared behind a long, low swell of sand fringed by sage and dotted by mesquite. They would reappear presently, coming out behind the ridge at a point near Adam.

Some minutes later he saw that the burros and driver had not only cleared the end of the ridge, but were now within a hundred yards of where he sat. The burros were trotting, with packs bobbing up and down. Only the old slouch hat of the prospector showed above the packs. Manifestly he was a short man.

"Say, but he's a walker!" ejaculated Adam.

Suddenly sight of that old slouch hat gave Adam a thrill. Then the man's shoulders appeared. How enormously broad! Then, as the burros veered to one side, the driver's whole stature was disclosed. What a stride he had, for a man so short. Almost he seemed as wide as he was long. His gait was rolling, ponderous. He wore old, gray, patched clothes that Adam wildly imagined he had seen somewhere.

Suddenly he yelled at the burros: "Hehaw! Gedap!"

That deep voice, those words, brought Adam leaping to his feet, transfixed and thrilling. Had he lost his mind? What trick of desert mirage or illusion! No — the burros were real — they kicked up the dust — rattled the pebbles in the sage; no — the man was real, however he seemed a ghost of Adam's past.

"Dismukes!" shouted Adam, hoarsely.

The prospector halted his long, rolling stride and looked. Then Adam plunged over sand and through sage. He could not believe his eyes. He must get his hands on this man, to prove reality. In a trice the intervening space was covered. Then Adam, breathless and aghast, gazed into a face that he knew, yet which held what he did not know.

"Howdy, Wansfell! Thought I'd meet you sooner or later," said the man.

His voice was unmistakable. He recognized Adam. Beyond any possibility of doubt — Dismukes! In the amaze and gladness of the moment Adam embraced this old savior and comrade and friend — embraced him as a long-lost brother or as a prodigal son. Then Adam released him, with sudden dawning consciousness that

Dismukes seemed to have no feeling whatever about this meeting.

"Dismukes! I had to grab you — just to feel if it was you. I'm knocked clean off my pins," declared Adam, breathing hard.

"Yes, it's me, Wansfell," replied Dismukes. His large, steady eyes, dark brown like those of an ox, held an exceeding and unutterable sadness.

"Back on the desert? *You!*" exclaimed Adam. "Dismukes, then you lost your gold — bad luck — something happened — you never went to the great cities — to spend your fortune — to live and live?"

"Yes, friend, I went," replied Dismukes.

A great awe fell upon Adam. His keen gaze, cleared of the mist of amaze, saw Dismukes truly. The ox eyes had the shadow of supreme tragedy. Their interest was far off, as if their sight had fixed on a dim, distant mountain range of the horizon. Yet they held peace. The broad face had thinned. Gone was the dark, healthy bronze! And the beard that had once been thick and grizzled was now scant and white. The whole face expressed resignation and peace. Those wonderful wide shoulders of Dismukes appeared just as wide, but they sagged, and the old, tremendous brawn was not there. Strangest of all, Dismukes wore the ragged gray prospector's garb which had been on his person when Adam saw him last. There! the yellow stain of Death Valley clay — and darker

471

stains — sight of which made Adam's flesh creep!

"Ah! So you went, after all," replied Adam, haltingly. "Well! Well! . . . Let's sit down, old comrade. Here on this stone. I confess my legs feel weak. . . . Never expected to see you again in this world!"

"Wansfell, no man can ever tell. It's folly to think an' toil an' hope for the future."

What strong, sad history of life revealed itself in that reply!

"Ah! . . . I — But never mind what I think. Dismukes, you've not been on the desert long."

"About a week. Outfitted at San Diego an' came over the mountain trail through El Campo. Landed in Frisco two weeks an' more ago. By ship from Japan."

"Did you have these old clothes hid away somewhere?" inquired Adam. "I remember them."

"No. I packed them wherever I went for the whole three years."

"Three years! Has it been that long?"

"Aye, friend Wansfell, three years."

Adam gazed out across the desert with slowly dimming eyes. The wasteland stretched there, vast and illimitable, the same as all the innumerable times he had gazed. Solemn and gray and old, indifferent to man, yet strengthening through its passionless fidelity to its own task!

"Dismukes, I want you to tell me where you went, what you did, why you came back," said

Adam, with earnestness that was entreaty.

Dismukes heaved a long sigh. He wagged the huge, shaggy head that was now gray. But he showed no more indication of emotion. How stolid he seemed — how locked in his aloofness!

"Yes, I'll tell you," he said. "Maybe it'll save you somethin' of what I went through."

Then he became lost in thought, perhaps calling upon memory, raking up the dead leaves of the past. Adam recalled that his own memory of Dismukes and the past brought note of the fact how the old prospector had loved to break his habit of silence, to talk about the desert, and to smoke his black pipe while he discoursed. But now speech did not easily flow and he did not smoke.

"Lookin' back, I seem to see myself as crazy," began Dismukes. "You'll remember how crazy. You'll remember before we parted up there on the Mohave at that borax camp where the young man was — who couldn't drive the mules. . . . Wansfell, from the minute I turned my back on you till now I've never thought of that. Did you drive the ornery mules?"

"Did I?" Adam's query was a grim assertion. "Every day for three months! You remember Old Butch, that gray devil of a mule. Well, Dismukes, the time came when *he* knew me. If I even picked up the long bull whip Old Butch would scream and run to lay his head on me."

"An' you saw the young driver through his trouble?"

"That I did. And it was more trouble than he told us then. The boss Carricks had was low-down and cunning. He'd got smitten with the lad's wife — a pretty girl, but frail in health. He kept Carricks on jobs away from home. We didn't meet the lad any too soon."

"Humph! That's got a familiar sound to me," declared Dismukes. "Wansfell, what'd you do to thet low-down boss?"

"Go on with *your* story," replied Adam.

"Aha! That's so. I want to make Two Palms Well before dark. . . . Wansfell, like a horned-toad on the desert, I changed my outside at Frisco. Alas! I imagined all within — blood — mind — soul had changed! . . . Went to Denver, St. Louis, an' looked at the sights, not much disappointed, because my time seemed far ahead. Then I went to my old home. There I had my first jar. Folks all dead! Not a relation livin'. Could not even find my mother's grave. No one remembered me an' I couldn't find any one I ever knew. The village had grown to a town. My old home was gone. The picture of it — the little gray cottage — the vines an' orchard — lived in my mind. I found the place. All gone! Three new houses there. Forty years is a long time! I didn't build the church or set out a park for the village of my boyhood. . . . Then I went on to Chicago, Philadelphia, New York. Stayed long in New York. At first it fascinated me. I felt I wanted to see it out of curiosity. I was lookin' for some place, somethin' I expected. But I never saw it. The hotels, theaters, saloons, gamblin' hells, an' worse — the operas an' parks an' churches — an' the wonderful stores — I saw them all. Men an' women like ants rushin' to an' fro. No rest, no sleep, no quiet, no peace! I met people, a few good, but most bad. An' in some hotels an' places I got to be well known. I got to have a name for throwin' gold around. Men of business sought my acquaintance, took me to dinners, made much of me — all to get me to invest in their schemes. Women! Aw! the women were my second disappointment! Wansfell, women are like desert mirages. Beautiful women, in silks an' satins, diamonds blazin' on bare necks an' arms, made eyes at me, talked soft an' sweet, an' flattered me an' praised me an' threw themselves at me — all because they thought I had stacks an' rolls an' bags of gold. Never a woman did I meet who liked *me*, who had any thought to hear my story, to learn my hope! Never a kind whisper! Never any keen eye that saw through my outside!

"Well, I wasn't seein' an' findin' the life I'd hoped for. That New York is as near hell as I ever got. I saw men with quiet faces an' women who seemed happy. But only in the passin' crowds. I never got to meet any of them. They had their homes an' troubles an' happiness, I figured, an' they were not lookin'

475

for anyone to fleece. It was my habit to get into a crowd an' watch, for I come to believe the mass of busy, workin' ordinary people were good. Maybe if I'd somehow made acquaintance with a few of them it 'd have been better. But that wasn't seein' life. I thought I knew what I wanted.

"All my yearnin's an' dreams seemed to pall on me. Where was the joy? Wansfell, the only joy I had was in findin' some poor beggar or bootblack or poor family, an' givin' them gold. The great city was full of them. An' I gave away thousands of dollars. God knows *that* was some good. An' now I see if I could have stuck it out, livin' among such people, I might have been of some use in the world. But, man! livin' was not possible in New York. All night the hotels roared. All night the streets hummed an' changed. There was as many people rushin' around by night as by day, an' different from each other, like bats an' hawks. I got restless an' half sick. I couldn't sleep. I seemed suffocatin' for fresh air. I wanted room to breathe. When I looked up at night I couldn't see the stars. Think of that for a desert man!

"At last I knew I couldn't find what I wanted in New York, an' I couldn't hunt any longer there. I had to leave. My plans called for goin' abroad. *Then* came a strange feelin' that I must have had all the time, but didn't realize. The West called me back. I seemed to want the Middle West, where I'd planned to buy the green farm. But you know I'm a man who sticks to his mind, when it's made up. There were London, Paris, Rome I'd dreamed about an' had planned to see. Well, I had a hell of a fight with somethin' in myself before I could get on that ship. Right off then I got seasick. Wansfell, the bite of a rattlesnake never made me half as sick as that dirty-gray, windy sea. The trip across was a nightmare. . . . London was a dreary place as big as the Mohave an' full of queer fishy-eyed people whom I couldn't understand. But I liked their slow, easy-goin' ways. Then Paris. . . . Wansfell, that Paris was a wonderful, glitterin' beautiful city, an' if a city had been a place for me, Paris would have been it. But I was lost. I couldn't speak French — couldn't learn a word. My tongue refused to twist round their queer words. All the same, I saw what I'd set out to see. . . . Wansfell, if a man fights despair for the women of the world, he'll get licked in Paris. An' the reason is, there you see the same thing in the homely, good, an' virtuous wives as you see in those terrible, fascinatin', dazzlin' actresses. What that somethin' is I couldn't guess. But you like all Frenchwomen. They're gay an' happy an' square. If I applied the truth of this desert to these Frenchwomen, I'd say the somethin' so fascinatin' in them is that the race is peterin' out an' the women are dyin' game.

"From Paris I went to Rome, an' there a queer state of mind came to me. I could look at temples an' old ruins without even seein' them — with my mind on my own country. All this travel idea, seein' an' learnin' an' doin', changed so that it was hateful. I cut out Egypt, an' I can't remember much of India an' Japan. But when I got on ship bound for Frisco I couldn't see anythin' for a different reason, an' that was tears. I'd come far to find joy of life, an' now I wept tears of joy because I was homeward bound. It was a great an' splendid feelin'!

"The Pacific isn't like the Atlantic. It's vast an' smooth an' peaceful, with swells like the mile-long ridges of the desert. I didn't get seasick. An' on that voyage I got some rest. Maybe the sea is like the desert. Anyway, it calmed me, an' I could think clear once more. As I walked the deck by day, or hung over the rail by night, my yearnin's an' dreams came back. When I reached Frisco I'd take train for the Middle West, an' somewhere I'd buy the green ranch an' settle down to peace an' quiet for the rest of my life. The hope was beautiful. I believed in it. That wild desire to search for the joy of life had to be buried. I had been wrong about that. It was only a dream — a boy's dream, on the hope of which I had spent the manhood of my best years. Ah! it was bitter — bitter to realize that. I — who had never given in to defeat! . . . But I conquered my regret because I knew I had just mistaken what I wanted. An' it was not wholly too late! . . . Wansfell, you've no idea of the size of the old earth. I've been round it. An' that Pacific! Oh, what an endless ocean of waters! It seemed eternal, like the sky. But — at last — I got to — Frisco."

Here Dismukes choked and broke down. The deep, rolling voice lost its strength for a moment. He drew a long, long breath that it hurt Adam to hear.

"Wansfell, when my feet once more touched land it was as though I'd really found happiness," presently went on Dismukes, clearing his throat of huskiness. "I was in the clouds. I could have kissed the very dirt. My own, my native land! . . . Now for the last leg of the journey — an' the little farm — the home to be — friends to make — perhaps a sweet-faced woman an' a child! Oh, it was as glorious as my lost dreams!

"But suddenly somethin' strange an' terrible seized hold of me. A land as strong as the wind gripped my heart. . . . *The desert called me!* . . . Day an' night I walked the streets. Fierce as the desert itself I fought. Oh, I fought my last an' hardest fight! . . . On one hand was the dream of my life — the hope of a home an' happiness — what I had slaved for. Forty years of toil! On the other hand the call of the desert! Loneliness, solitude, silence, the white, hot days, the starlit nights, the vast open desert, free and peaceful, the gray wastes, the colored mountains, sunrise and sunset. Ah! The desert was my only home. I belonged to the silence an' desolation. Forty years a wanderer on the desert, blindly seekin' gold! But, oh, it was not gold I wanted! Not gold! Nor fortune! That was my dream, my boyish dream. Gold did not nail me to the desert sands. That was only my idea. That was what brought me into the wastelands. I misunderstood the lure of the desert. I thought it was gold, but, no! For me the desert existed as the burrow for the fox. For me the desert linked my strange content to the past ages. For me the soul of the desert was my soul! . . . *I had to go back!* . . . I could live nowhere else. . . . Forty years! My youth — my manhood! . . . I'm old now — old! My dreams are done. . . . Oh, my God! . . . I HAD TO COME BACK!"

Adam sat confounded in grief, in shock. His lips were mute. Like a statue he gazed across the wasteland, so terribly magnified, so terribly illumined by the old prospector's revelation. How awful the gigantic red rock barriers! How awful the lonely, limitless expanse of sand! The eternal gray, the eternal monotony!

"Comrade, take the story of my life to heart," added Dismukes. "You're a young man still. Think of my forty years of hell, that now has made me a part of the desert. Think of how I set out upon my journey so full of wild, sweet hope! Think of my wonderful journey, through the glitterin' cities, round the world, only to find my hope a delusion! . . . A desert mirage!"

"Man, I cannot think!" burst out Adam. "I am stunned. . . . Oh, the pity of it — the sickening, pitiless fatality! Oh, my heart breaks for you! . . . Dismukes, of what use is hope? Oh, why do we fight? Where — where does joy abide for such as you and me?"

The great, rolling ox eyes gleamed upon Adam, strong with the soul of peace, of victory in their depths.

"Wansfell, joy an' happiness, whatever makes life worth livin', is in *you*. No man can go forth to find what he hasn't got within him."

Then he gazed away across the desert, across sand and cactus and mesquite, across the blue-hazed, canyon-streaked ranges toward the north.

"I go to Death Valley," he contined, slowly, in his deep voice. "I had left enough gold to grub-stake me. An' I go to Death Valley, but not to seek my fortune. It will be quiet and lonely there. An' I can think an' rest an' sleep. Perhaps I'll dig a little of the precious yellow dust, just to throw it away. God! . . . The man who loves gold is ruined. Passion makes men mad. . . . An' now I must go."

"Death Valley? No! No!" whispered Adam.

"Straight for Death Valley! It has called me across half the earth. I remember no desert place so lonely an' silent an' free. So different from the noisy world of men that crowds my mind still! There I shall find peace, perhaps my grave. See! life is all a hopin' to find! I go on my way. Wansfell, we never know what drives us.

481

But I am happy now. . . . Our trails have crossed for the last time. Good-by."

He wrung Adam's hand and quickly whirled to his burros.

"Hehaw! Gedap!" he shouted, with a smack on their haunches. Adam whispered a farewell he could not speak. Then, motionless, he watched the old prospector face the gray wastes toward the north and the beckoning mountains. Adam had an almost irresistible desire to run after Dismukes, to go with him. But the man wanted to be alone. What a stride he had! The fruitless quest had left him that at least. The same old rolling gait, the same doggedness! Dismukes was a man who could not be halted. Adam watched him — saw him at last merge and disappear in the gray, lonely sage. And then into Adam's strained sight seemed to play a quivering mirage — a vision of Death Valley, ghastly and white and naked, the abode of silence and decay set down under its dark-red walls — the end of the desert and the grave of Dismukes.

25

The November morning was keen and cold and Adam and Genie were on their way to spend the day at Andreas Canyon. Adam carried a lunch, a gun, and a book. Genie seemed so exuberant with wonderful spirits that she could scarcely keep her little moccasined feet on the sand. Adam had an unconscious joy in the sight of her.

A dim old Indian trail led up one of the slopes of Andreas Canyon, to which Adam called Genie's attention.

"We'll climb this some day — when it comes time to take you away," said Adam. "It's a hard climb, but the shortest way out. And you'll get to see the desert from the top of old Jacinto. That will be worth all the climb."

His words made Genie pensive. Of late the girl had become more and more beyond Adam's comprehension — wistful and sad and dreamy by turns, now like a bird and again like a thundercloud, but mostly a dancing, singing creature full of unutterable sweetness of life.

Beyond the oasis, some distance up the canyon, was a dense growth of mesquite and other brush. It surrounded a sandy glade in which bubbled forth a crystal spring of hot water. The bottom was clean white sand that boiled up in the center like shining bubbles. Indians in times past had laid stones around the pool. A small cottonwood tree on the west side of the glade had begun to change the green color of the leaves to amber and gold. All around the glade, like a wild, untrimmed hedge, the green and brown mesquites stood up, hiding the gray desert, insulating this cool, sandy, beautiful spot, hiding it away from the stern hardness outside.

Genie had never been here. Quickly she lost her pensiveness and began to sing like a lark. She kicked one moccasin one way and the other in another direction. Straightway she was on the stones, with her bare, slender, brown feet in the water.

"Ooooo! it's hot!" she cried, ecstatically. "But, oh, it's fine!" And she dipped them back.

"Genie, you stay here and amuse yourself," said Adam. "I'm going to climb. Maybe I'll be back soon — maybe not. You play and read, and eat the lunch when you're hungry."

"All right, Wanny," she replied, gayly. "But I should think you'd rather stay with me."

Adam had to be alone. He needed to be high above the desert, where he could look down. Another crisis in his transformation was painfully pending. The meeting with Dismukes had been of profound significance and its effect was going

484

to be far-reaching.

He climbed up the zigzag, dim trail, rising till the canyon yawned beneath him, and the green thicket where he had left Genie was but a dot. Then the way led round the slope of the great foothill, where he left the trail and climbed to the craggy summit. It was a round, bare peak of jagged bronze rock, and from this height half a mile above the desert the outlook was magnificent. Beyond and above him the gray walls and fringed peaks of San Jacinto towered, sculptored and grand against the azure blue.

Finding a comfortable seat with rest for his back, Adam faced the illimitable gulf of color and distance below. Always a height such as this, where, like a lonely eagle, he could command an unobstructed view, had been a charm, a strange delight of his desert years. Not wholly had love of climbing, or to see afar, or to feel alone, or to travel in beauty, been accountable for this habit.

Adam's first reward for this climb, before he had settled himself to watch the desert, was sight of a condor. Only rarely did Adam see this great and loneliest of lonely birds — king of the eagles and of the blue heights. Never had Adam seen one close. A wild, slate-colored bird, huge of build, with gristly neck and wonderful, clean-cut head, cruelly beaked! Even as Adam looked the condor pitched off the crag and spread his enormous wings.

A few flaps of those wide wings — then he

sailed out over the gulf, and around, rising as he circled. When he started he was below Adam; on the first lap of that circle he rose even with Adam's position; and when he came round again he sailed over Adam, perhaps fifty feet. Adam thrilled at the sight. The condor was peering down with gleaming, dark, uncanny eyes. He saw Adam. His keen head and great, crooked beak moved to and fro; the sun shone on his gray-flecked breast; every feather of his immense wings seemed to show, to quiver in the air, and the tip feathers were ragged and separate. He cut the air with a soft swish.

Around he sailed, widening his circle, rising higher, with never a movement of his wings. That fact, assured by Adam's sharp sight, was so marvelous that it fascinated him. What power enabled the condor to rise without propelling himself? No wind stirred down there under the peaks, so he could not lift himself by its aid. He sailed aloft. He came down on one slope of his circle, to rise up on the other, and always he went higher. How easily! How gracefully! He was peering down for sight of prey in which to sink cruel beak and talons. Once he crossed the sun and Adam saw his shadow on the gleaming rocks below. Then his circles widened across the deep canyon, high above the higher foothills, until he approached the lofty peak. Higher still, and here the winds of the heights caught him. How he breasted them, sailing on and up, soaring toward the blue!

Adam watched the bird with strained eyes that hurt but never tired. To watch him was one of the things Adam needed. On and ever upward soared the condor. His range had changed with the height. His speed had increased with the wind. His spirit had mounted as he climbed. The craggy gray peak might have harbored his nest and his mate, but he gave no sign. High over the lonely cold heights he soared. There, far above his domain, he circled level for a while, then swooped down like a falling star, miles across the sky, to sail, to soar, to rise again. Away across the heavens he flew, wide winged and free, king of the eagles and of the winds, lonely and grand in the blue. Never a movement of his wings! Higher he sailed. Higher he soared till he was a fading speck, till he was gone out of sight to his realm above.

"Gone!" sighed Adam. "He is gone and for all I know he may be a spirit of the wind. From his invisible abode in the heavens he can see the sheep on the crags — he can see me here — he can see Genie below — he can see the rabbit at his burrow. . . . Nature! Life! Oh, what use to think? What use to torture myself over mystery I can never solve? I learn one great truth only to find it involved in greater mystery."

Adam had realized the need of shocks, else the desert influence would insulate him forever in his physical life. The meeting with Dismukes had been one.

Why had Dismukes been compelled to come back to the desert? What was the lure of the silent places? How could men sacrifice friends, people, home, love, civilization for the solitude and loneliness of the wastelands? Where lay the infinite fascination in death and decay and desolation? Who could solve the desert secret?

Like white, living flames, Adam's thoughts leaped in his mind.

These wanderers of the wastelands, like Dismukes and himself, were not laboring under fancy or blindness or ignorance or imagination or delusion. They were certainly not actuated by a feeling for some nameless thing. The desert was a fact. The spell it cast was a fact. Also it began to dawn upon Adam that nothing in civilization, among glittering cities and moving people, in palaces or hovels, in wealth or poverty, in fame or ignominy, in any walk of worldly life, could cast a spell of enchantment, could swell women's hearts and claim men's souls like the desert. The secret then had to do with a powerful effect of the desert — that was to say, of lonely and desolate and wild places — upon the minds of human beings.

Adam remembered how Dismukes had loved to travel alone. If he had any selfishness in his great heart, it had been to gloat over the lonely places by himself. Even with Adam he seldom shared those moments of watching and listening. Always, some part of every day, he would spend alone on a ridge, on a height, or out on the sage, communing with this strange affinity of the desert. Adam had known Dismukes, at the end of a hard day's travel, to walk a mile and climb to a ledge, there to do nothing at all but watch and listen. It was habit. He did it without thinking. When Adam confronted him with the fact he was surprised. On Adam's side, this strange faculty or obsession, whatever it was, seemed very much more greatly marked. Dismukes had, or imagined he had, the need to seek gold. Adam had little to do but wander over the waste ways of the desert.

And now Adam, stirred to his depths by the culminating, fatal tragedy of Dismukes's life, and a passionate determination to understand it, delved into his mind and memory as never before, to discover forgotten lessons and larger growths. But not yet in his pondering did they prove to him why every day of his desert life, and particularly in the last few years, had he gone to this or that lonely spot for no reason at all except that it gave him strange, vague happiness. Here was an astounding fact. He could have seen the same beauty, color, grandeur, right from his camp. The hours he had passed thus were innumerable.

What had he done, what had gone on in his mind, during all these seemingly useless and wasted hours? Nothing! Merely nothing it seemed to sit for hours, gazing out over the desolate, gray-green, barren desert, to sit listening to the solitude, or the soft wind, or the seep of sand, or perhaps the notes of a lonely bird. Nothing, because most of all that time he did not have in his mind the significance of his presence there. He really did not know he was there. This state of apparent unconsciousness had never been known to Adam at all until Magdalene Virey had given him intimation of it. He had felt the thing, but had never thought about it. But during these three years that he had lived near San Jacinto it had grown until he gained a strange and fleeting power to exercise it voluntarily. Even this voluntary act seemed unthinking.

Adam, now, however, forced it to be a thinking act. And after many futile efforts he at last, for a lightning flash of an instant, seemed to capture the state of mind again. He recognized it because of an equally swift, vague joy that followed. Joy, he called it, for want of a better name. It was not joy. But it was wildly sweet — no — not so — but perhaps sweetly wild. That emotion, then, was the secret of the idle hours — the secret of the doing nothing. If he could only grasp the secret of the nothing! Looked at with profound thought, this nothing resolved itself into exactly what it had seemed to his first vague, wandering thought — merely listening, watching, smelling, feeling the desert. That was all. But now the sense of it began to assume tremendous importance. Adam believed himself to be not only on the track of the secret of the desert's influence, but also of life itself.

Adam realized that during these lonely hours he was one instant a primitive man and the next a thinking, or civilized man. The thinking man he understood; all difficulty of the problem lay hid in this other side of him. He could watch, he could feel without thinking. That seemed to be the state of the mind of an animal. Only it was a higher state — a state of intense, feeling, waiting, watching suspension! Adam divined that it was the mental state of the undeveloped savage, and that it brought fleeting moments of strange emotion.

Beyond all comprehension was the marvel of inscrutable nature. Somehow it had developed man. But the instincts of the ages were born with him when he was born. In blood, bone, tissue, heart, and brain! Wonder beyond that was the wonder that man had ever become civilized at all! Some infinite spirit was behind this.

In the illumination of his mind Adam saw much that had been mystery to him. When he had hunted meat, why had the chase been thrilling, exciting, pressing his heart hot against his side, sending his blood in gusts over his body? What a joy to run and leap after the quarry! Strange indeed had been his lust to kill beasts when, after killing, he was sorry. Stranger than this was a fact keen in his memory — the most vivid and intense feeling — come back from his starvation days when he had a wild rapture in pursuit of birds, rats, snakes that he had to kill with stones. Never, in all the years, had this rapture faded. Relic of his cruel boyhood days, when, like all boys, he had killed for the sake of killing, until some aspect of his bloody, quivering victim awakened conscience! Conscience then must be the great factor in human progress — the difference between savage and civilized man. Terribly strange for Adam to look at his brawny hands and remember what they had done to men! Over him, then, gushed the hot blood, over him quivered the muscular intensity, over him waved the fierce passion which, compared with that of his boyhood, was as the blaze of sun to a candle. He had killed men in ruthless justice, in strife of self-defense, but always afterward he had regretted. He had fought men in a terrible, furious joy, with eyes tingeing red, with nerves impervious to pain, with the salt taste of a fellow creature's blood sweet on his snarling lips, but always afterward he was full of wonder and shame.

Just under the skin of every man and every woman, perhaps stronger in one than another, flowed red blood in which primitive instincts still lived and would always live. That was the secret of the desert. The lonely, desolate land, the naked sand and rock-ribbed hills, the wilderness of silence and solitude stirred the instinctive memory of a primitive day. Men watched and listened unthinkingly in the wastelands, for what they knew not, but it was for the fleeting trancelike transformation back to savage nature. There were many reasons for which men became wanderers in the wastelands — love of gold; the need to forget or to remember; passion and crime and wanderlust; the appeal of beauty and sublimity — but what nailed them to the forbidding and inhospitable desert was the instinct of the savage. That was the secret of the spell of the desert. Men who had been confined to cities, chained to dull and humdrum toils, stagnating in the noisy haunts, sore and sick and deflated, standing for some impossible end, when let loose in the gray, iron-walled barrens of the desert were caught by a subtle and insidious enchantment that transfixed some, made beasts of most, and mysteriously bound all. Travelers passing across could not escape it, and they must always afterward remember the desert with a thrill of strange pleasure and of vague regret. Women who had been caught by circumstance and nailed to homes along the roads or edges of the desert must feel that nameless charm, though they hated the glaring, desolate void. Magdalene Virey, resigned to her doom in Death Valley, had responded to the nature that was in her.

Through this thing Adam saw the almost inconceivable progress of men upward. If progress had not been slow, nature would never have evolved him. And it seemed well that something of the wild and the primitive must forever remain instinctive in the human race. If the primitive were eliminated from men there would be no more progress. All the gladness of the senses lived in this law. The sweetness of the ages came back in thoughtless watching. The glory of the sunrise, the sadness of the sunset, the whisper of the wind and the murmur of the stream, the music of birds and their beauty — the magic of these came back from the dim, mystic dreamland of the primal day, from the childhood of the race. Nature was every man's mother. Nevertheless, the wonder and the splendor of life was the age-long progress of man toward unattainable perfection, the magnificent victory of humanity over mastery by primal instincts. And the fact that this seemed true to Adam made him wonder if the spirit of this marvelous life was not God.

The sun was westering when he descended the long, zigzag trail. He walked slowly, tired from his mental strain. And when he got down the sun was just tipping the ramparts above, flooding the canyon with golden haze and ruddy rays. Adam thought Genie, weary from long waiting, would be asleep on the sand, or at least reading, and that he could slip into the glade to surprise her. They played a game of this sort, and to her had gone most of the victories.

Like a panther he slid through the grasping mesquite boughs, and presently, coming to the denser brush, he stooped low to avoid making a rustle. As he moved along, bending so that he touched the sand with his hands, he came upon two fat beetles wagging and contesting over possession of some little particle. Scooping up a handful of sand, he buried them, and then, as they so ludicrously scrambled out, he gathered them up, intending, if he could get behind Genie unobserved, to drop them on her book or bare feet.

Thus it happened that he did not look ahead until after he had straightened up inside the glade. All before him seemed golden gleams and streaks of sunset rose. The air was thick with amber haze. Genie stood naked, ankle-deep in the bubbling spring. Like an opal her slender white body caught glimmer and sheen. Wondrously transparent she looked, for the sunlight seemed to shine through her! The red-gold tints of her hair burned like a woven cord of fire in bronze. Glistening crystal drops of water fell from her outstretched hands and her round arms gleamed where the white met the line of tan. The light of the sun shone upon her pensive, beautiful face as she stood wholly unaware of intrusion. Then she caught the sound of Adam's stifled gasp. She saw him. She burst into a scream of startled, wild laughter that rang with a trill through the dell.

Adam, breaking the spell of that transfixed instant, rushed headlong away.

26
●

Gaining the open, Adam strode swiftly down the trail to where the canyon spread wide and ended in the bowlder-strewn desert.

The world in which he moved seemed transfigured, radiant with the last glow of dying day, with a glory of golden gleam. His heart pounded and his blood flooded to and fro, swelling his veins. Life on the earth for him had been shot through and through with celestial fire. His feet were planted on the warm sands and his hands reached to touch the gray old bowlders. He needed these to assure himself that he had not been turned into the soft, cool wind or the slanting amber rays so thickly glistening with particles of dust, or the great, soaring king of the eagles. Adam crushed a bunch of odorous sage to his face, smelled it, breathed it, tasted it; and the bitter sweetness thrilled his senses. It was real. It was a part of the vast and glowing desert, of the wonderful earth, of the infinite universe that he yearned to incorporate into his being. The last glorious rays of the setting sun shone upon him and magnified his stature in a long, purple shadow. How the last warmth seemed to kiss his cheek as it sank behind the rim of the range! The huge bowlders were warm and alive under his hands. He pricked his fingers upon the *cholla* thorns just to see the ruddy drops of his life's current; and there was strange joy in the sting which proved him flesh and blood and nerve. He stood alone, as he had many thousands of times on the gray old desert, his feet on the sand, his knees in the sage; but the being alone then was inexpressibly different. It was as if he had, like the tarantula wasp, been born from a cocoon stage in a dark, dead cell, into a beautiful world of light, of freedom, of color, of beauty, of all that was life. He felt the glory of his beating heart, his throbbing pulse, his sight and all his sense. He turned his face to the cool, sweet, sage-scented breeze, and there he lifted it to the afterglow of sunset. Ah! the new, strange joy of life — the incalculable force of the natural man!

The luminous desert stretched before him, valley and mountain, and beyond them was other range and other valley, leading to the sea, and across its heaving bosom were other lands; and above him was the vast, deep-blue sky with its pale evening star, and beyond them began the infinite.

Adam felt himself a part of it all. His ecstasy was that he lived. Nature could not deny him. He stood there, young and strong and vital.

Then he heard Genie calling him. With a start he turned to answer. She was running down the trail. How swift, how little, how light! The desert had given her the freedom, the grace, the suppleness of its wild denizens. Like a fawn she bounded over the stones, and her hair caught the last gleams of glowing sunlight. When she neared Adam she checked her flying steps, pattering to a halt, one brown hand over her breast.

"Wheooo!" she burst out, panting. "I — couldn't — find — you. Why 'd — you come — so far?"

The something that had come between Adam's sight and the desert now surrounded Genie. Immeasurably she was transformed, and the change seemed a mystery.

"We must hurry back. It'll soon be dark. Come," he replied.

With step as free and swift as his she kept pace with him.

"Wanny, you stole up on me — tried to scare me — while I was bathing," she said, with arch reproach.

"Genie, it was an accident," he returned, hurriedly, and how strangely the blood tingled in his face! "I meant to scare you — yes. But I — I never thought — I never dreamed. . . . Genie, I give you my word. . . . Please say you believe me!"

"Why, Wanny," she said, in surprise, "of course I believe you! It's nothing to mind about. I didn't mind."

"Thank you. I — I'm glad you take it that

way," replied Adam. "I'm sorry I was so — so stupid."

"How funny you are!" she exclaimed, and her gay laugh pealed out. "What's there to be sorry about? . . . You see, I forgot it was getting late. . . . Ooooo! how good the water felt! I just couldn't get enough. . . . You did scare me just a little. I heard you — and was scared before I looked. . . . Wanny, I guess I was imagining things — dreaming, you call it. I was all wet, and looking at myself in the sunlight. I'd never seen myself like that. I'd read of mermaids with shining scales of gold, and nymphs of the woods catching falling blossoms. And I guess I thought I was them — and everything."

Then Adam scorned the old husk of worldliness that had incased his mind in his boyhood, and clung round it still. This child of nature had taught him many a thought-provoking lesson, and here was another, somehow elevating and on a level with his mental progress of the day. Genie had never lived in the world, nor had she been taught many of its customs. She was like a shy, wild young fawn; she was a dreaming, exuberant girl. Genie had been taught to write and study and read, and was far from being ignorant; but she had not understood the meaning of Adam's apology. What struck Adam so deeply and confounded him again was the fact that her innocent and sweet smile now, as she gazed up at him, was little different from the one upon her face when she saw him staring at her nude. She had been surprised at his concern and had laughed at his contrition. And that low, rippling laugh, so full of vital and natural life, seemed to blow, as the desert wind blew worn and withered leaves, all of Adam's recalled sophistications back into the past whence they had come.

Adam and Genie walked hand in hand down the long bowlder-strewn slope to the valley floor, where the *cholla* shone paling silver in gathering twilight, and the delicate crucifixion tree deceived the eye. The lonely November twilight deepened into night. The stars shone bright. The cool wind blew. The sage rustled.

Sleep did not soon woo Adam's eyelids this night, with the consequence that he awoke a little later than his usual hour. The rose of the dawn had bloomed.

Then Adam, on his knees by the brown running stream, in the midst of his ablutions, halted to stare at the sunrise. Had it ever before been so strangely beautiful? During his sleep the earth had revolved, and, lo! here was the sun again. Wonderful and perennial truth! Not only had it revolved, but it had gone on its mysterious journey, hurtling through space with inconceivable rapidity. While he slept! Again he had awakened. A thousand years ago he had awakened just like this, so it seemed, to the sunrise, to the loneliness of lonely places, to the beauty of nature, to the joy of life. He sensed some past state, which, when he thought about it, faded back illusively and was gone. But he knew he had lived somewhere before this. All of life was in him. The marvelous spirit he felt now would never die.

There dawned upon Adam a sudden consciousness of Genie's beauty. She was the last realized and the most beautiful creation of the desert around him.

It came to him as a great surprise. She, too, knelt at the stream, splashing the cool water, bathing her face, wetting the dark, gold-tinted locks and brushing them back. Curiously and absorbingly Adam gazed at her, with eyes from which some blinding shutter had fallen. Yes, she was beautiful. It seemed a simple fact that he had overlooked, yet it was amazing. It distracted him.

"Wanny, you're all eyes," cried Genie, gayly. "What's the matter with me? Why do you look so?"

"Genie, you're growing up," he replied, soberly.

"Well, you'd have known that before if you'd seen me sewing," she said.

"How old are you?" he asked.

"Guess I'm nearly seventeen," she said, and the words brought back the dreams.

"Why, you're a young lady!" ejaculated Adam. "And — and —" He had been about to add that she was beautiful, but he held his tongue.

"I guess that, too. . . . Hold out your arm."

Adam complied, and was further amazed to see, as she walked under his outstretched arm, that the glossy, wavy crown of her head almost touched it. She was as tall and slim and graceful as an arrowweed.

"There! I'll have you know you're a mighty big man," she said. "And if you weren't so big I'd come clear up to your shoulder."

"Genie, don't you want to leave this desert?" he queried, bluntly.

"Oh no," she replied, instantly. "I love it. And — and — please don't make me think of towns, of lots of people. I want to run wild like a road runner. I'd be perfectly happy if I didn't have to spend half the day mending these old clothes. . . . Wanny, if they get any worse they'll fall off me — and *then* I'll have to run around like you saw me yesterday! . . . Oh, but for the thorns, that 'd be grand!"

Her light, rippling laugh rang out, sweet and gay.

Adam waited for her later, in the shade of Taquitch Canyon, where from the topmost of a jumble of bowlders he watched a distant waterfall, white and green as it flashed over a dark cliff.

He watched her coming. Her ragged boy's garb with its patches and rents no longer hid her femininity and her charm from his eyes.

He saw anew. The litheness of her, the round and graceful figure from flying feet to glinting hair, cried aloud to the loneliness of Adam's heart the truth of her. An enchantment hung upon her very movements. She traveled from rock to rock, poising, balancing, leaping, and her curly hair danced on her head. Quick as those of a wildcat were her leaps. And her gay, sweet call or cry, birdlike and wild, echoed from the cliffs.

She was coming to Adam across the great jumble of rocks — a girl wonderful as a sprite. And her coming was suddenly realized as fulfillment of dreams. Adam faced the truth on some facts about his dreaming. Lonely hours on lonely slopes, of waiting and watching, had created the shadow of a woman or a girl gliding in the golden glow of the afternoon sunlight, coming to charm away forever the silence and solitude. So innumerable times he had dreamed, but never realized till now those dreams. She was coming, and the sleepy shade awoke to a gleam and a voice. The lacy waterfall shone white and its murmur seemed music of many streams. A canyon swallow twittered.

Adam thought how passing strange had been the tortures, the awakenings, and changings of his desert experience. And here was a vague dream fulfilled! This realization was unutterably sweet — so sweet because these years had been barren of youth, steeped in unconscious growing worship of beauty, spent alone with pains and toils. He watched her coming. Fresh as the foam of the waterfall, clean as the winds of the heights, wild as the wild young fawn — so she seemed! Youth and gayety — beauty and life!

But suddenly Adam seemed struck by an emotion, if not of terror, then of dread at some inconceivable and appalling nature of her presence. That emotion was of the distant past as was the vague peril of her approach. A girl — a woman creature — mystery of the ages — the giver of life as the sun gave heat — had come to him, out of the clouds or the desert sands, and the fatality of her coming was somewhat terrible.

Genie reached the huge bowlder upon which Adam sat and like a squirrel she ran up its steep side, to plump herself breathless and panting down against his knees.

"Ah! Old Taquitch — here's another — Indian maiden — for you to steal," she said, roguishly. "But before you — carry me up to the clouds — duck me under the waterfall!"

All the accumulated thought and emotion of recent hours concentrated in the gaze he fixed upon her face.

Her trilling laugh pealed out. She thought he was playing Taquitch, god of the heights. He was teasing her with his piercing eyes.

"Look! Look at me, O Taquitch!" she cried, with deep, pretended solemnity. "I am Ula, princess of the Coahuilas. I have left my father's house. I have seen the sun shining in your face,

oh, god of the lightnings! And I love — I love
— I love with all the Indian's heart. I will go
with you to the peaks. But never — never more
shall you steal another maiden!"

Adam scarcely heard Genie. He was piercing
through eyes and face to the mind and soul
and life and meaning of her beauty. Her skin
was creamy, golden brown, transparent, with
tiny tracery of veins underneath and faint tints
of rose. The low forehead and level brows
showed moist and soft and thoughtful under the
dark, damp curls with their amber glints. A
hint of desert leanness hid in the contour of
her oval face. Her mouth was strong with bowed
upper lip, the under sensitive and sad — a red,
sweet mouth, like a flower. And her eyes, now
meeting his so frankly, losing the mock solemnity and the fun, became deep-brown, crystal
gulfs of light and shade, of thought and feeling,
beautiful with the beauty of exquisite color, but
lovelier for the youth, the joy and wonder of
life, the innocence of soul.

"Wanny — are you — playing?" she asked,
tremulously, and her warm little hand clasped
his.

That changed the spell of her. To look at
her beauty was nothing comparable with the
warm throb of her young pulsing life. Out of
Adam's slow and painful and intense thought
at last evolved a nucleus of revelation. But those
clear eyes strangely checked this growing sense
of a truth about to overwhelm him. They made

him think, and thought had begun to waver and pale beside some subtler faculty of his being. Thus he realized the slow preponderance of feeling over thought, of body over soul, of physical over spiritual. And in this realization of unequal conflict he divined the meaning of his strange sense of peril in Genie's presence. The peril lay in the sophistication of his mind, not in Genie's beauty. Naturally as the mating of the birds he wanted her. That was all. It was like her simplicity, inevitable as life itself, and true to nature! But in his thoughts, flashing after comprehension, the simple fact loomed with staggering, overwhelming significance.

Bidding Genie rest or amuse herself, Adam climbed to a ledge above the waterfall, and there, with the mighty mass of mountain crowding out the light, he threw himself upon the bare stone.

Not long did he torment himself with wonder and fury and bewilderment over an indubitable fact. Almost at once he sank into a self-accusing state which grew from bad to worse, until he was sick, sore, base, and malignant in his arraignment of self. Again the old order of mind, the habit of youthful training, the learned precepts and maxims and laws, flooded back to augment his trouble. And when they got their sway he cursed himself, he hated himself, he beat his breast in the shame of an abasement terribly and inevitably and irretrievably true at that hour.

But this was a short-lived passion. It did not

ring true to Adam. It was his youth had suffered shame — the youth trained by his mother — the youth that had fallen upon wild and evil days at old Picacho. His youth flaming up with all its chivalry, its ideals, its sense of honor and modesty, its white-hot shame at even an unconscious wrong to a girl! Not the desert philosophy of manhood that saw nature clearly and saw it whole!

"Peace!" he cried, huskily, as if driving back a ghost of his youth. "I am no beast — no animal!"

Nay, he was a lonely wanderer of the wastelands, who many and many a time had dreamed himself sweetheart, lover, husband of all the beautiful women in the world Ah! it was his love of beauty, of life!

And so in his dreams, nature, like a panther in ambush, had come upon him unawares to grip him before he knew. Aye — he wanted Genie now — yearned for her with all that intense and longing desire which had falsely seemed love and joy of the whole living world. But it was not what it seemed. All the tenderness of a brother, all the affection of a father Adam had for Genie — emotions that now faded before the master spirit and the imperious flame of life. How little and pitiful arose the memory of Margarita Arallanes — how pale beside this blood fire of his senses! Life had failed him in his youth; life had cheated him. Yet he had arisen on stepping stones of agony to intenser love of that life. He had been faithful, while life had mocked him.

Passionate love of life, to see, to hear, to feel, to touch, had come to him with its saving grace, after the ruthless and violent strife of the desert had taught him to survive. But these were not the soul of nature. This was not nature's secret. He was a man, a creature of inherited instincts that the desert had intensified. In nature's eyes he was no different from the lonely desert bird or beast seeking its mate. The law was not wrong, but all the progress of mankind as represented in Adam's revolt made that law wrong.

When at last he had driven shame from his mind and justified his manhood over the instincts of which he could have no control, then he faced the ordeal.

Contending tides of passion and strife! That had been his desert life. And as the years had passed each new mounting tumult in heart or soul, each fight against men or elements, had exceeded the last. Would there never be an end? Was this his great ordeal — the last — before which he must go down in defeat? No — by all the gods false or true — no, it should never be! Thus he shot arrowy lightnings of soul at the fiery army of instincts trooping on to overwhelm his consciousness.

For a long time the ordeal never got so far as argument. It was revel of the senses, unleashed at last, untamed by the past, fiercer and stronger and more irresistible for all disuse. Melancholy and terrible was the truth that his desert years, so hard, so clean, so cold, so pure, the restraint of his enforced exile, had developed in him instincts masterless in their importunity. Life shrieking out of his flesh and blood for the future that nature demanded! There was revolt here, conscienceless revolt against the futility of manhood, voices from the old bones of his ancestors, from the dim and mystic past. Here at last was revealed the deepest secret of the desert, the eternal law men read in its lonely naked face — self-preservation and reproduction. The individual lived and fought and perished, but the species survived.

Adam's instinctive reaction seemed that of a savage into whose surging blood had been ejected some inhibitory current of humanism which chafed at the quivering shores of his veins and tried to dam the flood. He was like a strong man convulsed by fever. Like the strung thread of a bent bow he vibrated.

There came a knocking at the gate of his mind. The tempter! The voice of the serpent! Nature or devil, it was all one — a mighty and eloquent and persuasive force. It whispered to Adam that he was alone on the desert. Fate had been cruel. Love had betrayed him. Life had denied him. A criminal, surely not forgotten by justice, he could never leave the lonely wastelands to live. A motherless, fatherless girl, with no kith or kin, had been left in his care, and he had saved her, succored her. Care and health and love had made her beautiful. By all the laws of nature she was his, to hold, to cherish, to cheer the lonely, gray years. He had but to open his arms and call to her, reveal to her the mystery and glory of life, and she would be his forever. Unconsciously she herself leaned toward this fate, tempting him in all her innocence. She would grow into a glorious woman — the keen, sweet, fierce youth of her answering to the work of the desert. Were not all desert flowers more rare and vivid — were not all desert creatures more beautiful and strong than their like elsewhere? Genie would be his, as the eagle had its mate, and she would never know any other life. She would be compensation for his suffering, a companion for his wandering. Think! the joy of her, the thrill of her! The wonderful fire of her dark eyes and the dance of her curls and the red lips ripe for kisses! No man had any right to deny himself immortality. What was the world and its customs to him? Where was the all-wise and beneficent God who looked after the miserable and forlorn? Life was life, and that was everything. Beauty in life — that was eternal, the meaning of nature, and every man must love it, share it, and mark the image of himself upon the future. Lastly and most potent, the present fleeting hour that must soon pass! Let him grasp his precious jewel before it was too late — live in the moment. Life might be eternal, but not for him. Soon the seeping sand would nestle round his bleached bones and fill the sockets where once his eyes had burned. Genie was a gift of chance. He had wandered down into this valley, and now his life should never be lonely again. Lover of beauty and worshiper of nature, he had but to extend his arms to receive a treasure far greater than the gold of the desert, more beautiful than its flaming flowers, more mysterious than its fierce and inevitable life. A girl whose white body, like a transparent opal, let the sunshine through! A woman, gift of the ages to man, flame of love and life, most beautiful of all things quick or dead, a mystery for man to cherish, to love, to keep, to bind!

Then, at the instant when Adam's fall was imminent, and catastrophe leaned like the huge overhanging mountain mass, he wrestled up to fling the supremy of his soul into the teeth of nature.

"No! . . . No!" he gasped, hoarsely. "Not for me!"

At the last he saw clearly. The love he had for Genie now proclaimed itself. The other had not been love, whatever its greatness, its importunity, its almost blasting power. He was an outcast, and any day a man or men might seek him out to kill him or be killed. What madness was this of his to chain a joyous girl to his wandering steps? What but woe to her and remorse to him could ever come of such relation? Genie was so full of life and love that she hated to leave even the loneliness of the desert. To her, in the simplicity and adaptation of her nature, he was all. But she was a child, and the day he placed her in an environment where youth called to youth, and there were work, play, study, cheer, and love, he would become a memory. The kisses of her red ripe lips were not for him. The dance of her glinting curls, the flash of her speaking eyes, the gold-brown flesh of her, had been created by nature; and nature must go on with its inscrutable design, its eternal progress, leaving him outside the pale. The joy he was to feel in Genie must come of memory, when soon he had gone on down into the lonely wastelands. She would owe life and happiness to him, and, though she might not know it, he always would. A child, a girl, a woman — and some day perhaps a wife and mother — some happy man's blessing and joy — and these by the same inevitable nature that had tortured him would reward him in the solemn white days and the lonely starlit nights. For he had been and would be the creator of their smiles. How fierce and false had been his struggle, in the light of thought, when the truth was that he would give his life to spare Genie a moment's pain!

27

That afternoon when Adam returned to camp sore in body and spent in force, yet with strangely tranquil soul, there was an old Indian waiting for him. Genie had gone back long before Adam, and she sat on the sand, evidently having difficult but enjoyable conversation with the visitor.

At sight of his hard, craggy, bronze face, serried and seamed with the lines of years, it seemed that a bolt shot back in Adam's heart, opening a long-closed door.

"Charley Jim!" he ejaculated, in startled gladness.

"How, Eagle!" His deep voice, the familiar yet forgotten name, the lean brown hand, confirmed Adam's sight.

"Chief, the white man has not forgotten his Indian friend," replied Adam.

"Eagle no same boy like mescal stalk. Heap big! Many moon! Snows on the mountain!" said Charley Jim, with a gleam of a smile breaking the bronze face. His fingers touched the white hair over Adam's temples. Pathos and dignity marked the action.

513

"Boy no more, Charley Jim," returned Adam. "Eagle has his white feathers now!"

Genie burst into a trill of laughter.

"You funny old people! You make me feel old, too," she protested, and she ran away.

Charley Jim's somber eyes followed her, then returned to question Adam.

"She same girl here — long time — sick man's girl?" And he made signs to show the height of a child and the wellness of a man's lungs.

"Yes, chief. He her father. Dead. Mother dead, too," replied Adam, and he pointed to the two green graves across the stream.

"Ugh! No live good. No get well. . . . Eagle, sick man have brother — him dead. Jim find 'um. Him dig gold — no water — dead. . . . Jim find 'um heap bones."

It was thus Adam heard the story of the tragedy of Genie's uncle. Charley Jim told it more clearly, though just as briefly, in his own tongue. Moons before he had found a prospector's pack and then a pile of rags and bones half buried in the sand over in a valley beyond the Cottonwood Mountains. He recognized the man's pack as belonging to the brother of the sick man, Linwood, both of whom he knew. Adam could trust an Indian's memory. Genie's uncle had come to the not rare end of a wandering prospector's life. The old desert tragedy — thirst! All at once Adam's eyes seemed to burn blind with a red dim veil, and his tongue clove to the roof of his mouth, and through his body passed a cold shudder, and he had strange vision of himself staggering blindly in a circle, plunging madly for the false mirage. The haunting plague passed away. Adam turned to examine the few pack articles Charley Jim had brought for possible identification of the dead. One of these, a silver belt buckle of odd design, oxidized and tarnished, might possibly be remembered by Genie. Adam called her, placed it in her hands.

"Genie, did you ever see that?" he asked.

"Yes," she replied, with a start of recognition. "It was my father's. He gave it to my uncle."

Adam nodded to the Indian. "Chief, you were right."

"Oh, Wanny — it means he's found my uncle — dead!" exclaimed Genie, in awe.

"Yes, Genie," replied Adam, with a hand of sympathy upon her shoulder. "We know now. He'll never come back."

With the buckle in her hands the girl slowly walked toward the graves of her parents.

Charley Jim mounted his pony to ride away.

"Chief — tell me of Oella," said Adam.

The Indian gazed down upon Adam with somber eyes. Then his lean, sinewy hand swept up with stately and eloquent gesture to be pressed over his heart.

"Oella dead," he replied, sonorously, and then he looked beyond Adam, out across the lonesome land, beyond the ranges, perhaps to the realm of his red gods. Adam read the Indian gesture. Oella had died of a broken heart.

He stood there at the edge of the oasis, stricken mute, as his old Indian friend turned to go back across the valley to the Coahuila encampment. A broken heart! That superb Indian maiden, so lithe and tall and strong, so tranquil, so sure — serene of soul as the steady light of her midnight eyes — dead of a broken heart! She had loved him — a man alien to her race — a wanderer and a stranger within her gates, and when he had gone away life became unendurable. Another mystery of the lonely, gray, melancholy wastelands! Adam quivered there in the grip of it all.

Later when he returned to Genie it was to say, simply, "My dear, as soon as I can find my burros we pack for the long trail."

"No!" she exclaimed, with lighting eyes.

"Yes. I shall take you out to find you a home."

"Honest Injun?" she blazed at him, springing erect.

"Genie, I would not tease about that. We know your uncle is dead. The time to go has come. We'll start at sunrise."

Forgotten were Genie's dreams of yesterday! A day at her time of life meant change, growth, oblivion for what had been. With a cry of wondering delight she flung herself upon Adam, leaped and climbed to the great height of his face, and there, like a bird, she pecked at him with cool, sweet lips, and clung

516

to him in an ecstasy.

"Don't! . . . Still a child, Genie," he said, huskily, as he disengaged himself from her wild embrace. He meant that she was not still a child. It amazed him and hurt him to see her radiance at the thought of leaving the desert oasis which had been home for so long. Fickleness of youth! Yesterday she had wanted to live there forever; to-day the enchantments of new life, people, places, called alluringly. It was what Adam had expected. It was what he wanted for her. How clear had been his vision of the future! How truly, the moment he had fought down his selfish desires, had he read her innocent heart! His own swelled with gladness, numbing out the pang. For him, some little meed of praise! Not little was it to have conquered self — not little was it to have builded the happiness of an orphan!

Adam's burros had grow gray in their years of idle, contented life at the oasis. Like the road runners, they enjoyed the proximity of camp; and he found them shaggy and fat, half asleep while they grazed. He drove them back to the shade of the cottonwoods, where Genie, seeing this last and immutable proof of forthcoming departure, began to dance over the sand in wild glee.

"Genie, you'll do well to save some of your nimbleness," admonished Adam. "We'll have a load. You've got to climb the mountain and walk till I can buy another burro."

"Oh, Wanny, I'll fly!" she cried.

"Humph! I rather think you will fly the very first time a young fellow sees you — a big girl in those ragged boy's clothes."

Then Adam thrilled anew with the sweetness, the wonder of her. His cold heart warmed to the core. How he would live in the hope and happiness and love that surely must be awaiting this girl. His mention of a young fellow suddenly rendered Genie amazed, shy, bewildered.

"But — but — Wanny — you — you won't let any yo-young fellow see me *this* way!" she pleaded.

"How can I help it? You just wouldn't sew and make dresses. Now you're in for it. We'll meet a lot of lads. . . . And, Genie, just the other day you didn't care how *I* saw you."

"Oh, but you're different! You're my dad, my brother, old Taquitch, and everything."

"Thank you. That makes me feel a little better."

Suddenly she turned her dark eyes upon him, piercing now and dilating with thought.

"Wanny! Are you *sorry* to leave?"

"Yes," he replied, sadly.

"Then I'll stay, if you want me — ever — always," she said, very low. The golden flush paled on her cheek. She was a child, yet on the verge of womanhood.

"Genie, I'm sorry, but I'm glad, too. What I want most is to see you settled in a happy home, with a guardian, young friends about you

— all you want."

She appeared sober now, and Adam gathered that she had thought more seriously than he had given her credit for.

"Wanny, you're good, and your goodness makes you see all that for me. But a guardian — a happy home — all I want! . . . I'll be poor. I'll have to work for a living. I won't have *you!*"

Then suddenly she seemed about to weep. Her beautiful eyes dimmed. But Adam startled her out of her weakness.

"Poor! Well, Genie Linwood, you've got a surprise in store for you."

Wherewith he led her to the door of the hut and, tearing up the old wagon boards that had served as a floor, he dug in the sand underneath and dragged forth bag after bag, which he dropped at her feet with sodden, heavy thumps.

"Gold, Genie! Gold! Yours! . . . You'll be rich. . . . All this was dug by your father. I don't know how much, but it's a fortune. . . . Now what do you say?"

The rapture Adam had anticipated did not manifest itself. Genie seemed glad, certainly, but the significance of the gold did not really strike her.

"And you never told me! . . . Well, by the great horn spoon, I'm rich! . . . Wanny, will *you* be my guardian?"

"I will, till I can find you one," he replied, stoutly.

"Oh, never look for one — then I *will* have all I want!"

The last sunlight, the last starlight night, the last sunrise for Adam and Genie at the oasis, were beautiful memories of the past.

Adam, driving the burros along the dim old Indian trail, meditated on the inevitableness of the end of all things. For nearly three years he had seen that trail every few days and always he had speculated on the distant time when he would climb it with Genie. That hour had struck. Genie, with the light feet of an Indian, was behind him, now chattering like a magpie and then significantly silent. She had her bright face turned to the enchanting adventures of the calling future; she was turning her back upon the only home she could remember.

"Look, Genie, how gray and dry the canyon is," said Adam, hoping to divert her. "Just a little water in that white wash, and you know it never reaches the valley. It sinks in the sand. . . . Now look way above you — high over the foothills. See those gleams of white — those streaks of black. . . . Snow, Genie, and the pines and spruces!"

They camped at the edge of the spruces and pines. How sweet and cool and damp the air to desert dwellers! The wind sang through the trees with different tone. Adam, unpacking the burros, turned them loose, sure of their delight in the rich green grass. Genie, tired out with the long climb, fell upon one of the open packs to rest.

With his rifle Adam strode away among the scattered pines and clumps of spruce. The smell of this forest almost choked him, yet it seemed he could not smell and breathe enough. The dark-green, spear-pointed spruces and the brown-barked pines, so lofty and spreading, intoxicated his desert eyes. He looked and reveled, forgetting the gun in his hands, until his aimless steps frightened deer from right before him. Then, to shoot was habit, the result of which was regret. These deer were tame, not like the wary, telescope-eyed mountain sheep; and Adam, after his first exultant thrill — the old recurrent thrill from out the past — gazed down with sorrow at the sleek, beautiful deer he had slain. What dual character he had — what contrast of thrill and pang, of blood and brain, of desert and civilization, of physical and spiritual, of nature and — But he did not know what!

He laughed later, and Genie laughed, too, at how ravenous he was at supper, how delicious the venison tasted, how good it was to eat.

"Guess I'll give myself up as a bad job," he told her.

"Wanny, for me you'll always be Taquitch, giant of the desert and god of the clouds."

"Ah! You'll forget me in ten days after you meet *him!*" replied Adam, somewhat bitterly.

Genie could only stare her amaze.

"Forgive me, child. I don't mean that. I know you'll never forget me. . . . But you've been my — my little girl so long that it hurts to think of your being some other man's."

Then he was to see the marvel of Genie's first blush.

It was well that Adam had thought to pack extra blankets for Genie. She had never felt the nip of frost. And when night settled down black, with the wind rising, she needed to be warmly wrapped. Adam liked the keen air, and also the feel of the camp-fire heat upon his outstretched palms.

Next morning the sky was overcast with broken, scudding clouds, and a shrill wind tossed the tips of the pines. Genie crawled out of her blankets to her first experience of winter. When she dipped her hands into the water she squealed and jerked them out. Then at Adam's bantering laughter she bravely dashed into the ordeal of bathing face and hands with that icy water.

Adam did not have any particular objective point in mind. He felt strangely content to let circumstances of travel or chance or his old wandering instinct guide him.

They traveled leisurely through the foothills on the western side of the Sierra Madres, finding easy trails and good camp sites, and meeting Indians by the way. Six days out from the desert they reached a wagon road, and that led down to a beautiful country of soft velvety-green hills and narrow, pleasant valleys where clumps of live oaks grew, and here and there nestled a ranch.

So they traveled on. The country grew less rugged and some of it appeared to belong to great ranches, once the homes of the Spanish grandees. Late one afternoon travel brought them within sight of Santa Ysabel. Adam turned off the main road, in search of a place to camp, and, passing between two beautiful hills, came upon a little valley, all green with live oaks and brown with tilled ground. He saw horses, cattle, and finally a farmhouse, low and picturesque, of the vine-covered adobe style peculiar to a country first inhabited by the Spanish.

Adam went toward the house, which was mostly concealed by vines and oaks, and presently happened upon a scene that seldom gladdened the eyes of a desert wanderer. On a green plot under the trees several children stopped their play to stare at Adam, and one ran to the open door. There were white pigeons flying about the roof, and gray rabbits in the grass, and ducks wading in the brook. Adam heard the cackle of hens and the bray of a burro. A column of blue smoke lazily rose upward from a gray, adobe, fire-blackened oven.

Before Adam got to the door a woman appeared there, with the child at her skirts. She was middle-aged and stout, evidently a hard-working rancher's wife. She had a brown face, rather serious, but kind, Adam thought. And he looked keenly, because he was now getting into the civilized country that he expected would become Genie's home.

"Good evening, ma'am!" he said. "Will you let me camp out there by the oaks?"

"How d'ye do, stranger," she replied. "Yes, you're welcome. But you're only a mile or so from Santa Ysabel. There's a good inn."

"Time enough to go there to-morrow or next day," replied Adam. "You see, ma'am, I'm not alone. I've a young girl with me. We're from the desert. And I want her to have some — some decent clothes before I take her where there are people."

The woman laughed pleasantly.

"Your daughter?" she asked, with interest.

"No relation," replied Adam. "I — I was a friend of her mother, who died out on the desert."

"Stranger, you're welcome to my house overnight."

"Thank you, but I'd rather not trouble you. We'll be very comfortable. It's a nice place to camp."

"Come far?" asked the woman, whose honest blue eyes were taking stock of Adam.

"Yes, far for Genie. We've been about ten days coming over the mountains."

"Reckon you'd like some milk and eggs for supper?"

"Well, now, ma'am, if you only knew how

I would like some," returned Adam, heartily. "And poor Genie, who has fared so long on desert grub, she'd surely appreciate your kindness."

"I'll fetch some over, or send it by my boy," she said.

Adam returned thoughtfully to the little grove where he had elected to camp. This woman's kindness, the glint of sympathy in her eyes, brought him up short with the certitude that they were the very virtues he was looking for in the person to whom he intended to trust Genie. It behooved him from now on to go keenly at the task of finding that person. It would not be easy. For the present he meant to hide any hint of Genie's small fortune, and had cautioned her to that end.

Genie appeared tired and glad to sit on the green grassy bank. "I'll help — in a little while," she said. "Isn't this a pretty place? Oh, the grass feels so cool and smells so sweet! . . . Wanny, who'd you see at the house?"

"Some youngsters and a nice woman," replied Adam. It was on his tongue to tell Genie about the milk and eggs for supper, but in the interest of a surprise he kept silent.

Sunset had passed when Adam got the packs spread, the fire built, and supper under way.

At length the supper appeared to be about ready, except for the milk and eggs that had been promised. Adam set the pot and pan aside at the edge of the fire, and went off in search of some wood that would be needed later. He packed a big log of dead oak back to camp, bending under its weight.

When he looked up he saw a handsome, stalwart lad, bare-headed and in shirt sleeves, standing just beyond the fire, holding out with brown muscular arms a big pan of milk. The milk was spilling over the edges. And on one of his fingers hung a small bucket full of eggs. He had to balance himself carefully while he stooped to deposit the bucket of eggs on the ground.

"Hey, Johnnie, where'll I put the milk?" he called, cheerily.

Adam was astounded, and suddenly tickled to see Genie trying to hide behind one of the packs. She succeeded in hiding all but her head, which at the moment wore an old cap that made her look more than ever like a boy.

"My name's not Johnnie," she flashed, with spirit.

The lad appeared nonplused, probably more at the tone of voice than the speech. Then he laughed. Adam liked the sound of that laugh, its ring, its heartiness.

"Sammy, then. . . . Come get this milk," called the boy.

Genie maintained silence, but she glared over the top of the pack.

"Look here, bub," the lad went on, plaintively, "I can't stand this way all night. Mother wants the pan. . . . Boy, are you deaf? . . . Say, bub, I won't eat you."

"How dare you call me bub!" cried Genie, hotly.

"Well, I'll be doggoned!" exclaimed the young fellow. "Listen to the kid! . . . I'll call you worse than bub in a minute. Hurry, bubbie!"

Genie made a quick movement that whirled her around, with her cap flying off, and then she got to her knees. Thus, with face disclosed and blazing eyes, and curls no boy ever had, she presented a vastly different aspect.

"I'm no boy! I — I'm a — a lady!" she declared, with angry, trembling voice of outraged dignity.

"What!" gasped the lad. Then, in his amaze and horror, he dropped the pan of milk, that splashed all over, nearly drowning the fire.

"Hello! What's the trouble?" asked Adam, genially, appearing from the oaks.

"I — I — spilled the milk — mother sent," he replied, in confusion.

"That's too bad! No wonder, such a lot of milk! . . . What's your name?"

"It's Eugene — sir — Eugene Blair."

"Well, that's queer — Eugene Blair. . . . My name's Wansfell, and I'm glad to meet you," said Adam, offering his hand. "Now let me make you acquainted with Miss Eugenie Linwood."

The only acknowledgment Genie gave to her first introduction was a slow sinking down behind the pack. Her expression delighted Adam. As for the young man — he appeared to be about twenty years old — he was overcome with embarrassment.

"Glad to — to know you Miss — Miss Linwood," he gulped. "Please ex-excuse me. Mother never said — there was a — a girl. . . . And you looked so — I took you for a boy."

"That's all right, son," put in Adam, kindly. "Genie did look like a boy. So I've been telling her."

"Now — if you'll excuse me I'll run back after more milk," said the lad, hurriedly, and, grasping up the pan, he ran away.

"Well, Miss Know-it-all," said Adam, banteringly, "*what* did I tell you? Didn't I tell you we'd meet some nice young fellow?"

"He — he didn't see me — *all* of me," replied Genie, tragically.

"What? Why, a fellow with eyes like his could see right through that pack!" declared Adam.

"He called me bub!" suddenly exclaimed Genie, her tone changing from one of tragic woe to one of tragic resentment. "*Bub!* . . . The — the first boy I ever met in my whole life!"

"Why shouldn't he call you bub?" queried Adam. "There's no harm in that. And when he discovered his mistake he apologized like a little man."

"I *hate* him!" flashed Genie. "I'd starve to death before I'd eat his eggs and milk." With that she flounced off into the clump of oaks.

Adam was seeing Genie in a new light. It

528

amused him greatly, yet he could not help but look ruefully after her, somewhat uncertain. Feminine reactions were unknown quantities. Genie reminded him wonderfully of girls he had known when he was seventeen.

Presently young Blair returned with more milk, and also considerably more self-possession. Not seeing Genie, he evidently took the hint and quickly left.

"Come over after supper," called Adam, after him.

"All right," he replied, and then was gone.

Very shortly then Adam had supper prepared, to which he cheerfully invited Genie. She came reluctantly, with furtive eyes on the green beyond camp, and sat down to fold her feet under her, after the manner of an Indian. Adam, without any comment, served her supper, not omitting a generous quantity of fragrant fried eggs and a brimming cupful of creamy milk. Wherewith Genie utterly forgot, or magnificently disdained, any recollection of what she had said. She even asked for more. But she was vastly removed from the gay and lightsome Genie.

"What 'd you ask him back here for?" she demanded.

"I want to talk to him. Don't you?" replied Adam, innocently.

"Me! . . . When he called me bub?"

"Genie, be sensible. They're nice people. I think I'll camp here a day or so. We'll rest up, and that 'll give me time to look around."

"Look around! . . . What'll become of *me?*"
wailed Genie, miserably.

"You can watch camp. I dare say young Blair
will forget your rudeness and be nice to you."

Then Genie glared with terrible eyes upon
Adam, and she seemed between tears and rage.

"I — I never — never knew — you could
be like this."

"Like what? Genie, I declare, I'm half
ashamed of you! Nothing has happened. Only
this lad mistook you for a boy. Anyone would
think the world had come to an end. All because
you woke up and found out you had on boy's
clothes. Well, you've got to take your medicine
now. You *would* wear them. You never minded
me. You didn't care *how* I saw you!"

"I don't care how *he* saw me or sees me,
either, so there," declared Genie, enigmatically.

"Oh! Well, what's wrong, then?" queried
Adam, more curious than ever.

"I — he — it — it was what he called me,"
replied Genie, confusedly.

Adam gazed at her downcast face with spec-
ulative eyes, intuitively feeling that she had not
told the whole truth. He had anticipated trouble
with this spirited young wild creature from the
desert, once they got into civilization.

"Genie, I've been mostly in fun. Now I'm
serious. . . . I want you to be perfectly natural
and nice with these Blairs, or anyone else we
meet."

Manifestly she took that seriously enough.

Without another word she dragged her blankets and canvas away from the firelight, and at the edge of the gathering gloom under the oaks she made her bed and crawled into it.

A little while after dark, young Blair presented himself at Adam's fire, and took a seat to which he was invited.

"I suppose you folks are ranching it?" asked Adam, by way of opening conversation.

"It's hardly a ranch, though we have hopes," replied Blair. "Mother and I run the farm. My father's not — he's away."

"Looks like good soil. Plenty of water and fine grass," observed Adam.

"Best farming country all around — these valleys," declared the lad, warming to enthusiasm. "Ranchers taking it all up. Only a few valleys left. There's one just below this — about a hundred acres — if I could only get that! . . . But no such luck for me."

"You can never tell," replied Adam, in his quiet way. "You say ranchers are coming in?"

"Yes. San Diego is growing fast. People are buying out the Mexicans and Indians up in these hills. In a few years any rancher with one of these valleys will be rich."

"How much land do you own?"

"My mother bought this little farm here — ten acres — and the valley, which was about ninety. But my father — we lost the valley. And we manage to live here."

Adam's quick sympathy divined that something pertaining to the lad's father was bitter and unhappy. He questioned further about the farm, what they raised, where they marketed it, how many cattle, horses, chickens, ducks they had. In half an hour Adam knew the boy and liked him.

"You're pretty well educated for a farmer boy," remarked Adam.

"I went to school till I was sixteen. We're from Indiana — Vincennes. Father got the gold fever. We came West. Mother and I took to a surer way of living."

"You like ranching then?"

"Gee! but I'd love to be a real rancher! There's not only money in cattle and horses, on a big scale, but it's such a fine life. Outdoors all the time! . . . Oh, well, I *do* have the outdoors as much as anybody. But for mother and the kids — I'd like to do better by them."

"I saw the youngsters and I'd like to get acquainted. Tell me about them."

"Nothing much to tell. They're like little Indians. Tommy's three, Betty's four, Hal's five. He was a baby when we came West. The trip was too hard on him. He's been delicate. But he's slowly getting stronger."

"Well! You've a fine family. How are you going to educate them?"

"That's our problem. Mother and I must do our best — until — maybe we can send them to school at San Diego."

"When your ship comes in?"

"Yes; I'm always hoping for that. But first I'd like my ship to start out, so it can come back loaded."

The lad laughed. He was imaginative, full of fire and pathos, yet clear headed and courageous, neither blind to the handicap under which he labored nor morose at his fetters.

"Yes, if a man *waits* for his ship to come in — sometimes it never comes," said Adam.

"I suppose you'll be on your way to town early?" asked Blair, as he rose.

"Guess I'll not break camp to-morrow. Genie is tired. And I won't mind a little rest. Hope we'll see you again."

"Thank you. Good night."

When he was gone, Adam took to pacing along the edge of the oaks. In the light of the camp fire he saw the gleam of Genie's wide-open eyes. She had heard every word of Adam's conversation with young Blair. He felt a great sympathy for Genie. Like a child, she was face to face with new life, new sensations, poignant and bewildering. How might he best help her?

Next morning, when Adam returned from a look around, he discovered Genie up, puttering at the camp fire. She greeted him with undue cheerfulness. She was making a heroic effort to show that this situation was perfectly natural. She did pretty well, but Adam's keen eyes and sense gathered that Genie felt herself on the verge of great and tremendous events.

After breakfast Adam asked Genie to accompany him to the farmhouse. She went, but the free, lithe step wanted something of its old grace. Adam espied the children in the yard, and now he took cognizance of them. Tommy was a ragged, tousle-headed, chubby little rascal, ruddy cheeked and blue eyed. Betty resembled the lad, Eugene, having his fine dark eyes and open countenance. Hal was the largest, a red-headed, freckle-faced imp if Adam ever saw one. They regarded the newcomers with considerable interest. Genie approached them and offered to swing Betty, who was sitting in a clumsy little hammock-like affair made of barrel staves. And Adam, seeing the children's mother at the door, went that way.

"Good morning, Mrs. Blair!" he said. "We've come over to chat a bit and see your youngsters."

She greeted them smilingly, and came out wiping her hands on her apron. "Goodness knows we're glad to have you. Gene has gone to work. Won't you sit on the bench here? . . ."

Then she espied Genie. "For land's sake! That your girl in the boy's clothes? Gene told me what a dunce he'd been. . . . Oh, she's pretty! What shiny hair!"

"That's Genie. I want you to meet her — and then, Mrs. Blair, perhaps you can give an old desert codger a little advice," said Adam.

He called Genie, and she came readily, though not without shyness. Despite her garb and its rents, Adam could not but feel proud of her. Mrs. Blair's kindliness quickly put the girl at ease. After a little talk, in which Genie's part augured well for the impression she was to make upon people, Adam bade her play with the children.

"No wonder Gene spilled the milk!" ejaculated Mrs. Blair.

"Why?" queried Adam.

"The girl's more than pretty. Never saw such hair. And her eyes! They're not the color of hair and eyes I know."

"That's the desert's work, Mrs. Blair. On the desert nature makes color, as well as life, more vivid, more intense."

"And this Genie — isn't it odd — her name is like my boy Gene's — she's no relation of yours?"

Briefly then Adam related Genie's story and the circumstances of his association with her.

"Laws-a-me! Poor child! . . . And now she has no people — no home — not a friend in the world but you?"

"Not one. It's pretty sad, Mrs. Blair."

"Sad? It's worse than that. . . . Strikes me, though, Mr. Wansfell, you must be family and friends and all to that girl. . . . And let a mother tell you what a noble thing you've done — to give three years of your life to an orphan!"

"What I did was good for me. Better than anything I ever did before," replied Adam, earnestly. "I'd go on if it were possible. But Genie

535

needs a home, young people, work, to learn and live her life. And I — I must go back to the desert."

"Ah! So that's it!" exclaimed the woman, nodding. "My husband spoke just like you do. He took to the desert — sold my farm to get money to work his gold claims. Always he had to go back to the desert. . . . And now he'll never come home again."

"Yes, the desert claims many men. But I could and would sacrifice whatever the desert means to me, for Genie's sake, if it — if there was not a reason which makes that impossible."

"And now you're hunting a home for her?"

"Yes."

"She's well educated, you said?"

"Her mother was a school-teacher."

"Then she could teach children. . . . Things work out strangely in life, don't they? My Betty might be left alone. Any girl may become an orphan."

"Now, Mrs. Blair, will you be so kind as to take Genie, or go with us into town, and help us get some clothes for her? A few simple dresses and things she needs. I'd be helpless. And Genie knows so little. She ought to have a woman go with her."

"Indeed she shall have," declared Mrs. Blair. "I'll be only too glad to go. I need some things —" Then she struck her forehead with a plump hand. "I've a better idea. There's not much to be bought in the store at Santa Ysabel. But my neighbor up the valley — his name is Hunt — he has a granddaughter. They're city folks. They've been somebody once. This granddaughter is older than Genie — she's more of a woman's figure — and I heard her say only the other day that she brought a lot of outgrown dresses with her and didn't know what to do with them. All her clothes are fine — not like you buy out here. . . . I'll take Genie over there right this minute!"

Mrs. Blair got up and began to untie her apron. Kindliness beamed upon her countenance and she seemed to have acquired a more thoughtful eye.

"You're good indeed," said Adam, gratefully. "I thank you. It will be so much nicer for Genie. She dreaded this matter of clothes. You can tell Miss Hunt I'd be glad to pay —"

"Shucks! She wouldn't take your money. She's quality, I told you. And her name's not Hunt. That's her grandfather's name. I don't know what hers is — except he calls her Ruth."

Ruth! The sudden mention of that name seemed to Adam like a stab. What a queer, inexplicable sensation followed it!

"I'll be right out," declared Mrs. Blair, bustling into the house.

Adam called Genie to him and explained what was to happen. She grew radiant.

"Oh, Wanny, then I won't have to go into a town — to be laughed at — and I can get — get dressed like — like a lady — before

537

he sees me again!" she exclaimed, breathlessly.

"He? Who's that, Genie?" inquired Adam, dryly, though he knew he could guess very well.

Genie might have lived on the desert, like a shy, lonely, wild creature, but she was eternally feminine enough to bite her tongue at the slip she had made, and to blush charmingly.

Then Mrs. Blair bustled out again, in sunbonnet and shawl, and with the alacrity of excitement she led Genie away through the grove of oaks toward the other end of the valley.

Adam returned to camp, much relieved and pleased, yet finding suddenly that a grave, pondering mood had come upon him. In the still noon hour, when the sun was hot and the flies buzzed lazily, Adam would surely have succumbed to drowsiness had he not been vociferously hailed by some one. He sat up to hear one of the little Blairs call, "Say, my maw wants you to eat with us."

Adam lumbered up and, trying to accommodate his giant steps to those of the urchin, finally reached the house. He heard Mrs. Blair in the kitchen. Then something swift and white rushed upon Adam from somewhere.

"Look!" it cried, in ecstatic tones, and pirouetted before his dazzled eyes.

Genie! In a white dress, white slippers — all white, even to the rapt, beautiful, strangely transformed face! It was a Genie he could not recognize. Yet, however her dark gold-glinting tresses were brushed and arranged, he would have known their rare, rich color. And the eyes were Genie's — vivid like the heart of a magenta cactus flower, unutterably and terribly expressive of happiness. But all else — the girl's height and form and movement — had acquired something subtly feminine. The essence of woman breathed from her.

"Oh, Wanny, I've a whole *bundle* of dresses!" she cried, rapturously. "And I put this on to please you."

"Pleased! . . . Dear girl, I'm — I'm full of joy for you — overcome for myself," exclaimed Adam. How, in that moment, he blessed the nameless spirit which had come to him the day Genie's fate and future hung in the balance! What a victory for him to remember — seen now in the light of Genie's lovely face!

Then Mrs. Blair bustled in. Easy indeed was it to see how the happiness of others affected her. "It's good we have dinner at noon," she said, as she put dish after dish upon the table, "else we'd had to do with little. Sit at table, folks. . . . Children, you must wait. We've company. . . . Gene, come to dinner."

Adam found himself opposite Genie, who had suddenly seemed to lose her intensity, though not her glow. She had softened. The fierce joy had gone. Adam, watching her, received from her presence a thrill of expectancy, and realized that at least one of her sensations of the moment was being conveyed to him. Then Eugene entered. His face shone. He had wet his hair and brushed it and put on a coat. If something new and strange was happening to Genie, it had already happened to Eugene Blair.

"Folks, help yourselves and help each other," said Mrs. Blair.

Adam was ready for that. What a happy dinner! He ate with the relish of a desert man long used to sour dough and bacon, but he had keen ears for Mrs. Blair's chatter and eyes for Genie and Eugene. The mother, too, had a steady and thoughtful gaze for the young couple, and her mind was apparently upon weightier matters than her speech indicated.

"Well, folks," said Mrs. Blair, presently, "if you've all had enough, I'll call the children."

Eugene arose with alacrity. "Let's go outdoors," he said, stealing a shy look at Genie. She seemed to move in a trance. Adam went out, too, and found himself under the oaks. The very air was potent with the expectancy that Adam had sensed in the house. Something was about to happen. It puzzled him. Yet he liked the suspense. But he was nonplused. The young couple did not present a riddle. All the same, the instant Adam felt convinced of this he looked at them and lost his conviction. They did present a riddle. He had not seen any other lad and girl together for many years, but somehow he wagered to himself that if he had seen a thousand couples, this one would stand out strikingly.

Then Mrs. Blair appeared. She had the look of a woman to whom decision had come. The hospitality, the kindly interest in Genie, the happiness in seeing others made happy, were in abeyance to a strong, serious emotion.

"Mr. Wansfell, if you'll consent I'll give Genie a home here with me," she said.

"Consent! . . . I — I gladly do that," he replied, with strong agitation. "You are a — a good woman, Mrs. Blair. I am overwhelmed with gladness for Genie — for her luck. . . . It's so sudden — so unexpected."

"Some things happen that way," she replied. "They just come about. I took to Genie right off. So did my boy. I asked him — when we got back from our neighbor's — if it would not be a good idea to keep Genie. We are poor. It's one more to feed and clothe. But she can help. And she'll teach the children. That means a great deal to me and Gene. . . . He would be glad, he said. So I thought it over — and I've decided. We've your consent. . . . Now, Genie, will you stay and have a home with us?"

"Oh, I'll — I'll be so happy! I'll try so — so hard!" faltered Genie.

"Then — it's settled. My dear girl, we'll try to make you happy," declared Mrs. Blair, and, sitting beside Genie, she embraced her.

Adam's happiness was so acute it seemed pain. But was his feeling all happiness? What had Genie's quick look meant — the intense soul-searching flash she gave him when Mrs. Blair had said it was all settled? Genie's desert eyes saw separation from the man who had been savior, father, brother. One flash of eyes — then she was again lost in this immense and heart-numbing idea of a home. Adam saw Eugene look at her as his mother enfolded her. And Adam's heart suddenly lifted to exaltation. Youth to youth! The wonderful, the calling, the divine! The lad's look was soulful, absorbing, full of strange, deep melancholy, full of dreamy, distant, unconscious enchantment. What had seemed mysterious was now as clear as the sunlight. By some happy chance of life the homeless Genie had been guided to a good woman and a noble lad. Goodness was the commonest quality in the hearts of women; and nobility, in youth at least, flowered in the breast of every man.

And while Eugene thus gazed at Genie she lifted her eyelids, so heavy with their dreams, and met his gaze. Suddenly she sweetly, strangely blushed and looked away, at Adam, through him to the beyond. She seemed full of a vague, dreaming sweetness of life; a faint smile played round her lips; her face lost its scarlet wave for pearly whiteness; and tears splashed down upon her listless hands.

The moment, with all it revealed to Adam, swiftly passed.

"Gene, take her and show her the horses," said Mrs. Blair. "She said she loved horses. Show her all around. We'll let the work go by today."

Mrs. Blair talked awhile with Adam, asking

to know more about Genie, and confiding her own practical plans. Then she hustled off to look after the children, who had been forgotten.

Adam was left to the happiest and most grateful reflections of his life. Much good must come for him, for his lonely hours, when once more the wastelands claimed him; but that was the only thought he gave himself. Lounging back on the old rustic bench, he gave himself up to a growing delight of anticipation. These good Blairs did not dream that in offering Genie a home out of the kindliness of their hearts they had touched prosperity. They were poor. But Genie was rich. They meant to share with the orphan their little; they had no thought of anything Genie might share with them. Adam decided that he would buy the ninety acres, and the hundred in the valley beyond it; and horses, cattle, all the stock and implements for a fine ranch. Genie, innocent and bewildered child that she was, had utterly forgotten her bags of gold. On the next day, or soon, Adam meant to borrow Gene's horse and buggy and drive to Santa Ysabel and then to San Diego. He must find some good investment for the rest of Genie's gold, and a good bank, and some capable and reliable person to look after her affairs. How like a fairy story it would seem to Genie! What amazement and delight it would occasion Mrs. Blair! And as for the lad, no gold could enhance Genie's charm for him. Gene would love Genie! Adam had seen it written in their unconscious eyes. And Gene would have the working of the beautiful ranch his eager heart had longed for. For the first time Adam realized the worth of gold. Here it would be a golden harvest.

Dreaming thus, Adam was only faintly aware of voices and footsteps that drew nearer; and suddenly he seemed transfixed and thrilling, his gaze on a face he knew, the face on the miniature he carried — the lovely face of Ruth Virey.

28
●

"The foxes have holes — the birds of the air have nests!" cried Adam.

Was it he who lay there with aching heart and burning eyes? Ah! Again the lonely wasteland claimed him. That illimitable desert was home. Whose face was that limned on the clouds, and set into the beaten bossy mosaic of the sands, and sculptured in the contour of the dim, colored ranges?

His burros nipped the sage behind him as he lay, back against a stone, on the lofty height of the Sierra Madre divide, gazing down into that boundless void. What was it that had happened? Ah! He had fled! And he lived over again for the thousandth time, that week —

that fleeting week of transport with its endless regrets — in which he had found Genie a home, in which the daughter of Magdalene Virey had stormed his soul.

Vague and happy those first days when he bought the valley lands and flooded them with cattle — vague because of the slow gathering of insupportable and unconscious love — happy because he lived with Genie's rapture and her romance. Vivid were some of the memories — when he placed in Genie's little brown hands papers and deeds and bankbooks, and by a gesture, as if by magic, proclaimed her wondering sense the truth of a tale of Aladdin; when, to the serious-faced mother, pondering the costs, he announced her once more owner of the long-regretted land; when, to a fire-eyed lad, he had drawn aside the veil of the future.

But vague, mystic as a troubled dream, the inception of a love that rose like the blaze of the sun — vague as the opaque dawn of the desert! Whenever he looked up, by night or day, at task or idleness, there shone the lovely face, pale as a dawn-hazed star, a face like Magdalene Virey's, with all of its beauty, but naught of its passion; with all of its charm, yet none of its havoc. With youth, and bloom, and wide-open purple eyes, dark as midnight, staring at fate. And a voice like the voice of her mother, sweet, but not mocking, haunted the dreams of the man and lived in the winds.

"And you are a desert man," she had said.

545

"Yes — a desert man," he had replied.

"There's a place I want to go some day — when I am twenty-one. . . . Death Valley! Do you know it? My grandfather says I'm mad."

"Death Valley! For such as you? Stay — never go near that awful hell!"

The ghastly white pit and its naked red walls, the midnight furnace winds with their wailing roar, the long, long slopes to the avalanche graves! Ah! the torment of his heart, the tragedy he would hide, and the secret he must keep, and the miniature that burned in its place — they drew her with the invisible cords of life and fate. What he would spare her surged in the air that she breathed.

She had come to him under the oaks, and yet again, quitting her friends, drawn to the lonely desert man.

"They told me Genie's story," she said, and her eyes spoke eloquent praise her lips denied. "And so — her mother and father died on the desert. . . . Tell me, desert man, what does Death Valley look like?"

"It is night; it is hell — death and desolation — the grave of the desert, yellow and red and gray — lonely, lonely, lonely silent land!"

"But you love it! . . . Genie says the Indians call you Eagle — because you have the eye of the eagle. . . . Tell me . . . Tell me . . ."

And she made him talk, and she came again. Vague, sweet, first hours they were, with their drawing pain. Was it well to wake in the night, with eyes darker than the darkness, peering into his soul? Her mother's eyes — with all the glory and none of the shame! She had come another day and then the next, while time stood with its mocking wait.

Not vaguely came a scene: "I will tell you of the desert," and a part of his story followed, brief and hard.

"Ah! I would be a man," she said. "I would never run. I would never hide."

Mocking words from a tongue too sweet to mock! She had her mother's spirit. And Adam groped in the gloom, to the glee of his devils of scorn. The grass by day and the grass by night felt the impress of his face. Then love — first real love of youth, and noble passion of man — blazed as the sun in his face. From that revelation all was clear in the bursting light of calamity.

Ruth was coming under the oaks. She liked the cool shade and hated the glare. She was nineteen, with a woman's form and her mother's eyes — proud, sweet, aloof.

"Desert man, I am lonesome," she said. "My grandfather has gone again. He is chasing some new will-o'-the-wisp. Gold and mines, cattle and land — and now it's water. He has an ear for every man."

"Lonesome? You! What do you know of loneliness?" asked Adam.

"There's a loneliness of soul."

"Ah! but you are young. Go help Genie plan her home."

"Genie and Gene! Two people with but one voice! They cannot hear or see anyone but themselves. It's a pity to invade their paradise. *I* will not. . . . And, oh, how beautiful the world must be to them!"

"Ruth, is it not so to you?"

"Beautiful lands and greens and waters!" she exclaimed, in restless discontent. "But I cannot live on scenery. There is joy here, but none for me. . . . I lost my mother and I can't forget. She *had* to leave me and go with him — my father. My father who loved me as a child and hated me as a girl. Oh, it's all a mystery! She went with him to the desert. Gold mad — she said he was. She had her debt to pay. And *I* could not be taken to Death Valley."

"You have never heard from her since the parting?"

"Never. . . . And I am a woman now. Some day I will go to Death Valley."

"Why?" he asked.

"Because *they* went there."

"But no one lives long in that valley of death."

"Then I will find their graves," she said.

"Ruth, you must not. What good can come of your traveling there? I've told you of its desolate and forbidding nature. You are all wrong. Wait! Perhaps your mother will — perhaps you will hear of her some day."

"Oh, desert man, I was a child when we parted. I'm a woman now. I want to *know*. The mystery haunts me. *She* loved me — ah, so well! . . . Sometimes I cannot bear to live. My grandfather hides me in lonely places. We meet but few people, and those he repels. It is because of *me*. . . . Desert man, I am lonelier than was Genie. She is like a bird. She must have lived on the sun and the winds. But *I* am no child, and *I* am forlorn."

Brooding purple eyes of trouble, of longing, of discontent, of fire for life! The heart and soul of Ruth Virey — the heritage of need and unrest — shone from her eyes. All unconsciously she longed to be loved. She stood on the threshold of womanhood like a leaf in a storm.

"Talk with me, walk with me, desert man," she said, wistfully. "You were Taquitch for Genie. Be Eagle for me. Your eyes know the desert where my mother sleeps — where perhaps her spirit wanders. You soothe my troubled heart. Oh, I can feel *myself* with you, for you understand."

Thus Adam's soul was stormed. Magdalene Virey had presaged the future. In the dark stillness of the night, sleepless, haunted, tossed by torment, it was revealed to him that Magdalene Virey had risen out of the depths on noble love for him, and through that love she had seen with mystic eyes into the future. She had projected that love into the spirit of the desert, and it had guided Adam's wandering steps to her daughter Ruth. Was this only a wanderer's dream as he lay on the hills? Was it only a knot in the tangled skein of his desert life? Was it inscrutable design of a power he disdained?

Be what this might, the one great love of his years possessed him, fierce and resistless on its march to his defeat. It mocked his ordeal. It flaunted a banner in his face — noble love, noble passion, love of the soul, all that revered woman, wife, mother, and babe. He had found his mate. Strange how he remembered Margarita Arallanes and the wild boy's love of a day. Poor, pale, wasteful, sinful, lustful little gleam! And he recalled the spell of Genie — that strong call of nature in the wilderness. Above both he had risen. But Ruth Virey was *the* woman. He could win her. The truth beat at his temples, constricted his throat. Ruth was the flower of her mother's tragic longing to be loved. Ruth burned with that longing. And life was not to be denied. Magdalene Virey had given him this child of her agony. She trusted the fate of Ruth in his hands. She saw with superhuman eyes.

A deep tenderness for Ruth pervaded Adam's soul. Who, of all men, could love her, save her, content her as he? It was not thought of her kisses, of her embraces, that plucked at the roots of his will. Like a passing wave the thrill of such bliss went out to the might of a nobler tide. To save Ruth from the fate of her mother, from the peril of her own heart! And in the saving, a home — happiness — the tender smile of a mother — and the kiss of a child!

"But I am a criminal! I am a murderer! Any day I might be hanged before her very eyes!" he whispered, with his face in the grass, his fingers digging the turf. "Still — no one would ever recognize me now. . . . Ah! but *he* — that human wolf Collishaw — would not he know me? . . . Oh, if there be God — help me in my extremity!"

Once again he met her. As he rode up the valley at sunset she came out of the oak grove.

"I've been with Genie. Desert man, her happiness frightens me. Oh, I love her! You tell me of your hard, lonely, terrible desert life. Why, your ears should ring with bells of joy forever. It is *you* who have built her castle. What other deeds, like that, have you done — in those bitter years you tell of?"

"Not many, Ruth — perhaps not one."

"I don't believe you. I am learning you, desert man. And, oh, I wish you knew how it swells my heart to hear Genie tell of what you did for her. Every day she tells me something new. . . . Ah! and more — for to-day she said you would be leaving soon."

"Yes, Ruth — soon," he said.

"Back to the lonely sand?"

"Yes, back to the sage and sand and the big dark hills. Yes, it will be a lonely land," he replied, sadly.

"And you will wander down the trails until you meet some one — some woman or child or man — sick or miserable or lost — and then you will stop."

Adam had no answer.

"The Indians called you Eagle," she went on, and her tone startled him with its hint of remembered mockery. "You have the desert eye — you see so far. . . . But you don't see *here!* . . . Why should you waste your splendid strength, your magnificent manhood, wandering over the desert *if* it's only for unhappy people? Desert man, you are great. But you could do more good here — you could find more misery here. . . . I know one whose heart is breaking. And you've never *seen,* for all your eagle eye!"

"Listen, you morbid girl," he returned, stung as with fire. "I am not great. I am lost. I go to the desert because it is home. . . . Don't think of me! But look to yourself. Look into your heart. Fear it, Ruth Virey. You are a spoiled, dreamful, passionate child. But you have a mind and you have a will. You can conquer your unrest, your discontent. Revere the memory of your mother, but grieve no more. The past is dead. Learn to fight. You are no fighter. You are weak. You give in to loneliness, sadness, longing. Resolve to be a woman! You must live your life. Make it worth while. Every man, every woman, has a burden. Lift yours cheerfully and begin to climb. . . . Work for your grandfather. He needs your help. Love those with whom fate has placed you. And fight — fight the dark moods, the selfish thoughts, the hateful memories! Fight like a desert beast for your life. Work — work till you bruise those beautiful hands. Work with a hoe, if you can find nothing else. Love to see things grow green and flower and give fruit. Love the animals, the birds, and learn from them; love all nature, so that when you meet a man some day, *the* man, you can love him. That is what it means to be a woman. You are a beautiful, sweet, useless, petulant girl. But be so no more. Be a woman!"

Pale and shocked, with brimming eyes and tremulous lips, she replied:

"Stay — stay, desert man, and make me a woman!"

And those sad dark eyes and those sweet murmured words had made him flee — flee like a craven in the night. Yes, for Ruth's sake he had fled. Not a farewell to Genie — not a wave of his hand, but gone in the night — gone forever out of their lives!

"The foxes have holes — the birds of the air have nests!" cried Adam, to the listening silence.

Was it he who lay there with broken heart and magnified sight? Yes, wanderer of the wasteland again! Back to the lonely land! That limitless expanse of rock and sand was home. Was not that Ruth's face limned on the clouds? Did not her sad, reproachful eyes haunt him in the dim, purple distances?

From the lofty divide of the Sierra Madres Adam gazed down into the void he called home. Beyond the gray sands and far beyond the red reaches he saw across the California Desert into Arizona, and down into Mexico, and to the dim, blue Gulf.

Home! All the years of Adam's desert experience were needed to grasp the meaning of the stupendous scene. The eye of the eagle, the sight of the condor, supreme over the desert, most marvelous and delicate work of nature, could only behold, could only range that sun-blasted burned-out empire of the wastelands. Only the mind of man, the thought of man, could understand it. And for Adam it was home, and to his piercing eyes a thing, a place, a world, terribly true and beautiful and comforting, upon which he seemed driven to gaze and gaze, so that forever it must be limned on his vision and his memory.

The day was one of sunlight and storm, of blue sky, and purple clouds and fleecy white, of palls of swirling gray snow and dark veils of downward-streaming rain. The Sierra Madres rolled away on either side, range on range, rising to the north in the might of slow league-long mountain swell, until far against the stormy sky, stood the old white-capped heave of San Gorgonio looming over the gray Mohave; and to the south, like the wave undulations of a calm sea, sank the long low lines of the arid arm of desertland.

Beneath Adam piled the foothills, round and old and gray, sage gray, lavender gray, lilac gray, all so strangely gray — upheaved hills of aged earth and dust and stone. Hill by hill they lowered, with glaring gorges between, solitary hills and winding ranges and clustered domes, split by canyons and cleft by brushy ravines — miles and miles of foothills, reluctantly surrendering allegiance to the peaks above, moving downward as surely as the grains of their slopes, weathering and spreading at last in the sands.

Away and away flowed that gray Sahara with its specks of sage, ribbed by its ridges of dunes. Immense and unbounded it swept to its center, the Salton Sink — bowl of the desert — a great lake of colored silt, a ghastly, glaring stain on the earth, over which the storm clouds trailed their veils of rain, and shadows like colossal ships sailed the sandy main. Away to the southward it flowed, level and shining, at last to rise and meet the blue sky in lucent spurs of gold and white. This landmark contrasted singularly with the Salton Sink. It was the illusive and shifting line of the Superstition Mountains, where the wind sheeted the sands, and by night or day, like the changing of tides, went on with its mysterious transformation. These giant hills caught the sunlight through a rift in the broken clouds. And dim under the dunes showed the scalloped, dark shadows.

But these foothills and sand plains were only the edge of the desert. Beyond marched the mountain ranges. Vast, upheaved, crinkled crust of the naked earth, scored by fire, scarred by age, cracked by earthquake, and stained in the rusty reds and colored chocolates of the iron rocks! Down to the rim of the Salton Sink sheered a ragged range. Over it centered the lowering storm clouds, gray and drab and purple, with rays of the sun filtering through, lighting the grim, dark hardness, showing the smoky gloom. And where the ridge ran down to the desert, to make the lines of the sandy lake, it resembled a shore of the river Styx.

Beyond gleamed the Chocolate Mountains, sharp in the sunshine, canyoned and blue. And still beyond them, over the valley and far, rose the myriad mountains of Arizona, dim, hazed land, mystic land, like a land of desert dreams. In the distant south, around the blunt end of the Chocolates, came a valley winding palely green, with a line following its center, where the Rio Colorado meandered in its course to the blue waters of the Gulf. Over the shadowy shapes of mountains in haze, over the horizon of Arizona, there seemed a blank, pale wall of sky, strange to the eye. Was it the oblivion of sight, the infinitude of heaven? Piercing constant gaze at last brought to Adam the ghostly mountains of Mexico, the faintest of faint tracery of peaks, doubtful, then lost, the lonely Sonorian land.

"And that is my home!" he cried to the winds. Slow tears bathed his eyes, and, closing them, he rested his strained sight. A strange peace seemed to have stolen over him with his vision and grasp of the desert. A low, soft moan of wind in the crevices of rocks lulled his senses for the revel that was to come. He heard his burros nipping at the brush behind his back. From the heights an eagle shrilled its wild whistle of freedom and of solitude. One of the burros brayed, loud and bawling, a jarring note in a silence. Discordant sound it was, that yet brought a smile and a pang to Adam. For only yesterday — or was it long ago — what was it that had happened?

When he opened his eyes the desert under him and the infinity over him had been transfigured.

Only the full blaze of the sun! But a glory dwelt in the clouds and in the wide blue expanse of heaven. Silver-edged rents, purple ships in a golden sky, the long, fan-shaped rays of the sun, white rainbows of haze — these extended from the north across the arch to the open — a great peacefulness of light, deep and tender and blue.

Beneath lay the mirror of earth, the sun-fired ranges like chased and beaten gold, laid with shining jewels all around the resplendent desert. Mountains of porphyry marched down to the sands, rocks of bronze red blurred down to the sands. The white columnar pillars of the clouds seemed reflected in the desert, slow-gliding across the lucent wastes; and the mosaic of mountain and plain had its mirage in the sky. Above and below worked the alchemy of nature, mutable and evanescent, the dying of day, the passing of life.

29

Going down into the desert, Adam found that his steps were no longer wandering and aimless. And the nearer he got to the canyon pass in the Chocolates, the stronger grew his strange eagerness.

For years memory of that camp where he had fought starvation had drawn him like a magnet. He was weary with delving into the gulf of himself, trying to know his nature and heart and soul. Always he was beyond himself. No sooner was one mystery solved than another and deeper one presented itself; one victory gained then a more desperate trial faced him. He only knew the old camp called him resistlessly. Something would come to him there.

Travel and tasks of morn and eve were so habitual with him that they made little break in his thought. And that thought, like this desert steps, had traveled in a circle. He was nearing the places where he had begun his fight with physical forces. His every step brought him so much closer to the terrible deed that had so bitterly colored and directed his desert life.

He crossed the sandy basin from the Sierra Madres to the Chocolates in four days, two of his camps being dry. And on the fifth, in the afternoon, when the long shadows had begun to creep out from the mountains across sand and sage, he climbed the swelling, well-remembered slope where Charley Jim had lured the antelope, and gazed down into the oasis where he had all but starved to death, and where Oella had saved his life.

What struck him with gladness was to find the gray-green, lonely scene identical with the picture in his memory. How well he remembered! And it was twelve years — thirteen — fourteen years! Yet time had made little or no change in the oasis. Nature worked slowly in the desert.

His burros scented the water and trotted down the sage bank, bobbing their packs, kicking up little puffs of odorous dust. Adam stood still and gazed long. He seemed to be almost ready to draw a deep, full breath of melancholy joy. Then he descended to the sandy, rock-studded floor of the canyon, and on the wide white stream bed, where, as always, a slender stream tinkled over the pearly pebbles. How strange that he should fall into the exact course where once he had worn a trail! The flat stones upon which he stepped were as familiar as if he had trod them yesterday. But inside the palm grove time had made changes. The thatched huts were gone and the open places were overgrown with brush. No one had inhabited the oasis for many years.

Leisurely he pitched camp, working with a sense of comfort and pleasure at the anticipation of a permanent, or at least an indefinite, stay there. Of all his lonely camps on the desert, this had been the loneliest. He called it Lost Oasis. Here he could spend days and weeks, basking like a lizard in the sunshine, feeling his loneliness, listening to the silence; and he could climb to the heights and dream, and watch, and live again those wonderful, revealing, unthinking moments when he went back to savage nature.

After his work and meal were finished, and sunset was coloring the sky, Adam wandered around through the willows and along the stream. He stood for some time looking down upon the sandy bar where he had stumbled in pursuit of the rattlesnake and it had bitten him in the face. And then he went from one familiar place to another, sitting at last in the twilight, under the palms where Oella had nursed and fed him back to life and strength. Where was she now — that tranquil, somber-eyed Indian maiden who had refused to wed one of her race and who had died of a broken heart? The twilight seemed prophetic, the rustling palms seemed whispering. Both sadness and pleasure mingled in Adam's return.

But the nameless something, the vague assurance of content, the end of that restless, strange sense of hurrying onward still to seek, to find — these feelings seemed about to come to him, yet held tantalizingly aloof. To-morrow surely! He was tired with his long travel, and it would take a little time once more to adjust himself to loneliness. The perfect peace of loneliness had not yet come back to him. His mind was too full to attend to the seeing, listening, feeling that constituted harmony with the desert. Yet something was beginning to come between remembrances of the immediate past and the insistent premonitions of the present. When he lay down in his blankets to hear the low rustle of the wind in the palms and to see the haunting stars, it was to realize that they were the same as always, but that he himself had changed.

Next day he climbed to the heights where he had learned to hunt mountain sheep, where he had learned the watching, listening, primitive joy of the Indian. He thrilled in the climb, he breathed deep of the keen, cold wind, he gazed afar with piercing eyes. Hours, like those of a lonely eagle on a crag, Adam spent there, and he wooed back to him the watching, listening power with its reward of sweet, wild elation. But as the westering sun sent him down the mountain, he felt a vague regret. The indefinable something eluded him.

In the dusk Adam walked along the rim of the slope above the oasis. He had watched the sunset fade over the desert, and the shading of twilight, and the gathering of dusk.

He wondered what it would mean to him now to be lost without water or food down there in the wasteland. Would panic seize him? He imagined it would be only as long as he was not sure of death. When he realized that, he would find strength and peace to meet his doom. But what agony to look up at the starlit heaven and breathe farewell to beautiful life, to the strong, sweet wine of nature, to the memory of love!

To die alone down there? Ah! Why did his thoughts turn to death? To lie down on the sand and the sage of the desert, in the dead darkness of night, would be terrible. Yet, would it really be? Would not something come to his soul? A strong man's farewell to life, out there on the lonesome desert, would be elemental and natural. But the hour of facing death — how sad, lonely, tragic! Yet it had been bravely met by countless men over all the desolate deserts of the dreary world. All men did not feel alike. Perhaps the strongest, bravest, calmest, would suffer the least. Still, it was Adam's conviction that to look up at the indifferent heavens and to send a hopeless cry out across the desert, realizing the end, remembering with anguish the faces of loved ones, would indeed be a bursting of the heart.

Life was so short. Hope and love so futile! Home and family — ah! a brother — should be treasured, and lived for with all the power of blood and mind. Friends should be precious. It was realization that a man needed.

A crescent beautiful moon soared up over the dark bulk of the mountain. Adam paced to and fro in a sandy glade of the oasis. All the immensity of desert and infinity of sky seemed to be at work to overwhelm him. The stars — so white, wonderful, watching, eyes of heaven, remorseless and wise! Not a sigh of wind stirred under the palms, not a quiver of a leaf. Nature seemed so strange, beautiful, waiting. All waited! Was it for him? The shadows on the white sand wrote Adam's story of wild youth and crime and flight and agony and passion and love. How sad the low chirp of insects! Adam paced there a long time, thinking thoughts he never had before, feeling things he never felt before — realizing the brevity of life, the soul of sorrow, the truth of nature, the sweetness of women, the glory of children, the happiness of work and home.

Something was charging the air around Adam; something was surging deep in his soul.

What was the meaning of that which confounded his emotions? Adam's soul seemed trembling on the verge of a great lesson, that had been hidden all the years and now began to dawn upon him in the glory of the firmament — in the immensity of the earth — in the sense of endless space — in the meaning of time — in the nothingness of man.

Suddenly a faint coldness, not of wind nor of chill air, but of something intangible, stole over Adam. He shivered. He had felt it before, though never so strong. And his sense of loneliness vanished. He was not alone! All around he peered, not frightened or aghast, but uncertain, vaguely conscious of a sense that seemed unnatural. The shadow of his lofty form showed dark on the sand. It walked with him as he walked. Was there a spirit in keeping with his steps?

Disturbed in mind, Adam went to bed. When he awoke there had come to him in the night, in his sleep or in his dreams, whispered words from Genie's mother, ringing words from Ruth Virey, "I will come to you out on the desert." Mrs. Linwood had meant that to be proof of immortal life of the soul — of God. And Ruth had rung at him: "I would be a man. I would never run. I would never hide!"

Then the still, small voice of conscience became a clarion. Torment seized Adam. The lonely lure of the desert had betrayed him. There was no rest — no peace. He was driven. He had dreamed of himself as a wanderer driven down the naked shingles of the desert. No dream, but reality!

He spent the day upon the heights, feeling that there, if anywhere, he might shake this burden of his consciousness. In vain! He was a civilized man, and only in rare moments could he go back to the forgetfulness of the savage. He had a soul. It was a living flame. The heights failed him. A haunting whisper breathed in the wind and an invisible spirit kept pace with his steps. And at last, in slow-mounting swell of heart, with terror in his soul, he faced the south. Ah! How sharp the pang in his breast! Picacho! There, purple against the sky, seemingly close, stood up the turreted and castled peak under the shadow of which lay the grave of his brother. And Adam sent out a lonely and terrible cry down the winds toward the place that resistlessly called him. He was called and he must go. He had wandered in a circle. All his steps had bent toward the scene of his crime. From the first to the last he had been wandering back to his punishment. He saw it now. That was the call — that the guide — that the nameless something charging the air.

Realization gave him a moment's savageness — the power of body over mind. Heart and blood and pulse and nerve burst red hot to the fight, and to passionate love of liberty, of life. He was in the grasp of a giant of the ages. He fought as he had fought thirst, starvation, loneliness — as he had fought the desert and the wild beasts and wilder men of that desert. The deep and powerful instinct which he had conquered for Genie's sake — the noble emotion of love and bliss that he had overcome for Ruth's sake — what were these compared to the hell in his heart now? It was love of life that made him a fierce wild cat of the desert. Had not the desert taught him its secret to survive, to breathe, to see, to listen, to live?

Thus the I of Adam's soul was arraigned in pitiless strife with the Me of his body. Like a wild and hunted creature he roamed the mountain top, halting at the old resting places, there to sit like a stone, to lie on his face, to writhe and fight and cry in his torment. At sunset he staggered down the trail, spent and haggard, to take up useless tasks, to find food tasteless and sleep impossible. Thus passed the next day and yet another, before there came a break in his passion and his strength.

The violence of physical effort wore itself out. He remained in camp, still locked in deadly grip with himself, but wearing to that end in which his conscience would rise supreme, or he would sink forever debased.

A perfect white night came in which Adam felt that the oasis and its environment presented a soul-quieting scene. What incredible paradox that he must go to nature for the strength to save himself from himself! To the nature that made him a savage — that urged in him the strife of the wolf! The moon, half full, shone overhead in a cloudless blue sky where great white stars twinkled. No wind stirred. The palms drooped, sad and graceful, strangely quiet. They were meant for wind. The shadows they cast were of nameless shapes. A wavering dark line of horizon wandered away to be lost in the wilderness. So still, so tranquil, so sweet the night! There were only two sounds — the melancholy notes of a night hawk, and the low, faint moan from the desert. The desert to Adam seemed a vast river, flowing slowly, down the levels of the earth to distant gates. Its moan was one of immutable power and motive. By this soft, low, strange moan the world seemed to be dominated. A spirit was out there in the gloom — a spirit from the illimitable, star-studded infinite above. And it was this spirit that came, at rare intervals, and whispered to Adam's consciousness. Madman or knave, he was being conquered.

"I would never hide!" Ruth Virey had said in passionate scorn.

She was like her mother, wonderful as steel in her will. Yet these women seemed all heart. They transcended men in love, in sacrifice, in that living flame of soul, turbulent and un-quenchable as the fire of the sun.

"I'll hide no more!" burst from Adam, and the whisper startled him, like those soundless whispers in the shadows.

He could live no longer a life in hiding. He must stand, in his own consciousness, if only for a moment, free to look any man in the face, free to be worthy to love Ruth Virey, free as the eagle of his spirit. He would no longer hide from man, from punishment. Love of that purple-eyed girl had been a stinging, quickening spur. But it was only instrumental in the overthrow of fear. Some other power, not physical, not love, but cold, pure, passionless, spiritual, had been drawing him like a wavering compass needle to its pole.

Was it the faith Genie's dying mother had placed in God? Was it a godlike something in him which conflicted with nature? Was it the strange progress of life, inscrutable and inflexible, that dragged men down or lifted them up, made them base or made them great?

The darkness of his mind, the blackness of the abyss of his soul, seemed about to be illumined. But the truth held aloof. Yet could he not see what constituted greatness in any man? What was it to be great? The beasts of the desert and the birds recognized it — strength — speed — ferocity — tenacity of life. The Indians worshiped greatness so that they looked up and prayed to their gods. They worshiped stature, and power and skill of hand, and fleetness of foot, and above all — endurance. More, they endowed their great chieftains with wisdom. But above all — to endure pain, heat, shock, all of the desert hardships, all of the agonies of life — to endure — that was their symbol of greatness.

Adam asked no other for himself or for any

man. To endure and to surmount the ills of life! Any man could be great. He had his choice. To realize at last — to face the inevitable fight in any walk of life — to work and to endure — to slave and to suffer in silence — to stand like a savage the bloody bruises and broken bones — to bite the tongue and hold back the gasp — to plod on down the trails or the roads or the streets and to be true to an ideal — to endure the stings and blows of misfortune — to bear up under loss — to fight the bitterness of defeat and the weakness of grief — to be victor over anger — to smile when tears were close — to resist disease and evil men and base instincts — to hate hate and to love love — to go on when it would seem good to die — to seek ever the glory and the dream — to look up with unquenchable faith in something evermore about to be — that was what any man could do and so be great!

At midnight Adam paced under the palms. All seemed dim, gray, cool, spectral, rustling, whispering. The old familiar sounds were there, only rendered different by his mood. Midnight was haunting. Somehow the desert with its mustering shadows, dark and vast and strange, resembled his soul and his destiny and the mystery of himself. How sweet the loneliness and solitude of the oasis! There under the palms he could walk and be himself, with only the eye of nature and of spirit on him in this final hour of his extremity.

Happiness was not imperative; self-indulgence was not essential to life. Adam realized he had done wonderful things — perhaps noble things. But nothing great! Perhaps all his agony had been preparation for this supreme ordeal.

How saving and splendid would it be, if out of his stultified youth, with its blinded love of brother and its weakness of will — if out of the bitter sting of infidelity and his fatal, tragic deed — if out of the long torture of hardship of the desert and its strife and its contact with souls as wild as his — how glorious it would be if out of this terrible tide of dark, contending years, so full of remorse and fear and endless atonement, there should rise a man who, trained now in the desert's ferocity to survive, should use that force to a noble aim, and, climbing beyond his nature, sacrifice himself to the old biblical law — a life for a life — and with faith in unknown future lend his spirit to the progress of the ages!

Adam divined that he did not belong to himself. What he wanted for himself, selfishly, was not commensurable with the need of others in this life. He was concerned here with many ideals, the highest of which was sacrifice, that the evil of him should not go on. Since he had loved Ruth Virey the whole value of life had shifted. Life was sweet, but no longer if he had to hide, no longer under the ban of crime. The stain must be washed away. By slow and gradual change, by torments innumerable, had he come to this realization. He had deceived himself by love of life. But the truth in him was the truth of the immortality of his soul, just as it was truth that he inherited instincts of the savage. Life was renewal. Every base, selfish man held back its spirituality.

"No more! No more!" cried Adam, looking up.

And in that cry he accepted the spirit of life, the mighty being that pulsated there in the darkness, the whispering voice of Genie's mother, the love of Ruth that never was to be his, the strange, desperate fights with his instincts, the stranger fight of his renunciation — he accepted these on faith as his idea of God.

"I will give my life for my brother's," he said. "I will offer myself in punishment for my crime. I will pay with my body that I may save my soul!"

30
•

Adam lingered in his travel through the beautiful Palo Verde Valley, and at last reached the long swell of desert slope that led down to the Rio Colorado.

Tranquil and sad was his gaze on the majestic river as it swirled red and sullen between its wide green borders toward the upflung wilderness of colored peaks he remembered so well.

All the day he strode behind his faithful burros, here high on the river bank where he could see the somber flood rolling to the south, and there low in the willow-shaded trail. And though he had an eye for the green, dry coverts and the wide, winding valley, he seemed to see most vividly the scenes of boyhood and of home. And the memory revived the love he had borne his brother Guerd. High on the grassy hill at the old village school — he was there once again, wild and gay, playing the games, tagging at the heels of his idol.

The miles slipped by under his tireless stride. Hour by hour he had quickened his pace. And when sunset caught him with its call to camp, he could see the grand purple bulk of old Picacho looming in the sky. Twilight and dusk and night, and the lonely camp fire! He heard the sullen gurgle of the river in the weeds and he saw the trains of stars reflected along its swirling surface. A killdeer, most mournful of birds, pealed his plaintive, lonely cry. Across the blue-black sky, gleamed a shooting star. The wind stirred in the leaves, gently and low, and fanned the glowing embers, and bore the white ashes away into the darkness. Shadows played from the flickering blaze, fantastic and weird, like dancing specters in the gloom. Adam watched the gleaming river rolling on to its grave in the Gulf. Like all things, it died, was dispersed, and had rebirth in other climes. Then he watched the stars at their grand and blazing task.

On the afternoon of the third day he turned under the red bluff into the basin of Picacho. Long the trail had been overgrown and dim, and cattle tracks were scarce. The wide willow and mesquite flat, with its groves of cotton-woods, had grown denser, wilder, no more criss-crossed by trails. Adam had slowed down now, and he skirted the edge of the thicket till he reached the bank of bronze rock that had flowed down from the peaks in ages past. The *ocatillas*, so pearly gray, softly green, and vividly scarlet, grew there just the same as long ago when he had plucked a flower for the dusky hair of Margarita. He welcomed sight of them, for they were of the past.

And here, side by side, stood the crucifixion tree and the *palo verde* under which Margarita had told him their legends. The years had made no change that Adam could discern. The smoke tree and the green tree raised their delicate, exquisite, leafless foliage against the blue of sky, beautiful and soft, hiding from the eye the harsh law of their desert nature.

Adam tarried here. His wandering steps were nearing their end. And he gazed across the river at the wilderness of Arizona peaks. It seemed he knew every one. Had he seen them yesterday or long ago?

The sculptured turrets of Picacho were taking on a crown of gold, and from the sheer, ragged bluffs of the purple mass shadows and hazes and rays were streaming down into the valley. One golden streak slanted from the wind-worn hole in the rim. Solemn and noble the castled mountain towered in the sky. In its lonely grandeur there was strength.

One moment longer Adam watched and listened, absorbing the color and glory and wildness, stung to the depths of his heart by his farewell to loneliness. He retrograded one last instant to the savage who sensed but did not think. He thrilled to the old, mysterious, fading instinct. Then, as in answer to a sonorous call in his ear, he measured slow and laboring strides through the aisles to the river.

His burros scratched their packs on the thorny

mesquites to get down to the arrowweed and willow. Where once had been open bank, now all was green except for a narrow sandy aisle. The dock was gone. A sunken barge lay on a bar, and moored to its end were two leaky skiffs. Traffic and trade had departed from the river landing. Adam remembered a prospector had told him that the mill had been moved from the river up to the mine under the peak. So now, he thought, supplies and traffic must come and go by way of Yuma.

He drove his burros down the sandy aisle. A glimpse of an old adobe wall, gray through the mesquites, stopped his heart. He went on. The house of Arallanes was a roofless ruin, the vacant windows and doors staring darkly, the walls crumbling to the sands. The shed where Adam had slept was now half hidden by mesquites. The *ocatilla* poles were bleached and rotten and the brush was gone from the roof; but the sandy floor looked as clean and white as the day Adam had spread his blankets there. Fourteen years! Silent he stood, and the low, mournful wind was a knell. The past could never be undone.

He went back to the lane and to the open. Old stone walls were all that appeared left of the houses he expected to see. Over the trees, far up the slope, he espied the ruins of the dismantled mill. Unreal it looked there, out of place, marring the majestic sweep of the slope.

His keen desert nostrils detected smoke before

he saw blue columns rising through the green. He passed a plot of sand-mounded graves. Had they been there? How fierce a pang pierced his heart! Rude stones marked the graves, and on one a single wooden cross, crude and weathered, slanted away. Adam peered low at the lettering — M. A. And swiftly he swung erect.

There was a cluster of houses farther on, low and squat, a few of them new, but most of them Adam remembered. A post-office sign marked this village of Picacho. The stone-fronted store looked just the same, and the loungers there might never have moved from their tracks in fourteen years. But the faces were strange.

A lean old man, gray and peaked, detached himself from the group and tottered toward Adam with his cane in the sand.

"Wal, stranger, howdy! You down from up-river?"

His voice twanged a chord of memory. Merryvale! Slowly the tide of emotion rose in Adam's breast. He peered down into the gray old face, with its narrow, half-shut eyes and its sunken cheeks. Yes, it was Merryvale.

"Howdy, friend!" replied Adam. "Yes, I come from up the river."

"Strange in these parts, I reckon?"

"Yes. But I — I was here years ago."

"Wal, I knowed you was strange because you come in by the river. Travelers nowadays go round the mountain. Prospectors never come any more. The glory of Picacho has faded."

"Aren't they working the mill?" queried Adam, quickly.

"Haw! Haw! The mill will never grind with ore that is gone! No work these last five years. The mill has rusted out — fallen to ruin. And the gold of old Picacho is gone. But, stranger, she hummed while she lasted. Millions in gold — millions in gold!"

He wagged his lean old head and chuckled.

"I knew a man here once by the name of Arallanes. What has become of him?"

"Arallanes? Wal, I do recollect him. I was watchman at the mill an' he was boss of the gang. His daughter was knifed by a greaser named Felix. . . . Arallanes left here these ten years ago an' he's never been back."

"His — daughter! . . . Is that her grave back there — the sunken mound of sand — with the wooden cross?"

"I reckon that's Margarita's grave. She was a pretty wench — mad about men — an' there's some who said she got her just deserts."

The broad river gleamed yellow through the breaks in the mesquites. Ponderous and swirling, it glided on round the bend. Adam's gaze then sought the peak. The vast, stormy, purple mass, like a mountain of cloud, shone with sunset crown of silver.

Somewhere near, hidden by the trees, a Mexican broke the stillness with song — wild, sensuous, Spanish love, in its haunting melody.

"I knew another man here," began Adam, with the words a sonorous knell in his ear. "His name was Collishaw. . . . What's become of him?"

"Collishaw? Never will forgit *him!*" declared the old man, grimly. "Last I heard he was cheatin' Injuns out of water rights over here at Walters — an' still lookin' fer somebody to hang. . . . Haw! Haw! That Collishaw was a Texas sheriff."

Suddenly Adam bent lower, so that his face was on a level with Merryvale's.

"Don't you recognize me?"

"Wal, I shore don't, stranger," declared the other. "I've been nigh fifty years in the West an' never seen your like yet. If I had I'd never forgot."

"Merryvale, do you remember a lad who shot off your fishing line one day? Do you remember how you took interest in him — told him of Western ways — that he must be a man?"

"Shore I remember that lad!" exclaimed Merryvale, bluntly. He was old, but he was still keen. "How'd you know about him?"

"I am Adam Larey!"

The old man's eyes grew piercing. Intensely he gazed, bending closer, strong and thrilling now, with the zest of earlier experience sharp in his expression.

"I know you now. It's Adam. I'd knowed them eyes among a thousand, if I'd only looked. Eagle's eyes, Adam, once seen never forgot! . . .

An' look at the giant of him! Wal, you make me feel young again. . . . Adam, lad, I ain't never forgot ye — never! Shake hands with old Merryvale."

Agitated, with tremulous voice and shaking hands, he grasped Adam, almost embracing him, his gray old face alight with gladness.

"It's good to see you, Merryvale — to learn you've not forgotten me — all these years."

"Lad, you was like my own! . . . But who'd ever know you now? You've white hair, Adam, an' — ah! I see the desert in your face."

"Old friend, did you ever hear of Wansfell?"

"Wansfell? You mean thet wanderer the prospectors tell about? . . . Shore, I've been hearin' tales of him these many years."

"I am Wansfell," replied Adam.

"*So help me God!* . . . Wansfell? . . . You, Adam, the kindly lad! . . . Didn't I tell you what a hell of a man you'd be when you grew up?"

Adam drew Merryvale aside from the curiously gathering loungers.

"Old friend, you are responsible for Wansfell. . . . And now, before we tell — before I go — I want you to take me to — to — my — my brother's grave?"

Merryvale stared.

"*What?*" he ejaculated, and again his keen old eyes searched Adam's.

"Yes. The grave — of my brother — Guerd," whispered Adam.

"Say, man! . . . You think Guerd Larey's buried *here?* . . . Thet's why you come back?"

Astonishment seemed to dominate Merryvale, to hold in check other emotions.

"My friend," replied Adam, "I came to see his grave — to make my peace with him and God — and to give myself up to the law."

"Give yourself — up — to the law!" gasped Merryvale. "Have you gone desert mad?"

"No. I'm right in my mind," returned Adam, patiently. "I owe it to my conscience, Merryvale. . . . Fourteen years of torture! Any punishment I may suffer here, compared with those long years, will be as nothing. . . . It will be happiness to give myself up."

Merryvale's lean jaw quivered as the astonishment and concern left his face. A light of divination began to dawn there.

"But what do you want to give yourself up for?" he demanded.

"I told you. My conscience. My need to stand right with myself. To pay!"

"I mean — what 'd you do? . . . *What for?*"

"Old friend, you've grown thick of wits," rejoined Adam. "Because of my crime."

"An' what was thet, Adam Larey?" queried Merryvale, sharply.

"The crime of Cain," replied Adam, sadly. "Come, friend — take me to my brother's grave."

Merryvale seemed galvanized from age to youth.

"Your brother's grave! . . . Guerd Larey's grave? By heaven! I wish I could take you to it! . . . Adam, you're out of your head. You *are* desert mad. . . . Bless you, lad, you've made a terrible mistake! You're not what you think you are. You've hid in the desert fourteen years — you've gone through hell — you've become Wansfell — all for nothin'! . . . My God! to think of thet! . . . Adam, you're no murderer. Your brother is not dead. He wasn't even bad hurt. No — no — Guerd Larey's alive — alive — alive!"

Zane Grey was born Pearl Zane Gray at Zanesville, Ohio in 1872. He was graduated from the University of Pennsylvania in 1896 with a degree in dentistry. He practiced in New York City while striving to make a living by writing. He married Lina Elise Roth in 1905 and with her financial assistance he published his first novel himself, BETTY ZANE (1903). Closing his dental office, the Greys moved into a cottage on the Delaware River, near Lackawaxen, Pennsylvania. Grey took his first trip to Arizona in 1907 and, following his return, wrote THE HERITAGE OF THE DESERT (1910). The profound effect that the desert had had on him was so vibrantly captured that it still comes alive for a reader. Grey couldn't have been more fortunate in his choice of a mate. Trained in English at Hunter College, Lina Grey proofread every manuscript Grey wrote, polished his prose, and she effectively managed their financial affairs. Grey's early novels were serialized in pulp magazines but by 1918 he had graduated to the slick magazine market. Motion picture rights brought in a fortune and, with 108 films based on his work, Grey set a record yet to be equaled by any other author. Zane Grey was not a realistic writer, but rather one who charted the interiors of the soul through encounters with the wilderness. He provided

characters no more realistic than one finds in Balzac, Dickens, or Thomas Mann, but nonetheless they have a vital story to tell. "There was so much unexpressed feeling that could not be entirely portrayed," Loren Grey, Grey's younger son and a noted psychologist, once recalled, "that, in later years, he would weep when re-reading one of his own books." More than stories, Grey fashioned psycho-dramas of the human soul in its odyssey to the center of the psyche. They may not be the stuff of the real world, but without them the real world has no meaning — which may go a long way to explain the hold he has held on an enraptured public ever since that first Western romance in 1910.

We hope you have enjoyed this Large Print book. Other Thorndike Press or Chivers Press Large Print books are available at your library or directly from the publishers. For more information about current and upcoming titles, please call or write, without obligation, to:

Thorndike Press
P.O. Box 159
Thorndike, Maine 04986
USA
Tel. (800) 223-6121 (U.S. & Canada)
In Maine call collect: (207) 948-2962

OR

Chivers Press Limited
Windsor Bridge Road
Bath BA2 3AX
England
Tel. (0225) 335336

All our Large Print titles are designed for easy reading, and all our books are made to last.